AF244197

CLASSICS
OF
RUSSIAN
LITERATURE

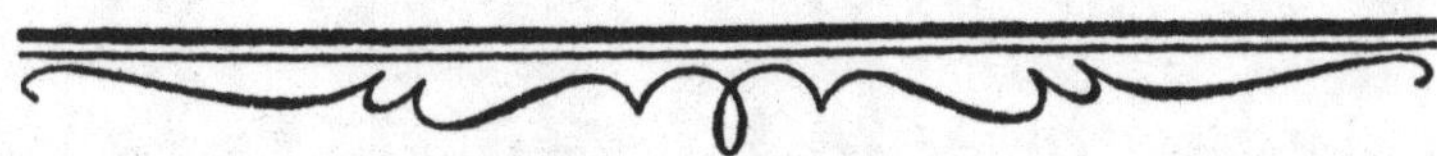

A.P. CHEKHOV

SHORT NOVELS
and
STORIES

University Press of the Pacific
Honolulu, Hawaii

Short Novels and Stories

by
A. P. Chekhov

Translated from the Russian by Ivy Litvinov
Designed by B. Trifonov

ISBN 0-89875-321-X

Copyright © 2001 by University Press of the Pacific

Reprinted from the Original edition

University Press of the Pacific
Honolulu, Hawaii
http://www.universitypressofthepacific.com

All rights reserved, including the right to reproduce
this book, or portions thereof, in any form.

CONTENTS

DEATH OF A CLERK

It was an excellent night when the excellent clerk, Ivan Dmitrich Chervyakov* sat in the second row of the stalls, enjoying "Les Cloches de Corneville" with the aid of opera-glasses. He watched the stage and thought himself the happiest of mortals, when all of a sudden. . . . "All of a sudden" has become a hackneyed expression, but how can authors help using it, since life is full of surprises? All of a sudden, then, his face puckered up, his eyes rolled heavenwards, his breath was suspended. . . turning his face away from the opera-glasses, he doubled up in his seat and—a-shoo! That is to say he sneezed. Now everyone has a right to sneeze wherever he likes. Peasants, police inspectors, even privy councillors sneeze. Everyone sneezes—everyone. Chervyakov felt no embarrassment, dabbed at his nose with his pocket handkerchief, and, like a well-bred man, looked round to see whether his sneezing had incommoded anyone. And then he did feel embarrassed. For he saw a little old man sitting in the first row, just in front of him, carefully wiping his bald cranium and neck with his glove, muttering something the while. Chervyakov recognized in the

* From word *chervyak*, worm.—*Tr.*

old man, Civil General Brizhalov of the Ministry for Communications.

"I sneezed over him!" thought Chervyakov. "He's not my chief, it's true, but still it's very awkward. I must apologize."

Chervyakov leaned forward with a little cough, and whispered in the General's ear:

"I beg your pardon, Your Excellency, I sneezed.... I didn't mean to...."

"Don't mention it."

"Do forgive me. I ... it wasn't premeditated!"

"Can't you keep quiet, for goodness' sake! Let me listen!"

Chervyakov, somewhat disconcerted, smiled sheepishly and tried to turn his attention to the stage. He watched the actors, but no longer felt the happiest of mortals. He was devoured by remorse. Walking up to Brizhalov in the interval, he hung about for a while and at last, conquering his timidity, mumbled:

"I sneezed at you, Your Excellency.... Pardon me.... You know.... I didn't mean...."

"Oh, really ... I had forgotten it, must you go on?" the General said, his underlip twitching impatiently.

"He says he's forgotten, but I don't like the look in his eyes," thought Chervyakov, glancing distrustfully in the General's direction. "Doesn't want to talk to me. I must explain to him that I didn't mean to ... that it's a law of nature, otherwise he might think I meant to spit on him. Even if he doesn't think so now, he might afterwards!..."

When he got home, Chervyakov told his wife of his ungentlemanly conduct. It seemed to him that his wife received his story with undue levity. True, she was alarmed for a moment, but finding Brizhalov was not "our" chief, she was reassured.

"I think you ought to go and apologize, though," she said. "Or he'll think you don't know how to behave in company."

"That's it! I tried to apologize, but he was so strange. Didn't say a word of sense. Besides, there was no time for talking."

Next day Chervyakov put on his new official frock-coat, had his hair cut, and went to explain his conduct to Brizhalov. The General's reception-room was full of petitioners, and the General himself was there, receiving petitions. After interviewing a few of them, the General raised his eyes to Chervyakov's face.

"Last night, in The Arcadia, if you remember, Your Excellency," began the clerk. "I—er—sneezed, and—er—happened to ... I beg...."

"Pshaw, what nonsense!" said the General. "What can I do for you?" he asked, addressing the next man.

"Won't listen to me!" thought Chervyakov, turning pale. "It means he's angry.... I can't leave it at that.... I must explain to him...."

When the General, having received the last petitioner, turned to go back to his private apartment, Chervyakov pursued him, muttering:

"Excuse me, Your Excellency! Nothing but my heart-felt repentance emboldens me to trouble Your Excellency...."

The General looked as if he were going to cry, and waved him away.

"You are laughing at me, Sir!" he said and shut the door in his face.

"Laughing!" thought Chervyakov. "I don't see anything funny in it. Doesn't he understand, and he a General? Very well, I won't bother the fine gentleman with my apologies any more. Devil take him! I'll write him a letter, I won't go to him any more! I won't, and that's all!"

Such were Chervyakov's thoughts as he walked home. But he did not write the letter. He thought and thought but could not think how to word it. So he had to go to the General the next day, to get things straight.

"I ventured to trouble you yesterday, Your Excellency," he began when the General turned a questioning glance upon him, "not to laugh at you, as Your Excellency suggested. I came to bring my apologies for having inconvenienced you by sneezing.... As for laughing at you, I would never think of such a thing. How would I dare to! If we took it into our heads to laugh at people, there would be no respect left ... no respect for superiors...."

 "Get out of here!" barked the General, livid and shaking with rage.

"I beg your pardon?" whispered Chervyakov, numb with terror.

"Get out!" repeated the General, stamping his foot.

Chervyakov felt as if something had snapped inside him. He neither heard nor saw anything as he backed towards the door, walked out into the street and wandered on. He stumbled mechanically home, lay down on the sofa, just as he was, in his official frock-coat, and died.

1883

CHAMELEON

Police Inspector Ochumelov* crossed the market-place in a new great-coat holding a bundle in his hand. After him strode a red-haired constable carrying a sieve filled to the brim with confiscated gooseberries. All around was silence. ... There was not a soul in the market-place. ... The open doors of small shops and taverns gaped drearily out at God's world, like so many hungry jaws. There were not even any beggars standing near them.

All of a sudden the sound of a voice came to Ochumelov's ears. "So you'd bite, would you, you cur! Don't let it go, lads! Biting is not allowed nowadays. Hold it! Ow!"

A dog's whine was heard. Ochumelov glanced in the direction of the sound and this is what he saw: a dog came running out of the timber-yard of the merchant Pichugin on three legs, pursued by a man in a starched print shirt and an unbuttoned waistcoat, his whole body bent forward; the man stumbled and caught hold of the dog by one of its hind-legs. There was another whine, and again a shout of: "Don't let it go!" Drowsy faces

* From word *ochumeli*, crazed —*Tr.*

were thrust out of shops, and in no time a crowd which seemed to have sprung out of the earth had gathered around the timber-yard.

"Looks like a public disturbance, Your Honour!" said the constable.

Ochumelov turned, and marched up to the crowd. Right in front of the gate of the yard he saw the abovementioned individual in the unbuttoned waistcoat, who stood there with his right hand raised, displaying a bleeding finger to the crowd. The words: "I'll give it to you, you devil!" seemed to be written on his tipsy countenance, and the finger itself looked like a banner of victory. Ochumelov recognized in this individual Khryukin,* the goldsmith. In the very middle of the crowd, its forelegs well apart, sat the culprit, its whole body a-tremble—a white *borzoi* pup, with a pointed nose and a yellow spot on its back. In its tearful eyes was an expression of misery and horror.

"What's all this about?" asked Ochumelov, shouldering his way through the crowd. "What are you doing here? Why are you holding up your finger? Who shouted?"

"I was walking along, Your Honour, as quiet as a lamb," began Khryukin, coughing into his fist. "I had business about some wood with Mitri Mitrich here, and suddenly, for no reason whatever, that nuisance bit my finger. Excuse me, but I'm a working man.... Mine is a very intricate trade. Make them pay me compensation—perhaps I won't be able to move this finger for a week. It doesn't say in the law, Your Honour, that we have to put up with ferocious animals. If everyone's to start biting, life won't be worth living...."

"H'm...well, well," said Ochumelov severely, coughing and twitching his eyebrows. "Well, well ... whose dog is it? I shan't leave it at this. I'll teach people to

* Khryu-khryu—pig's grunt.—*Tr.*

let dogs run about! It's time something was done about gentlemen who are not willing to obey the regulations! He'll get such a fine, the scoundrel—I'll teach him what it means to let dogs and cattle of all sorts rove about! I'll show him what's what! Eldirin," he continued, turning to the constable, "find out whose dog it is, and draw up a statement. And the dog must be exterminated without delay. It's probably mad ... whose dog is it, I ask?"

"I think it belongs to General Zhigalov," said a voice from the crowd.

"General Zhigalov! H'm. Help me off with my coat, Eldirin. ... Phew, how hot it is! It must be going to rain." He turned to Khryukin: "One thing I don't understand—how did it happen to bite you? How could it have got at your finger? Such a little dog, and you such a strapping fellow! You must have scratched your finger with a nail, and then taken it into your head to get paid for it. I know you fellows! A set of devils!"

"He burned the end of its nose with a lighted cigarette for a joke, Your Honour, and it snapped at him, it's nobody's fool! That Khryukin's always up to some mischief, Your Honour!"

"None of your lies, Squinty! You didn't see me do it, so why lie? His Honour is a wise gentleman, he knows who's lying and who's telling a god's truth. May the justice of the peace try me if I'm lying! It says in the law ... all men are equal now. I have a brother in the police myself, if you want to know...."

"Don't argue!"

"No, that isn't the General's dog," remarked the constable profoundly. "The General hasn't got a dog like that. All his dogs are pointers."

"Are you sure?"

"Quite sure, Your Honour."

"And you're right! The General's dogs are expensive, breed-dogs, and this one—just look at it! Ugly, mangy cur! Why should anyone keep a dog like that? Are you crazy? If a dog like that were to find itself in Moscow or Petersburg, d'you know what would happen to it? Nobody would worry about the law, it would be got rid of in a minute. You're a victim, Khryukin, and mind you don't leave it at that. He must be taught a lesson! It's high time...."

"Perhaps it is the General's after all," said the constable, thinking aloud. "You can't tell by looking at it. I saw one just like it in his yard the other day.'

"Of course it's the General's!" came the voice from the crowd.

"H'm! Help me on with my coat, Eldirin.... I felt a gust of wind. I'm shivery. Take it to the General's and ask them. Say I found it, and sent it. And tell them not to let it into the street. Perhaps it's an expensive dog, and it'll soon get spoilt if every brute thinks he can stick cigarettes into its nose. A dog's a delicate creature. And you put down your hand, blockhead! Stop showing everyone your silly finger. It's your own fault...."

"Here comes the General's chef, we'll ask him.... Hi, there, Prokhor! Come here, old man! Have a look at this dog... is it yours?"

"What next! We've never had one like that in our lives!"

"No need to make any more enquiries," said Ochumelov. "It's a stray. What's the good of standing here talking. You've been told it's a stray, so a stray it is. Destroy it and have done with the matter."

"It isn't ours," continued Prokhor. "It belongs to the General's brother, who came a short time ago. Our General takes no interest in *borzois*. His brother now, he likes...."

"What, has the General's brother come? Vladimir Ivanich?" exclaimed Ochumelov, an ecstatic smile spreading over his features. "Fancy that! And I didn't know. Come to stay?"

"That's right."

"Just fancy! Wanted to see his brother! And I didn't know. So it's *his* dog? Very glad! Take it ... it's a nice little doggie! Snap at his finger? Ha-ha-ha! Come now, don't tremble! Gr-gr ... the little rascal's angry... What a pup!"

Prokhor called the dog and walked out of the timber-yard with it. The crowd laughed at Khryukin.

"I'll have you yet!" Ochumelov threatened him, and, wrapping his great-coat round him, he continued his way across the market-place.

1884

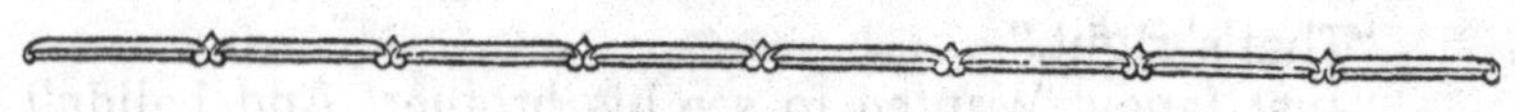

THE MASK

A fancy-dress charity ball, or, as the local young ladies preferred to call it, a *bal paré*, was being given in the X. Social Club.

It was twelve o'clock, midnight. The non-dancing intellectuals who wore no masks—there were five of them—sat round the big table in the reading-room, their noses and beards buried in the sheets of newspapers, reading, dozing, and, in the words of the special correspondent of the Moscow and Petersburg newspapers—a most liberally-inclined gentleman "meditated."

The music of a quadrille floated in from the ball-room. Waiters constantly thundered past the door with a clattering of dishes. But within the reading-room a profound stillness reigned.

A low, muffled voice which sounded as if it came from the chimney suddenly broke the silence.

"We'll be more comfortable here, I think. Come on! This way, fellows!"

The door opened and a broad-shouldered, stocky individual in a coachman's livery, with peacock's feathers in his hat, wearing a mask, entered the reading-room. He was followed by two ladies, also in masks, and a

waiter carrying a tray. On the tray were a squat
bottle of liqueur, three bottles of red wine, and several
glasses.

"This way. It'll be cooler here," said the man. "Put
the tray on the table. Sit down, Mesdemoiselles. *Je vous
pris à la trimontra!* And you, gentlemen, make room. . .
you're in the way."

He swayed slightly, brushing several magazines from
the top of the table.

"Put it down. And you move out of the way, you reading gentlemen. This is no time for your newspapers and
politics . . . put them away!"

"I would ask you to be a little quieter," said one
of the intellectuals, regarding the masked man through
his spectacles. "This is a reading-room, not a bar. . . .
This is no place for drinking."

"Who says so? Isn't the table steady, or will the ceiling come down on us? Funny! But I have no time for
talking. Put down your papers. . . . You've had your read
and it'll have to do for you. You're too clever as it 's,
besides you'll spoil your eyes, but what's more important is—I won't have it, and that's all about it."

The waiter put the tray on the table and stood at
the door, a napkin over his arm. The ladies immediately
started on the red wine.

"And to think that there are clever people who pre-
fer newspapers to drinks like this," said the man with
the peacock feathers, pouring himself out a liqueur. "It's
my belief, honoured sirs, that you are so fond of newspapers because you have no money for drinks. Am I
right? Haw-haw! Look at them reading. . . . And what is
written in your newspapers? You in the spectacles! Give
us some facts! Haw-haw! Stop it now! None of your airs
and graces! Have a drink!"

The man with the peacock feathers reached out and
tore the newspaper out of the hands of the gentleman in
spectacles. The latter went red and pale by turns, gaz-

ing in astonishment at the other intellectuals, and they returned his gaze.

"You forget yourself, my good sir," he cried. "You are turning the reading-room into a tavern, you see fit to create disorder, to snatch newspapers out of people's hands. I won't have it! You don't know whom you are addressing, my good sir. I am bank-manager Zhestyakov...."

"I don't care a hoot if you *are* Zhestyakov. And this will show you what I think of your newspapers."

The man held up the paper and tore it into fragments.

"What's the meaning of this, gentlemen?" muttered Zhestyakov, half-stunned with rage. "It's extremely strange, it's, it's ... simply flabbergasting!"

"Now he's angry!" laughed the man. "Oh, dear, how frightened I am! Look how my knees are shaking! Now listen to me, Honoured Sirs. Joking apart, I don't feel like talking to you.... You see I want to be alone with these mesdemoiselles, I want to enjoy myself, so please don't make any trouble, and, just go.... There's the door. Mr. Belebukhin! Get out of here! What are you turning up your snout like that for? When I say go, go! Quick march, before you are thrown out."

"What did you say?" asked Belebukhin, treasurer of the Orphans' Court, flushing and shrugging his shoulders. "I fail to understand. An insolent fellow bursts into the room and all of a sudden begins saying God knows what."

"An insolent fellow did you say?" shouted the man with the peacock feathers, working himself up into a rage and banging on the table with his fists, making the glasses on the tray jump. "Who d'you think you're talking to? You think, just because I'm wearing a mask you can call me what you like. Aren't you a hot-headed fellow! Get out when I tell you! And the bank manager can make himself scarce, too. Get out the lot of you, I don't want a single rascal left in the room! Come on now—go to your pig-sties."

"We'll see about that," said Zhestyakov, whose very glasses seemed to be sweating with agitation. "I'll show you! Hi, there, call one of the masters of ceremonies!"

A minute later a little red-haired master of ceremonies, sporting a scrap of blue ribbon in his lapel, came into the room panting from his exertions in the dance.

"Kindly leave the room," he began. "This is no place for drinking. Go to the refreshment-room, please."

"And where did *you* spring from?" asked the masked individual. "I didn't call you, did I?"

"No impertinence, if you please, and kindly go."

"Look here, my dear man. . . . I give you exactly one minute. . . . Since you are a master of ceremonies, and an important personage here, just march these artistes out. My mesdemoiselles don't like having strangers around. . . . They're shy, and I want to get my money's worth and see them in a state of nature. . . ."

"This boor doesn't seem to understand he's not in a pig-sty!" shouted Zhestyakov. "Call Yevstrat Spiridonich!"

"Yevstrat Spiridonich!" sounded all over the club. "Where is Yevstrat Spiridonich?"

Yevstrat Spiridonich, an old man in police uniform, was not slow to put in an appearance.

"Kindly leave the room," he said huskily, his ferocious eyes goggling, and the ends of his dyed moustache twitching.

"You frightened me!" said the man, laughing delightedly. "You did, by God! What a figure of fun, God strike me dead! Whiskered like a cat, eyes popping. . . . Haw-haw-haw!"

"No arguing, now!" yelled Yevstrat Spiridonich at the top of his voice, shaking with rage. "Get out or I'll have you chucked out!"

The reading-room was in an uproar. Yevstrat Spiridonich, red as a lobster, shouted and stamped. Zhestyakov shouted. Belebukhin shouted. All the intellectuals shouted, but their voices were drowned by the low, throaty, muffled bass of the masked man. In the general perturbation the dancing ceased and the guests poured out of the ball-room into the reading-room.

Summoning for the sake of effect all the police then on the club premises, Yevstrat Spiridonich sat down to write out a report.

"Write away!" said the masked man, thrusting his finger beneath the pen. "Now what will happen to poor me? Oh, poor me! Why are you set on ruining a poor orphan? Haw-haw! Go on, then! Is the report ready? Has everybody signed it? Now look! One, two, three. . . ."

He got up, drew himself to his full height, and tore off his mask. After exposing his drunken countenance and looking round at everyone to enjoy the effect produced, he fell back into his chair and laughed uproariously. And the effect was indeed remarkable. The intellectuals exchanged bewildered glances and turned pale, some were seen to scratch the backs of their heads. Yevstrat Spiridonich cleared his throat, like a man who has unconsciously perpetrated a terrible blunder.

Everyone recognized in the brawler hereditary honourable citizen Pyatigorov, the local millionaire-manufacturer, notorious for his rowdiness, his philanthropy and, as the local press never tired of remarking, his respect for education.

"Well, are you going?" asked Pyatigorov, after a short pause.

The intellectuals tiptoed out of the reading-room without uttering a word, and Pyatigorov locked the door behind them.

"You knew it was Pyatigorov," said Yevstrat Spiridonich in a husky undertone a little later, shaking by his shoulder the waiter who had brought wine into the reading-room. "Why didn't you say anything?"

"I was told not to."

"Told not to! Wait till I give you a month in quod, you rogue, you'll know the meaning of told not to. Get out! And you're a fine set, gentlemen," he continued, turning to the intellectuals. "Raising a riot. As if you couldn't leave the reading-room for ten minutes! Well, you made the mess and it's for you to get out of it. Oh, sirs, sirs.... I don't like your ways, before God, I don't...."

The intellectuals roamed about the club dejected, miserable, penitent, whispering to one another, like people who sense disaster. Their wives and daughters, hearing that Pyatigorov had been "insulted" and was offended, fell quiet and began leaving for their homes. The dancing ceased.

At two o'clock in the morning Pyatigorov came out of the reading-room; he was reeling drunk. Going into the ball-room he sat down beside the band and dozed to the sound of the music, till at last, his head bowed mournfully, he began to snore.

"Stop playing!" cried the masters of ceremonies, waving at the musicians. "Sh.... Yegor Nilich is asleep."

"Would you like me to see you home, Yegor Nilich?" enquired Belebukhin, bending down to the millionaire's ear.

Pyatigorov protruded his lips as if trying to blow a fly off his cheek.

"Would you like me to see you home?" repeated Belebukhin. Or shall I tell them to bring your carriage round?"

"Hey? What? Ha! It's you.... What d'you want?"

"To see you home ... time to go bye-bye."

"Home. I want to go home ... take me home...."

Beaming with satisfaction, Belebukhin helped Pyatigorov to his feet. The rest of the intellectuals came running up, wreathed in smiles, and together they lifted

the hereditary honourable citizen to his feet, and bore
him with elaborate care to his carriage.

"Only an artist, a man of talent, could have taken in
a whole company like that," babbled Zhestyakov cheerfully, helping the millionaire into his carriage. "I'm literally amazed, Yegor Nilich. I can't stop laughing, even
now... ha-ha.... And we all got so excited and fussy!
Ha-ha! Believe me I never laughed so much in the
theatre. Such depths of humour! I shall remember this
unforgettable evening all my life."

After seeing off Pyatigorov the intellectuals felt
cheered and consoled.

"He shook hands with me," boasted Zhestyakov, in
high glee. "So it's all right, he isn't angry."

"Let's hope so!" sighed Yevstrat Spiridonich. "He's
a scoundrel, a bad lot but—he's our benefactor. You've
got to be careful."

1884

WOE

Turner Grigory Petrov, who had a well-established reputation both as a splendid craftsman and the most hardened drunkard and ne'er-do-well in the whole Galchino district, was taking his sick wife to the Zemstvo hospital. He had to drive thirty versts, and the road was appalling; even the postman could scarcely cope with it, not to mention a lazy fellow like turner Grigory. A chill, harsh wind blew in his face. Snow-flakes whirled in great clouds, and it was hard to make out if the snow came from the sky or the earth. Neither fields, telegraph-posts, nor woods could be seen for the snow, and when a particularly violent gust of wind descended upon Grigory, not even the shaft-bow was visible. The feeble, aged mare plodded forward at a snail's pace. She needed all her energy for drawing a hoof at a time out of the deep snow and straining forward with her head.... The turner was in a hurry. He jumped up and down on the seat restlessly, every now and then lashing at the horse's back.

"Don't cry, Matryona," he muttered. "Try and bear it. We'll soon be at the hospital, God willing, and they'll see to you in a jiffy.... Pavel Ivanich will give you

some drops, or tell them to bleed you, or perhaps he
will be so good as to have you rubbed with spirits, it
draws the pain from the side, you know. Pavel Ivanich
will do his best. . . . He'll shout and stamp his foot,
and then he'll do what he can. . . . He's a nice gentleman, very kind, God bless him. . . . As soon as we get
there he'll come running out of his house, and start
swearing: 'What? Why?' he'll shout. 'Why didn't you
come earlier? Am I a dog, to look after you devils the
whole day? Why didn't you come in the morning? Get
out! Come tomorrow!' And I will say: 'Mr. Doctor! Pavel Ivanich! Your Honour!'—Gee up, you devil, gee up!"

The turner lashed at the horse and rambled on, not
looking at his wife.

" 'Your Honour! As God is my witness . . . I swear by
the Holy Cross that I left home early in the morning.
How could I get here in time when the Lord in his wrath
sent a blizzard like this? You can see for yourself. . . .
Even a good horse would not be able to make it, and
mine—look at it!—it's not a horse, it's a disgrace!' And
Pavel Ivanich will frown and shout: 'I know you! You'll
always find an excuse! Especially you, Grigory! I know
you well. I suppose you stopped on the way five times
at taverns.' And I'll say: 'Your Honour! Am I a heart-
less beast, a heathen? My old woman ready to give up
the ghost, dying, and me to be running into taverns!
How can you say such things? To hell with the taverns!'
Then Pavel Ivanich will tell them to carry you into the
hospital. And I will bow down before him: 'Pavel Ivanich! Your Honour! We thank you humbly! Forgive us,
poor fools and sinners. Do not judge us harshly, we're
only muzhiks! We deserve to be kicked out, and you
come out into the snow to meet us.' And Pavel Ivanich
will look as if he was ready to strike me, and will say:
'Instead of flopping down at my feet, you'd better stop
swilling vodka, you fool, and have some pity on your
old woman. You ought to be whipped!' 'Whipped, Pavel

Ivanich, God knows we ought to be whipped! But how can we help falling at your feet and bowing before you, when you are our benefactor, our own father? Your Honour! It's the truth I'm saying, before God it is—spit in my eye if I go back on it! The moment my Matryona here gets better, the moment she is herself again, I'll make you whatever you are good enough to order. A cigarette-case, if you like, of speckled birch, croquet-balls, skittles as good as foreign ones. . . I'll do anything for you! And I won't take a kopek from you. They'd take four rubles from you in Moscow for a cigarette-case like that, and I won't take a kopek." And the doctor will laugh and say: 'All right! All right! That'll do. A pity you're such a drunkard, though.' I know how to talk to the gentry, old woman. The gentleman doesn't live that I couldn't get round. If only God helps us not to lose our way! What a blizzard! I can hardly see for the snow."

The turner muttered incessantly, letting his tongue run on mechanically, to stifle his uneasiness. But though he had words and to spare at his command, but the thoughts and questions in his head were still more numerous. Grief had taken the turner unawares, like a bolt from the blue, and he was at his wit's end, unable to recover, to become his normal self again, to think. Up till now he had lived a carefree life, in a kind of drunken stupor, knowing neither grief nor joy, and all of a sudden he felt excruciating pain at his heart. The lighthearted idler and drunkard suddenly found himself in the position of a busy, preoccupied man, a man in a hurry, at odds with nature herself.

As the turner remembered it, the grief had begun the evening before. When he had returned home the evening before, tipsy as usual, and begun, from ancient habit, to swear and brandish his fists, his wife had looked at her tyrant as she had never looked at him before. The usual expression of her old eyes was as martyred

and meek as that of a dog which is beaten plentifully
and fed sparsely, but now they were stern and still, like
the eyes of saints in icons, or of dying people. The grief
had begun with those strange, disturbing eyes. The bewildered turner had begged a neighbour to lend him
his horse, and now he was taking his wife to the hospital, in the hope that Pavel Ivanich with his powders and
salves would bring back the familiar expression to the
old woman's eyes.

"Mind, Matryona," he muttered, "if Pavel Ivanich
asks you if I beat you, say: 'Oh, no Sir!' And I'll never
beat you any more. By the Holy Cross I won't! You know
I never really meant it when I beat you. I only beat you
for want of something better to do. I'm fond of you.
Another man wouldn't care, but I take you to the hospital... I'm doing all I can. And in a blizzard like this!
Thy will, Oh Lord! If only the Lord would help us not
to lose our way! How's your side, Matryona? Why
don't you say something? I ask you—does your side
hurt?"

He thought it queer that the snow did not melt on the
old woman's face, queer that the face itself seemed to
have lengthened, and was such an earthy-grey colour,
like soiled wax, and looked so stern, so grave.

"Old fool!" muttered the turner. "I ask you in good
faith, before God, and you.... Old fool! I won't take you
to Pavel Ivanich, so there!"

The turner let the reins hang loose, and gave himself up to his thoughts. He could not bring himself to
turn and look at the old woman—he was afraid. To
keep on questioning her without getting any reply
frightened him, too. At last, to put an end to the suspense, without looking at the old woman he felt her
cold hand. When he let go of it, it fell back like a stone.

"She's dead! Ah me! Ah me!"

And the turner wept. What he felt was not so much
grief, as vexation. How quickly things happen in this

life, he thought to himself. His grief had hardly begun, and now all was over. He had hardly begun to live with his old woman, to speak his heart to her, to cherish her, when she died. . . . He had lived with her forty years, and these forty years had passed in a kind of mist. What with drinking, fighting and want, life had passed almost unnoticed. And the old woman had died at the very moment when he had felt that he loved her, that he could not live without her, that he had wronged her terribly.

"She used to go begging," he remembered. "I sent her to beg for bread, I did! Ah me, ah me! She could have lived another ten years, poor fool, and now she thinks I was really like that. Holy Mother, where am I going? It's burying she needs now, not a doctor! Gee up, you!"

Grigory turned the horse's head and lashed out at it with all his might. The road got worse and worse every hour. Now he could not see the shaft-bow at all. Every now and then the sleigh bumped against a young fir-tree, some dark object scratched the turner's hand and flashed before his eyes, and once more he could see nothing but a whirling whiteness.

"If one could only start life over again. . ." thought the turner.

He remembered that forty years ago Matryona had been young, pretty, gay, that she had come from a prosperous home. They had married her to him because of his skill. They had had everything required for a happy life, but ever since the moment, after the wedding was over, he had flung himself, dead-drunk, on the stove-ledge, he had seemed unable to wake up properly. He could remember the wedding, but what happened after it he could not for the life of him remember, except drinking, sleeping and fighting. And so forty years had been wasted.

The white clouds of whirling snow began gradually to turn grey. Dusk was falling.

"Where am I going?" the turner again asked himself. "I must bury her, and I keep on driving towards
the hospital. I must have gone out of my mind!"

Again he turned the horse's head, again he beat it.
The mare, mustering up all her energies, snorted and
started off at a trot. The turner lashed at her again
and again.... He heard a thud somewhere behind him
and knew, without looking back, that it was the head
of the corpse banging against the side of the sleigh. And
it kept getting darker and darker, the wind colder and
harsher....

"To begin life over again," thought the turner. "I'd
get myself new instruments, and take orders ... and
I'd give her the money ... I would!"

And then he let go of the reins, started looking for
them, tried to pick them up, but in vain; his hands would
not move....

"Never mind," he thought. "The mare will go of herself, she knows the way. If I could get a nap, now.... I
could have a rest till it's time for the funeral and the
service."

The turner shut his eyes and dozed. A little later
he heard the horse come to a stop. Opening his eyes he
found himself in front of something dark, like a hut or
a hay-rick.

He knew he ought to get off the sleigh and find out
where he was, but there was such a languor in all his
limbs that he could not have stirred, even to save himself from freezing to death.... He slept peacefully.

He waked up in a big room with whitewashed walls.
Bright sunlight was streaming through the window.
The turner could see that there were people in the room
and his first thought was to appear dignified and knowing.

"We must have a service for the old woman," he
said. "The priest will have to be told."

"All right, all right! You just keep still," a voice
interrupted him.

"Why, it's Pavel Ivanich," cried the turner in astonishment, suddenly catching sight of the doctor. "Your Honour! Benefactor!"

He tried to jump out of bed and prostrate himself before medical science, but felt that his arms and legs would not obey him.

"Your Honour! Where are my feet? Where are my hands?"

"Say good-bye to your hands and feet.... You got them frozen. Come, come, what are you crying for? You've had your life, and thank God for it! I suppose you're over sixty, you've had your day."

"Woe! woe, Your Honour! Forgive me! If I could only live another six years!"

"What for?"

"It wasn't my horse, I shall have to give it back.... I shall have to bury my old woman. Oh, how quickly everything happens in this world. Your Honour! Pavel Ivanich! A cigarette-case of the best speckled birch! I'll make you a croquet-set...."

The doctor went out of the room with a wave of his hand. All over with the turner.

1885

VANKA

N ine-year-old Vanka Zhukov, who had been apprenticed three months ago to Alyakhin the shoemaker, did not go to bed on Christmas eve. He waited till his master and mistress and the senior apprentices had gone to church, and then took from the cupboard a bottle of ink and a pen with a rusty nib, spread out a crumpled sheet of paper, and was all ready to write. Before tracing the first letter he glanced several times anxiously at the door and window, peered at the dark icon, with shelves holding cobbler's lasts stretching on either side of it, and gave a quivering sigh. The paper lay on the bench, and Vanka knelt on the floor at the bench.

"Dear Grandad Konstantin Makarich," he wrote. "I am writing a letter to you. I send you Christmas greetings and hope God will send you his blessings. I have no father and no Mummie and you are all I have left."

Vanka raised his eyes to the dark window-pane, in which the reflection of the candle flickered, and in his imagination distinctly saw his grandfather, Konstantin Makarich, who was night watchman on the estate of some gentlefolk called Zhivarev. He was a small, lean old man about sixty-five, but remarkably lively and agile, with a smiling face and eyes bleary with drink.

In the day-time he either slept in the back kitchen, or
sat joking with the cook and the kitchen-maids, and
in the night, wrapped in a great sheepskin coat, he walked
round and round the estate, sounding his rattle. After him, with drooping heads, went old Kashtanka and
another dog, called Eel, on account of his black coat
and long, weasel-like body. Eel was wonderfully re-
spectful and insinuating, and turned the same appealing
glance on friends and strangers alike, but he inspired
confidence in no one. His deferential manner and docil-
ity were a cloak for the most Jesuitical spite and malice. He was an adept at stealing up, to snap at a foot,
creeping into the ice-house, or snatching a peasant's
chicken. His hind-legs had been slashed again and again,
twice he had been strung up, he was beaten within an
inch of his life every week, but he survived it all.

Grandad was probably standing at the gate at this
moment, screwing up his eyes to look at the bright red
light coming from the church windows, or stumping
about in his felt boots, fooling with the servants. His
rattle would be fastened to his belt. He would be throwing out his arms and hugging himself against the cold,
or, with his old man's titter, pinching a maid, or one
of the cooks.

"Have a nip," he would say, holding out his snuff-
box to the women.

The women would take a pinch and sneeze. Grandfather would be overcome with delight, breaking out into
jolly laughter, and shouting:

"Good for frozen noses!"

Even the dogs would be given snuff. Kashtanka
would sneeze, shake her head and walk away, offended.
But Eel, too polite to sneeze, would wag his tail. And
the weather was glorious. The air still, transparent,
fresh. It was a dark night, but the whole village, with its
white roofs, the smoke rising from the chimneys, the
trees, silver with rime, the snow-drifts, could be seen

distinctly. The sky was sprinkled with gaily twinkling stars, and the Milky Way stood out as clearly as if newly scrubbed for the holiday and polished with snow. ...

Vanka sighed, dipped his pen in the ink, and went on writing:

"And yesterday I had such a hiding. The master took me by the hair and dragged me out into the yard and beat me with the stirrup-strap because by mistake I went to sleep rocking their baby. And one day last week the mistress told me to gut a herring and I began from the tail and she picked up the herring and rubbed my face with the head. The other apprentices make fun of me they send me to the tavern for vodka and make me steal the masters cucumbers and the master beats me with the first thing he finds. And there is nothing to eat. They give me bread in the morning and gruel for dinner and in the evening bread again but I never get tea or cabbage soup they gobble it all up themselves. And they make me sleep in the passage and when their baby cries I dont get any sleep at all I have to rock it. Dear Grandad for the dear Lords sake take me away from here take me home to the village I cant bear it any longer. Oh Grandad I beg and implore you and I will always pray for you do take me away from here or I'll die. ..."

Vanka's lips twitched, he rubbed his eyes with a black fist and gave a sob.

"I will grind your snuff for you," he went on. "I will pray for you and you can flog me as hard as you like if I am naughty. And if you think there is nothing for me to do I will ask the steward to take pity on me and let me clean the boots or I will go as a shepherd-boy instead of Fedya. Dear Grandad I cant stand it it is killing me. I thought I would run away on foot to the village but I have no boots and I was afraid of the frost. And when I grow up to be a man I will look after you and I will not let anyone hurt you and when you die I will pray for your soul like I do for my Mummie.

"Moscow is such a big town there are so many gentle-
mens houses and such a lot of horses and no sheep and
the dogs are not a bit fierce. The boys dont go about with
the star at Christmas and they dont let you sing in church
and once I saw them selling fish-hooks in the shop all
together with the lines and for any fish you like very
good ones and there was one would hold a sheat-fish
weighing a pood and I have seen shops where there are
all sorts of guns just like the master has at home they
must cost a hundred rubles each. And in the butchers
shops there are grouse and wood-cock and hares but the
people in the shop dont say where they were shot.

"Dear Grandad when they have a Christmas tree at
the big house take a gilded nut for me and put it away
in the green chest. Ask Miss Olga Ignatyevna tell her
its for Vanka."

Vanka gave a sharp sigh and once more gazed at
the window-pane. He remembered his grandfather going
to get a Christmas tree for the gentry, and taking his
grandson with him. Oh what happy times those had been!
Grandfather would give a chuckle, and the frost-bound
wood chuckled, and Vanka, following their example,
chuckled, too. Before chopping down the fir-tree, Grandfather would smoke a pipe, take a long pinch of snuff,
and laugh at the shivering Vanka.... The young fir-
trees, coated with rime, stood motionless, waiting to see
which one of them was to die. And suddenly a hare would
come leaping over a snow-drift, swift as an arrow....
Grandfather could never help shouting:

"Stop it, stop it ... stop it! Oh, you stub-tailed devil!"

Grandfather would drag the tree to the big house, and
they would start decorating it.... Miss Olga Ignatyevna,
Vanka's favourite, was the busiest of all. While Pelageya,
Vanka's mother, was alive and in service at the big house,
Olga Ignatyevna used to give Vanka sweets, and amuse
herself by teaching him to read, write and count to a hundred, and even to dance the quadrille. But when Pelageya

died, the orphaned Vanka was sent down to the back kitchen to his grandfather, and from there to Moscow, to Alyakhin the shoemaker. . . .

"Come to me dear Grandad," continued Vanka. "I beg you for Christs sake take me away from here. Pity me unhappy orphan they beat me all the time and I am always hungry and I am so miserable here I cant tell you I cry all the time. And one day the master hit me over the head with a last and I fell down and thought I would never get up again. I have such a miserable life worse than a dogs. And I send my love to Alyona one-eyed Yegor and the coachman and dont give my concertina to anyone. I remain your grandson Ivan Zhukov dear Grandad come."

Vanka folded the sheet of paper in four and put it into an envelope which he had bought the day before for a kopek. . . . Then he paused to think, dipped his pen into the ink-pot, wrote: *"GRANDAD"* scratched his head, thought again, and added: *"KONSTANTIN MAKARICH*

THE VILLAGE"

Pleased that no one had prevented him from writing, he put on his cap and ran out into the street without putting his coat on over his shirt.

The men at the butcher's told him, when he asked them the day before, that letters are put into letter-boxes, and from these boxes sent all over the world on mail coaches with three horses and drunken drivers and jingling bells. Vanka ran as far as the nearest letter-box and dropped his precious letter into the slit. . . .

An hour later, lulled by rosy hopes, he was fast asleep. . . . He dreamed of a stove. On the stove-ledge sat his grandfather, his bare feet dangling, reading the letter to the cooks. . . . Eel was walking backwards and forwards in front of the stove, wagging his tail. . . .

1886

ANTAGONISTS

Some time after nine o'clock on a dark September night, Andrei, six-year-old, and the only son of Doctor Kirilov, Zemstvo medical officer, died of diphtheria. The doctor's wife had just sunk on to her knees at the side of the cot, in the first paroxysm of despair, when the front-door bell rang shrilly.

Owing to the diphtheria the servants had been sent out of the house in the morning. Kirilov, just as he was, in his shirt-sleeves, his waistcoat unbuttoned, went to open the door, not even wiping his wet face and carbolic-stained hands. It was dark in the hall, and all he could make out of the man who entered was his height, which was average, his white muffler, and his large face, which was so pale that it seemed to light up the hall....

"Is the doctor at home?" he asked quickly.

"I am at home," replied Kirilov. "What do you want?"

"Oh! Glad to meet you!" said the man in a tone of relief, groping for the doctor's hand in the dark, and pressing it heartily between his two hands when he found it. "Very glad...very glad! We have met before. My name is Abogin.... I had the pleasure of meeting you in the summer at the Gnuchevs. I'm so glad I found you in. Come with me at once, I implore you...my wife is dangerously ill. I have my carriage here."

The voice and movements of the newcomer showed that he was in a state of extreme agitation. He was breathing fast, and spoke in a rapid, trembling voice, as if he had only just escaped from a fire or a mad dog, and he expressed himself with child-like artlessness. He spoke in short, broken phrases, as people who are terrified and overwhelmed are apt to, and uttered a number of irrelevant words having nothing to do with the case.

"I was afraid I wouldn't find you in," he went on. "All the way here I went through agonies.... Put on your coat and come, for God's sake.... It began like this: Papchinsky came to see me—Alexander Semyonovich, you know him. We sat talking for a while, and then we went to the table, and had tea. Suddenly my wife cried out, put her hand on her heart, and fell back in her chair. We carried her to her bed and ... I rubbed her temples with ammonia and sprinkled her with water ... but she lay there like the dead.... I'm so afraid it's aneurism.... Come.... Her father died of aneurism...."

Kirilov listened in silence as if he did not understand Russian.

When Abogin again mentioned Papchinsky and his wife's father, and again searched for Kirilov's hand in the darkness, the doctor threw back his head and drawled out indifferently:

"Sorry I can't go to your house. Five minutes ago my—son died."

"No, really!" whispered Abogin, retreating a step. "My God, what an inopportune moment I have chosen. What an unlucky day—it's really remarkable. What a coincidence... who would have thought it!"

He seized the door-handle, his head bent, as if lost in thought. Apparently he was undecided whether to go or to continue his entreaties.

"Listen!" he said passionately, seizing Kirilov by the

shirt-sleeve. "I understand your situation perfectly. God knows I'm ashamed to try and gain your attention at such a moment, but what am I to do? Judge for yourself—where am I to go? There's not a single other doctor in the place but you. Come, for God's sake! I don't ask you for myself. It's not I who am ill."

A silence ensued. Kirilov turned his back on Abogin, stood thus for a minute or two, and then went slowly out of the hall into the sitting-room. Judging by his irresolute, mechanical gait, by the absorption with which, once in the room, he straightened the fringed shade on the unlit lamp, and glanced into a thick book lying on the table, he had neither intentions nor desires at that moment, and was thinking of nothing. He had probably quite forgotten that there was a stranger standing in the hall. The dusk and quiet of the room seemed only to increase his stupefaction.

Going from the sitting-room into his study, he raised his right foot higher than necessary, and groped for the frame of the door, while his whole figure expressed a kind of bewilderment, as if he had found himself in a strange house, or had got drunk for the first time in his life, and was now yielding, bewildered, to the new sensation. A broad strip of light spread across one of the walls of the study and over the book-shelves; this light, together with the heavy, pungent odour of carbolic and ether, came from the door into the bedroom, which was ajar.... The doctor sank into a chair at the table. For a moment he gazed drowsily at his books, lit up by the ray of light, and then got up again and went into the bedroom.

Here, in the bedroom, a deathly stillness reigned. Here the veriest trifle bore eloquent testimony to the tempest which had so recently raged, and had now subsided into weariness, here all was repose. A candle standing on a stool amidst a crowd of bottles, boxes and jars, and a big lamp on the chest-of-drawers, lit up the

whole room. On a bed right under the window lay a
little boy with his eyes open and an expression of wonder on his face. He did not move, but his open eyes
seemed to get darker every moment, and to be going
deeper and deeper into his skull. Her hands on his
body, and her face hidden in the bed-clothes, the mother
knelt at the bed-side. Like the child, she also did not
move, but what potential movement there was in the
curves of her body and in her arms! She pressed against
the bed with her whole being, with force and avidity,
as if fearing to disturb the quiet easeful pose her exhausted body had at last found for itself. Blankets,
scraps of linen, basins, the water standing in pools on
the floor, the brushes and spoons lying about, the white
bottle of lime-water, the very air, heavy and close—all
was resting and seemed to be plunged in profound
peace.

The doctor stood beside his wife, thrust his hands
into his trousers pockets and, his head on one side, fixed
his gaze on his son. His face expressed indifference, and
only the drops glistening on his beard showed that he
had recently wept.

The repellence and horror associated with the idea
of death were lacking in the bedroom. In the prevailing paralysis, the mother's pose, the indifference
stamped on the features of the father, there was something almost attractive, something touching, that subtle,
imperceptible beauty of human grief, which people will
not quickly learn to understand, still less to describe,
and which, probably, can only be conveyed by music.
And there was beauty in the sombre stillness. Kirilov
and his wife said nothing, did not weep, as if, in addition to the burden of their grief they felt the poetry of
their situation. Just as in its time their youth had passed,
their right to have children had vanished for ever with
this boy. The doctor was forty-four years old, he was
already grey, and looked an old man. His faded, dell

cate wife was thirty-five. Andrei was not merely their only child, he was their last.

Unlike his wife, the doctor belonged to those natures which feel the need for action in moments of mental suffering. After standing a few minutes beside his wife, he went out of the bedroom, still lifting his right foot unnecessarily high, into a tiny room half filled up by a wide sofa. From here he went into the kitchen. Wandering about near the stove and the bed of the cook, he bent down and went through a low door into the hall.

There he once more was confronted by the white muffler and the pallid countenance.

"At last," sighed Abogin, putting his hand on the door handle. "Come, please do!"

The doctor started, glanced at him, and remembered. . . .

"But I told you I couldn't," he said, suddenly coming back to life. "How very extraordinary. . . ."

"I'm not a graven image. Doctor, I understand your situation perfectly. I feel for you!" said Abogin in imploring tones, laying his hand on his muffler. "But I don't ask you for myself. My wife is dying. If you had heard that shriek, seen her face, you would understand my importunity. My God, and I thought you had gone to dress! Doctor, time is precious. Come, I beg you."

"I cannot go with you," said the doctor, uttering each word distinctly, and stepping into the sitting-room.

Abogin followed him and seized him by the sleeve.

"You are in great trouble, I understand you, but it is not to cure a toothache, not just for a diagnosis, that I ask you to come, it is to save a human life." He continued in a begging voice: "This life stands above personal grief. Come now, I ask you to display courage, heroism. In the name of humanity!"

"Humanity—that's a two-edged weapon," said Kirilov testily. "In the name of that same humanity I ask

you not to take me away. Extraordinary, really! I can
hardly stand on my feet, and you try to intimidate me
with the word 'humanity.' I am fit for nothing just
now.... Nothing will induce me to go, and besides I
have no one to leave my wife with. No, no...."

Kirilov retreated a step, keeping the other off with a
thrust of his hands.

"Please don't ask me any more," he continued, in sudden panic. "Excuse me ... according to Volume XIII of
the code I am bound to go with you, and you have the
right to drag me with you by the coat-collar. Very well,
do so, but ... I am fit for nothing.... I'm not even in a
state to speak.... Excuse me...."

"You shouldn't use that tone to me, Doctor," said Abogin, once more tugging at the doctor's sleeve. "What do I
care about Volume XIII? I have no right whatever to force
you against your will. If you are coming, then come! If
not, it can't be helped, I appeal not to your inclinations
but to your heart. A young woman is dying. You say
your son has just died—then of all people you ought to
understand my anguish!"

Abogin's voice trembled with agitation. There was
much more persuasive power in the trembling and the
tones of his voice than in his words. Abogin was sincere,
but it was remarkable that all his phrases sounded stilted,
callous, unnecessarily florid, and seemed an offence both
to the atmosphere of the doctor's flat, and to the woman
dying somewhere far away. He felt it himself, and, fearing he could not make himself understood, tried his utmost to make his voice soft and appealing, so as to get
his way, if not by words, then by sincerity of accent. It
may be asserted that phrases, however beautiful and deep,
only affect the indifferent, and do not always satisfy those
who are happy or grief-stricken. This is why the highest
expression of happiness or grief is more often than not
silence. Lovers understand each other better when they
are silent, and a passionate, ardent speech over a grave

only touches outsiders, and seems cold and insignificant
to the widow and children.

Kirilov stood in silence. When Abogin pronounced a
few more phrases about the high calling of a doctor,
self-sacrifice, and so on, the doctor asked morosely:

"Is it far?"

"Only about thirteen or fourteen versts. My horses
are excellent, Doctor. I give you my word of honour
they'll take you there and back within an hour. Only
one hour!"

These last words weighed more with the doctor than
the references to humanity and the calling of a doctor.
After a moment's consideration, he said, sighing:

"Very well. Let's go."

He went into his study with a rapid gait, now become quite steady, and a moment after appeared in a long
frock-coat. The delighted Abogin walked beside him with
short, shuffling steps, helped him on with his coat, and
went out of the house with him.

It was dark outside, but lighter than in the hall. The
tall, stooping figure of the doctor, his narrow beard, and
aquiline nose were clearly outlined against the darkness.
Abogin, besides his pallid face, now displayed a big
head and a student's cap which hardly covered the
crown. The muffler showed white only in front, at the
back it was hidden by his long hair.

"Believe me, I shall know how to show my appre-
ciation for your magnanimity," he murmured, as he
seated the doctor in the carriage. "We'll be there in no
time. Luka, old chap, drive as fast as you can.
Please do!"

The coachman drove rapidly. At first they passed a
row of ugly buildings ranged along the court-yard of
the hospital. They were all in darkness, but for a bright
light streaming across the front-garden from a window
right at the back of the yard, and three windows in the
top storey of one of the hospital buildings, in which

the panes seemed paler than the surrounding air. Then
the carriage plunged into thick darkness, and there was
a smell of damp and mushrooms and the sound of rustling leaves. Among the branches, the crows, aroused by
the noise of the wheels, raised startled, plaintive
cries, as if they knew the doctor's son was dead, and
Abogin's wife was ill. But soon single trees, and then
thickets, began to flash by. A pond on the surface of
which reposed great black shadows, gleamed sombrely
and the carriage rolled over open country. The cawing
of the crows became hollower, and soon died altogether.

Kirilov and Abogin hardly spoke the whole way.
Only once Abogin sighed, murmuring:

"Agonizing situation. You never love those near to
you as you do when you fear to lose them."

And when the carriage slowed down to ford the river,
Kirilov suddenly started, and moved in his seat, as if
alarmed by the splashing of the water.

"Look here, let me go," he said mournfully. "I'll
come to you later on. I only want to send my assistant
to my wife. After all, she's quite alone."

Abogin said nothing. The carriage swayed, its
wheels knocking against the stones, emerged on the
sandy shore and rolled onwards. In his misery Kirilov
fidgeted and glanced around him. Behind them, by the
dim light of the stars could be seen the road and the
willows on the river bank, vanishing in the gloom. To
the right extended a plain, as smooth and boundless
as the sky. In the distance dim lights gleamed on it
here and there, probably above peat marshes. To the
left, parallel to the road, stretched a hillside, shaggy
with bushes, and above it the big red crescent moon
hung motionless, slightly veiled by the mist, and surrounded by tiny cloudlets, which seemed to be watching it from all sides, and mounting guard over it, so
that it should not go away.

The whole of nature seemed to be pervaded with despair and disease. Like a fallen woman alone in a dark room, trying not to think about the past, the earth was haunted by memories of spring and summer, waiting in apathy for the inevitable arrival of winter. Wherever one looked nature presented a dark, endlessly deep, chilly pit out of which neither Kirilov, Abogin, nor the red crescent moon could ever clamber....

The nearer the carriage approached its destination, the more impatient became Abogin. He moved about, jumped up, looked ahead over the coachman's shoulder. And when at last the carriage drew up in front of a porch picturesquely draped with a striped canvas curtain, and he looked up at the lighted windows on the second floor, his breath coming faster and louder.

"If anything happens, I will never get over it," he said, accompanying the doctor into the hall, and rubbing his hands in his agitation. "But there are no sounds of perturbation, so everything must be all right, so far," he added, straining his ears in the silence.

Neither voices nor footsteps were to be heard in the hall, and the whole house seemed asleep, despite the brilliant lights. Now the doctor and Abogin, who had hitherto been in the dark, could see each other properly. The doctor was tall, stoop-shouldered, and dressed in a slovenly manner. He was not good-looking. His thick, almost negroid lips, aquiline nose, and languid, indifferent glance, held something which was unpleasantly harsh, cold and severe. His unbrushed hair, sunken temples, the premature greyness of his long, narrow beard, with the chin gleaming through it here and there, the earthy pallor of his skin, his negligent awkward manners, all suggested habitual want, deprivation, weariness of life, lack of interest in people. To look at his inexpressive figure you would never have thought this man had a wife, that he could weep for a child. Abogin represented something very different. He was a

stocky, massive, fair man, with a big head, and marked,
but pudgy features, elegantly attired according to the
latest fashion. There was something aristocratic and leo-
nine in his bearing, his tightly buttoned frock-coat, his
mane of hair, and his face. He held up his head as he
walked, his chest thrust well forward, spoke in a pleasant baritone, while an almost feminine elegance displayed itself in the way in which he removed his muffler, and smoothed his hair. Even his pallor, and the
childish timidity with which he glanced up the stairs
while taking off his overcoat, did not mar the general
impression or affect the state of good nourishment, the
health, and the self-confidence which emanated from his
whole figure.

"Nobody about and not a sound," he said, as he
mounted the stairs. "And no fuss. Let's hope...."

He conducted the doctor through the hall into a big
room, in which hovered the black shape of a grand-
piano, and a candelabra hung from the ceiling enveloped in a white loose-cover. From this room they went
into a small drawing-room, very snug and pleasant,
veiled in a kind of rosy twilight.

"Sit down here and wait, Doctor," said Abogin.
"I'll be back in a minute. I'll go and tell them you're
here."

Kirilov was left alone. The luxury of the drawing-
room, the pleasant twilight, his very presence in a
strange unfamiliar house, an adventure in itself, seemed
not to make the faintest impression on him. He sat down
in an arm-chair and inspected his carbolic-stained fingers. He barely observed a crimson lamp-shade and, a
'cello-case, but glancing towards the ticking clock he did
notice a stuffed wolf, as massive and well-nourished as
Abogin himself.

All was quiet. Far away in one of the other rooms
someone exclaimed "Ah!" loudly, a glass door, apparently on a wardrobe, clattered, and all was silence

once more. After five minutes or so Kirilov stopped looking at his hands and raised his eyes towards the door through which Abogin had disappeared.

Abogin was standing in the door-way, but he was not the same man who had gone out of the room. His look of nourishment and refined elegance had deserted him, his face, hands, and pose were stamped with a repulsive air of something which was neither horror exactly, nor physical distress. His nose, lips, moustache, all his features, were twitching, as if they wanted to wrench themselves from his face, there was a gleam of pain in his eyes. . . .

He strode with long, heavy steps into the middle of the drawing-room, and then bent forward, groaned, and shook his fists.

"She deceived me!" he shouted, stressing the middle syllable of the word "deceived." "Deceived me! Left me! Fell ill and sent me for the doctor simply to run away with that jackanapes Papchinsky! My God!"

Abogin strode heavily up to the doctor, shook his pudgy white fists into the latter's face, and howled out:

"Left me! Deceived me! Why all that lying? My God! My God! Why that filthy, swindling trick, that treacherous, fiendish game? What harm did I ever do her? She's left me!"

Tears rolled down his cheeks. He turned on his heel and began pacing up and down the drawing-room. In his short frock-coat, fashionable narrow trousers, which made his legs look too thin for his body, with his big head and mane of hair, he was now more like a lion than ever. A look of curiosity flashed across the doctor's indifferent features. He rose and looked at Abogin.

"But where is the patient?" he asked.

"Patient! Patient!" shouted Abogin, laughing and crying and still brandishing his fists. "She's not a patient, she's an accursed female! How base! How shabby! Satan himself, you would think, could not have invented anything more revolting. Sent me away so that she could run off, run away with that jackanapes, that dull wag, that pimp! Oh, God, I would rather she had died! I shall never get over it. Never!"

The doctor drew himself up. He blinked, his eyes filled with tears, his narrow beard wagged from left to right as his jaws moved.

"Excuse me—what is the meaning of all this?" he asked, looking round curiously. "My child has died, my wife is overcome with grief, alone in the house.... I can hardly stand myself, I haven't slept for three nights... and what do I find? I have been made to play a part in some vulgar farce, to act as a kind of stage property. I—I don't understand."

Abogin opened one fist, flung a crumpled sheet of note-paper on the floor and trampled on it as if it were an insect he wanted to destroy.

"And I noticed nothing, understood nothing," he said through clenched teeth, shaking his fist in front of his face, with an expression as if someone had just trodden on his corn. "I never noticed the way he came every day, never noticed that he came in a carriage today. Why a carriage? And I, blind fool, never noticed! Blind fool!"

"I—I don't understand," muttered the doctor. "What does it all mean? It's sheer contempt of the individual, it's a mockery of human suffering. It's simply impossible—I never heard of such a thing in my life!"

With blank incredulity, like a man who has only just begun to realize that he has been deeply insulted, the doctor shrugged his shoulders, and flung out both his hands, and, unable either to speak or act, sank into the arm-chair.

"So you don't love me any more, you love another— very well then, but why the deception, why the base, treacherous trick!" exclaimed Abogin tearfully. "What's the good of it? And what was it for? What harm did I ever do you? Doctor!" he cried impetuously, going up to

Kirilov. "You have been the involuntary witness of my misfortune, and I will not conceal the truth from you. I swear to you, I loved that woman, I worshipped her, I was her slave. I sacrificed everything for her. Quarrelled with my people, threw up my work, gave up music, forgave her things I would never have forgiven my mother or sister.... I never gave her a harsh look.... I never gave her the slightest grounds. What are all the lies for? I did not demand love, but why this base deception? If you didn't love me, then why not say so, frankly —you knew my views on all this...."

With tears in his eyes, and trembling all over, Abogin poured out his whole heart before the doctor, in perfect sincerity. He spoke passionately, his hands pressed to his heart, revealing his domestic secrets without the slightest hesitation, actually seeming to be glad that these secrets had at last escaped from him. If he could have gone on talking for another hour in this way, completely unbosomed himself, he would no doubt have felt better. Who knows? If the doctor had heard him out with friendly sympathy, perhaps, as so often happens, he would have reconciled himself to his fate without a murmur, and without committing unnecessary follies.... But this was not to be. While Abogin was speaking, a noticeable change came over the doctor's face. The indifference and wonder stamped on his features gradually gave way to an expression of bitter resentment, indignation and wrath. His features became still more harsh, unyielding and disagreeable. When Abogin held in front of his eyes the photograph of a good-looking young woman whose face was as stern and blank as a nun's and asked him whether anyone could believe that a woman with a face like that could lie, the doctor suddenly sprang to his feet, with a savage gleam in his eyes, and said, rudely, emphasizing every word:

"Why are you telling me all this? I am not interested. I will not listen to you!" Here he began to shout, bang-

ing on the table with his fist. "I don't need your trivial
secrets, damn them! Don't dare to speak to me about
such trash. Perhaps you think I haven't been sufficiently
insulted yet? You consider me a servant whom you can
insult with impunity. Is that it?"

Abogin backed away from Kirilov and stared at him
in amazement.

"What did you bring me here for?" continued the
doctor, his beard wagging. "You married for want of
something better to do, you can play out your melo-
drama for the same reason, but what's it to do with
me? What have I to do with your love affairs? Leave me
in peace! Go in for gentlemanly fisticuffs, show off your
humane ideals, play—" (here the doctor shot a glance at
the 'cello-case), "play your double-bass and trombone,
fatten like a gelded cockerel, but don't dare to trifle with
human beings. If you can't respect them, leave them alone!"

"Excuse me, but what does all this mean?" said
Abogin, his face flushing.

"It means that it is base and ignoble to play with
people like this. I'm a doctor, you consider doctors, and
all workers who do not smell of eau-de-Cologne and
prostitution, your lackeys, people of *mauvais ton*. Do so,
if you like, but you have no right to use a suffering man
as stage property."

"How dare you say that to me?" said Abogin softly,
his face again twitching, this time with obvious rage.

"How dare *you*, knowing of my sorrow, bring me here
to listen to your vapourings?" shouted the doctor, banging on the table again. "What gives you the right to mock
at another's grief?"

"You must be mad!" cried Abogin. "How ungenerous.
I am profoundly unhappy myself, and ... and...."

"Unhappy!" echoed the doctor scornfully. "Don't use
that word, it has no application to you. Rotters, who cannot meet their bills, also call themselves unhappy. A
cockerel, suffering from adiposity, is unhappy, too."

"You forget yourself, my dear Sir!" squealed Abogin. "For such words ... blows are dealt. D'you understand me?"

Abogin fumbled hastily in the pocket of his jacket, brought out a bill-fold, extracted from it two notes and slapped them down on the table.

"That's for your visit," he said, his nostrils quivering. "You are paid."

"Don't dare to offer me money!" shouted the doctor, sweeping the notes on to the floor. "Insults cannot be repaid with money."

Abogin and the doctor confronted one another, furiously exchanging unmerited insults. They had probably never in their lives, even in delirium, uttered so many unjust, cruel and absurd remarks. In both, the egoism of the sufferer was roused. Those who suffer are egoistic, angry, unjust, and cruel, and less able to understand one another than really stupid people. Misfortune, far from uniting people, separates them, and even when it might be supposed that similarity of misfortune ought to bring people together, they show themselves a great deal more unjust and ruthless than do those who are comparatively content.

"Be so kind as to send me home!" shouted the doctor breathlessly.

Abogin rang a hand-bell sharply. When no one appeared in answer to his summons, he rang again, and flung the bell angrily on the floor. It struck the carpet with a hollow sound, uttering a plaintive, expiring moan. A footman appeared.

"Where have you been hiding, damn you?" shouted his master, rushing at him with clenched fists. "Where were you just now? Go and order the carriage for this gentleman, and get the brougham ready for me. Wait!" he cried, when the footman turned to go. "Let not a single traitor be left in this house tomorrow. Out with them all! I shall engage new servants! Swine!"

While waiting for the carriages Abogin and the doctor maintained silence. His well-nourished expression and subtle elegance had returned to the former. He paced up and down the room, tossing his head with a noble gesture, and seemed to be planning something. His wrath had not yet subsided, but he endeavoured to look as if he did not notice the presence of his enemy. The doctor stood still, holding on to the table with one hand and regarding Abogin with the profound, ugly, almost cynical contempt of which only the poor and miserable are capable, when confronted by satiety and elegance.

When, a little later, the doctor was seated in the carriage on his way home, the scornful expression still remained in his eyes. It was dark, much darker than it had been an hour ago. The red crescent moon had disappeared behind the hill and the guardian clouds lay in dark patches around the stars. Wheels could be heard on the road behind, and a brougham with red lamps gleaming overtook the doctor. It was Abogin, intent on protesting, on committing follies. . . .

All the way home the doctor thought, not of his wife nor of Andrei, but of Abogin and of the people inhabiting the house he had just left. His thoughts were unjust and cruel. He condemned Abogin, Abogin's wife, Papchinsky, everyone living in a rosy perfumed dusk, and gave himself up to hatred and contempt for them all the way, till his very heart ached. And an attitude to these people which was quite unjust took firm root in his mind.

Time will pass, and Kirilov's grief will pass, but the unjust attitude, unworthy of a human heart, will not pass, but will remain with the doctor till the day of his death.

1887

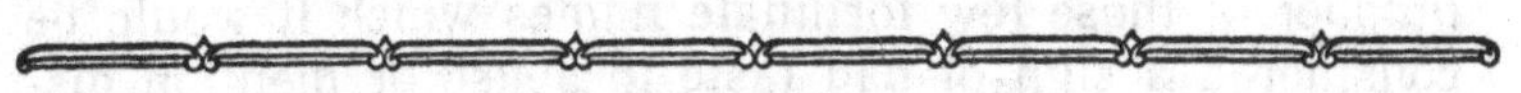

DULL STORY

(FROM AN OLD MAN'S NOTE-BOOK)

I

There lives in Russia a certain Nikolai Stepanovich, a highly esteemed professor, a privy councillor, a knight of many orders. He possesses so many medals, both Russian and foreign, that when he has occasion to wear them all, the students dub him "the icon-stand." He moves in the most aristocratic circles, and for at least twenty-five or thirty years there is not a single famous savant in Russia with whom he has not been on intimate terms. There is no one for him to make friends with now, but looking back to the past we find in the long list of his distinguished friends such names as Pirogov, Kavelin, and the poet Nekrassov, all of whom bestowed their warm, sincere friendship upon him. He is an honorary member of all Russian Universities, and three foreign ones. And so on, and so on. All this, and a great deal more, constitute what is called my name.

This name of mine is a famous one. In Russia every educated person knows it, and abroad it is mentioned from the chairs of universities, and never without the terms "distinguished and honourable." It belongs to the number of those few fortunate names which it would be considered a sign of bad taste to abuse or mention disrespectfully in public or in the press. And that is as it should be. After all my name is closely associated with the idea of one who is famous, richly endowed by nature, and of indisputable usefulness. I am as hard-working and tough as a camel, and this counts for much, and I am talented, which counts for still more. It may as well be added that I am an honest, well-bred, unassuming fellow. I never poke my nose into literature or politics or seek popularity in arguments with the ignorant, nor do I speechify at banquets or over the graves of my colleagues.... My name as a scientist is untarnished, and there is nothing to complain of. It is a fortunate name.

The bearer of this name, myself that is to say, is a man of sixty-two, bald, with false teeth and an incurable tic. My person is as insignificant and unlovely as my name is brilliant and lovely. My head and hands shake from sheer weakness. My neck is like the finger-board of a double bass, as Turgenev says of one of his heroines, my chest is hollow, my back narrow. When I speak or give lectures my mouth droops to one side. When I smile my face is covered with the wrinkles of age and approaching death. There is nothing impressive in my puny self, unless it be that, when overtaken by the tic, an expression comes over my face which must suggest to anyone who looks at me the stern, impressive thought: "This man will probably soon die."

I can still lecture fairly well. As before I know how to keep the attention of my audience for two hours on end. My enthusiasm, my command of language and my wit make the defects of my voice pass unnoticed, though it is dry and harsh and I sometimes drone like a preacher. But I am a poor writer. That section of my brain which controls my talent as an author no longer serves me. My memory has become weak, there is a lack of logical sequence in my thoughts, and when I commit them to paper

it always seems to me that I have lost the flair required
for their integration, my composition is monotonous, my
phrases jejune and timid. I often fail to write what I
want to; by the time I come to the end I find I have forgotten the beginning. I often forget the simplest words,
and always have to waste a great deal of energy to avoid
superfluous phrases and unnecessary subordinate clauses
in my letters—obvious signs of the decline of my mental
processes. And it is noteworthy that the simpler the letter, the greater the strain on my powers. I feel much
more at home writing a scientific article than inditing a
congratulatory epistle or a business report. Another
thing—I find it a great deal easier to write in German or
English than in Russian.

With regard to my present life I must first and foremost mention the insomnia to which I have lately been a
martyr. If I were asked: what is the main, basic feature
of your existence? I would reply—insomnia. According
to my time-honoured practice I undress and get into bed
precisely at midnight. I fall asleep almost at once, but
wake up at about two, feeling as if I had not slept at
all. I have to get out of bed and light the lamp. For an
hour or two I pace the floor of my room, staring at the
familiar pictures and photographs in it. When I am tired
of walking up and down, I seat myself at my desk. I sit
there motionless, thinking of nothing, and feeling no
desire for anything. If a book lies before me I move it
mechanically towards me and read without the slightest
interest. In this way I recently read quite mechanically,
in a single night, a whole novel, with the strange title
"What the Swallow Sang Of." Sometimes I try to occupy
my mind by counting to a thousand, or conjuring up the
face of some friend of mine, and endeavouring to recall
in what year and under what circumstances he joined the
Faculty.

I like listening to sounds. Sometimes, two doors away,
my daughter Liza mutters something rapidly in her sleep,

or my wife passes through the drawing-room with a candle in her hand, invariably dropping the match-box; sometimes the shrinking panels of the wardrobe creak, or the wick in the lamp begins humming suddenly; and all these sounds affect me strangely.

Not to sleep at night means to be conscious the whole time that one is abnormal and I wait impatiently for the morning and the day to come, when it is natural to be awake. Many tedious hours pass before the cock in the yard begins to crow. This is my first deliverer. When the cock crows I know that the hall-porter will wake up in an hour, and for some reason, unknown to me, go upstairs, coughing irritably. And then the window-panes will begin gradually to pale, and the sound of voices will come from the street. . . .

The day begins for me with the appearance in my bedroom of my wife. She comes in in her skirt, washed and smelling of eau-de-Cologne, but with her hair down, trying to look as if her visit were quite casual, invariably saying the same thing:

"Excuse me, I just looked in. . . . Another bad night?"

Then she extinguishes the lamp, sits down at the table, and begins talking. Though no prophet, I know in advance what she will say. The same every morning. Usually, after anxious enquiries as to my health, she suddenly remembers our officer son, serving in Warsaw. After the twentieth of each month we send him fifty rubles—and it is chiefly this which serves as the theme of our conversation.

"Of course it's hard for us," sighs my wife. "But until he is firmly established in life it is our duty to help him. The poor boy lives among strangers, his pay is very low. . . . But if you like we'll send him forty rubles next month, instead of fifty. What d'you think?"

Daily experience might have taught my wife that our expenditure is not diminished by constant discussion, but my wife has no use for experience, and talks every morn-

ing about our officer and the price of bread, which, thank
God, has gone down, while sugar has gone up two
kopeks—and all this with an air of telling me something new.

I listen, agree mechanically, and, no doubt, because
I have not slept all night, strange, futile musings take
possession of my mind. I look at my wife in childish
amazement. I ask myself in astonishment: is it possible that
this corpulent, clumsy old woman, whose face expresses
petty cares and anxiety as to a crust of bread, whose
eyes are dulled by perpetual preoccupation with debt and
want, who is capable of talking of nothing but expenses
and whose smiles are evoked by nothing but lowered
prices, is it possible that this woman was once that slender Varya, whom I loved so ardently for her fine, clear
mind, her pure soul, her beauty, and, as Othello loved
Desdemona, "that she did pity me" in the vicissitudes
of my scientific work. Is it possible that this is my wife,
Varya, who one day bore me a son?

I gaze intently at the puffy face of this dumpy old
woman, searching for my Varya in her, but nothing of the
past remains excepting her anxiety about my health and
her way of calling my salary, *our* salary, my cap, *our* cap.
It grieves me to look at her, and I humour her by letting
her run on as long as she likes, and do not even say a word
when she criticizes people unjustly, or nags at me for not
taking private practice and not publishing a text-book.

Our conversations always end in the same way. My
wife suddenly remembers I haven't had my tea, and
starts up.

"What am I thinking of?" she says. "The samovar has
been on the table for ages, and here I sit chattering.
I'm sure I don't know what my memory's coming to!"

She moves rapidly towards the door, stopping there
to say:

"We owe Yegor five months' wages. Did you know?
How many times have I told you that it doesn't do to let

the servants' wages run on! It's ever so much easier to
pay ten rubles every month than to pay fifty rubles for
five months."

Once outside the door, she stops again, saying:

"There's nobody I pity as I do our poor Liza. The poor
girl goes to the conservatoire, is continually in good
society, and look how she's dressed! It's a disgrace to
show oneself in the street in such a winter-coat! If she
were anyone else's daughter it wouldn't matter so much,
but everyone knows her father's a famous professor, a
privy councillor."

And at last, having reproached me with my reputation
and my rank, she goes. Thus begins my day. It continues in no better fashion.

While I am drinking my tea my daughter Liza comes
into my room in her hat and coat, carrying her music,
all ready to go to the conservatoire. She is twenty-two
years old, but looks even younger, a handsome girl rather
like my wife in her youth. She kisses me tenderly on
my temple and drops a kiss on my hand, and says:

"Good morning, Daddy. How are you?"

When she was little she was very fond of ices, and
I often had to take her to the confectioner's. Ices were for
her a gauge for all that was best. If she wanted to praise
me she would say: "You're an ice-cream, Papa." One of
her fingers she called pistachio, another cream, and another raspberry, and so on. When she used to come and
greet me in the mornings I would seat her on my knee
and kiss her fingers, naming them: "Cream, pistachio,
lemon. . . ."

And I still kiss Liza's fingers for old time's sake, murmuring: "Pistachio, cream, lemon," but the effect is not
the same. I am as cold as an ice-cream myself, and feel
shamefaced. When my daughter comes to me and touches
my temple with her lips, I start as if a bee had stung me,
give a strained smile and turn away my face. Ever since
I began suffering from insomnia my mind is obsessed

with the thought: my daughter continually sees me, an old man and a celebrity, blush painfully because I am behind with the footman's wages. She continually sees how my anxiety about petty debts makes me stop working and pace the floor in thought, and yet does not come to me (without telling her mother) and whisper: "Father, take my watch, my bracelets, my ear-rings, my dresses— pawn them, you need money. . . ." She sees how her mother and I, yielding to false shame, try to conceal our poverty from others, and yet she does not decline the expensive pleasure of studying music. God forbid that I should accept her watch, her bracelets, or her sacrifice! That is not what I want.

And this brings me to the thought of my son, the Warsaw officer. He is a wise, honourable, sober fellow. But that is not enough for me. It seems to me that if my father were an old man, and I knew that there were moments in which he blushed for his poverty, I would give up my commission to another, and hire myself out as a worker. Such thoughts about my children poison my existence. What is the use of them? Only a narrow-minded or embittered person cherishes rancour against ordinary human beings for not being heroes. But enough of this.

At a quarter to ten I must go and give a lecture to my dear boys. I dress and set off along the road I have been familiar with for thirty years now, a road which has its history for me. On the site of the big grey house with the chemist's shop on the ground floor was once a small ale-shop and in this ale-shop I thought out my thesis and wrote my first love letter to Varya. I wrote in pencil on a sheet of paper with the printed heading "Historia morbi." And over there is the grocer's shop, formerly owned by a little Jew who sold me cigarettes on tick, and afterwards by a stout woman who was fond of students because "they all had a mother at home"; the present owner is a red-haired tradesman, perfectly indifferent, who sits all day drinking tea from a copper kettle. And here come the gloomy gates, long in need of repair, of the University; a bored yardman in a sheepskin, holding a broom... heaps of snow. ... Surely such gates do not produce a very inspiring impression on some lad, fresh from the country, who imagines that the temple of sciences really is a temple! The dilapidated state of the university buildings, the gloom of its corridors, its soot-stained walls, the inadequate lighting, the miserable aspect of the stairs, cloak-room, and benches, probably occupy an honourable place in the history of Russian pessimism, among the causes of susceptibility. ... And here is our park. It seems to have become neither better nor worse since I was a student. I never liked it. It would be a great deal better if there were lofty pines and sturdy oaks here, instead of the consumptive lime-trees, yellow acacias, and skimpy, clipped lilac bushes. The student, whose state of mind is largely influenced by his surroundings, should meet with nothing that is not lofty, purposeful and elegant in the place where he studies. The Lord preserve him from sickly trees, broken window-panes, shabby walls and doors upholstered in torn oil-cloth.

As I approach the wing of the building in which I work, the door flies open and I am welcomed by an old colleague, the hall porter, who was born in the same year as myself, and bears the same name—Nikolai. He lets me in, grunting:

"A frosty day, Your Excellency!"

Or, if my coat is wet:

"Raining, Your Honour!"

Then he runs ahead of me to open all the doors I must pass through. In my private office he carefully helps me off with my coat, always managing to give me some tidbit of university news. Thanks to the intimacy existing between the porters and night watchmen in the University, he is posted in everything that is going on in all four faculties, in the office, in the rector's room, and in the library. There is nothing he does not know. When some such event as the resignation of the rector or one of the deans is the subject of general speculation, I hear him speaking to the young night watchman of the likeliest candidates for these places, explaining that such a one has not been approved by the minister, such a one has refused the post himself, and going into fantastic details as to certain mysterious documents received at the office, of secret conversations said to have been held between the minister and the patron, and so on. Apart from these details he almost always turns out to have been right. His descriptions of each candidate are distinctly original, but they are nevertheless correct. If you should require to know the year in which someone presented his thesis, joined the university staff, resigned, or died, you have only to draw on the extraordinary memory of this veteran, who, not content with supplying you with year, month and date, will also inform you of the circumstances in which this or that event took place. His was the ready memory of a lover.

He is the guardian of the University's traditions. He has inherited from his predecessors of the porter fraternity a store of legends pertaining to university life, has contributed to this wealth, treasures of his own, amassed during his years of service, and should you wish it can relate many a story, both brief and lengthy. He can tell you of remarkable sages who knew all there was to know, of extraordinary workers who could go for weeks without sleep, of innumerable martyrs and victims of science. In his stories good triumphs over evil, the weak invariably conquer the strong, the sage gets the upper hand of the fool, and the humble overcome the proud and old.... It is not necessary to accept these legends and marvels at their face value, but something essential remains after you have passed them through the filter of your mind—our splendid traditions, and the names of true heroes, acknowledged by all.

In our society all that is known of the scientific world is summed up in tales of the extraordinary absent-mindedness of old professors, and a few witticisms ascribed impartially to Gruber, myself, and Babukhin. This is not much for a society with claims to culture. If society really loved science, scientists, and students as Nikolai does, our literature would long have been enriched by epics, legends and tales—all of which, unfortunately, it at present lacks.

After telling me the news, Nikolai's features assume an expression of severity, and we embark upon a business talk. If an outsider could hear Nikolai employing scientific terminology with such freedom, he would no doubt think he was a scientist in military uniform. As a matter of fact, however, the tales of the erudition of university porters are greatly exaggerated. True, Nikolai knows upwards of a hundred Latin names, can put a skeleton together, occasionally prepare the materials for demonstration, or amuse the students with some lengthy scientific quotation, but such a simple thing as, for instance, the theory of the circulation of the blood, is just as obscure to him now as it was twenty years ago.

Seated at the desk, bending low over a book, or some chemical preparation, is my prosector Pyotr Ignatevich, a hard-working, unassuming but mediocre individual, about thirty-five years old, already going bald and sporting a "corporation." He works from morning to night, is an indefatigable reader, and remembers all he reads, and this makes him worth his weight in gold for me. For the rest he is a dray-horse, or, in other words, a learned dullard. The characteristics of a human dray-horse which distinguish him from a man of talent are narrowness of outlook and sharply limited specialization. Apart from his speciality he is as simple as a child. I remember going into my office one morning, and saying:

"Think what a misfortune! They say Skobelev is dead."

Nikolai crossed himself, but Pyotr Ignatevich turned to me and asked:

"Who's Skobelev?"

Another time—a little earlier—I told him that Professor Perov had died. The worthy Pyotr Ignatevich said:

"What was his subject?"

I used to think that Patti herself might sing right into his ear, that hordes of Chinese might invade Russia, that there might be an earthquake, and he would not turn a hair, but would go on quietly gazing into his microscope with one eye screwed up. In a word, Hecuba was nothing at all to him. I would have given much to see how this dry stick slept with his wife.

Another of his distinguishing features is his blind faith in the infallibility of science, especially of all that is written by Germans. He is sure of himself and his preparations, knows what is the goal of life, and is perfectly immune to the doubts and disillusionment which make the hair of the talented turn grey. He bows slavishly to authority and feels no need for independent thought. It is hard to shake his convictions, impossible to argue with him. How can one argue with a man who is profoundly convinced that medicine is the most perfect of the sciences, doctors the best people in the world, medical traditions the best traditions existing? The only survival of the bad old traditions of the medical profession is the white tie doctors still affect. The scientist and the educated man merely bow to the traditions of the University as a whole, without specific application to the various faculties—medical, law and the rest. But you will never get Pyotr Ignatevich to agree with you here, and he is ready to argue about it till the day of judgement.

I can clearly envisage his future. In the course of his life he will make a few hundred impeccably correct preparations, write a number of arid, extremely praiseworthy notes, and about a dozen conscientious translations, but he will never do anything out of the common.

This requires imagination, inventiveness, intuition, all of which Pyotr Ignatevich lacks entirely. To put it briefly, this is not a master, but a servant, of science.

Pyotr Ignatevich, Nikolai, and I speak in undertones. We feel a little ill at ease. The knowledge that an audience is murmuring like an ocean on the other side of the door is always chastening. Thirty years have not accustomed me to this sensation, and I experience it every morning. I button up my frock-coat nervously, put unnecessary questions to Nikolai, show temper. . . . Anyone might think I was afraid. but this is not cowardice, it is something different, something I can neither put a name to or give a description of.

I look at my watch for no reason whatever, and remark:

"Well! Time to go."

We proceed in the following order: in front goes Nikolai with the demonstration material or the diagrams, after him, myself, and after me, his head modestly bent, trudges the dray-horse. Or, when necessary, a corpse is borne in front on a stretcher, after the corpse comes Nikolai, and so on. At my appearance the students rise, then sit down and the murmuring of the sea suddenly ceases. A calm sets in.

I know what I am going to lecture on, but I do not know *how* I shall lecture, what I shall begin and end with. There is not a single ready-made phrase in my head. But the moment I glance at my audience (ranged before me in an amphitheatre), and pronounce the stereotyped, "at our last lecture we stopped at," phrases pour out of me in endless sequence and I am off. I speak rapidly and fervently, and apparently the power does not exist that could interrupt the flow of my speech. To lecture well, that is to say, to interest and benefit your hearers, practice and experience are required as well as talent, the speaker must have a perfectly clear conception of his own abilities and of the abilities of his hearers, as well as a clear grasp of his subject. In addition to all this he must possess a certain craftiness, and never lose sight of his audience for a second.

A good conductor, while conveying the composer's meaning, performs a dozen activities simultaneously, following the score, waving his baton, keeping an eye on the singer, pointing now to the drum, now to the French horn, and so on. It is just the same with me, when lecturing. I am faced by a hundred and fifty faces, all differing from one another, and three hundred eyes staring straight into my face. It is my business to conquer this hydra-headed monster. So long as I am fully aware, all the time I am lecturing, of the measure of its attention, and its reasoning powers, I have it in control. My other enemy resides within my own bosom. This is the infinite variety of forms, phenomena and laws, and the multitude of thoughts, my own and others, springing from this variety.

I must be continually and skilfully extracting from this vast mass of material that which is most important and essential, and, keeping pace with my own words, present my thought in the form most accessible for the monster's mind, and capable of exciting its interest, while at the same time seeing to it that my thoughts are conveyed not as they accumulate, but in the order required for the presentation of the picture I intend to convey. Further I have to try to speak in a pleasing and cultivated manner, to keep my definitions brief and precise, and my phrases as simple and elegant as possible. Every moment I have to remind myself that there is only an hour and forty minutes at my disposal. In a word, I have plenty to do. At one and the same time I must incorporate in myself the scientist, the teacher, and the orator, and woe betide me if the orator gets the upper hand of the teacher and the scientist, or vice versa!

I lecture a quarter of an hour, or perhaps half an hour, and suddenly notice that the students are beginning to stare at the ceiling, at Pyotr Ignatevich; somebody fumbles for his handkerchief, somebody else settles himself comfortably in his seat, a third smiles at his own thoughts. This means their attention is beginning to wear thin. Measures must be taken. I use the first opportunity to introduce a pun. All the hundred and fifty faces smile broadly, the eyes gleam, the murmur of the sea is heard for a brief moment. . . . I join in the laugh, too, their attention is renewed, and I can go on.

No debates, entertainments, or games ever gave me so much pleasure as lecturing. Only while lecturing have I been able to give myself up whole-heartedly to my ruling passion, only then have I realized that inspiration is no invention of the poets, but really exists. Hercules never felt such exquisite fatigue after his amorous feats as I used to after a lecture.

That was how it used to be. Now lecturing causes me nothing but torture. Hardly half an hour passes before I begin to feel an unconquerable weakness in my legs and shoulders. I sit down, but I am not used to lecturing in a sitting position. The next minute I get up, and continue on my feet, then sit down again. My mouth feels dry, my voice gets husky, my head swims. . . . In order to conceal my state from my audience I sip water, cough, blow my nose, as if hampered by a cold, produce puns at random, and end up by announcing the interval sooner than I ought to. But it is chiefly shame that I feel.

My conscience and my mind tell me that the best thing for me now to do would be to deliver a farewell lecture to my boys, to say my last word to them, to give them my blessing, and yield my post to another, younger and stronger than myself. But—God forgive me!—I have not the courage to follow the dictates of conscience.

Unfortunately, I am neither a philosopher nor a theologian. I know very well that I have not more than six months to live. It might be thought I should be chiefly occupied with questions of my latter end, and of the dreams which may come to me in "that sleep of death." But somehow my soul does not seem inclined to ponder these problems, though my mind acknowledges that they are all-important. Now, on the threshold of death, the only thing that interests me is what interested me twenty or thirty years ago—science. Even when I am breathing my last I am sure I shall still believe that science is the most important, beautiful and essential thing in the life of man, that it always has been and always will be the highest manifestation of love, that by means of science alone man will conquer nature and himself. This belief may be naive and fundamentally incorrect, but it is not my fault that I believe as I do. I am unable to suppress this belief of mine.

But that is not the point. I only ask indulgence for my weakness, and for it to be understood that to tear from his professorship and his students a man who is less affected by the final goal of the universe than by the future development of the marrow, would be tantamount to nailing him down in his coffin while he is still alive.

My insomnia and the consequent tense struggle against the weakness which overcomes me, lead to a strange phenomenon. While lecturing, tears rise to my throat, my eyelids begin to itch, and I feel a strange, hysterical desire to throw out my arms and complain loudly. I feel an impulse to shout in a loud voice that fate has doomed a well-known man like myself to capital punishment, that in six months or so another will be swaying my hearers. I should like to cry out that I have been poisoned. New thoughts, hitherto quite strange to me, are poisoning the last days of my life, stinging my brain like gnats. And at such times I feel the horror of my situation so keenly that I should like my hearers to be horrified, to jump up from their seats, and rush panic-stricken and shrieking to the exit.

Such moments are hard to endure.

II

After a lecture I stay at home and work. I read magazines and treatises, or prepare for my next lecture, sometimes I write a little. I work spasmodically, for there are visitors to be received.

The door-bell rings. A colleague has called to consult me on a matter of business. He enters with his hat and his stick in his hands, stretching out both these articles towards me, and saying:

"I've come just for a minute—only a minute! Don't get up, *Collega*! I only want to say two words to you."

We begin with a display of our extraordinary politeness, our pleasure in seeing each other. I try to force him into a chair, and he tries to force me to sit down. At the same time we cautiously stroke each other in the region of the waistcoat, touching a button, as if feeling each other, and afraid of burning our fingers. Both of us laugh, though we have not said anything funny. Once seated, we bend our heads towards each other and start talking in undertones. However cordial our relations we feel obliged to gild our speech after the Chinese manner, with "as you so justly remark," or "as I had the honour to inform you," to laugh at one another's witticisms, even when these are somewhat inept. Having come to an end of our business, my friend rises abruptly, with a wave of the hand in the direction of my desk, and begins to take his leave. Again we feel one another and laugh. I accompany him into the hall, where I help him on with his coat, he doing his utmost to reject this high honour. Then, when Yegor opens the front door for him, my friend assures me I will catch cold, and I pretend to be ready to go right out-of-doors with him. When at last I return to my study my face goes on smiling, as if it could not stop.

A little later there is another ring at the bell. Someone comes into the hall, is a long time removing his street

68

clothes and clearing his throat. Yegor announces that a
student wishes to see me. "Let him come in," I say. In a
few seconds a young man of pleasing appearance enters
the room. For nearly a year now there have been strained
relations between us. He makes a deplorable showing at
my examinations, and I give him the lowest marks.
Every year there are about seven young people of this
sort, whom, in the language of the students, I "pitch into"
or "pluck." Those who fail in their examinations owing to
lack of ability or illness as a rule bear their cross patiently and do not try to bargain with me. Only optimists,
easy-going individuals, whose appetite and regular
attendance at the opera are interfered with by failure in
examinations, try to bargain with me. I am indulgent
with the former, but the latter I pitch into unmercifully
all the year round.

"Sit down," I say to my visitor. "What can I do
for you?"

"Excuse me for troubling you, Professor," he begins,
stuttering and looking away. "I would not venture to
trouble you, but for ... I've sat for your examination five
times, and ... flunked it again. Please be so kind as to
give me a pass, because...."

The argument which the idlers produce in their favour
is always the same: they have passed all the other examinations splendidly, and only flunked mine, which is the
more extraordinary in that they have always studied my
subject zealously, and know it thoroughly. If they were
plucked, it was owing to some incomprehensible misunderstanding.

"I'm sorry, my friend," I say to my visitor. "I cannot give you a pass. Go and study your notes again, and
then come to me. We'll see, then."

A pause. I take pleasure in causing a certain amount
of discomfort to a student who prefers beer and the opera
to science, and remark, with a sigh:

"In my opinion, the best thing for you to do now is

to leave the medical faculty altogether. If, with your ability, you are quite unable to pass the examinations, it can only be that you have neither the desire to be a doctor, nor the necessary vocation."

The optimist's face lengthens.

"Excuse me, Professor," he says, with a nervous laugh. "That would be a very strange thing for me to do. To study five years and suddenly ... leave!"

"Not at all. Better to have wasted five years than all your life remain in an occupation which is not to your taste."

But the next moment I feel sorry for him and hasten to add:

"However, you know best. Go and study a little more and come to me when you are ready."

"When?" enquires the idler in hollow tones.

"Whenever you like. Tomorrow, if you are ready."

I read clearly the message in his good-natured eyes: "I can come, but you'll flunk me again, you know you will, you beast!"

"Of course," I continued, "sitting fifteen times for my examination will not make you a learned man, but it may train your will. And that's something, at least."

A pause ensues. I rise, waiting for my visitor to retire, but he stands there, looking at the window, fingering his youthful beard, and meditating. The thing is becoming wearisome.

The optimist has a pleasant mellow voice, and intelligent, mocking eyes, but his complacent features are somewhat blurred by frequent potations of beer and prolonged repose on sofas. No doubt he could tell me much that would be interesting to hear about the opera, his love affairs, his comrades (to whom he is deeply attached), but unfortunately such things are not discussed between us. ... I would gladly listen to him. ...

"Professor! I give you my word of honour that, if you pass me, I'll...."

When it comes to his "word of honour," I give a wave of the hand, and sit down at my desk. The student thinks a little longer and then says despondently:

"In that case, good-bye.... Excuse me!"

"Good-bye, my friend. Good luck to you!"

He leaves the room with faltering steps, slowly puts on his coat in the hall, and, once out, probably has another long "think." Dismissing me from his thoughts as "that old devil," he makes for a cheap restaurant to drink beer and dine, and then goes home to bed. Peace to your ashes, honest toiler!

A third ring. In comes a young doctor in a new black suit, gold-framed spectacles and the inevitable white tie. He introduces himself. I ask him to be seated and enquire his business. The youthful high priest of sciences begins telling me, not without emotion, that he passed his doctor's examinations this year, and has now only to write his thesis. He would like to work with me, under my aegis and I would oblige him infinitely by suggesting a theme for his thesis.

"I should be happy to be of use, *Collega*," I say. "But first let us define clearly what a thesis is. The word is usually supposed to connote an essay arising out of independent work. That is so, is it not? An essay written to another's theme and under another's guidance, has another name...."

The aspirant makes no reply. I jump out of my chair in an outburst of indignation.

"What makes you all come to me, I wonder?" I exclaim angrily. "Do I keep a shop? I do not deal in themes! For the hundredth time I would beg you all to leave me in peace! Excuse me if I seem rude, but really I'm sick of this!"

The aspirant still says not a word, but a faint blush appears above his cheek-bones. His face expresses profound respect for my famous name and erudition, but his eyes show me that he despises my voice, my pitiful physique, and my nervous gesticulations. He finds me an eccentric figure in my wrath.

"I don't keep a shop!" I repeat angrily. "It's really extraordinary! Why don't you want to be independent? Why is liberty so odious to you?"

I go on and on and he still maintains silence. At last I begin to quieten down, but of course I will give in to him. The aspirant will receive from me some worn-out theme, write under my direction a paper of no earthly use to anyone, come out the victor in a wearisome debate, and receive a scientific degree which will never do him any good.

The bell rings constantly, but I will limit myself to recounting only the first four. When the bell rings for the fourth time I hear familiar footsteps, the rustle of a dress, a voice I love. . . .

Eighteen years ago a friend of mine, an eye-specialist, died leaving a seven-year-old daughter, Katya, and about sixty thousand rubles. He appointed me as her guardian in his will. Katya lived in my family till she was ten, when she was sent to a boarding-school, and only came back to us for the summer holidays. I had no time to look after her upbringing, had only brief opportunities for observing her, and can therefore say very little about her childhood.

My earliest memory of her, and one which I hold dear, is the wonderful confidence with which she came into my home and allowed herself to be treated by the doctors in illness—a confidence which always lit up her face. She might be sitting apart with a swollen and bandaged cheek, but invariably taking the utmost interest in all going on around her: whether watching me writing and turning over the pages of a book, or my wife bustling about, or the cook peeling potatoes in the kitchen, or the gambols of a dog, her eyes always expressed the same thought: "Everything that goes on in the world is wise and wonderful." She was extremely curious, and loved talking to me. Sometimes she would sit opposite me at the other side of the table, following my movements and putting questions to me. She wanted to know what I was reading, what I did at the University, whether I was not afraid of corpses, what I did with my salary.

"Do the students at the University fight?" she would ask.

"Yes, darling, they do."

"And do you make them stand in the corner?"

"Oh, yes!"

She thought it so funny that the students fought and I made them stand in the corner that she laughed. She was a gentle, patient, good child. I often watched her when she was deprived of something, unjustly punished, or left with her curiosity unsatisfied. At such moments sadness would be blended with the expression of permanent confidence on her face, but that was all. I did not know how to stand up for her, but when I saw her look sad I felt a longing to draw her close to me, and pity her, like an old nurse: "My blessed little orphan!"

I remember, too, how fond of dressing and scenting herself she was. In that respect she was like me. I, too, like fine clothes and expensive scent.

I regret that I never had time nor inclination to follow the development of what became Katya's ruling passion from her fourteenth or fifteenth year. I refer to her ardent love for the theatre. When she came home from boarding-school for the summer there was nothing she spoke about with such satisfaction and ardour, as plays and actors. She fairly wore us out with her incessant chatter about the theatre. My wife and children would not listen to her. I was the only one who had not the courage to refuse her my attention. When she felt the desire to share her enthusiasm with someone, she would come into my study and say in a beseeching voice:

"Nikolai Stepanich, may I talk to you about the theatre?"

I would point to the clock and say:

"I give you half an hour. Go ahead."

Later on she got into the habit of bringing home dozens of portraits of actors and actresses, the objects of her adoration. Then she tried her hand at amateur theatricals and at last, when her school days were over, she announced to me that she was born to be an actress.

I never shared Katya's theatrical enthusiasm. In my opinion, if a play is any good there is no need, for the production of the desired effect, to trouble actors. Reading is quite enough. If a play is bad, then no acting will make it good.

In my youth I went often to the theatre, and my family still engage a box twice a year, and take me there "to air myself." This does not entitle me to judge of the theatre, of course, and I will not say much about it. In my opinion the theatre has not become any better than it was thirty or forty years ago. I am still unable either in the passages or the foyer, to find a glass of water to drink; the cloak-room attendants still fine me twenty kopeks for my coat, though there would seem to be nothing reprehensible in wearing warm clothes in the winter; music is still quite unnecessarily played during the intervals, adding something new and unwanted to the impression made by the play. Men still go to the bar for a drink during the intervals. And since no progress is to be observed in trifles, there would be no good in my looking for it in greater matters. When an actor, steeped from head to foot in theatrical traditions and prejudices, declaims an ordinary simple monologue like "To be or not to be" without simplicity, hissing for no reason whatever and shaking all over, or when he tries to convince me at all costs that Chatsky, who held forth to fools, and was in love with a fool of a girl, is a very clever man, and that *Wit Works Woe* is not a boring play, it seems to me that the old routine which used to bore me forty years ago, when I was entertained with classical wailings and chest-smiting, still emanates from the stage. And I leave the theatre every time a greater conservative than I entered it.

The credulous, sentimental crowd may allow itself to be persuaded that the modern theatre is a school. But those who hold proper ideas of what a school should be will not swallow such bait. I do not know how things will be in fifty or a hundred years, but in modern conditions the theatre can serve as nothing but entertainment. And this entertainment is too costly for us to go on enjoying it. It filches from the State thousands of young, healthy, gifted men and women, who, if they had not devoted themselves to the theatre, might have been excellent doctors, tillers of the soil, teachers, or officers. It filches from the public their evening hours, the best time for intellectual work and friendly converse. Not to mention the financial expenditure and the moral injury inflicted upon the spectators when they see murder, adultery, or slander, glorified on the stage.

Katya, however, was of quite another opinion. She assured me that the theatre, even in its present state, is more important than lectures and books, more important than anything else in the world. The theatre is a force uniting within itself all the arts, and actors are missionaries. No art or science exercises such a powerful and unequivocal influence on the human spirit as the stage, and it is not for nothing that even the most mediocre actor is more popular than the greatest scientist or artist. And no other public activities gives such enjoyment and satisfaction as acting gives to actors.

And one fine day Katya joined a theatrical company and went away, to Ufa, I think, taking with her quite a lot of money, a mass of rainbow-hued hopes, and an aristocratic approach to the theatre.

Her first letters, written on the way, were wonderful I read them, lost in admiration that these small sheets of paper could contain so much youth, spiritual purity,

blessed innocence, combined with a subtle, practical
judgement which would have done honour to the finest
masculine mind. The Volga, the scenery, the towns she
visited, her comrades, her successes and her failures she
did not so much describe, as sing. Every line breathed
the confidence that I was accustomed to see on her face,
and withal there were innumerable mistakes in gram-
mar, and hardly any punctuation whatever.

Six months had hardly passed when I received an
extremely poetical and enthusiastic letter, beginning with
the words: "I have fallen in love." To this letter was ap-
pended a photograph of a young man with a clean-
shaven face, wearing a broad-brimmed hat, and carrying a plaid rug over one shoulder. The next few letters
were just as wonderful, but now punctuation marks began to make their appearance, there were no more gram-
mar mistakes, and the letters themselves smacked
strongly of male influence. Katya now wrote to tell me
how nice it would be to build a big theatre somewhere
on the Volga, on co-operative lines, of course, and get
some wealthy merchants and shipowners to contribute
to this enterprise. There would be plenty of money, the
box-office receipts would be enormous, the actors would
work for mutual profits. . . . This might be all very well,
I told myself, but such ideas could only come from a
masculine mind.

However that may have been, a year or two later
everything was apparently still going well. Katya was
in love, believed in her cause, and was happy. But after
this I began to observe obvious signs of weariness in
her letters. In the first place Katya began complaining
to me of her comrades—this was the first and most ominous symptom. If a young scientist or writer begins his
activities by complaining bitterly of scientists or writers, it means he is already fatigued, and not fit for his
work. Katya wrote me that her comrades did not attend
rehearsals and never knew their parts. The absurdity of

the plays produced, and the behaviour of the actors on
the stage, showed that each one of them felt the utmost
contempt for the audience. In the interests of box-office
receipts, which was the sole topic of conversation, actresses demeaned themselves by singing chansonnettes,
and tragic actors sang couplets in which deceived hus-
bands and the pregnancy of unfaithful wives was made
fun of. It was quite a wonder that provincial theatres
still survived, and that they could continue in such a
meagre and corrupt vein.

In reply I sent Katya a long, and, I am afraid, an
extremely tedious letter. Among other things I wrote:
"I have often had talks with old actors, high-minded
people who have been good enough to bestow their affection on me. From conversation with them I could see
that their work is ruled not so much by their own minds
and wills as by the fashion and mood prevailing among
audiences. The best of them, in their time, have had to
act in tragedies and operettas, in Parisian farces, and in
pantomime, and in every case they believed themselves
to be following the right path, and doing good. So you
see the root of the evil must be sought for not in the
actors, but deeper, in art itself, and in the attitude of
society towards art." This letter of mine only irritated
Katya. "We are talking at cross purposes," she replied.
"I did not write to you about high-minded people
who bestowed their affection upon you, but about a
band of rotters with nothing high-souled about them.
They are a horde of savages, only in the theatre because
unable to find employment anywhere else, and only calling themselves actors out of insolence. Not a single talented person, but any amount of mediocrities, drunk-
ards, schemers, and backbiters. I can never tell you how
bitter it is to me that the art I love so much should
have fallen into the hands of people I detest, that the
best minds only see this evil from a distance, do not
desire to approach it more nearly, and, instead of sym-

pathizing, write heavy-handed commonplaces and go in for utterly superfluous moralizing...." And so on, all in the same manner.

Some more time elapsed, and I received the following epistle: "I have been cruelly deceived. I cannot go on living. Make use of my money as you see fit. I have loved you as my father and only friend. Farewell."

And so it turned out that "he," too, belonged to the horde of savages. After this, as far as I could make out from certain hints, there had been an attempt at suicide. Katya, it seems, tried to poison herself. She must have had a serious illness after this, for the next letter I received was from Yalta, where she had probably gone on doctor's orders. Her last letter to me contained a request to send her a thousand rubles to Yalta as quickly as possible, and ended with the words: "Forgive me if my letter is gloomy. Yesterday I buried my child." She lived in the Crimea for about a year, and then came home.

She had been away for some four years, during the whole of which time it must be admitted that I played a strange and not very admirable part with regard to her. In the early days, when she announced her intention of going on the stage, wrote to me about her love, had fits of extravagance, compelling me to send, now a thousand, now two thousand rubles, when she wrote to me of her desire to die, and then of the death of her child, I lost my head and my only part in her destiny was to think constantly of her and write her long, dull letters, which I might as well have left unwritten. And yet, was not I in the place of a father to her, did not I love her as my own daughter?

At present Katya lives a quarter of a mile from me. She has rented a five-room apartment and furnished it very comfortably, with that taste which is all her own. If anyone should undertake to describe the atmosphere in which she lives, the emphasis would have to be on its languor. Soft couches and soft chairs for the lazy body, soft carpets for the lazy feet, dim, faded, blurred colours for the lazy eyes. And for the lazy soul, an abundance of cheap fans on the walls and small pictures in which originality of execution prevails over subject, abundance of little tables, shelves, everywhere perfectly superfluous and worthless objects, odd scraps of material, curtains. . . . All this, and the obvious avoidance of bright colours, symmetry, and space, reveals, as well as spiritual laziness, the perversion of natural taste. Katya lies on a couch for days on end, reading—mainly novels and short stories. She only goes out once a day, in the afternoon, to come and see me.

I go on working and Katya sits not far off on the sofa, silently drawing the folds of her shawl round her, as if she were cold. Either because I am fond of her, or because I got used to her frequent visits when she was still a little girl, her presence does not prevent me from concentrating. Every now and then I toss an idle question at her, and she gives me a brief reply. Or, feeling the need of a moment's relaxation, I turn and look at her as she skims absently through a medical magazine or a newspaper. And then I observe that her face no longer wears its former expression of confidence. It is now cold, apathetic, abstracted, like the faces of passengers forced to wait a long time for their train. She still dresses well, with her former simplicity of taste, but she is no longer neat and trim. Her dress and hair show signs of contact with the couches and rocking-chairs on which she reposes all day. And she is no longer curious to know everything as she used to be. She no longer puts any questions to me—as if, having experienced all that life had to offer, she no longer expects to hear anything new.

A little before five, signs of life are heard in the sitting-room and drawing-room. This means that Liza has come back from the conservatoire and brought some girl friends with her. Somebody can be heard playing the piano, somebody sings a note or two, laughter rings out. In the dining-room Yegor is laying the table, rattling the dishes.

"Good-bye," says Katya. "I won't go in to them, to-day. They must excuse me. I have no time. Come and see me."

When I see her to the front door she inspects me severely from head to foot and says crossly:

"You get thinner and thinner. Why don't you have treatment? I shall make Sergei Fedorovich come and see you. Let him examine you."

"Don't do that, Katya."

"I can't understand what your people are thinking about! A fine family you have!"

She jerks on her coat, a couple of hair-pins invariably fall on the floor from her carelessly done hair. She is too lazy, and in too much of a hurry to set her hair to rights, merely pushing a tumbled curl under her hat before leaving.

When I go into the dining-room my wife asks me:

"Has Katya been with you? Why didn't she come to see us? It looks so odd...."

"Oh, Mamma," says Liza reproachfully. "If she doesn't want to come, she can stay away. We don't have to go down on our knees to her."

"Whatever you say, it's rude. To sit three hours in the study and never give us a thought. But she can do as she likes, of course."

Varya and Liza both detest Katya. I cannot understand their hatred, indeed, it would probably take another woman to do so. I am ready to swear that hardly one of the hundred-and-fifty youths I see almost daily in my lecture hall, or of the hundreds of middle-aged men I meet in the course of a week, would be able to understand this hatred and disgust for Katya's past, for the fact that she had born a child out of wedlock, this

hatred for the illegitimate child itself. At the same time
I cannot think of a single woman or girl of my acquaintance who would not, consciously or unconsciously,
cherish the same feelings. And this not because women
are more virtuous than men—after all, virtue and purity differ very slightly from vice, if they are not free
from malice. I put it down to the backwardness of wom-
en. The melancholy sympathy and vague remorse felt
by the modern man at the sight of misfortune seem to
me to show much more culture and moral development
than hatred and disgust. The modern woman is as
lachrymose and callous as were women in medieval
times. And in my opinion those who advocate a man's
upbringing for her are in the right.

My wife also dislikes Katya for having been on the
stage, for her ingratitude, her pride, her eccentricity, for
all those innumerable defects which one woman can
always find in another.

In addition to the home-circle there are two or three
girl friends of my daughter at the dinner-table, and
Liza's admirer and suitor, Alexander Adolfovich Gnekker, a fair young man, about thirty years old, of middle height, stout, broad-shouldered, with reddish
whiskers and a dyed moustache, which give his smooth,
fat face a doll-like appearance. He wears a very short
jacket, a fancy waistcoat, checked trousers very wide
at the top and very narrow at the bottom, and flat-soled
tan shoes. He has bulging, prawn-like eyes, his tie is
like the neck of a prawn, and it even seems to me that
this young man smells of prawn soup. He visits us
every day, but none of us knows where he comes from,
where he was educated, and what he lives on. Though
he neither sings nor plays himself, he has something to
do with music and singing, sells mysterious grand-
pianos to mysterious customers, is continually at the
conservatoire, knows all the celebrities, and acts the host
at concerts. He utters oracular musical criticisms and

I have observed that everyone hastens to agree with him.

Rich people always have hangers-on, and it is the same with science and the arts. I don't suppose there is a single art or science free from the presence of "foreign bodies" such as Mr. Gnekker. I am not a musician and may be mistaken about Gnekker, whom, moreover, I know very little. But his authoritative air and the complacency with which he stands near the piano and listens when anyone plays or sings, strike me as suspicious.

You may be the acme of gentility and a privy councillor, but if you have a daughter, you are never safe from the atmosphere of middle-class vulgarity which courting, match-making and weddings will introduce into your house and your mood. I for one can never reconcile myself to the triumphant expression on my wife's face whenever Gnekker visits us, or to the bottles of Lafitte, port and sherry, which are placed on the table solely on his account, so that he should see with his own eyes the luxurious scale on which we live. Nor can I endure the staccato laugh which Liza has learned in the conservatoire, or her way of narrowing her eyes when we have male visitors. But the main thing is that I cannot for the life of me understand why a person utterly alien to my habits, my science, the whole manner of my life, utterly different from the sort of people I like, should come every day to my house, and dine with me every day. My wife and the servants whisper mysteriously that he is "the fiancé," but even so I cannot make out why he should be here. He arouses in me the same astonishment I should feel if a Zulu were to be given a place at the table beside me. I find it strange, too, that my daughter, whom I still regard as a child, should love this tie, these eyes, these pudgy cheeks. . . .

In the old days I used either to enjoy my dinner, or, at the worst, be indifferent to it, but now it arouses in me nothing but boredom and irritation. Ever since I became an "Excellency," and was made dean of the faculty, my wife and daughter have for some reason considered it necessary to introduce changes into our *menu* and the etiquette of our table. Instead of the plain dishes to which I have been accustomed from the days when I was a student, and later, a medico, I am now fed on soup-purée, with white blobs floating about in it, and on kidneys in madeira sauce. My new rank and celebrity have deprived me for ever of cabbage soup, with delicious pies, of goose and apple sauce, of bream and buckwheat. They have also deprived me of Agasha, the housemaid, a jolly garrulous old woman, in whose place Yegor, a dull-witted, pompous fellow, serves the dinner, wearing a white cotton glove on his right hand. The intervals between courses seem longer than they really are, because there is nothing to fill them up with. Gone are the old gaiety, the easy chatter, jokes, laughter, the mutual caresses, the joyousness felt by the children, my wife, and myself, when we used to come together round the table. For a busy man like myself dinner was a time of rest and re-union, and for my wife and children it was a treat, brief, it is true, but bright and gay, when they knew that for half an hour I belonged, not to the students, not to science, but to themselves and no one else. Gone is the ability to get slightly tipsy on a glass of wine, gone are Agasha, bream and buckwheat, the noisy enjoyment with which every trifling dinner-time incident, such as a fight under the table between the cat and the dog, or the time when Katya's bandage fell from her cheek into her soup.

It would be as unappetizing to describe our present dinners as it is to eat them. My wife, who always looks worried, now sits there with an expression of ostentatious solemnity on her face. She glances uneasily at our plates, saying: "I see you don't like the meat.... You know, you don't, so why not say so?" And I have to reply: "Not at all, my dear! It's delicious!" And she:

"You always stand up for me, Nikolai Stepanich, you
never say what you really think. But why does Alexander Adolfovich eat so little?" and this goes on
throughout the meal. Liza utters her staccato laugh and
narrows her eyes. I look from one to the other and it is
at dinner-time that I realize with the utmost clarity,
that the inner life of both of them has long escaped my
observation. I feel as if there had once been a time when
I lived at home with my real family, and that now I am
dining out with a not-real wife and regarding a not-
real Liza. A startling change has taken place in them
both, and I somehow failed to observe the long process
leading to this change, so that it is no wonder I am
unable to understand it now.   What has brought this
change about? I cannot say. Perhaps the real trouble is
that the Lord has not endowed my wife and daughter
with the powers possessed by myself. I have accustomed
myself to resist external influences from my childhood
up, and have trained myself in this. Such vicissitudes
of life as fame, rank, the transfer from mere sufficiency
to living beyond one's means, the acquaintance of celebrities, and so on, have made hardly any impressions
on me, my integrity has remained untouched by them.
But all this has fallen like an avalanche upon my wife
and Liza, weak and untrained as they were, and crushed
them.

Gnekker and the young ladies discuss fugues, coun-
ter-point, singers, pianists, Bach and Brahms, and my
wife, lest she should be considered an ignoramus, smiles
sympathetically, mumuring: "Exquisite. . . .   No, really!
Just fancy. . . ." Gnekker eats heartily and utters ponderous witticisms, listening condescendingly to the remarks
of the young ladies. Every now and then he has an impulse to speak bad French and then, for some reason, he
sees fit to dub me *votre excellence.*

But I am morose. Apparently I embarrass them, and
they embarrass me. I have never before felt any stir-

rings of snobbishness, but now I am tortured by something of the kind. I endeavour to see nothing but bad traits in Gnekker. This does not take me long, and soon I fall to worrying over the fact that a rank outsider should play the role of suitor in my house. His presence has a bad effect on me in another way, too. As a rule, left to myself, or in the company of those I like, I do not think of my own merits, or if I should do so for a moment, they seem as trifling to me as if I had only been a qualified scientist for a very short time. But in the company of people like Gnekker my merits seem to tower like a mountain, its peak disappearing into the clouds, and Gnekkers creeping about at its foot, almost invisible to the eye.

After dinner I retire to my study and smoke my pipe, the only one for the whole day, all that is left of my bad old habit of smoking from morning till night. While I smoke my wife comes to sit and talk to me. Just as I do in the morning, I know beforehand what she will talk about.

"We must have a serious talk, Nikolai Stepanich," she begins. "About Liza, I mean.... You might display a little interest, after all...."

"What do you mean?"

"You pretend not to notice anything, it's too bad. You have no right to be so easy-going. Gnekker has intentions towards Liza.... What do you think about it?"

"I can't say he's no good, since I don't know him, but I've told you again and again that I don't like him."

"But you can't ... you can't...."

She gets up and paces the floor nervously.

"You can't take a serious thing like that so lightly," she says. "When it is a question of your daughter's happiness all personal considerations must be abandoned. I know you don't like him. Very well, then ... suppose we refuse him now, break it off, can we be sure that Liza will not hold it against us all her life? Suitors

are not so very plentiful nowadays, and it is possible
that no other will turn up.... He is very much in love
with Liza, and as far as I can see she likes him, too....
I know he has no definite position, but we can't help that.
Let's hope he'll settle down one day. He comes from a
good family, and has plenty of money."

"How do you know?"

"He told me so. His father has a big house in Kharkov and an estate in the neighbourhood. You'll have to
go to Kharkov, Nikolai Stepanich, you know!"

"What for?"

"You'll be able to find out when you're on the spot....
You know some of the professors there, they'll help you.
I'd go myself, but I'm only a woman. I can't...."

"I'm not going to Kharkov," I say gruffly.

My wife gives way to alarm, an expression of extreme anguish appearing on her face.

"For God's sake, Nikolai Stepanich!" she implores
me, sobbing. "For God's sake, lift this burden from my
shoulders! I'm so unhappy!"

It pains me to see her like this.

"Very well, Varya," I say kindly. "I'll go to Kharkov, since you want me to, I'll do whatever you like."

She presses her handkerchief to her eyes and goes to
her room to cry. I am left alone.

Soon after, the lamp is brought in. Familiar shadows, long ago become tedious to me, are thrown on
the walls by the arm-chairs and the lamp-shade, and the
sight of them reminds me that night has come and that
my accursed insomnia will soon begin. I go to bed, get
up again and walk up and down the room, then go back
to bed.... As a rule it is after dinner, at night-fall, that
my nervous excitement reaches its highest point. I begin crying for no apparent reason, hiding my head under
the pillow. At such moments I am always afraid someone will come in, or that I will suddenly die, I am
ashamed of my tears, and am altogether in a pitiable

condition. I feel I can no longer bear to look at my lamp, my books, the shadows on the floor, I can no longer bear to listen to the sound of voices coming from the drawing-room. An invisible, incomprehensible force pushes me violently out of the house. I leap up, throw on my clothes, and go out, taking every precaution not to be noticed by any of the household. Where am I to go?

The answer to this question has long been in my mind—to Katya.

III

Usually I find her lying on a Turkish sofa or on a couch, reading. When she sees me she raises her head languidly, sits up and stretches out her hand to me.

"Lolling about as usual!" I say, after a short pause for rest. "It's very bad for you. Why don't you find something to do?"

"What?"

"You ought to find something to do, I tell you."

"But what? There's no choice for a woman between going to a factory or going on the stage."

"Very well, then, since it's not to be a factory, why not go on the stage?"

She makes no answer.

"Why don't you get married?" I say, half in earnest.

"There's no one to marry. And why should I?"

"You can't go on like this."

"Without a husband? What does it matter? There are plenty of men, if that was what I wanted."

"That's not nice, Katya."

"What isn't?"

"What you just said."

Seeing she had upset me, and anxious to soften the bad impression she had made, Katya says:

"Come with me. Come here! This way!"

She leads me into a small, snug room and points to a desk in it.

"Look ... I got it ready for you. You will work
here. Come every day and bring your work with you.
They won't let you work in peace in your own home.
Will you work here? Do say you will!"

Not to grieve her by a refusal I tell her I will, and
that I like the room very much. Then we both sit down
in the snug little room and start talking.

Warm, cosy surroundings and a sympathetic companion no longer arouse in me, as formerly, feelings of
gratification, but are a powerful incentive to complaints
and grumbling. I feel as if a little self-pity and complaining might do me good.

"Things are bad, dearie," I begin, sighing deeply.
"Very bad."

"What's the matter?"

"It's like this, my dear. The highest and most sacred
prerogative of kings is the right to pardon. And I have
always felt myself a king, for I have availed myself of
this prerogative extensively. I never judged, was always
indulgent, showered my pardons right and left on all.
When others protested and raged, I merely advised and
persuaded. My whole life I have endeavoured to make my
company tolerable for my family, my servants. And this
attitude of mine influenced all who had to do with me,
I know it did. But now I am a king no longer. Something
which would only be excusable in a slave is going on
inside me—bitter thoughts pass through my mind day
and night and feelings such as I never harboured before
have made a nest in my heart. I feel hatred and contempt,
indignation, wrath, and fear. I have become overween-
ingly severe, exacting, irritable, rude, suspicious. That
which would formerly have merely caused me to per-
petrate a pun and laugh good-humouredly, now evokes
in me dark feelings. My very sense of logic fails me—
formerly it was only money itself which I despised, now
I cherish bitterness with regard not to money, but to the
rich, as if they were to blame. Formerly I detested

tyranny and violence, but now I detest those who use violence, as if it was they, and not we who are unable to bring out the good in one another, who are to blame. What can be the meaning of all this? If my new thoughts and feelings arise from altered convictions, then what is the cause of this change in my convictions? Can it be that the world has become worse and I have become better, or is it that till now I have been blind and indifferent? If the change arises from a general decline of physical and mental powers—I'm a sick man, you know, I lose weight every day—then my situation is indeed pitiful. For it would mean that these thoughts are abnormal, morbid, that I ought to be ashamed of them, regard them as insignificant."

"It's nothing to do with your illness," Katya interrupted me. "It's just that your eyes have been opened, that's all. You now see what you refused to see before. In my opinion the first thing for you to do is to make a final break with your family and leave them."

"You're talking nonsense."

"You don't care for them—why play the hypocrite? Is that what you call a family? Nonentities! If they were to die today, tomorrow nobody would notice they weren't there."

Katya despises my wife and daughter just as much as they hate her. Nowadays one hardly likes to speak of the right of people to despise one another. But if one adopts Katya's point of view and acknowledges the existence of such a right, it becomes impossible to deny that she has just as much right to despise my wife and Liza as they have to detest her.

"Nonentities!" she repeats. "Have you had dinner today? How is it they remembered to call you to the table? How is it they still remember your existence?"

"Katya," I say sternly. "I ask you to stop talking like that."

"And do you suppose it's fun for me to talk about

them? I should be delighted not to know them at all.
Listen to me, my dear—drop everything and go away. Go
abroad! And the sooner the better."

"What nonsense! And what about the University?"

"Drop the University, too! What's the University to
you? What do you get from it? You've been giving lectures for thirty years, and where are your pupils? How
many of them have become famous? Try and count them.
It doesn't need talent and honesty like yours to produce
all these doctors who can only exploit ignorance, and
amass thousands of rubles. You are not needed!"

"For heaven's sake, how blunt you are!" I exclaim,
appalled. "Stop, or I shall go! I don't know how to reply
to this sort of talk!"

The maid comes in and announces that tea is served.
Beside the samovar, I am glad to say, a change comes
over our conversation. Having poured out my complaints,
I now wish to indulge in another weakness of the aged—
reminiscences. I tell Katya about my past, to my own
astonishment informing her of things I had no idea still
survived in my memory. And she listens to me with
sympathetic admiration, with pride, and with bated
breath. I am particularly fond of telling her of my days
in the seminary, and of my dreams of getting into the
University.

"I used to walk about the garden of the seminary,"
I tell her. "From some distant tavern the wind bears the
droning of a concertina and the sound of singing, or
a troika dashes past the wall of the seminary with bells
jingling, and this is quite enough for me to feel joy welling up, not only in my breast, but in my stomach, legs,
arms. . . . I would listen to the concertina, or to the sound
of the receding bells, and imagine myself a doctor, and
paint imaginary pictures, one more exquisite than another. And, behold, my dreams have come true! I have
had more than I dared to hope for. For thirty years I have
been a beloved professor, have had wonderful friends,

enjoyed an honourable popularity. I have known love, married for passionate love, had children. In short, looking back, I see my life as a beautiful composition, the work of a master. Now it only remains for me not to spoil the finale. This requires that I die like a man. If death is really a peril, then it must be faced in a way worthy of a teacher, a scientist and the citizen of a Christian state, with a cheerful, peaceful spirit. But I *am* spoiling the finale. Drowning, I run to you for help, and you tell me: drown, that's what you have to do."

But suddenly the front-door bell rings. Katya and I both recognize the ring, and say:

"It must be Mikhail Fedorovich."

And indeed, a minute later, in comes my philologist friend, Mikhail Fedorovich, tall, svelte, fifty years old, with thick grey hair, black eyebrows, and clean-shaven cheeks. He is a good man and a wonderful comrade. He comes of an ancient family of aristocrats, all more or less fortunate and gifted, all playing an important part in the history of our literature and education. He is himself clever, talented, highly-educated, but not without eccentricities. We are all a little strange one way or another, but there is something extraordinary about his eccentricities, and not without danger for his friends. Among the latter I know many who are quite unable to see his innumerable virtues, on account of these eccentricities.

He comes into the room slowly, drawing off his gloves and saying in deep tones:

"Good evening. Having tea? Splendid! It's devilish cold."

Then he sits down at the table, pours himself out a glass of tea, and starts talking immediately. The distinguishing feature of his conversation is a tone of permanent facetiousness, a peculiar blend of philosophy and drollery, reminiscent of the grave-diggers in *Hamlet*. His talk is always of serious things, but he never talks seriously. His criticisms are invariably harsh and abusive, but his gentle, smooth, facetious manner takes the sting out of the abuse and harshness, and one soon gets used to his ways. Every evening he brings half a dozen university anecdotes which he invariably begins to relate when he sits down to table.

"God Almighty!" he sighs, twitching his black eyebrows humorously, "what funny folk there are in this world!"

"Tell us," says Katya.

"As I was leaving the lecture hall today, I met that old fool of ours N. N.... He was walking along with his horsy chin thrust out, as usual, looking for someone to complain to about his headaches, his wife, or the students, who stay away from his lectures. 'He's seen me,' I thought, 'I'm in for it, now....'"

And so on. Or he would begin like this:

"I was at our Z.'s public lecture yesterday. I'm really astonished that our alma mater—whisper it not in Gath!—risks showing imbeciles like Z. in public. Why, he's notorious throughout Europe as a dunce. You could comb Europe and not find another like him. You know how he lectures, as if he were sucking sweets—um, um—then he takes fright, loses his place, (his thoughts move about as quickly as an archbishop on a bicycle), and, worst of all, nobody knows what it is he wants to say. As dull as ditch-water.... It's as boring as listening to the graduation speech (and what could be worse than that?), in the university hall."

Here he goes off at a tangent.

"Three years ago—Nikolai Stepanich here will remember—it fell to me to make this speech. Hot, stuffy, my official frock-coat tight under the arm-pits—phew! I spoke for half an hour, an hour, an hour and a half, two hours.... Well, I thought to myself, thank God there are only ten more pages left. And the last four pages were

quite unnecessary, I intended to leave them out. So that
leaves only six, I said to myself. But what do you think!
I looked up for a moment and saw a beribboned general
and an archbishop sitting side by side in the front row.
The poor things were stiff with boredom, blinking to keep
their eyes open, and at the same time trying to look as
if they were listening, and understood and liked what
I was saying. Well, if you like it, I thought to myself,
you shall have it. So there. And I read all through the
last four pages."

When he talks, only his eyes and eyebrows seem to
smile, as is usually the way with sarcastic individuals.
There is neither dislike nor ill-humour in his eyes at
such times, nothing but waggishness and a kind of vixen-
ish slyness only seen on the faces of very observant persons. While I am speaking of his eyes I may as well mention another of his peculiarities. When he takes a glass
from Katya, or listens to her remarks, or follows her
with his eyes if she happens to go out of the room for a
moment, I catch a look of humility, entreaty, innocence
in his glance.

The maid removes the samovar and places on the
table a large hunk of cheese, some fruit, and a bottle of
Crimean champagne, a rather poor wine which Katya
got fond of while living in the Crimea. Mikhail Fedorovich takes two packs of cards from the what-not, and
begins playing patience. He asserts that some games of
patience demand the greatest concentration and attention, but he nevertheless talks all the time he is laying
out the cards. Katya keeps a keen eye on them, helping
him more by gestures and mimicry than by words. She
never drinks more than two small glasses of wine the
whole evening, I sip at half a tumbler. The rest falls to
the lot of Mikhail Fedorovich, who can drink a great
deal without getting drunk.

Over the game of patience we solve a variety of problems, mainly of the loftiest order, and most of our

shafts are directed at what is dearest of all to us—
science.

"Science has outlived its age, God knows," says
Mikhail Fedorovich dropping out a word or two at a
time. "Its day is done. Oh, yes. . . . Humanity is beginning
to feel the need for putting something else in its place.
It sprang from the soil of prejudice, nourished itself on
prejudice, and is now itself the quintessence of prejudice,
like its defunct grandmothers—alchemy, metaphysics, and
philosophy. After all what has science given humanity?
The difference between the learned Europeans and the
Chinese, who get along without any science whatever, is
trifling, purely external. The Chinese have no use for
science, and what have they lost?"

"Flies have no use for science, either," I say. "But
what does it prove?"

"Don't get angry, Nikolai Stepanich. I wouldn't talk
like this to anyone else. . . . I'm more cautious than you
think, I wouldn't dream of saying such things in public—
God forbid! The mass of humanity cherish the prejudice
that science and art are loftier things than agriculture
and commerce, loftier than industry. Our sect is kept alive
on this prejudice and it is not for you and me to destroy
it. God forbid!"

During the process of the game Youth comes in for
plenty of abuse.

"The public are deteriorating," sighs Mikhail Fedorovich. "I'm not thinking about ideals and all that—if
only they knew how to work and think! Well may one say
with the poet: 'Sadly I watch the coming generation'!"

"Yes, they've deteriorated terribly," agrees Katya.
"Can you mention a single distinguished pupil of yours
during the last five—or, for that matter—ten years?"

"I don't know about the other professors, but I can't
think of anyone myself."

"In my time," continues Katya, "I've met lots of your
students and young savants, and lots of actors. . . . And

what do you think? I've never happened to come across
a single interesting person—not to mention heroic or
talented individuals. They're all colourless, mediocre,
puffed up, affected...."

All this talk about deterioration invariably makes me
feel as if I had accidentally overheard something unpleasant about my daughter. Such sweeping accusations,
based upon threadbare commonplaces, bugbears such as
deterioration, lack of ideals, or references to the glorious
past, vex me. Any accusation, even when made in the
presence of ladies, should be formulated with the utmost
exactitude, otherwise it is no accusation, but mere backbiting, unworthy of decent people.

I am an old man, I have been working thirty years,
but I observe neither deterioration, nor lack of ideals, and
do not consider that the present is worse than the past.
Nikolai the porter, whose experience on the matter is
worth something, says the students of today are neither
better nor worse than those of former times.

If I were to be asked what it is I do not like about
my present students, I should not be able to give an
answer at once, or say much, but I should not be vague.
I know their defects and therefore do not need to resort
to blurred commonplaces. I wish they didn't smoke and
drink so much, and marry so late. I don't like their
recklessness and that callousness of theirs which frequently leads to indifference to the presence of necessitous
students among them, and the failure to pay up their
arrears to the Society for Aid to Needy Students. They
have no knowledge of foreign languages and express
themselves incorrectly in Russian. Only yesterday my
colleague the professor of hygienics complained to me
that he has to give twice as many lectures as he used to,
on account of their weakness in physics and their complete
ignorance of meteorology. They are easily swayed by the
latest writers, even when these are by no means the best,
but utterly indifferent to classics like Shakespeare, Marcus

Aurelius, Epictetus, or Pascal, and it is in this inability to distinguish the great from the small that their lack of everyday common sense shows itself most of all. Instead of trying to solve complicated questions of a more or less social character (land settlement, for instance) by scientific investigation and experience—the ways most appropriate to their vocation and perfectly at their disposal—they merely draw up subscription lists. They gladly become internes, assistants, laboratory employees, non-resident physicians, and are content to occupy these posts up to the age of forty, though independence of mind, the demand for liberty of thought and personal initiative are not less necessary in science than in, let us say, art or commerce. I have plenty of pupils and students, but no assistants or successors, and therefore, though I love and admire them, I am not proud of them. And so on and so on. ...

But such defects, however numerous, can only make one who is timid and pusillanimous fall into pessimistic or abusive mood. They all bear a transitory, accidental stamp, and depend entirely on circumstances. Ten years are quite enough for them to disappear or yield to other, fresh defects, which are quite inevitable, and will, in their turn, alarm timid souls. The sins of the students frequently annoy me, but this annoyance is nothing in comparison with the joy I have felt in the course of thirty years, when talking to my students, lecturing to them, watching their mutual relations and comparing them to those of the outside world.

Mikhail Fedorovich continues to gibe, Katya to listen to him, and neither of them notices the profound abyss towards which so apparently blameless an amusement as criticizing their neighbours is gradually leading them. Neither of them notices that ordinary talk is gradually degenerating into mere taunts and jeers, and they actually stoop to backbiting.

"It's extraordinary the people one meets," says
Mikhail Fedorovich. "I went to see our Yegor Petrovich
yesterday, and found one of your medicos there, a third-
year man, I believe. What a face, a regular Dobrolyubov,
profound meditation stamped on his brow. We got talking.
'Look here, young man,' I said to him. 'I read somewhere
that some German, I forget his name, has produced a new
alkaloid, idiotine, from the human brain.' And what do
you think? He believed me, his face showed his respect—
'look what science can do!' was written on it. And the
other day I went to the theatre. I sat down. Just in front
of me in the next row were two individuals—one seemed
to be a law-student, one of the 'comrades,' the other, a
shaggy fellow, was a medico. The medical student was
as drunk as a lord. Didn't pay the slightest attention to
the stage. Just sat there dozing and nodding. But every
time some actor started on a monologue in a loud voice
or simply raised his voice, our medico started, nudged
his neighbour, and asked: 'What did he say? Was it
sublime?' 'Exceedingly sublime,' replied the law student.
'Br-r-r-ravo!' shouted the medico. 'Sublime! B-r-ravo!'
The drunken sot goes to the theatre, not for the sake
of art, mark you! He must have sublimity!"

And Katya listens and laughs. There is something
disconcerting about her laughter, it is a kind of rapid
and rhythmical inhalation and exhalation, as if she were
playing the concertina, and the only sign of mirth on her
face shows in her nostrils. My spirits sink and I do not
know what to say. I flare up, jump out of my chair, and
shout:

"Stop it! You sit there like a couple of toads and
poison the air with your breath. Enough of that!"

And I start to go home, without waiting for them to
finish their backbiting. It's time anyhow—eleven o'clock.

"I'll stay a little longer," says Mikhail Fedorovich.
"May I, Yekaterina Vladimirovna?"

"Of course," replies Katya.

"Bene. In that case be so good as to let us have another bottle."

They both accompany me to the hall with candles in their hands, and while I am getting into my overcoat Mikhail Fedorovich says:

"You're looking terribly thin and old, lately, Nikolai Stepanich. What's the matter? Are you ill?"

"A little."

"And won't see a doctor," puts in Katya morosely.

"Why don't you consult someone? You can't go on like this! The Lord helps those who help themselves, my friend. Give your people my regards and my apologies for not visiting them. I'll come and say good-bye in a few days, before I go abroad. Really I will. I'm leaving next week."

I leave Katya in a state of irritation, alarmed by the talk of my illness, and displeased with myself. After all, I ask myself, why not go and consult one of my colleagues? And immediately I picture to myself my colleague, after examining me, going over to the window in silence, thinking a while, and then turning to me, and trying to prevent me from reading the truth on his face, saying in casual tones: "So far I see nothing special, but I would nevertheless advise you, colleague, to give up working. . . ." And this deprives me of my last hope.

Which of us does not cherish some hope? When I diagnose for myself, and treat myself, I can now and then hope that it is my ignorance which deceives me, that I am mistaken about the albumen and sugar I discover in my urine, about the state of my heart, and about the dropsical symptoms I have already twice noticed of a morning. When, with the ardour of a hypochondriac, I look through text-books on therapy, changing my medicine daily, I keep thinking that I shall come upon something consoling. How petty it all is!

Whether the sky is covered with clouds, or the moon and the stars shine, I look up at the heavens and think how soon death will be coming for me. It might be supposed that at such times my thoughts would be profound, vivid, deep as the sky itself.... But nothing of the sort. I think about myself, my wife, Liza, Gnekker, my students—in a word about people. My thoughts are mean, trifling, I try to hoodwink myself, and all the time my attitude to life might be expressed in the words of the famous Arakcheyev, who, in a private letter, wrote: "There must be something bad in all that is good in this world, and the bad always preponderates over the good." In other words—everything is loathsome, there is nothing to live for, and those sixty-two years already spent must be regarded as wasted. I catch myself in such thoughts and try to persuade myself that they are casual, passing thoughts, and have no deep roots in my being, but next moment I think:

"If this is so, what makes you want to go to those two toads every night?"

And I make myself a vow never to go and see Katya again while perfectly aware that I shall go the next day.

When I have pulled at my front-door bell and gone upstairs I feel as if I no longer had a family, and had no desire to get it back. Clearly the new thoughts suggested by Arakcheyev's words have no casual or transitory place in my being, but rule my whole existence. Tortured by conscience, wretched, languid, scarcely moving my limbs, as if I carried a ton weight about with me, I get into bed and soon fall asleep.

And then ... insomnia....

IV

With the arrival of summer, life changes.

One fine morning Liza comes into my room and says jocosely:

"Come on, Your Excellency! Everything's ready."

My Excellency is led out into the street, seated in a

droshky, and driven off. As I drive I idly read the street notices from right to left. I read the word 'traktir' (tavern) backwards—'Ritkart'. This would make a very good name for a baroness—Baroness Ritkart. We pass a cemetery when we are in open country, and this makes not the slightest impression on me, though I will be lying in it so soon. Then our way lies through a wood, and through open country again. Nothing interests me. After a two hours' drive My Excellency is taken into a country cottage, and ensconced in a small, bright room on the ground-floor, with blue wallpaper.

The night passes as usual in insomnia, but in the morning, instead of waking up and listening to my wife's conversation, I stay in bed. I am not exactly asleep, but in that drowsy state of semi-oblivion, when one knows that one is not asleep, but goes on dreaming. At noon I rise and sit down at my desk from sheer habit, though I do not work, but amuse myself with French yellowbacks, sent to me by Katya. It would, of course, be more patriotic to read Russian writers, but I have to admit that I am not particularly fond of them. With the exception of the works of a few acknowledged masters, the whole of modern literature strikes me not as literature but as a kind of home-industry, existing solely on the sufferance of the public and not finding a ready market for its wares. The best products of home-industries can never be described as excellent and cannot sincerely be praised without a qualifying "but." And this holds good for those literary novelties which I have read during the last ten or fifteen years—not a single remarkable one, no getting away from the "buts." "Clever, lofty, but not brilliant; brilliant, lofty, but not clever, or, finally—brilliant, clever, but not lofty."

Not that I consider all French books brilliant, clever and lofty. *They* do not satisfy me, either. But they are not quite as dull as Russian books, and it is no exception to find in them that salient quality—the sense of individual liberty—which no Russian authors possess. I cannot recall a single modern book in which the author does not endeavour, from the very first page, to screen himself behind convention and compromise. One writer is afraid to mention a naked body, another binds himself hand and foot by psychological analysis, a third must have a "warm attitude to human beings," a fourth purposely smears whole pages with descriptions of scenery, for fear of being suspected of "tendencies". . . . One wishes to make himself out a true bourgeois at all cost in his writings, another poses as an aristocrat, and so on. We have design, cautiousness, circumspection, but no freedom, no courage to write as one likes, and therefore no originality.

All this applies to what is known as belles-lettres.

When it comes to serious articles by Russian authors, on such subjects, let us say, as sociology, art, etc., I avoid them from sheer timidity. In my childhood and youth I was afraid of hall-porters and theatre-attendants, a fear which has remained with me to this day. I am still afraid of them. They say we only fear what we do not understand. And it really is hard to understand why hall-porters and theatre-attendants are so pompous, so arrogant, so augustly rude And I experience the same vague fear when I read serious articles. Their extraordinary pomposity, their Olympian facetiousness, their familiar handling of foreign authors, their ability to make much out of nothing with such remarkable skill, are incomprehensible and alarming to me, so unlike the modesty, the quiet gentlemanly tone to which I am accustomed when reading the works of our medical and naturalist authors. I find it almost as hard to read the translations made or edited by serious Russian writers as to read their own articles. The Olympian, condescending tone of the preface, the multitude of translator's notes, preventing me from concentrating on the text itself, the question-marks and "sics" in brackets, with which the generous translator sprinkles the whole article or book, seem to me like so many attacks on the author's individuality and my own independence as a reader.

I was once invited to give an expert opinion at the district law-court. During the interval one of my colleagues (also an expert) drew my attention to the rude way in which the prosecutor addressed the accused, among whom were two educated women. I do not think I exaggerated in the least when I said to my colleague that this rudeness was no worse than the treatment of one another by the authors of serious articles. Indeed this rudeness is so marked that it is hard to speak calmly of it. Either they treat one another, or the writers they are criticizing, with an exaggerated respect amounting to servility, or, on the contrary, couch their opinions in terms very much bolder than those in which I refer in these notes, and in my thoughts, to my future son-in-law. Imputations of insanity, of dubious intentions, and even of all sorts of crimes, compose the usual adornments of serious articles. And all this, as our young doctors like to say in their "articles," *ultima ratio.* Such an attitude cannot but affect the morals of the younger generation of writers and I am therefore no whit astonished to find, in the new books which have enriched our belles-lettres during the last ten or fifteen years, heroes who drink too much vodka, and heroines who are insufficiently chaste. I read my French novels and glance out of the open window. I can see the tops of the palings in the fence round my front-garden, two or three sickly-looking trees, and, beyond the fence, a field, terminated by a broad belt of pine-trees. I often watch a boy and girl, both fair-haired and ragged, climbing on to the fence and laughing at my bald head. In their bright eyes I can read their thought: "Look at the baldy!" These are almost the only ones who care nothing either for my reputation or my rank.

I do not have visitors every day now. I will speak only of the visits of Nikolai and of Pyotr Ignatevich.

Nikolai usually comes to see me on holidays, ostensibly about business, but chiefly for the sake of seeing me. He is extremely tipsy, a thing which never happens to him in the winter.

"Well—how's everything?" I ask, going out to him on the porch.

"Your Excellency," he says, laying his hand on his heart and gazing at me with the ecstasy of a lover. "Your Excellency! As God is my witness! May God strike me dead! *Gaudeamus igitur juvenestus. . . .*"

And he eagerly kisses my shoulder, my sleeves, and my coat-buttons.

"Everything all right over there?" I ask.

"Your Excellency! As God is my judge. . . ."

He soon tires me out with his incessant invocations of God and I send him to the kitchen where they will give him dinner. Pyotr Ignatevich comes to me on holidays, too, on purpose to see me and share his thoughts with me. He usually sits down not far from the table, modest, neat and clean, rational, not venturing to cross his legs or lean on the edge of the table. And he never ceases in his gentle, even tones to give me, in smooth, bookish language, what he considers extremely interesting and piquant items of information gleaned by him from magazines and books. All these tidbits are exactly alike, and belong to the same type: some Frenchman has made a discovery, someone else—a German—has exposed him, proving that this discovery was made as long ago as 1870 by some American, and a third—also a German—has outwitted them both, proving to them that they have deceived themselves, and taken air-bubbles seen through the microscope for a dark pigment. Pyotr Ignatevich, even when his intention is to entertain me, speaks at length and in detail, as if he were defending a thesis, with a long list of the bibliographical sources of his information, trying hard to make no mistakes in his dates, the issue of the magazines or names, and taking care always to call Petit, Jean Jacques Petit. Sometimes he stays to dinner, relating all through the meal similar piquant stories, driving us all frantic with boredom Should Gnekker cr Liza turn the conversation to fugues or counterpoint, Brahms or Bach, he lowers his eyes in modest confusion. He is ashamed that such trivialities should be mentioned in the presence of serious persons like myself and him.

In my present mood five minutes of his company bore me as much as if I had been seeing and hearing him for an age. I detest the poor man. My spirits droop beneath his gentle, even tones and bookish language, his anecdotes drive me into a stupor. He has nothing but the kindest feelings for me and all he says is for the sole purpose of giving me pleasure, and I reward him by gazing steadily at him as if I wanted to hypnotize him, saying to myself over and over again: "Go, go, go...." But he does not respond to suggestion, and stays, and stays, and stays....

All the while he is with me I cannot shake off the thought: "It is quite possible that when I die he will be appointed in my place," and my unfortunate lecture-hall appears to me in the guise of an oasis in which my springs have dried up, and I am rude, silent, morose with Pyotr Ignatevich, as if he, and not myself were to blame for such thoughts. When he starts on his usual lauding of German scientists I no longer answer him jokingly, but mutter glumly: "Your Germans are a pack of asses...."

I know I am behaving like the late Professor Nikita Krilov who, when bathing at Reval with Pirogov, was furious with the water for being cold and said: "Those blasted Germans!" I behave badly to Pyotr Ignatevich, but when he leaves, and I see from the window his grey hat bobbing up and down past the fence, I have an impulse to call him back and say: "Forgive me, old man."

Dinner is still more tedious than it was in the winter. That same Gnekker whom I now despise and detest dines with us almost every day. Formerly I endured his presence in silence, but now I direct the shafts of my wit against him, making my wife and Liza blush. Carried away by angry feelings, I often utter absurdities without knowing why. Thus it once happened that I fixed my scornful glance on Gnekker, and declaimed, without the slightest provocation:

> *"The eagle lower than the chick may fly,*
> *But never will the chicken reach the sky."*

And what is most vexatious of all is that the chicken Gnekker turned out to be a great deal wiser than the eagle professor. Conscious that my wife and daughter are on his side, he maintains the following tactics: to reply to my taunts with indulgent silence (the old man is a bit barmy, no use arguing with him), or else to rally me good-humouredly. It is quite surprising to see how petty a man can become. I am capable, throughout the whole meal, of indulging in a day-dream, in which Gnekker turns out to be a swindler, my wife and Liza see their error, and I taunt them—indulging in these and similar fantasies when I have one foot in the grave.

I am now a witness of scenes formerly only known to me by hearsay. Much as it pains me I will describe one which occurred a few days ago atfer dinner.

I am sitting in my room, smoking my pipe. My wife comes in as her custom is, sits down, and begins saying how nice it would be for me to go to Kharkov while the weather is warm and I am free, there to discover what sort of man our Gnekker really is.

"Very well, I'll go," I agree.

My wife, gratified, gets up and goes to the door, but turns back on the threshold, to say:

"Oh, and another thing! I know you'll be cross, but it's my duty to warn you. . . . Excuse me, Nikolai Stepanich, but all our friends, and the neighbours, too, are beginning to notice how often you go and see Katya.

She is clever and well-educated and a charming companion, but you must admit it looks rather odd for a man of your age and social standing to take pleasure in her company. ... Besides, she has such a reputation."

The blood suddenly rushes to my heart, sparks seem to be showering from my eyes, I spring up and shout at the top of my voice, clutching my temples and stamping my foot:

"Leave me alone! Leave me alone! Go away!"

My face must look awful, and my voice must sound very strange, for my wife turns pale, screaming loudly, and shouting desperately, also at the top of her voice. Hearing our cries Liza and Gnekker come running in, followed by Yegor.... "Leave me alone!" I repeat. "Get out! Leave me alone!"

My legs go quite numb, as if they no longer existed, I feel myself falling into somebody's arms, half aware of the sound of someone sobbing, and sink into a swoon, which lasts for two or three hours.

To return to Katya. She comes to me every day just before night-fall, and this of course cannot pass unnoticed either by friends or neighbours. She comes in for a few minutes, and takes me out for a drive. She has her own horse and a new barouche, purchased this summer. Altogether she lives on a grand scale. She has rented an expensive country villa with a big garden, and has had all her furniture moved into it, and keeps two maids and a coachman.... I often ask her:

"What will you live on when you have run through the money your father left you, Katya?"

"We'll see," she replies.

"You ought to have more respect for this money, my dear. A good man worked hard to accumulate it."

"You've told me that before. I know."

At first we drive over open country, then through the pine-wood I can see from my window. Nature still strikes me as beautiful, although an imp whispers in my ear that

all these pines and firs, these birds, the white clouds in
the sky, will not notice my absence in three or four
months' time, after I am dead. Katya likes taking the
reins, the good weather and my presence beside her make
her happy. She is in high spirits and does not indulge
in caustic remarks.

"You're a good man, Nikolai Stepanich," she says. "You
are a rare specimen, and no actor could impersonate you.
Quite a poor actor could impersonate me or Mikhail
Fedorovich, but nobody could do you. I envy you, I envy
you terribly. After all, who do I consider myself to be?
What am I?"

After a moment's pause for thought, she asks me:

"I'm an undesirable type, aren't I, Nikolai Stepanich?
I am, aren't I?"

"Yes, you are."

"H'm... what can I do about it?"

How am I to answer her? It is easy to say: "Work,"
or "Give all you have to the poor," or "Know thyself!"
and because this is so easy to say, I find nothing to say
in reply to her.

My therapeutist colleagues tell their students to
"individualize each separate case" when giving medical
treatment. And the moment one begins to follow this
advice one sees how futile are the remedies recommended
in the text-books as the best standard treatment, when
it comes to individual cases. It is just the same when it
is not the body, but the mind which is sick. But I must
give her some sort of reply, and I say:

"You have too much time on your hands, my dear. You
must find something to do. Now why don't you go on
the stage again, since you feel a vocation?"

"I can't."

"Why do you put on such martyred airs? I don't like
it, my dear. It's all your own fault. Remember you began
by picking faults in people and society, but did nothing
to improve the one or the other. You did not resist evil

but only tired yourself out, you were a victim, not of struggle, but of your own weakness of will. But you were young and inexperienced then, everything might go differently now. Come, try again! You will work, serve the glorious cause of art...."

"Don't be a hypocrite, Nikolai Stepanich!" Katya interrupts me. "Let's decide once and for all to talk about actors, actresses, and writers, but leave art in peace. You're a fine, rare person, but you don't know enough about art to call it sacred with any conviction. You have no flair for art, no ear. You have been busy all your life and have had no time to cultivate this flair. And altogether.... I hate all this talk about art," she continues irately, "hate it! People vulgarize it enough, in all conscience."

"Who vulgarizes it?"

"Some by incessant drinking, the press by its flippancy, wise folk by their philosophizings."

"Philosophy has nothing to do with it."

"Oh, yes, it has. When people philosophize they show they understand nothing."

To prevent the conversation from degenerating into mere taunts, I hasten to change the subject, and then say nothing for a long time. Only when we emerge from the woods and approach Katya's villa do I return to the former subject of conversation and say:

"But you haven't told me why you don't want to go back to the stage."

"Nikolai Stepanich, that's cruel!" she cries, and suddenly blushes all over. "Do you want me to put the truth into words? Very well then, since that's what you like. I have no talent. No talent, and ... and lots of vanity. There you are!"

After making this admission, she turns her face away from me, tugging violently at the reins to conceal the trembling of her hands.

As we drive up to Katya's villa we see in the distance

Mikhail Fedorovich, strolling in front of the gate, and impatiently awaiting us.

"Again that Mikhail Fedorovich!" says Katya in vexation. "Do take him away from me. He's a bore, he's nothing but a dry stick! I've had enough of him!"

Mikhail Fedorovich was to have left for abroad long ago, but keeps putting off his departure from week to week. A change has come over him of late. His face is drawn, wine affects him now, a thing that never happened before, and grey hairs have appeared in his black eyebrows. When the carriage draws up in front of the gate, he cannot conceal his joy and impatience. He makes a great fuss about helping Katya and myself to get out, bombards us with questions, laughs, and rubs his hands, and the humble, imploring, innocent expression which I formerly only noticed in his glance has now spread to his other features. He rejoices and at the same time is ashamed of his joy, ashamed of his habit of visiting Katya every evening, and considers it necessary to explain his visit by some obvious absurdity, such as: "I was driving by on business, and thought I'd drop in for a few minutes."

We all three go into the house. At first we have tea, and then all the objects I have so long been familiar with appear on the table—the two packs of cards, the big hunk of cheese, the fruit, the bottle of Crimean champagne. The subjects of our conversation are not new, either, they are the same ones we discussed in the winter. The University, the students, literature and the theatre all come in for their share of obloquy. The atmosphere becomes turbid and close with malicious gossip, poisoned by the breath not of two toads, as in the winter, but of three. The maid who serves us now hears, in addition to the deep velvety laughter, and gasping accordion-like gusts, unpleasant, staccato laughs, like the tee-heeing of stage comic generals.

V

There are nights made terrible by thunder, lightning and torrents of rain—"sparrows' nights," the Russian country people call them. Such a night once played itself out in my own life.

I waked up just after midnight and leaped out of bed. I had taken it into my head that I was going to die on the spot. What made me think this? I felt no bodily sensation pointing to a rapid end, nothing but a consciousness of horror, as if I had just seen some vast ominous glow in the sky.

Hastily lighting the lamp, I drank some water out of the carafe, and rushed over to the open window. It was a beautiful night, the air fragrant with the scent of new-mown hay and some other sweet smell. I could see the tops of the palings, the drowsy summit of the sickly trees growing beside the window, the road, the dark belt of the woods. The moon shone serene and bright in a cloudless sky. Perfect stillness, not a leaf stirring. It seemed to me that everything was looking at me, listening to me, ready to watch me die....

Very sinister. I closed the window and rushed back to my bed. I tried to take my pulse, and, unable to find it in my wrist, fumbled for it at the temples, then under my chin, and again in my wrist, and wherever I touched myself I was cold and clammy with sweat. My breath became more and more rapid, my whole frame trembled, my insides were in a state of violent upheaval, and I felt as if my face and the bald spot on my head were covered with cobwebs.

What was to be done? Call my family? No, I couldn't do that. What could my wife and Liza do for me if they were to come?

I hid my head under the pillow, covered my eyes, and waited.... My back was cold, and I felt as if my

110

spine were being sucked inwards, and as if death must inevitably come creeping up to me from behind....

A sound suddenly broke the silence of the night: kee-vee, kee-vee. I did not know where it came from—from within myself, or out-of-doors.

"Kee-vee, kee-vee!"

God, how terrible it was! I wanted to take another drink of water, but was afraid to open my eyes or raise my head from the pillow. I was in the grip of senseless, animal terror, unable to understand what it was I was afraid of—was it that I wanted to go on living, or that some new, unknown pain awaited me?

From the room overhead someone was groaning, or perhaps, laughing.... I strained my ears. A little later steps were heard on the stairs. Someone hurried down, and then ran up again. Then steps could again be heard descending; someone stopped outside my door, and listened.

"Who's there?" I cried.

The door opened, I opened my eyes boldly and saw my wife. Her face was pale and her eyes red with weeping.

"Are you awake, Nikolai Stepanich?" she asked.

"What's the matter?"

"For God's sake, come and see Liza. She's in an awful state...."

"In a minute," I muttered, glad not to be alone any more. "I'll come ... just a minute."

I followed my wife, listening to what she told me, but too much agitated to understand her words. Spots of light danced on the stairs from the candle in her hand, our long shadows trembled, I stumbled over the hem of my dressing gown, and I felt as if someone were chasing me and trying to grab at my back. "I shall die this very moment, on the stairs," I told myself. "This very moment...." But the stairs came to an end, and we approached Liza's bedroom along a dark corridor terminating in a wide Italian window. She was sitting on the side of her bed with nothing on but a chemise, moaning, her bare legs dangling.

"O, my God, my God," she muttered, blinking at the candle. "I can't, I can't...."

"Liza, my child," I said. "What's the matter with you?"

When she saw me she gave a cry and threw herself on my shoulder.

"Daddy, my kind Daddy," she sobbed. "My good Daddy.... My darling, my pet.... I don't know what's the matter with me.... I'm so unhappy!"

She put her arms round me, kissing me and uttering the affectionate words I used to hear from her when she was a little girl.

"Calm yourself, my child," I said. "God bless you! Don't cry! I'm unhappy, too."

I tried to cover her up, my wife gave her something to drink, and the two of us moved awkwardly round the bed. My shoulder brushed against hers, reminding me of the days when we used to give our children their baths together.

"Do something for her!" my wife implored me. "Do something!"

What could I do? There was nothing I could do. The poor child had something on her mind, but I understood nothing, knew nothing, and could only murmur:

"Don't cry, don't cry ... it'll pass ... go to sleep...."

As if to spite us, a dog began howling somewhere outside, first softly and irresolutely, and then loudly, ranging from a high soprano to deep bass notes. I had never before attached any significance to omens, such as the howling of dogs or the hooting of owls, but this time I felt a pang of anguish at my heart, and hastened to explain the reason for this howling to myself.

"Nonsense!" I told myself. "Merely the influence of one living creature on another. My violent nervous tension must have communicated itself to my wife, to Liza, to the dog, that's all. . . . Transfers of this sort are the true explanation of forebodings, visions, and the like. . . ."

When, a little later, I returned to my room to write out a prescription for Liza, I no longer thought about my own sudden demise, I simply felt so depressed and wretched, that it is a pity I did not die then and there. I stood motionless in the middle of the room for a long time, trying to think what to prescribe for Liza, but the groans overhead ceased and I decided not to prescribe anything, but still stood there. . . .

Deathly silence, a silence which, as some writer puts it, seemed to ring in the ears. Time passed slowly, the strips of moonlight on the window-still did not change their places, they seemed to be fixed there. . . . Dawn would be long in coming.

Suddenly the gate creaked and someone stole towards the house, breaking off a twig from one of the sickly trees and tapping cautiously at my window-pane with it.

"Nikolai Stepanich!" I heard someone whisper. "Nikolai Stepanich!"

I opened the window and thought I must be dreaming. Beneath the sill, pressed against the wall, stood a woman in a black dress, brilliantly lit up by the moonlight, and gazing at me from great eyes. Her face was pale, stern and unreal in the moonlight, as if carved from marble, but her chin was trembling.

"It's me," she said. "Me—Katya."

Moonlight makes all women's eyes seem big and black, everyone looks taller and paler, and probably for this reason I had not recognized her at once.

"What's the matter?"

"Don't be angry with me," she said. "I suddenly felt so unbearably miserable. I couldn't stand it and I came here in my carriage. I saw a light in your window and I thought I would knock. . . . Forgive me. . . . Oh, if you only knew how unhappy I was! What are you doing just now?"

"Nothing... I can't sleep...."

"I had a sort of foreboding. But of course it's all nonsense."

Her eyebrows shot up, tears shone in her eyes and her whole face was irradiated, as if by a bright light, by that familiar expression of confidence I had not seen for such a long time.

"Nikolai Stepanich," she pleaded, stretching out her arms towards me. "My darling, I beg you, I implore you.... If you do not scorn my friendship and my respect for you, do what I ask you...."

"What is it?"

"Take my money from me."

"Now what have you taken into your head? What do I want your money for?"

"You could go away and get yourself cured. You need medical treatment. Will you take it? Will you? Will you, my darling?"

She gazed eagerly into my face and said again: "Will you? Do say you will!"

"No, my dear, I will not," I said. "But thank you."

She turned her back on me and bent her head. No doubt there had been something in the tone of my refusal which did not admit of further talk about money.

"Go home to bed," I said. "We'll meet tomorrow."

"So you don't consider me your friend?" she asked dismally.

"I didn't say that. But your money is no use to me now."

"Oh, sorry!" she said, lowering her voice a whole octave. "I understand. To borrow from a person like me— a retired actress.... Oh well, good-bye."

And she went away so swiftly that I did not even have time to say good-bye to her.

I am in Kharkov.

Since it would have been no use to try and struggle against my present mood, and indeed beyond my strength, I determined that my last days on earth should be, at least outwardly irreproachable. If I have not *been* all that I should for my family, as I am well aware is the case, I could at least endeavour to *do* what they wanted. Since I am to go to Kharkov, to Kharkov I will go. Moreover of late I have become so indifferent to everything that I don't care in the least where I go—to Kharkov, to Paris, or to Berdichev.

I arrived here at about noon, and put up at a hotel not far from the cathedral. The movement of the train made me feel sick, and there was a draught in the compartment, and now I sit on the side of the bed, clutching my temples and waiting for my tic to begin. I ought to go and see my friends among the professors here but lack the inclination and the strength.

The old waiter comes to ask if I have brought bed-linen with me. I keep him for five minutes and question him about Gnekker, on whose account I am here. The porter turns out to be a native of Kharkov, knows the town inside out, but cannot think of a single householder by the name of Gnekker. I ask him about estates in the neighbourhood, with the same result.

The clock in the passage strikes one o'clock, two o'clock, three o'clock.... These last few months of sitting and waiting for death seem to me longer than the whole of the rest of my life put together. Never before have I been able to endure the slow passage of time so patiently. Formerly, when waiting at the station for a train to come, or sitting through an examination, every quarter of an hour seemed an eternity, now I can sit motionless on the side of my bed all night, and realize with complete indifference, that tomorrow and the day after tomorrow, the nights will be just as long and uneventful. ...

The clock in the passage strikes five ... six ... seven. ... It is getting dark.

There is a dull pain in my cheek—that is the tic beginning. In order to occupy my thoughts I go back to the point of view which was mine before I became indifferent, and ask myself: why am I, a famous man, a privy councillor, sitting on the side of this bed with a strange, grey blanket, in a tiny hotel-room? Why am I looking at this cheap iron wash-stand and listening to the ticking of the wretched clock in the passage? Is this worthy of my reputation, my high social position? I reply to these questions with a sneer. I am amused at the simplicity with which, in my youth, I exaggerated the importance of fame and of the extraordinary position I supposed celebrities to occupy. I am famous, my name is pronounced with reverence, my portrait has appeared in the *Niva* and the *Universal Illustrated Magazine*, I have actually read my own biography in a German magazine—and what of all this? Here I am, all alone in a strange town, on a strange bed, rubbing my aching cheek with the palm of my hand. ... Domestic vicissitudes, the implacability of creditors, the rudeness of railway employees, the inconvenience of the passport system, the expensive and unwholesome food in station buffets, the universal ignorance and rudeness—all this and a great deal more which it would take too long to enumerate, concerns me no less than it does any nonentity, who is unknown outside the street in which he lives. Then what is there so distinctive about my situation? Say I am the most famous man in the world, a hero of whom my country is proud; all papers publish bulletins on the state of my health, every post brings me letters of sympathy from my colleagues, pupils, and the general public, yet none of these things can prevent me from dying in a strange bed, wretched, utterly solitary. ... No one is to blame for this, of course,

and I, sinful mortal that I am, have no love for popularity.
I feel as if it had betrayed me.

I fall asleep towards ten, sleeping soundly despite
the tic, and would probably have slept a long time if
someone had not waked me. Soon after one there came
a knock at the door.

"Who's there?"

"A telegram."

"You could have kept it till tomorrow," I said angrily,
taking the telegram from the porter. "Now I shan't be
able to get to sleep again."

"Excuse me. Your light was on, so I thought you were
awake."

I opened the telegram, and looked for the signature.
It was from my wife. What does she want?

"Gnekker and Liza married secretly yesterday. Come
back."

I felt a moment of alarm on reading it. But it was
not so much the action of Liza and Gnekker which alarmed
me, as the indifference with which I received the news
of their marriage. They say it is philosophers and sages
who are indifferent. This is not true—indifference is
paralysis of the soul, premature death.

I got back into bed and began trying to think
of something to occupy my mind. What should I think
about? Everything seemed to have been thought out,
and there was now nothing capable of arousing my
thoughts.

When day began to break I sat up in bed, embracing
my knees, and made an effort, for want of something
better to do, to understand myself. "Know thyself!" is
splendid and useful advice, but the ancients forgot to
point out how to follow it.

Formerly, when desirous of understanding myself or
another, I fixed my attention not on actions, which do not
depend on the individual, but on his desires. Tell me
what you desire and I will tell you what you are.

And now I subject myself to examination: what do I desire?

I should like our wives, our children, our friends, and our pupils to love us, not our reputations, a firm, or a label, but ordinary human beings. What else? I should like to have assistants and disciples. What else? I should like to wake up in a hundred years' time, and have a glimpse, only a passing glimpse, of the state of science. I should like to live another ten years. . . . What else?

That's all. I thought and thought and could think of nothing. And think as I would, it was clear to me, however far-flung my thoughts, that something essential, the main thing, was lacking from my desires. My passion for science, my desire to go on living, my sitting up in the strange bed, my attempts to know myself, all these thoughts, sensations and conceptions of mine had nothing in common with one another, nothing which might weave them into a single whole. Each thought and feeling was isolated within me, and the most skilful psychologist would fail to find in all my criticisms of science, the theatre, literature, my pupils, in all the pictures which my imagination painted, anything which might be called a general idea, or serve as a god for a living man.

And if this is missing, then everything is missing.

Given such poverty of spirit, any serious indisposition, the fear of death, the influence of circumstances and people, is sufficient to upset and break into smithereens everything I have been accustomed to regard as my mental outlook, everything in which I used to see the meaning and joy of life. It is therefore no wonder that the last months of my life are being darkened by thoughts and feelings worthy of a slave or a savage, that I have become too indifferent to look at the dawn. When that which is higher and stronger than all external influences is lacking in an individual, a violent cold in the head is quite enough to unhinge him and make him see an owl in every bird, hear a dog's howl in every sound. And all his pessimism and optimism, all his thoughts, lofty or petty, are only important as symptoms.

I am defeated. That being so, there is no point in going on thinking, no point in talking. I will sit and wait silently for the inevitable.

The next morning the porter brought me tea and a copy of the local newspaper. I glanced mechanically through the advertisements on the front page, the leading article, the extracts from other newspapers and magazines, the news.... Among other items I found the following piece of information in the news column: "Yesterday the well-known scientist, Honoured Professor Nikolai Stepanovich N., arrived at Kharkov by the express train, and is staying at the N. hotel."

Great names apparently exist in order to live a life of their own, apart from that of their possessors. My name is now walking about Kharkov with perfect nonchalance. In three months' time it will blaze like the sun itself in gilt letters on a tombstone, while I myself am already moss-grown....

A light tap on the door. Somebody wants to see me.

"Who's there? Come in."

The door opens and I retreat a step in my astonishment, hastily drawing the folds of my dressing-gown round me. Katya stands before me.

"Hullo," she says, breathing heavily after her ascent of the stairs. "You weren't expecting me? I ... I came here, too."

She sat down and went on talking, stammering slightly and avoiding my glance.

"Why don't you speak to me? I came here, too.... I came today. I heard you were staying in this hotel and I came to see you."

"I'm delighted to see you," I said, shrugging my shoulders, "but I'm astonished. It's like a bolt from the blue. What brings you here?"

"Me? I just thought I'd come."

Silence. Suddenly she rose abruptly and came towards me.

"Nikolai Stepanich," she said, turning pale and pressing her hands to her breast. "Nikolai Stepanich! I can't go on living like this! I can't! For God's sake, tell me, tell me quickly, this moment—what am I to do! Tell me what I am to do!"

"What can I tell you?" I said in astonishment. "I have nothing to tell you."

"Tell me, I implore you!" she continued, gasping, and trembling all over. "I swear I can't go on like this! It's too much for me!"

She sank on to a chair and fell to sobbing. She threw back her head, wrung her hands, stamped on the floor. Her hat fell off and hung on its elastic, her hair came down.

"Help me! Help me!" she implored me. "I can't go on any longer!"

She took a handkerchief out of her reticule, and with it came some letters which fell from her knees to the floor. I picked them up and recognized on one the writing of Mikhail Fedorovich, accidentally catching sight of a fragment of a word—"passiona-"

"There is nothing I can tell you, Katya," I said.

"Help me!" she sobbed, seizing my hand and covering it with kisses. "You are my father, my only friend! You are wise, educated, you have lived a long time! You have been a teacher. Tell me—what am I to do?"

"On my soul, Katya, I don't know."

I was embarrassed, confused, touched by her sobs, and scarcely able to stand on my feet.

"Let's have breakfast, Katya," I said, with a strained smile. "Do stop crying."

And then I added in faltering accents:

"I shall soon be gone, Katya."

"One word, only one word," she exclaimed, weeping and stretching out her arms to me. "What am I to do?"

"What a funny girl you are!" I muttered. "I don't

understand. A clever girl like you and all of a sudden off you go in tears!"

Silence ensued. Katya set her hair to rights and put on her hat, then she crumpled up the letters and thrust them back into her reticule, and all this silently, without haste. Her face, the front of her dress and her gloves were soaked with tears, but her expression had become severe and cold.... Looking at her I felt almost ashamed at the consciousness that I was happier than she. I had only noticed in myself the lack of what my philosopher colleagues call a general idea a short time before my death, in the evening of my days, and the soul of this poor creature will find no haven for a lifetime, a whole lifetime!

"Let's have breakfast, Katya," I said.

"No thanks," she replied coldly.

Another minute passed in silence.

"I don't like Kharkov," I said. "It's very dingy. A dingy sort of town."

"I suppose it is. Ugly. I shan't be here long ... between journeys, I'm leaving today."

"Where are you going?"

"To the Crimea ... to the Caucasus, I mean."

"Really? For long?"

"I don't know."

Katya gets up and holds out her hand to me, smiling coldly, and not looking at me.

I want to ask her: "So you won't be at my funeral?" But she does not look at me, her hand is cold, like the hand of a stranger. I accompany her to the door in silence. Now she has left me, is passing down the long passage without looking back. She knows I am looking after her, when she gets to the turn she will surely look back.

But she does not. Her black dress disappears, the sound of her footsteps ceases.... Good-bye, my precious!

1889

THE GRASSHOPPER

I

All Olga Ivanovna's friends and acquaintances went to her wedding.

"Look at him—there *is* something about him, isn't there?" she said to her friends, nodding towards her husband—apparently anxious to explain how it was that she had agreed to marry a commonplace, in no way remarkable man.

Ossip Stepanovich Dimov, her husband, was a doctor with the rank of titular counsellor. He worked in two hospitals, in one as non-resident physician, and in the other as prosector. From nine till noon he received out-patients and visited his ward, and in the afternoon took the horse-tram to another hospital, where he performed post-mortems on patients who had died there. His private practice amounted to very little, about 500 rubles a year. And that is all. There is nothing more to say about him. Whereas Olga Ivanovna and her friends and acquaint-ances were by no means ordinary people. Each of them was distinguished in some way or other, and not alto-gether unknown, having already made a name and gained a certain celebrity, or, if not exactly celebrated yet, all gave promise of a brilliant future. One was an actor, whose genuine dramatic talents had already found recognition; he was elegant, clever and discreet, recited beautifully, and gave Olga Ivanovna lessons in elocution; another was an opera singer, fat and good-humoured, who assured Olga Ivanovna with a sigh that she was ruining herself—if she were not so lazy, if she would only take herself in hand, she would make a fine singer; as well as these there were several artists, chief among them Ryabovsky, who went in for painting problem pictures, animals and landscapes, and was an extremely handsome fair young man of about twenty-five, whose pictures made a hit at exhibitions—his latest had fetched five hundred rubles. He used to finish off Olga Ivanovna's sketches for her, and always said that something might come of her painting. Then there was a 'celloist who could make his 'cello "weep," and who declared openly that of all the women whom he knew, the only one capable of accompanying him was Olga Ivanovna. And the writer, young, but already well known, who had produced short novels, plays and stories. Who else? Oh, yes, there was Vasili Vasilievich, a genteel land-owner, amateur book-illustrator and creator of vignettes; he had a true feeling for the old Russian style, and for the legendary epic. He could produce veritable miracles on paper, on china, and on smoked plates. Amidst this artistic, liberal society, these favourites of fortune, who while perfectly urbane and well-bred, only remembered the existence of doctors when they were ill, and in whose ears the name of Dimov was equivalent to such common names as Sidorov or Tarasov, Dimov seemed like a stranger, superfluous, small, though he was actually very tall and broad-shouldered. His frock-coat seemed to have been made for someone else, and he had a beard like a tradesman's. Of course, if he had been a writer or an artist everyone would have said that his beard made him look like Zola.

The actor told Olga Ivanovna that with her flaxen hair

and in her wedding attire, she was exactly like a slender cherry-tree, when covered in the spring with delicate white blossom.

"No, but listen!" Olga Ivanovna said, seizing him by the hand. "How could it have happened? Listen to me, listen.... My father and Dimov worked in the same hospital, you know. When poor father fell ill Dimov watched by his bed-side day and night. Such a self-sacrifice! Listen, Ryabovsky! And you listen, writer, you'll find it very interesting. Come nearer. Such self-sacrifice, such sincere sympathy. I didn't sleep at night, either, I sat by my father, and all of a sudden—I won the heart of the lusty youth—just like that! My Dimov was head-over-ears in love. How queer fate can be! Well, after my father died Dimov came to see me sometimes, and we sometimes met out-of-doors, and one fine day—lo and behold—a proposal, like a bolt from the blue! I cried all night, I fell madly in love, too. And here I am a married woman. There *is* something strong, something powerful, bearish, about him, isn't there, now? He's three-quarter face to us now, the light's all wrong, but when he turns full face just have a look at his forehead. What have you to say to such a forehead, Ryabovsky? Dimov, we're talking about you!" she shouted to her husband. "Come here! Give Ryabovsky your honest hand.... That's right. You must be friends."

Dimov held his hand out to Ryabovsky with a naive, good-humoured smile.

"Delighted," he said. "There was a Ryabovsky with me at college. He's no relation of yours, I suppose?"

II

Olga Ivanovna was twenty-two, Dimov, thirty-one. They had a wonderful life after their marriage. Olga Ivanovna covered the walls of her drawing-room with sketches, framed and unframed, by herself and her friends, and surrounded the grand-piano and the furniture with an artistic jumble of Chinese parasols, easels, many-coloured drapes, daggers, small busts, photographs. . . . In the dining-room she hung cheap coloured prints, bast shoes, and scythes on the wall, and grouped a scythe and a rake in the corner, thus achieving a dining-room *à la russe*. She draped the ceiling and walls of the bedroom with dark cloth, to make it look like a cave, hung a Venetian lantern over the beds, and placed a figure holding an halberd at the door. And everyone said that the young couple had made themselves a very cosy nest.

Olga Ivanovna got up at eleven every day, played the piano, or, if there was sunshine, painted in oils. A little after twelve she went to her dressmaker. She and Dimov had very little money, only just enough for their needs, and if she was to appear constantly in new dresses, and look effective, the dressmaker and she had to resort to all sorts of cunning. Again and again sheer miracles were achieved, and a thing of utter enchantment, not a dress, but a dream, was created from an old, dyed frock and some odd bits of tulle and lace. From the dressmaker Olga Ivanovna usually went on to an actress friend, and while she was about it tried to wangle tickets for some first-night, or somebody's "benefit." From the actress she had to visit an artist's studio, or go to a picture-show, and then on to some celebrity to invite him to her house, to return a call, or simply to chatter. And everywhere she was greeted with gaiety and cordiality and assured that she was good, sweet, unusual. . . . Those whom she called celebrated and great received her as one of themselves, on an equal footing, and declared unanimously that with her gifts, taste and mind, she would come to something big, if only she would stop wasting her talents in so many directions. She sang, played the piano, painted in oils, modelled in clay, acted in amateur theatricals, and all this not just anyhow, but displaying real talent. Whatever she did, whether it was making lanterns for illuminations, dressing up, or simply tying somebody's tie, turned out artistic, graceful, charming. But in nothing did her talents display themselves so vividly as in her ability to strike up lightning friendships and get on intimate terms with celebrated folk. The moment anyone distinguished himself in the very slightest degree, or got himself talked about, she scraped up an acquaintance with him, made friends instantly, and invited him to her house. Every time she made a new acquaintance was a veritable red-letter day for her. She worshipped the famous, she was proud of them, she dreamed of them every night. She thirsted for celebrities and could never slake this thirst. Old friends disappeared and were forgotten, new ones came to take their place, but she soon grew tired of these, too, or they disappointed her, and she began eagerly seeking new friends, new celebrities, and, when she had found them, looking for others. And why?

Between four and five she had dinner at home with her husband. His simplicity, common sense and good-humour reduced her to a state of admiration and ecstasy. She was continually jumping up, flinging her arms round his neck, and showering kisses on him.

"You are a wise, high-minded man, Dimov," she told him. "But you have one very grave defect. You take no interest whatever in art. You quite ignore music and painting."

"I don't understand them," he said humbly. "I have worked at natural science and medicine my whole life, and I never had any time to go in for art."

"But that's awful, Dimov!"

"Why? Your friends know nothing about natural science or medicine, and you don't hold it against them. Everyone to his own. I don't understand landscapes or operas, but I look at it this way: since some clever people devote their whole lives to them, and other clever people pay enormous sums for them, they must be necessary. I don't understand, but that doesn't mean that I ignore them."

"Let me press your honest hand!

After dinner Olga Ivanovna paid calls, then she went to the theatre or a concert, and did not get home till after midnight. And this went on every day.

On Wednesday evenings she was at home to visitors. There was no card playing or dancing on these Wednesday evenings, and the company entertained themselves with the arts. The well-known actor recited, the singer sang, the artists made drawings in Olga's innumerable albums, the 'celloist played, and the hostess herself drew, modelled, sang and played accompaniments. In the intervals between reciting, playing and singing, they talked and argued about literature, the theatre, art. There were no ladies present, for Olga Ivanovna considered all women, except actresses and her dress-maker, trivial and boring. There was not a single Wednesday evening when the hostess did not start at every ring at the door-bell, saying with a triumphant countenance: "It's him!" by which pronoun she indicated some newly invited celebrity. Dimov was never in the drawing-room, and nobody so much as remembered his existence. But precisely at half-past eleven, the door into the dining-room opened and Dimov appeared in the door-way, with his good-natured, gentle smile, rubbing the palms of his hands together, and saying:

"Come to supper, gentlemen!"

Everyone filed into the dining-room, and every time their eyes were greeted by the same objects: a dish of oysters, a round of ham or veal, sardines, cheese, caviare, pickled mushrooms, vodka and two decanters of wine.

"My darling *maître d'hôtel*," Olga Ivanovna would say, clasping her hands in ecstasy. "You're simply charming! Do look at his forehead, everyone! Dimov, turn your profile to us! Look, everyone—the face of a Bengal tiger, and an expression as sweet and kind as a doe's! You pet!"

The guests ate, glancing at Dimov, and thinking: "He really is a nice chap"; but they soon forgot about him and went on talking about the theatre, music, art.

The young couple were happy, and their life went smoothly on. True, the third week of their honeymoon did not pass quite happily, indeed it was sad. Dimov caught erysipelas at the hospital, and had to stay in bed six days and have his beautiful black hair cropped to the roots. Olga Ivanovna sat at his bed-side weeping bitterly, but when he got a little better she tied a white kerchief over his cropped head and began painting him as a Bedouin. And they both thought it great fun. Three days after he had quite recovered and begun going to the hospital again, a fresh misfortune overtook him.

"I have no luck, Mums," he said to her one day at dinner. "I had four post-mortems today, and I got two of my fingers cut at once. And I only noticed after I got home."

Olga Ivanovna was alarmed. He smiled and said it was a trifle and that he often cut his hands during post-mortems.

"I get carried away, Mums, and then I'm absent-minded."

Olga Ivanovna nervously awaited the onset of blood poisoning, and prayed every night that it might be averted; it all passed off harmlessly. And the old happy, tranquil life, untouched by grief or anxiety, was resumed. The present was splendid, and soon spring would be coming, smiling at them from afar, and promising a hundred joys. Happiness would go on for ever. For April, May and June there would be the country cottage a long way from Moscow, walks, sketches, fishing, nightingales, and then, from July right up to the autumn, the artists' excursion on the Volga, an excursion in which Olga Ivanovna, as a permanent member of their circle, would take part. She had already had herself made two travelling costumes of crash, and had bought paints, brushes, canvas and a new palette for the journey. Ryabovsky visited her almost every day to see how her painting was getting on. When she showed him her work he would thrust his hands deep into his pockets, compress his lips firmly, sniff and say:

"Well, well.... That cloud screams: that's not an evening light. The foreground is a bit messy, and there's something, you know what I mean—lacking.... Your hut looks as if it had been squashed and was whining piteously.... Make that corner darker. But on the whole it's not so dusty.... I'm pleased."

And the more obscure his way of speaking, the more easily Olga Ivanovna understood what he meant.

III

On Whitmonday Dimov went out in the afternoon and bought some snacks and sweets to take to his wife in the country. He had not seen her for a fortnight, and missed her sorely. In the railway carriage and afterwards, while trying to find his cottage in a thick copse, he felt the pangs of hunger, and indulged in dreams of sitting down to a leisurely supper with his wife, and afterwards tumbling into bed. It cheered him up to look at his parcel, which contained caviare, cheese, and smoked fish.

By the time he had found and recognized the cottage the sun had gone down. The elderly servant told him that the mistress was not at home, but that she would probably soon be back. The cottage, a highly unattractive structure, with low ceilings, note-paper on the walls, and uneven floors, full of gaps, contained only three rooms. In one was a bed, in the next canvases, paint-brushes, a piece of dirty paper, men's coats and hats on chairs and window-sills; and in the third Dimov came upon three strange men. Two were dark and bearded, and the third was clean-shaven and stout, an actor apparently. A samovar was steaming on the table.

"What do you want?" asked the actor in a bass voice, casting an unfriendly glance at Dimov. "To see Olga Ivanovna? Wait a minute. She'll be here soon."

Dimov sat down and waited. One of the dark men, looking at him with drowsy languor, poured out some tea, and asked:

"Have some tea?"

Dimov was both hungry and thirsty, but he refused the tea so as not to take the edge off his appetite. Soon steps were heard and a familiar laugh. A door banged and Olga Ivanovna burst into the room, in a broad-brimmed hat, carrying a box; after her, holding a big parasol and a folding stool, came Ryabovsky, red-cheeked and in high spirits.

"Dimov!" screamed Olga Ivanovna, flushing up with delight. "Dimov!" she repeated, laying her head and both her hands on his chest. "It's you! Why haven't you been for such a long time? Why? Why?"

"When could I, Mums? I'm always busy, and when I have any free time it always happens there's no suitable train."

"Oh, how glad I am to see you! I dreamed of you all night, all night, I was afraid you were ill or something. Oh, if only you know what a darling you are, and how lucky it is you came! You are my deliverer! You're the only one who can save me! There's going to be the most original wedding here tomorrow," she went on, laughing and re-tying her husband's tie. "The telegraph-operator at the station is going to be married, Chikeldeyev his name is. Good-looking boy, and no fool, there's something strong, bearish about his face, you know. . . . He could sit for the portrait of a youthful Varangian. All we summer visitors take an interest in him and have given our word of honour to be at his wedding. . . . He's hard-up, lonely, shy, it would be a sin to refuse him our sympathy. Fancy, the wedding will be just after the service, and everyone is going straight from the church to the home of the bride. . . . The grove, the singing of birds, spots of sun on the grass, you know, and all of us coloured spots against a bright green background—ever so original, just like the French expressionists. But, Dimov, what am I to wear at church?" said Olga Ivanovna, making a dolorous face. "I have nothing here, literally nothing. No dress, no flowers, no gloves. . . . You simply must save me! Your coming just now means fate intended you to save me. Take my keys, darling, go home, and get me my pink dress out of the wardrobe. You know it, it's hanging right in front. . . . And on the floor of the box-room you'll see two cardboard boxes. When you open the top one you'll see nothing but tulle, tulle, tulle and all sorts of scraps, and underneath them, flowers. Take out all the flowers very carefully, try not to crumple them, my pet, I'll choose something from them afterwards. And buy me a pair of gloves."

"Very well," said Dimov. "I'll go back tomorrow and send them."

"Tomorrow?" repeated Olga Ivanovna, gazing at him in consternation. You couldn't possibly be in time tomorrow! The first train leaves at nine tomorrow, and the wedding's at eleven. No, ducky, you'll have to go today, you'll simply have to! If you can't come tomorrow yourself, send everything with a messenger. Go on, now. . . . The train will be here soon. Don't be late, my pet."

"All right."

"How I hate to let you go!" said Olga Ivanovna, and tears welled up in her eyes. "What a fool I was to promise the telegraph-operator!"

Dimov, gulping down a glass of tea and picking up a cracknel, smiled meekly and went to the station. The caviare, cheese and smoked fish were eaten by the two dark men and the fat actor.

On a still moonlit night in July, Olga Ivanovna stood on the deck of a Volga steamer, looking in turns at the water and the exquisite river bank. Beside her stood Ryabovsky, telling her that the black shadows on the surface of the water were not shadows but a dream, that it would be good to forget everything, to die, to become a memory, surrounded by this magical, gleaming water, this infinite sky, these mournful, pensive banks, all speaking to us of the vanity of our lives, and of the existence of something higher, something eternal, blissful. The past was trivial and devoid of interest, the future was blank, and even this divine, never-to-be-repeated night would soon end, would become part of eternity—why, then, live?

And Olga Ivanovna listened in turn to Ryabovsky's voice and to the silence of the night, and told herself that she was immortal, that she would never die. The opalescent water, which was like nothing she had ever before seen, the sky, the banks, the black shadows, and the unaccountable joy filling her soul, all told her that she would one day be a great artist, and that somewhere, beyond the distance, beyond the moonlit night, in infinite space, there awaited her success, glory, the love of the people.... When she gazed long and unblinkingly into the distance she seemed to see crowds, lights, the sounds of solemn music, cries of enthusiasm, herself in a white dress, and flowers raining upon her from all sides. She told herself, too, that beside her, leaning on the rail, stood a truly great man, a genius, one of God's elect.... Everything he had done up to now was wonderful, fresh, unusual, and the work he would do in time, when his extraordinary talent had matured with the years, would be striking, immeasurably lofty, and all this could be seen in his face, in his way of expressing himself, and in his attitude to nature. He had his own special language for describing the shadows, the hues of evening, the brilliance of the moon-

light, and the charm of his power over nature was almost
irresistible. He was good-looking, too, and original, and
his life, independent, free, without earthly ties, was like
the life of a bird.

"It's getting chilly," said Olga Ivanovna, and she
shivered.

Ryabovsky wrapped his coat round her, saying mournfully:

"I feel I am in your power. I am a slave. What makes
you so fascinating today?"

He gazed at her all the time, never looking away, and
there was something terrible in his eyes, she was afraid
to look at him.

"I am madly in love with you. . ." he whispered, breathing on her cheek. "Only say the word and I will stop
living, throw up art. . ." he murmured, profoundly
stirred. "Love me, love me. . . ."

"Don't talk like that," said Olga Ivanovna, closing
her eyes. "It's awful. And what about Dimov?"

"What does Dimov matter? Why Dimov? What have
I to do with Dimov? The Volga, the moon, beauty, my love,
my ecstasy, but no Dimov. . . . Oh, I know nothing. . . . I
don't need the past, give me only one moment . . . one
little moment!"

Olga Ivanovna's heart beat violently. She tried to
think of her husband, but the entire past, her wedding,
Dimov, her Wednesday evenings, now seemed to her
small, insignificant, dull, useless, and far, far away. . . .
And after all—what did Dimov matter? Why Dimov?
What had she to do with Dimov? Was there really such
a person, wasn't he just a dream?

"The happiness he has had is quite enough for an
ordinary man like him," she told herself, covering her
face with her hands. "Let them judge *there,* let them curse
me, I will go to my ruin, yes, to my ruin, just to spite
them. . . . One should try everything once. Oh God, how
terrifying, and how lovely!"

"Well? Well?" murmured the artist, putting his arms round her and eagerly kissing the hands with which she was feebly trying to push him away. "Do you love me? Do you? Oh, what a night! What a divine night!"

"Yes, what a night!" she whispered, looking into his eyes, which were shining with tears, and then, looking away quickly, she put her arms round him and kissed him firmly on the lips.

"We'll be at Kineshma in a minute," said someone from the other side of the deck. Heavy steps were heard. It was the man from the refreshment-room passing.

"Listen," called Olga Ivanovna to him, laughing and crying from joy. "Bring us some wine."

The artist, pale with agitation, sat down on a bench, looking at Olga Ivanovna with adoring, grateful eyes, and then shut his own, and said with a weary smile:

"I'm tired."

And he laid his head on the rail.

V

The second of September was a warm, still day, but misty. A light fog had hovered over the Volga in the early morning, and after nine o'clock it began to drizzle. And there was not the slightest hope of its clearing up. At breakfast Ryabovsky had told Olga Ivanovna that painting was the most ungrateful and tedious of the arts, that he was no artist, that no one but fools believed in his talent, and suddenly, without the faintest warning, seized a knife and slashed at his most successful sketch. After breakfast he sat moodily at the window and looked out at the river. And the Volga, no longer shining, was dimmed, dull, cold-looking. Everything spoke of the approach of the sad, bleak autumn. It seemed as if the lush green carpets on the banks, the diamond-like reflections of the sun's rays, the transparent, blue distance, and all the elegant show of nature had been taken from the Volga

and laid away in a chest till next spring, and the crows
flew over the river, teasing it: "Bare! Bare!" Ryabovsky
listened to their cawing and told himself that he had
painted himself out and lost his talent, that everything
in the world was conventional, relative, idiotic, and that
he should never have got mixed up with this woman....
In a word he was dejected and depressed....

Olga Ivanovna sat on the bed on the other side of the
partition, passing her fingers through her beautiful flaxen
hair, seeing herself in imagination in her drawing-room,
in the bedroom, in her husband's study. Her imagination
bore her to the theatre, to the dressmaker, to her celebrated friends. What were they doing at this moment? Did
they ever think of her? The season had begun and it was
time to think of her Wednesday evenings. And Dimov?
Dear Dimov! How meekly and with what childish plain-
tiveness he kept begging her in his letters to come home.
Every month he sent her 75 rubles, and when she wrote
him that she had borrowed a hundred rubles from the
artists he sent her another hundred. What a good, generous man! The journey had tired Olga Ivanovna, she was
bored, she was longing to get away from these peasants,
from the smell of damp rising from the river, to shake off
the feeling of physical uncleanliness which never left her,
while living in peasant huts and migrating from village
to village. If Ryabovsky had not given the artists his word
of honour that he would stay with them till the twentieth
of September they could have gone away this very day.
And wouldn't that have been nice!

"My God," groaned Ryabovsky. "Whenever will the
sun come out? I can't go on with a sunlit landscape when
there isn't any sun."

"You have a sketch with a cloudy sky," said Olga
Ivanovna, coming out from behind the partition. "Don't
you remember—with a wood in the right foreground and
a herd of cows and geese on the left. You might finish
it now."

"For God's sake!" The artist made a grimace of distaste. "Finish! Do you really consider me too much of a fool to know what I ought to do?"

"How you have changed to me," sighed Olga Ivanovna.

"And a good thing, too!"

Olga Ivanovna's features twitched, she crossed over to the stove, and stood there, crying.

"And now tears—if that isn't the limit! Stop it! I have a thousand reasons for crying, but I don't cry."

"Reasons!" sobbed Olga Ivanovna. "The chief reason of all is that you are sick of me. Yes, you are!" And her sobs increased. "The whole truth is that you are ashamed of our love. You are afraid of the artists noticing, though there's no concealing it, and they've known about it for ages."

"Olga, I ask you only one thing," said the artist in imploring tones, placing his hand on his heart. "Only one thing—leave me alone! That's all I want from you."

"But swear that you still love me!"

"This is torture!" the artist hissed through clenched teeth, and he leaped to his feet. "It'll end in my throwing myself into the Volga or going mad! Leave me alone!"

"Kill me, then, go on, kill me!" cried Olga Ivanovna. "Kill me!"

She burst out sobbing and went behind the partition again. The rain rustled on the straw thatch. Ryabovsky clutched at his head and paced up and down the room for a time, and then, an expression of determination on his face, as if he were clinching an argument with someone, he put on his cap, threw his gun over his shoulder, and went out of the hut.

After he had gone, Olga Ivanovna lay on her bed for a long time, crying. At first she thought how nice it would be to take poison, and for Ryabovsky to find her dead when he came back, but very soon her thoughts flew back to her drawing-room, to her husband's study, and

she saw herself sitting quite still beside Dimov, enjoying
the physical sensations of peace and cleanliness, and then
seated in the theatre listening to Mazzini. And the yearn-
ing for civilization, for the noises of the city, for celebrated men, struck a pang to her heart. A country-woman
came into the hut and began heating the stove with lei-
sured movements, in preparation for cooking dinner.
There was a smell of smouldering wood, and the air
turned blue with smoke. The artists came in in their
muddy high-boots, their faces wet with rain, looked at
one another's sketches and consoled themselves by the
reflection that the Volga had its charm even in bad
weather. And the pendulum of the cheap clock on the wall
went tick-tick-tick. Chilly flies clustered in the corner next
to the icons, buzzing faintly, and cockroaches crawled
about in the bulging files under the benches.

Ryabovsky returned to the hut at sunset. He flung his
cap on the table, sank on to the bench, pale, exhausted,
still in his muddy boots, and closed his eyes.

"I'm tired," he said, his eyebrows twitching in the
effort to lift his eyelids.

Olga Ivanovna, in her anxiety to ingratiate herself,
and show him that she was not really angry, went over
to him, kissed him in silence, and passed a comb through
his fair hair. She felt a sudden desire to comb his hair.

"What's this?" he said, starting as if something
clammy had touched him, and opening his eyes. "What's
this? Leave me in peace, I beg you!"

He pushed her from him and moved away and she
caught an expression of disgust and annoyance on his
face. Just then the woman came up to him, holding a
plate of cabbage soup carefully in both hands, and Olga
Ivanovna noticed that her thick thumbs were wet with
the soup. And the dirty woman with her skirt drawn tight
over her stomach, the cabbage soup, which Ryabovsky fell
upon eagerly, the hut, this life which had at first seemed
so delightful in its simplicity and artistic disorder, now

struck her as appalling. Suddenly affronted, she said coldly:

"We shall have to part for a time, or we shall quarrel outright, from sheer boredom. I'm sick of all this! I shall leave today."

"How? On a broomstick?"

"Today's Thursday, so the steamer will arive at nine-thirty."

"Will it? Oh, yes.... Very well, go then," said Ryabovsky softly, wiping his lips with a towel, for want of a napkin. "It's dull for you here, and I'm not such an egoist as to try and detain you. Go, we'll meet again after the 20th."

Olga Ivanovna started packing with a light heart, her cheeks flaming with satisfaction. "Could it really be," she asked herself, "that she would soon be sitting in her drawing-room, painting, sleeping in a bedroom, and dining with a cloth on the table?" A load seemed to fall from her shoulders, and she was no longer angry with the artist.

"I'll leave you my paints and brushes, Ryabusha," she called out. "If there are any left over you can bring them back.... Now mind you don't get lazy when I'm not here, don't indulge in the blues—work! You're a brick, Ryabusha!"

At nine o'clock Ryabovsky kissed her good-bye, so as not to have to kiss her on the deck in front of the artists, she was sure, and saw her to the landing-stage. The steamer soon hove in sight and bore her away.

She was home in two and a half days. Without removing her hat and waterproof, breathing heavily in her agitation, she went into the drawing-room, and from there to the dining-room. Dimov was seated at the table in his shirt sleeves, his waistcoat unbuttoned, sharpening a knife on the prongs of a fork; on a plate before him was a roasted grouse. Olga Ivanovna had entered the flat with the conviction that she must conceal everything from

her husband, and that she had the ability and strength
to do this, but at the sight of his broad, meek, joyful
smile and the happiness shining in his eyes she felt that
it would be as base and detestable, as impossible for
her to deceive such a man as it would be to slander, to
steal, or to murder, and she then and there decided to
tell him all that had occurred. Allowing him to kiss and
embrace her, she sank down on her knees before him and
covered her face with her hands.

"What is it? What is it, Mums?" he asked her tenderly. "Did you miss me so?"

She lifted her face, red with shame, and cast a guilty
look, full of entreaty at him, but shame and fear prevented
her from telling him the truth.

"It's nothing. . ." she said. "I'm just. . . ."

"Let's sit down," he said, raising her, and seating
her at the table. "That's the way. . . . Have some grouse.
You're hungry, poor darling."

She inhaled the familiar atmosphere eagerly, and ate
some grouse, while he gazed at her affectionately, laughing with delight.

VI

It was apparently some time in the middle of the
winter that Dimov began to suspect that he was being
deceived. He could no longer look his wife in the eyes,
as if it were he whose conscience was not clear, no longer
smiled joyfully when he met her, and in order to be as
little alone with her as possible often brought home to
dinner his friend Korostelev, a crop-headed little man
with puckered features, who started buttoning and un-
buttoning his coat from sheer embarrassment whenever
Olga Ivanovna addressed him, and then fell to tweaking
the left side of his moustache with his right hand. During
dinner the doctors remarked that when the diaphragm
was too high up, palpitations sometimes occurred, or that

there had been a great deal of nervous disease lately,
or that Dimov, the evening before, performing a post-
mortem on a patient said to have died of pernicious ane-
mia, had discovered cancer of the pancreas. And they
seemed to carry on this medical conversation just to give
Olga Ivanovna an excuse not to talk, that is, not to lie.
After dinner Korostelev would sit down at the piano, and
Dimov would sigh and call out:

"Come on, old boy! What are you waiting for? Give
us something nice and sad."

His shoulders raised and his fingers outspread, Korostelev would strike a few chords and begin singing in
a tenor voice: "Show me, show me the place in our country, where the Russian muzhik does not groan!" and Dimov would give another sigh, prop his head on his fist
and plunge into thought.

Olga Ivanovna had now begun to behave extremely
incautiously. She woke up every morning in the worst
possible spirits, to the thought that she no longer loved
Ryabovsky, and that it was all over between them, thank
God. But after she had had a cup of coffee she would
remind herself that Ryabovsky had robbed her of her
husband and that she was now left without a husband,
and without Ryabovsky. Then she would remember that
her friends were speaking of some marvellous picture
Ryabovsky was finishing for a show, a kind of mixture
of landscape and problem picture, in the style of Polenov,
and that everyone who visited his studio was in ecstasies
about it. But he had created this picture under her influence, she told herself, he had improved enormously,
thanks to her influence. Her influence had been so beneficial, so real, that if she were to leave him he might go
all to pieces. She remembered, moreover, that the last
time he had come to see her he had worn a grey coat
with silvery threads in it and a new tie, and had asked
her in languishing tones: "Do I look nice?" And he had
certainly looked very nice, in his smart coat, with his long

curls and blue eyes (or at least she had thought so), and he had been very affectionate with her.

Remembering all this and more, and forming her own conclusions, Olga Ivanovna would dress and go in a state of great excitement to Ryabovsky's studio. She usually found him in excellent spirits and full of admiration for his picture, which really was very good. When he was in a playful mood, he would fool about and parry serious questions with a joke. Olga Ivanovna was jealous of the picture and detested it, but always stood in front of it in polite silence for five minutes, and then would say, sighing as people sigh in a shrine:

"Yes, you never painted anything like it before. You know, it quite frightens me."

Then she would implore him to love her, not to throw her over, to pity her, poor, unhappy thing. She would weep, kiss his hands, try to drag an assurance of love out of him, pointing out that without her good influence he would stray from the path and be lost. Then, having thoroughly upset him and humiliated herself, she would go to the dressmaker or to an actress friend about a theatre-ticket.

On the days when she did not find him in his studio she left him a note threatening to take poison, if he did not come to see her that very day. Alarmed, he would go to her and stay to dinner. Unabashed by the presence of her husband, he would make insulting remarks to her, she repaying him in his own coin. They both felt that they were in each other's way, that they were tyrants and enemies, and this infuriated them, and in their fury they did not notice how indecent their behaviour was and that even the crop-headed Korostelev could not fail to understand everything. After dinner Ryabovsky would bid them a hasty farewell and go.

"Where are you going?" Olga Ivanovna would ask him in the hall, looking at him with hatred.

Frowning and narrowing his eyes he would name some

lady whom they both knew, and it was obvious that he
was making fun of her jealousy and wanted to annoy
her. She would go to her bedroom and lie down. In her
jealousy, rage, humiliation and shame she would bite the
pillow and sob loudly. Then Dimov would leave Korostelev
in the drawing-room and step into the bedroom, looking
shy and embarassed, and say in a low voice:

"Don't cry so, Mums! What's the good? You ought to
keep quiet about it. You mustn't let people see. . . . What's
done can't be undone, you know."

Unable to control her jealousy, which made her very
temples throb, and telling herself that it was not too late
to put things right, she would get up and wash, powder
her tear-stained face, and rush off to the lady he had
mentioned. Not finding Ryabovsky there, she would drive
to another, and another. . . . At first she felt shame in
these journeys, but she soon got used to them, and sometimes visited all the women she knew in a single evening,
in her search for Ryabovsky, and they all understood her
motive.

Once she said to Ryabovsky, of her husband:

"That man oppresses me with his magnanimity."

This phrase pleased her so much that whenever she
met any of the artists who were in the secret of her affair
with Ryabovsky, she would mention her husband, saying,
with a powerful gesture:

"That man oppresses me with his magnanimity."

Their routine of life went on just the same as the
preceding year. On Wednesday evenings there were the
at-homes. The actor recited, the artists drew, the 'celloist
played, the singer sang, and invariably at half past
eleven the door into the dining-room opened and Dimov
said, smiling: "Come to supper, gentlemen."

As before, Olga Ivanovna sought out great men,
found them, and, still not satisfied, went to look for
others. As before, she came home late every night, but
Dimov was never asleep when she returned, as he had

been the year before, but sat working at something in his study. He went to bed at three and got up at eight.

One evening when she was taking a last look at herself in the glass before going to the theatre, Dimov came into the bedroom in a frock-coat and white tie. He smiled meekly and looked straight into her eyes, as he used to formerly. His face was radiant.

"I've just presented my thesis," he said, sitting down and smoothing the knees of his trousers.

"Was it a success?" asked Olga Ivanovna.

"Wasn't it just?" he laughed, craning his neck to catch sight of his wife's face in the mirror, for she still stood with her back towards him putting the finishing touches to her hair. "Wasn't it just?" he repeated. "And it's highly probable, you know, that they'll make me docent in general pathology. It looks very like it."

It was obvious, from his blissful, radiant expression that if Olga Ivanovna had shared his joy and triumph he would have forgiven her all, both present and future, and would have forgotten all, but she understood neither what a docent was nor what general pathology meant, besides she was afraid of being late for the theatre, and so she said nothing.

He sat on for a few minutes, and then, smiling apologetically, went away.

VII

It had been a most restless day.

Dimov had a violent headache. He had no breakfast and did not go to the hospital, but lay all day on the couch in his study. Olga Ivanovna went off as usual to Ryabovsky soon after twelve, to show him a sketch for a still life that she had made, and ask him why he had not been to see her the day before. She knew her sketch was poor, and had only painted it so as to have an excuse to go and see the artist.

She went in without ringing and while she was taking off her galoshes in the hall she thought she heard soft steps in the studio, accompanied by the rustle of a woman's dress, and when she glanced hastily in she was just in time to catch a glimpse of a brown skirt, which flashed by one moment and disappeared the next behind a large canvas over which a sheet of black calico was draped, covering the easel and reaching to the floor. There could be no doubt that a woman was hiding there. How often had Olga Ivanovna found herself a hiding place behind this canvas! Ryabovsky, obviously profoundly embarrassed, stretched out both his hands towards her, as if astonished to see her, and said with a strained smile:

"A-a-ah! Glad to see you! What's your news?"

Olga Ivanovna's eyes filled with tears. She felt ashamed and wretched, and would not for anything in the world have spoken in front of that other woman, her rival, that liar, who was now standing behind the canvas and no doubt laughing up her sleeve.

"I just wanted to show you my sketch," she said, in a high, timid voice, and her lips quivered. "It's a nature-morte."

"A-a-a-h, a sketch. . . ."

The artist took the sketch in his hands, and, his eyes fixed on it, strolled, as it were absent-mindedly into the next room.

Olga Ivanovna followed him submissively.

"Nature-morte, of the very best sort," he muttered, mechanically seeking rhymes, "kur-ort, sport, port, short. . . ."

The sound of hasty steps and the rustling of skirts came from the studio. This meant *she* had gone. Olga Ivanovna felt an impulse to cry out, to hit the artist over the head with something heavy, and run away, but she was blinded with tears, crushed with shame, and felt she was no longer Olga Ivanovna, the artist, but some wretched little pigmy.

"I'm tired," said the artist in languishing tones, looking at the sketch and trying to shake off his fatigue with a toss of his head. "It's quite nice, of course, but it's a sketch today, and a sketch last year and in a month's time another sketch.... Aren't you sick of them? In your place I would give up art and go in for music or something seriously. You're not an artist, you know, you're a musician. But if you only knew how tired I am! I'll tell them to bring us some tea, shall I?"

He went out of the room and Olga Ivanovna could hear him speaking something to his man-servant. To avoid a leave-taking and a scene, above all to prevent herself from bursting out crying, she ran out into the hall before Ryabovsky had time to get back, put on her galoshes, and went out. Once in the street she breathed more freely, feeling that she had shaken off Ryabovsky, art, and the unendurable sense of humiliation she had undergone in the studio, for good and all. This was the end.

She went to her dressmaker, then to Barnai, who had only just come back, from Barnai to a music-shop, thinking all the time of the cold, ruthless and dignified letter she would write to Ryabovsky, and of how she would go to the Crimea with Dimov in the spring or summer, there to shake off the past for ever, and begin a new life.

She got home quite late, but instead of going to her room to undress she went straight to the drawing-room to compose her letter. Ryabovsky had told her she was not an artist, and in revenge she would now tell him that he painted the same picture year after year, that he said the same things day after day, that he had gone off, that he would never achieve any more than he had already achieved. She intended to add that he was greatly indebted to her good influence and that if he was now behaving badly it was because her influence had been stultified by all sorts of disreputable creatures, like the one who had hidden behind the picture today.

"Mums," called Dimov from his study, without opening the door. "Mums."

"What d'you want?"

"Don't come near me, Mums, but just come to the door. That's right. I caught diphtheria a day or two ago in the hospital and ... I feel very bad. Send for Korostelev."

Olga Ivanovna always called her husband by his surname, as she did all her men friends. His name was Ossip, and she did not like, for it reminded her of Gogol's Ossip and a silly pun on the names Ossip and Arkhip. But now she exclaimed:

"Oh, Ossip, it can't be true!"

"Send for him. I feel bad. .." said Dimov from inside the room, and she could hear him walk over to the sofa and lie down. "Send for him." His voice sounded hollow.

"Can it really be?" thought Olga Ivanovna, cold with horror. "Why, it's dangerous!"

Without knowing why she lit a candle and took it to her bedroom, and while trying to decide what she ought to do, she caught sight of herself in the looking-glass. With her pale, frightened face, in her jacket with the high, puffy sleeves, and yellow flounces in front, and the eccentric diagonal stripes on her skirt, she saw herself as an awful fright, a revolting creature. An infinite pity for Dimov surged up within her, for his boundless love for her, his young life and even his lonely bed, in which he had not slept for so long, and she remembered his invariable meek, submissive smile. She wept bitterly and wrote an imploring note to Korostelev. It was two o'clock in the morning.

VIII

When Olga Ivanovna, her head heavy from lack of sleep, her hair not done, a guilty expression on her face, and looking quite plain, came out of her bedroom soon after seven the next morning, a gentleman with a black

beard, a doctor apparently, passed her in the hall. There
was a smell of medicaments. Korostelev was standing at
the door in the study, tweaking the left side of his
moustache with his right hand.

"Sorry, but I can't let you go to him," he said morosely
to Olga Ivanovna. "You might catch it. And besides,
there's no point in your going to him. He's delirious."

"Has he really got diphtheria?" whispered Olga
Ivanovna.

"I would have everyone who courts danger needlessly
sent to prison," muttered Korostelev, not answering her
question. "D'you know how he got infected? He sucked
up pus from the throat of a little boy with diphtheria.
And what for? Sheer folly, imbecility!"

"Is it very dangerous?" asked Olga Ivanovna.

"Yes, they say it's a very bad case. What we ought
to do is to send for Shreck."

A red-haired little man with a long nose and a Jewish
accent came, and after him a tall, stooping, shaggy man,
rather like an archdeacon, and then a younger man, stout
and red-faced, wearing spectacles. They were all doctors
who came to take turns at the bed-side of their comrade.
Korostelev, who did not go home when his watch was
over, wandered about the rooms like a ghost. The maid
made tea for the doctors and was always running to the
chemist's, so there was no one to do the rooms. It was
very quiet, very dreary.

Olga Ivanovna sat in her bedroom telling herself that
God was punishing her for deceiving her husband. The
silent, unmurmuring, enigmatic being, his individuality
sapped by good-nature, yielding, weakened by excess of
kindness, now lay on the couch, suffering in silence. If
he had complained, if he had even raved in delirium, the
doctors keeping watch over him would have discovered
that it was not only diphtheria that was to blame. They
might have asked Korostelev, he knew all, and it was
not for nothing that he regarded his friend's wife with

eyes which seemed to say that it was she who was the evil genius, and that the diphtheria was merely her ally. She forgot the moonlit night on the Volga, the assurances of love, the poetic life in the peasant hut, and remembered only that she had plunged head and shoulders into something foul and sticky, from which she would never be able to wash herself clean—and all out of sheer caprice, for the sake of trivial amusement.

"What a liar I have been!" she said to herself, remembering the restless love which had existed betw en Ryabovsky and herself. "A curse on it all!"

At four o'clock she had dinner with Korostelev. He ate nothing, only drinking some red wine and frowning. She, too, ate nothing. She prayed silently, promising God that if Dimov recovered, she would love him again and be a faithful wife. And then, forgetting her troubles for a moment, she would look at Korostelev and wonder: "Surely it must be a bore to be such an insignificant, obscure person, with such a puckered-up face and such bad manners!" And again it seemed to her that God might strike her down this very moment for, in her fear of infection, never once having been in her husband's study. Her prevailing mood was a feeling of dull misery and the conviction that her life was ruined and spoilt beyond repair....

After dinner the dusk soon fell. When Olga Ivanovna went into the drawing-room she found Korostelev asleep on the sofa, his head on a silk cushion embroidered in gilt thread. "Hup-wah," he snored. "Hup-wah."

The doctors, coming and going on their visits to the bed-side, were quite unaware of all this irregularity. The strange man snoring in the drawing-room, the pictures on the walls, the eccentric furniture, the mistress of the house going about with her hair not done and her dress in disarray, all this was now incapable of arousing the slightest interest. One of the doctors happened to laugh at something, and the laugh sounded strangely timid, making everyone feel uneasy.

When Olga Ivanovna next went into the drawing-room Korostelev was awake sitting up on the sofa, smoking.

"The diphtheria has settled in the nasal cavities," he said in an undertone. "His heart is already beginning to show the strain. Things look bad, bad."

"Why don't you send for Shreck?" asked Olga Ivanovna.

"He's been It was he who noticed that the diphtheria had gone into the nose. And who's Shreck, anyhow? There's no such thing as Shreck, really. He's Shreck and I'm Korostelev, and that's all."

Time passed with agonizing slowness. Olga Ivanovna, fully dressed, lay dozing on her bed, unmade since the morning. The whole flat seemed to be filled from floor to ceiling by a huge block of iron, and she felt that if only this block could be removed, everyone would cheer up. Waking with a start, she realized that it was not a block of iron but Dimov's illness.

"Nature-morte, port," she said to herself, again falling into a doze, "sport, kur-ort. . . . And who's Shreck? Shreck, treck . . . wreck . . . kreck. And where are all my friends? Do they know we are in trouble? Oh, God, save us, have mercy. . . . Shreck, treck. . . ."

And again the block of iron. . . . Time dragged on endlessly, though the clock on the floor below seemed to be always striking the hour. And every now and then there came rings at the bell; the doctors coming to Dimov. . . . The maid came into the room holding a tray with an empty glass on it.

"Shall I do your bed, Ma'am?" she asked.

Getting no reply she went out again. The clock downstairs struck the hour, Olga Ivanovna dreamed it was raining on the Volga, and again someone came into her room, a stranger apparently. But the next moment she recognized Korostelev, and sat up in bed.

"What's the time?" she asked.

"About three."

"How is he?"

"How is he? I came to tell you he's dying."

He swallowed a sob, and sat down on the bed beside her, wiping away his tears with his cuff. She did not take it in at first, but went suddenly cold and crossed herself slowly.

"Dying," he repeated in a high voice and again sobbed. "Dying, because he sacrificed himself. What a loss to science!" he said with bitter emphasis. "In comparison with all the rest of us he was a great man, a remarkable man. What a gift! What hopes he inspired in us all!" went on Korostelev, wringing his hands. "My God, my God, he would have been such a scientist, such a rare scientist! Ossip Dimov, Ossip Dimov, what have you done? Oh God!"

In his despair Korostelev covered his face with both hands.

"And what moral force!" he continued, getting more and more angry with someone. "Kind, pure, affectionate soul—crystal-clear! He served science and he died in the cause of science. Worked like a horse, day and night, nobody spared him, and he, young, learned, a future professor, had to look for private practice, sit up at night doing translations, to pay for those—miserable rags!"

Korostelev looked at Olga Ivanovna with loathing, seized the sheet in both his hands and tore angrily at it, as if it were to blame.

"He did not spare himself and nobody spared him. But what's the good of talking?"

"Yes, he was a remarkable man," came in deep tones from the drawing-room.

Olga Ivanovna went back in memory over her whole life with him, from beginning to end, in the utmost detail, and suddenly realized that he really had been a remarkable man, an unusual man, a great man, in comparison with all the others she had known. And remembering the attitude to him of her late father, and of all his colleagues she realized that they had all seen in him a future celebrity. The walls, the ceilings, the lamp and the carpet on the floor winked mockingly at her, as if trying to say: "You've missed your chance!" She rushed weeping out of the bedroom, almost running into a strange man in the drawing-room and burst into the study to her husband. He lay motionless on the couch, a blanket covering him up to the waist. His face was terribly drawn and thin and had that greyish yellow tinge never seen on the living. Only his forehead, his black eyebrows and his familiar smile showed that it was Dimov. Olga Ivanovna touched his breast, his brow and his hands with rapid movements. The breast was still warm, but the brow and hands were unpleasantly cold. And the half-shut eyes gazed, not at Olga Ivanovna, but at the blanket.

"Dimov!" she called out loud. "Dimov!"

She wanted to explain to him that it had all been a mistake, that everything was not yet lost, that life might yet be beautiful and happy, that he was an unusual, a remarkable, a great man, and that she would worship him all her life, would kneel before him, would feel a sacred awe of him. . . .

"Dimov!" she called, shaking him by the shoulder, unable to believe that he would never again wake up, "Dimov, Dimov, I say!"

And in the drawing-room Korostelev was saying to the maid:

"What is there to ask about? Go round to the church and ask where the almswomen live. They'll wash the body and put everything in order—they'll do all that is necessary."

1892

WARD No. 6

I

In the hospital yard is a small annexe, surrounded by
a regular jungle of burdock, stinging nettles and wild
hemp. The roof is rusty, the chimney crumbling, the rotting porch-steps are overgrown with grass, and there are
only faint vestiges of plaster on the walls. It faces the
hospital and its back is turned towards a field from
which it is separated by a discoloured fence bristling
with nails. The upward-pointing nails, the fence, and
the annexe itself, have that dismal, God-forsaken look
characteristic of our hospital and prison buildings.

If you are not afraid of the nettles, come with me
along the narrow path leading to the annexe and let us
peep inside. As we open the front door we find ourselves
in a passage. Mountains of hospital rubbish are piled
against the walls and the stove. This ragged, useless
trash—mattresses, old dressing-gowns, under-drawers,
striped blue shirts, worn-out boots—is jumbled together in a malodorous heap.

The watchman Nikita, an old soldier with mouldy-
looking stripes on his coat-sleeve, and a pipe always
between his teeth, reposes on the top of this rubbish. His

shaggy eyebrows lend to his grim, drink-sodden face
the expression of a Russian sheep-dog; his nose is red;
small, lean and wiry, there is nevertheless something
imposing about his carriage, and his fists are massive.
He is one of those single-minded, reliable, efficient and
dull-witted persons who value order above everything
else in the world, and believe that there is nothing like
a good beating. He showers blows indiscriminately on
faces, chests and backs, convinced that there is no other
way to keep order.

From here we enter a spacious room which occupies
the whole annexe, except for the space taken up by the
passage. The walls are painted a muddy blue, the ceiling
is black with soot like the beams of an old-time hut, with
no chimney, indicating that the stoves smoke in the winter, filling the room with poisonous fumes. The windows
are hideous with inside iron bars, the floor discoloured
and splintery. The place smells of sour cabbage, smoking
lamps, bugs and ammonia, and when you first go in, this
stench makes you think you are entering a menagerie.

The beds are screwed into the floor. Men clothed in
blue hospital gowns and old-fashioned night-caps are
sitting and lying on them. They are mental patients.

There are five of them. Only one of them belongs to
the upper classes, the rest are from the common people.
The one nearest to the door, a tall, lean man with a
glossy red moustache and eyes red with weeping, sits
with his head on his fists, staring fixedly in front of him.
Day and night he grieves, nodding, sighing, giving wry
smiles; he seldom joins in the general conversation and
as a rule does not answer when spoken to. He takes
his food and drink mechanically when it is brought to
him. Judging by his painful, almost incessant cough and
the hectic flush on his cheeks, he is in the early stages
of consumption.

The next bed is occupied by a small, lively, extremely
agile old man with a pointed beard and hair as black

and curly as a Negro's. In the day-time he struts about
the room, from window to window, or sits on his bed
with his legs crossed beneath him, alternately whistling
as indefatigably as a bullfinch, singing in a low voice,
or simply tittering. Even in the night he displays his
child-like gaiety and lively temperament, getting up to
say his prayers, that is to beat his chest with his doubled fists, and to fumble at the doors. He is Moses, the
Jewish hat-maker, and has been mad these twenty years,
ever since his shop was burned down.

He is the only inhabitant of Ward No. 6 who is per-
mitted to leave the building and even go through the
hospital yard and into the street. He has enjoyed this
privilege for years, probably because he has been so
long in the hospital and is such a quiet, harmless fool,
the butt of the town, whose appearance, surrounded by
a crowd of small boys and dogs, has become a part of
everyday life. In his hospital gown, absurd night-cap
and slippers, sometimes barefoot and quite naked beneath the gown, he roams the streets, stopping at gates
and in front of little shops, begging for a kopek. He gets
some *kvass** at one place, a bit of bread, or a kopek at
another, and returns to the annexe rich and content.
Everything he brings back is taken from him by Nikita.
The soldier does this roughly, angrily, turning the man's
pockets inside out and calling God to witness that he
will never again let the Jew go out into the streets, and
that there is nothing worse than disorder.

Moses is an obliging soul. He brings his room-mates
water when they are thirsty, covers them up when
they are asleep, promises to bring home a kopek for
each of them and make new caps for all; it is he who
feeds with a spoon his neighbour on the left—a paralytic. He does this not from compassion or from any humane motive, but merely following the example, and

* Kind of cider made from fermented bread.—*Tr.*

involuntarily submitting to the influence of his neighbour on the right, Gromov.

Ivan Dmitrich Gromov, a man about thirty-three years
old, who comes of a good family and was once a bailiff
and the secretary of a provincial government office, suf-
fers from persecution mania. He either lies huddled up on
his bed or paces backwards and forwards as if he were
taking a constitutional, and is rarely to be found sitting.
He is in a state of perpetual excitement and agitation,
always tense with vague, indefinite expectations. At the
slightest rustle in the passage or noise in the yard he lifts
his head and listens—have they come for him? Is it him
they are looking for? At such moments his face expresses
extreme perturbation and loathing.

I like his broad, pale, unhappy face with the high
cheek-bones, a face in which, as in a mirror, is reflected
a soul tormented by incessant struggle and fear. His
grimaces are queer and morbid, but the subtle lines
which profound and genuine suffering has drawn on his
face are sensitive and intelligent, and there is a warm,
sane light in his eyes. I like the man, always polite, kind
and considerate with everyone but Nikita. If anyone
drops a button or a spoon, he leaps from his bed and
picks it up. He wishes everyone "good morning" when
he gets up, and says "good night" before going to bed.

His insanity manifests itself, apart from his grimaces
and the continual strain under which he labours, in
the following ways: sometimes in the evenings, he draws
his robe round him, and, trembling all over, his teeth
chattering, he walks rapidly up and down the room and
between the beds. He is then like a man in the grip of
a violent fever. From the way in which he suddenly halts
and looks at his room-mates it would appear that he
had something very important to tell them, but evidently
realizing that nobody will listen to him or understand
him, he tosses his head impatiently and resumes his
walking. Soon, however, the desire to talk overrules all

other considerations and he lets himself go, pouring out eager, impassioned effusions. His speech, wild and disconnected as the ravings of a fever-patient, is not always intelligible, but there is something in his words and accents that is singularly appealing. When he speaks, you can hear both the sane human being and the madman in him. It would be hard to put down on paper his wild ravings. He discourses of human baseness, of that oppression which destroys truth, of the beautiful life that will one day dawn in this world, of the iron bars on the windows which remind him continually of the stupidity and cruelty of the oppressors. The result is an incoherent, clumsy blend of songs which, though old, have not yet been sung to the end.

II

Some twelve or fifteen years ago there lived in his own house in the main street of the town a certain official by the name of Gromov, a steady well-to-do man. He had two sons: Sergei and Ivan. Sergei, after completing three years of study at the University, contracted galloping consumption and died, and this death was the beginning of a series of disasters which overtook the Gromov family. A week after Sergei's funeral the old man was sued for forgery and embezzlement, and died soon after in the prison hospital of typhus. His house and property were sold at auction, and Ivan Dmitrich and his mother were left without any means of support.

While his father was alive Ivan Dmitrich lived in Petersburg, studying at the University, and receiving 60 or 70 rubles from home every month, so that he had never known want, but now he was forced to make drastic changes in his way of life. He had to work from morning till night, giving lessons for trifling payment, copying documents, and even so he went hungry, for he sent all he earned to his mother. Ivan Dmitrich was not fit for this sort of life; he lost heart, fell ill, left the University and went home. Here, in the small town, he got work as a teacher in the district school through influential friends, but finding he was unable to get on with his colleagues or win the sympathy of the pupils, he soon gave up the post. His mother died. He was without a job for about six months, living on bread and water, and then took the post of bailiff. This last post he held till discharged for reasons of health.

He had never, even in his student days, appeared robust. He was always pale and thin, subject to colds, eating little and sleeping badly. A single glass of wine made him giddy and hysterical. He was drawn to his fellow-mortals, but owing to his irritable and suspicious disposition, there was no one with whom he was on intimate terms, no one he could call a friend. He invariably referred to the townsmen with contempt, declaring that their gross ignorance and drowsy animal existence made him sick. His voice was shrill, and he spoke loudly and passionately, always either in wrathful indignation or in ecstasy and amazement, and always sincerely. Whatever you spoke to him about, he would manage to turn the conversation to his favourite subject: the atmosphere in our town is stifling, life is dull, society devoid of higher interests, dragging out a dreary, meaningless existence only enlivened by violence, coarse debauchery and hypocrisy; knaves are well-fed and well-clad while honest folk live from hand to mouth; schools, a progressive local newspaper, a theatre, public lectures and the co-operation of all the intellectual forces, is what is needed; society must be made aware of all this, be made to see how shocking it is. In judging his fellow-men he laid the paint on thick, but his pallette held only black and white, it admitted of no fine shades; according to him, mankind consisted of honest people and knaves, there was no intermediate category. Of women and love he spoke with ardent enthusiasm, though he had never been in love.

Despite his censoriousness and nervous irritability he was liked in our town, and behind his back referred to affectionately as Vanya. His delicacy, his readiness to oblige, his high principles and moral integrity combined with his shabby coat, sickly appearance and the afflictions which had befallen his family, all tended to create a warm, friendly feeling for him, tinged with melancholy; then he was well-educated and well-read, his fellow-citizens said there was nothing he did not know, and he was regarded by everyone as a kind of walking encyclopaedia.

He was a great reader. He would sit in the club by the hour, tugging nervously at his small beard and turning over the pages of magazines and books; and his face showed that he was not so much reading as devouring their contents, hardly giving himself time to turn them over in his mind. Reading had evidently become a morbid habit with him, for he fell upon everything that came his way with equal avidity, even though it was nothing more interesting than last year's papers and almanacs. At home he always read lying down.

III

One autumn morning Ivan Dmitrich, his coat-collar turned up, plodded through the slush of side-streets and backyards on his way to hand a writ of execution to some citizen. He was in his usual morning mood, which was bad. In one of the side-streets he met two manacled men, under an armed convoy of four. Ivan Dmitrich was used to such meetings which invariably roused in him feelings of pity and embarrassment, but this time he was strangely and unaccountably affected. For some reason it suddenly came into his head that there was nothing to prevent him from being manacled himself and

led like these prisoners through the muddy streets to
the prison. On his way home from delivering the writ,
he met a police inspector of his acquaintance near the
post-office; the latter, after exchanging greetings with
him, accompanied him for a few paces, and somehow
this struck Gromov as suspicious. When he got home,
the thought of the prisoners and the soldiers with their
rifles haunted him all day, and a strange mental dis-
quietude prevented him from reading, and concentrating
on his thoughts. He did not light his lamp in the evening, and could not sleep for thinking of how he, too,
might be arrested, manacled and thrown into prison. He
knew he was guilty of no crime, and could guarantee
that he would never murder, commit arson, or steal; but
was it not possible to commit a crime as it were accidentally, without meaning to? Besides, were there not
such things as fraud or even miscarriage of justice? Does
not the popular saying: "nobody is safe from the poor-
house or the prison" reflect the experience of ages? And
in the present state of legal proceedings what could be
more likely than a miscarriage of justice? Such people
as judges, police authorities and doctors, who regard
human suffering in a strictly official light, become in
the course of time and from habit so callous that they
cannot, even if they wanted to, treat their clients in
any but a formal way; in this respect there is no difference between them and the peasant slaughtering sheep
and calves in his backyard, perfectly oblivious to the
blood. And once this formal, callous attitude has been
established, only one thing is needed to make a judge
deprive an innocent person of his rights and sentence
him to hard labour—time. Just the time necessary for
the observation of the few formalities for which the judge
receives his salary, and all will be over. And then
you may seek justice and protection in the small dirty
town two hundred versts away from the nearest railway station! And is it not absurd to think of justice

when every act of oppression is regarded by society as rational and expedient, and every act of clemency, such as an acquittal, is greeted with an outburst of unsatisfied revengeful feelings?

The next morning Ivan Dmitrich rose from his bed in a state of abject terror, with cold sweat breaking out on his brow, and the conviction that he might be arrested any minute. Since the oppressive thoughts of the day before would not leave him, he told himself that there must be some real ground for them. After all, they could not have entered his mind without some good reason. A policeman passed his window at a leisurely pace: what could that mean? Two men stopped opposite his house and stood silent. Why were they silent?

Days and nights of anguish ensued for Ivan Dmitrich. He thought everyone who passed his windows or entered his yard was a spy or a detective. The district police inspector was in the habit of driving along the street in his carriage and pair every day at noon; he drove from his country estate to the police office, but to Ivan Dmitrich it seemed he was driving too fast, and that there was a significant look on his face; he was probably hastening to announce that there was a dangerous criminal living in the town. Every time the doorbell rang, or there was a knock at the gate, Ivan Dmitrich started; he felt uneasy if his landlady had a visitor he had not seen before; when he met a policeman or a gendarme he smiled and whistled a tune to appear at ease. He lay awake all night for fear of being arrested, but snored loudly and sighed drowsily to make the landlady think he was asleep; for if he did not sleep, would not it mean he had something on his conscience—and what a clue that would be! Facts and common sense assured him that his fears were absurd and morbid, that there was nothing terrible in arrest or imprisonment if one took a broad view of things—so long as one's conscience was clear; but the saner and more logical his reasoning, the greater, the acuter became his restlessness. He was like the hermit who tried to clear himself a spot in the jungle, but found that the trees and bushes grew all the denser under the axe. Realizing the futility of it, Ivan Dmitrich at last gave up reason, and surrendered himself to terror and despair.

He began to seek solitude and shun society. His work, which he had always detested, had now become quite intolerable to him. He was afraid someone might play him a dirty trick, slip a bribe into his pocket without his noticing, and then expose him, that he would let some error which would be tantamount to forgery creep into the official papers or that he would lose money which did not belong to him. It was quite remarkable how ingenious and versatile his mind had become, now that he daily invented a thousand reasons why he should tremble for his honour and freedom. On the other hand, his interest in the outside world and in reading was weakening, his memory had deteriorated considerably.

In the spring, after the snow had melted, the corpses of an old woman and a little boy, both in a state of decomposition, and bearing the signs of death by violence, were found in the gully outside the cemetery. The whole town talked of nothing but these corpses and the unknown murderers. To prevent people from thinking he was the murderer, Ivan Dmitrich walked about the streets with a smile on his face and when he met his acquaintances, he would assure them, paling and flushing by turns, that there was no crime so base as that of killing the weak and defenceless. But he soon got tired of perpetual dissembling and decided that the best thing for a man in his position to do would be to hide in the cellar. He spent a day, the night following, and another day in the cellar, got chilled to the bone and sneaked back to his own room like a thief as soon as it was dark. He stood still in the middle of the room till daybreak, listening. Just before daybreak some stove-makers came

to the landlady. Ivan Dmitrich was perfectly aware that
they had come to repair the kitchen stove, but fear whispered to him they were policemen disguised as stove-
makers. He crept quietly out of the house, without stopping to put on his hat and coat, and rushed panic-stricken
into the street. Dogs ran after him barking, a man shouted behind him, the wind whistled in his ears, and it
seemed to Ivan Dmitrich that all the violence in the world
had accumulated behind his back and was chasing him.

He was stopped and brought home, and his landlady
sent for the doctor. Doctor Andrei Yefimich, of whom
there will be more to say hereafter, prescribed cold com-
presses and laurel drops, shook his head sadly and went
away, telling the landlady he would not come any more,
it was no good trying to prevent people from going mad.
Since he had no money to live on and to pay for medical
treatment, Ivan Dmitrich was sent to the hospital, where
they found a place for him in the ward for venereal patients. He did not sleep at night, was irritable, and disturbed the other patients, and soon, on the orders of
Andrei Yefimich, he was transferred to Ward No. 6.

In a year nobody in the town remembered Ivan Dmitrich, and his books, which his landlady dumped into a
sleigh under the roof of a lean-to, were all taken by the
neighbouring boys.

IV

The neighbour to the left of Ivan Dmitrich was, as
has already been said, Moses the Jew, and his right-hand
neighbour was a rotund, bloated peasant, with a blank,
absolutely meaningless countenance, an inert, gluttonous,
unclean animal, who had long forgotten what it was to
think or to feel, and who exuded a pungent, stifling
odour.

Nikita, whose duty it was to look after this man, beat
him savagely, with all his might, not sparing his own

fists; and it was not so much the fact that he was beaten which was so appalling—one gets used to that sort of thing—but that the stupefied beast did not react to the assault either by sound, gesture or the flicker of an eyelid, merely rocking from side to side like a heavy barrel.

The fifth and last inhabitant of Ward No. 6 is a townsman, formerly a mail-sorter at the post-office; he is a sparse, lean, fair-haired man with a kind but slightly roguish face. To judge by the serene and cheerful look in his intelligent eyes he knows how to take care of himself and cherishes some important and delightful secret. He hides something under his pillow or his mattress which he shows no one, not for fear of it being taken away from him or stolen, but from bashfulness. Sometimes he walks up to the window, and, with his back to the others, hangs something on his chest and looks down at it; if anyone should come up to him at such a moment, he will tear this something off his chest and display extreme embarrassment. But it is not very hard to divine his secret.

"You may congratulate me," he sometimes says to Ivan Dmitrich, "I have been recommended for a Stanislavus of the second order with a star. The second order with a star is usually given only to foreigners, but for some reason they want to make an exception in my favour." And he adds with a smile and a shrug: "I must say I never expected it!"

"I know nothing about these matters," answers Ivan Dmitrich grimly.

"But you know what I mean to get sooner or later?" continues the former mail-sorter narrowing his eyes slyly. "I am sure to get the Swedish 'Polar Star.' Such an order is worth taking a little trouble for. A white cross and a black ribbon. Very pretty."

Life is probably nowhere so monotonous as it is in the hospital annexe. In the morning all the patients except the paralytic and the fat peasant go out into the passage and wash in a great wooden bowl, drying themselves on the skirts of their gowns; after that they drink tea out of tin mugs brought by Nikita from the main building. Each is allowed one mugful. At noon they have soup made from sour cabbage and porridge, and supper consists of the porridge left over from dinner. Between meals they lie on their beds, sleep, gaze out of the windows or pace up and down the room. Thus it goes on from day to day. Even the former mail-sorter talks of the same orders all the time.

A fresh face is not often seen in Ward No. 6. The doctor has long stopped taking any more mental cases, and not many people from the outside world care to visit lunatic asylums. Once every two months Semyon Lazarich, the barber, visits the ward. We will not describe how he cuts the patients' hair, and how Nikita aids him in it, nor the panic spread among the patients at the sight of the drunken, smiling barber.

Apart from the barber nobody visits the annexe. The patients have to put up with the undiluted company of Nikita, day after day. Of late, however, a strange rumour has begun to be spread in the hospital. They say the doctor has begun visiting Ward No. 6 regularly.

V

This is indeed a strange rumour!

Doctor Andrei Yefimich Ragin is a remarkable man in his way. He is said to have been very religious in his early youth, and to have set his heart on an ecclesiastic career, intending, on leaving high school in 1863, to enter the ecclesiastical academy, had not his father, who practised medicine and was a surgeon, held him up to ridicule, declaring that he would no longer regard him as his son if he became a priest. I do not know how

much truth there is in all this, but I have often heard
Andrei Yefimich confess he never felt a vocation for medicine or for any particular branch of science.

However that may be, after graduating from the medical department he did not take orders. He was not
remarkable for his piety, and was no more like a clergy-
man at the beginning of his medical career than he is
now.

He is a heavy, coarse peasant type; his face, beard,
straight hair and strong, ungainly frame suggest the
proprietor of a wayside inn, well-fed, stubborn and
harsh. His grim countenance is covered with a network
of blue veins, the eyes are small, the nose is red. He is
tall and broad-shouldered, with enormous hands and
feet, and looks as if he could fell an ox with his bare
fists. But he walks softly and his gait is cautious, furtive; encountering anyone in a narrow passage, he is the
first to stop and give way, saying, "sorry!" not as you
might expect in a deep voice, but in reedy, gentle tones.
He has a small tumour on his neck which prevents him
from wearing stiff collars, and therefore he goes about
in soft linen or cotton shirts. He does not dress like a
doctor at all. A suit lasts him ten years, and when he
does get a new one, which he usually buys at a slop-
shop kept by a Jew, it looks just as worn and crumpled
as the old suit; he receives patients, dines or visits
friends in the same coat; and there is no stinginess in
this, nothing but sheer disregard for his personal appearance.

When Andrei Yefimich came to our town to take up
his post, the "charitable institution" was in an appalling state. One could hardly breathe in the wards, the
corridors, or the hospital yard for the stench. Hospital
attendants, nurses and their families slept in the wards,
along with the patients. Everyone complained that cockroaches, bugs and mice made life impossible. The surgical department was never free of erysipelas. There were

only two scalpels in the whole hospital, and not a single
thermometer, the bath-tubs were used for storing potatoes. The superintendent, the matron and the medical
assistant robbed the patients of their food, and as for
the old doctor who had held the post before Andrei Yefimich, it was said that he speculated in the spirits allotted to the hospital and kept a veritable harem, recruited
from nurses and female patients. The inhabitants of the
town were well aware of this disgraceful state of affairs,
they even exaggerated it, but no one seemed to take it to
heart. Some excused it all by saying that only peasants
and the lower classes were treated in the hospital and
that they could have nothing to complain of since they
were much worse off at home than in the hospital: would
you feed them on ortolans? Others pleaded that the town
could not be expected to keep a decent hospital without
the aid of the Zemstvo; one should be grateful for any
hospital, even a bad one. And the Zemstvo, which had
not been open long itself, did not start a hospital of its
own either in the town or its vicinity, because, as they
said, there was one already.

Andrei Yefimich's first inspection of the hospital drove
him to the conclusion that it was an immoral institution, highly detrimental to the health of the community.
In his opinion the wisest thing to do would be to dis-
charge the patients and close the hospital. But he reasoned that for this something more than his will would be
required, and that it would be no good anyhow; if one
sweeps away all the dirt, both moral and physical from
one place, it is sure to gather in another; one must wait
for it to disappear of itself. Besides, since people had
opened a hospital and tolerated it, it meant they needed it; ignorant prejudice, and all this everyday filth and
abomination are necessary things, for in time they will
be converted into something useful, as dung becomes
fertile soil. There are no good things in the world which
have not originally sprung from foulness.

When he started on his duties, Andrei Yefimich seems to have made very little fuss about all this disorder. He merely asked hospital attendants and nurses not to spend the night in the wards, and had a couple of cupboards for surgical instruments installed; the superintendent, the matron, and the erysipelas all stayed where they were.

Andrei Yefimich strongly appreciates wisdom and honesty, but he has not the strength of character, the confidence in his own rights, which would enable him to organize the life round him on an honest and rational footing. He is not the man to give orders, to prohibit, to insist. It almost seemed as if he had taken a vow never to raise his voice or use the imperative mood. He finds it hard to say "give me," or "bring me"; when he feels hungry, he gives a hesitant cough and says to his cook: "What about some tea?..." or "What about dinner?" As for telling the superintendent to stop stealing, or sacking him, or abolishing the unnecessary sinecure, that is quite beyond his strength. When people lie to Andrei Yefimich, or flatter him, or bring him an obviously false account to sign, he turns as red as a lobster and, feeling like a criminal, signs the paper; when the patients complain to him of hunger and rough treatment, he feels embarrassed and mutters apologetically:

"All right, I'll look into it.... There must be some misunderstanding...."

At first Andrei Yefimich worked with zeal, receiving patients every day up till dinner-time, performing operations and even going in for obstetrics. The ladies maintained he was very attentive and diagnosed illnesses marvellously, especially those of women or children. As time went on, however, he grew disheartened by the monotony and obvious inefficiency of the work. One day he would receive 30 patients; and lo! the next day there would be 35, the day after 40, and so on, from day to day, from year to year, the death-rate in the town never decreas-

167

ing, and fresh patients streaming in. It was impossible to give any serious aid to the 40 out-patients who came in the course of the morning, so that his work was necessarily a fraud, do what he might. If in a given year he received 12,000 out-patients, it meant, by the simplest reckoning, that 12,000 men and women had been deceived. To take the serious cases into the hospital and treat them according to the rules of science was impossible, too, for though there were plenty of rules, there was no science: and quite apart from philosophy, merely to stick pedantically to the rules, like the other doctors, would have demanded, first and foremost, cleanliness and ventilation, and not filth, wholesome food and not stinking sour-cabbage soup, helpful assistants, and not thieves.

Besides, why prevent people from dying, since death is the normal and legitimate end of life? What if the life of some shop-keeper or clerk is prolonged by five or ten years? And if the aim of medicine is to ease suffering by giving drugs, the question inevitably arises: why should suffering be eased? In the first place, suffering is supposed to aid mankind in achieving perfection, and in the second place, if mankind learns to ease suffering by means of pills and powders, people will abandon the religion and philosophy in which they have hitherto found, not merely protection from all ills, but happiness itself. Pushkin endured agonizing sufferings on his deathbed, Heine lay paralyzed for years before he died; why then should an Andrei Yefimich, or a Matryona Savishna, whose trivial lives, but for suffering, would be as devoid of significance as the life of an amoeba, be free from sickness?

Oppressed by such arguments, Andrei Yefimich lost heart and gave up going to the hospital every day.

This is his daily routine. He usually gets up about eight in the morning, dresses and drinks tea. Then he sits in his study and reads, or goes to the hospital. In the dark narrow hospital corridor he finds out-patients waiting to be admitted. Male and female hospital attendants rush past them, their boots clattering over the brick floor, emaciated in-patients saunter by in their gowns, dead bodies and pots of night-soil are borne out, children howl, and sharp draughts rake the corridor. Andrei Yefimich is aware that such conditions are a torture to feverish, consumptive, or merely nervous patients, but what is to be done about it? In the reception-room he is greeted by his assistant Sergei Sergeich, a fat little man with a plump, clean-shaven, well-washed face, easy, gentle manners, wearing a new loose-fitting suit, and looking much more like a senator than a medical assistant. He has an extensive practice in the town, wears a white tie, and considers he knows more than the doctor, who has no practice. In the corner of the reception-room is an iconostasis with a great icon in it and a heavy icon-lamp hanging before it; nearby is a sconce for votive candles shrouded in white linen. Portraits of bishops, a view of the Svyatogorsk Monastery, and wreaths of dried cornflowers adorn the walls. Sergei Sergeich is religious and a stickler for ecclesiastical propriety. It was he who had the icon put up in the hospital; on Sundays he orders one of the patients to read a prayer, after which Sergei Sergeich himself makes the rounds of the wards, swinging the censer to and fro and spreading the smell of incense.

The patients are numerous, and time is short, so that the doctor must restrict himself to a few questions to each patient and prescribe some medicine or other, mostly embrocation or castor-oil. Andrei Yefimich leans his

cheek against his fist and falls into a reverie, questioning the patients mechanically. Sergei Sergeich is also
seated, rubbing the palms of his hands together and occasionally putting in a word.

"We suffer sickness and endure poverty," he says,
"because we do not pray to our merciful Lord. Yes, indeed!"

Andrei Yefimich does not perform operations during
reception hours; he has long got out of the habit of oper-
ating, and the sight of blood upsets him. When he has
to open a child's mouth to look down its throat, and
the child bawls and tries to push him away with his
little fists, the noise makes Andrei Yefimich giddy, and
tears come to his eyes. He hastens to write out a prescription and waves his arms for the mother to take her
child away.

He soon gets tired of the patients' timidity and stupidity, the presence of the ritual-loving Sergei Sergeich,
the pictures on the walls, and his own questions, which
he has not varied these twenty years and more. After
receiving five or six patients, he goes home. The rest are
received by the assistant.

Pleasantly conscious that he has long ago, thank
God, got rid of all private practice, and that nobody will
interrupt him, Andrei Yefimich settles down to his books
the moment he gets home. He reads a great deal, and
always with pleasure. Half his salary goes on books,
and three of the six rooms in his apartment are crammed
with books and old magazines. His favourite reading is history and philosophy; the only medical magazine he subscribes to is *The Physician,* which he invariably starts reading from the end. He reads uninterrupt-
edly for hours at a time, without experiencing the slightest fatigue. He does not read as rapidly and impetuously
as Ivan Dmitrich used to, but slowly, with insight, often
dwelling on places which either give him pleasure or
are hard to understand. There is always a carafe of vod-

ka standing near his book, and a salted cucumber or spiced apple lying straight on the baize top of his desk Every half-hour, without taking his eyes from the page, he pours himself out a wine-glass of vodka, feels for the cucumber, and takes a bite from it.

At three o'clock he goes cautiously to the kitchen door, gives a little cough and says:

"What about dinner, Darya?"

After dinner, a badly served, rather tasteless affair, Andrei Yefimich walks from room to room with folded arms, thinking. The clock strikes four, then five, but Andrei Yefimich is still walking and thinking. Every now and then the kitchen door creaks and Darya's blowzy red face appears.

"Isn't it time for your beer, Andrei Yefimich?" she asks anxiously.

"Not quite," he answers. "A little later, just a little. . . ."

Towards evening comes the postmaster Mikhail Averyanich, the only man in the town whose company Andrei Yefimich does not find irksome. Mikhail Averyanich was a rich landowner in his day and served in the cavalry; but he ran through his fortune and was driven by want to take a job in the post-office in his old age. He looks hale and hearty, has luxurious white whiskers, good manners and a loud but pleasant voice. He is kind and sensitive, though hot-tempered. If a member of the public makes a protest at the post-office, disagrees or merely argues a point, Mikhail Averyanich turns crimson and trembles violently, and he shouts in a voice of thunder: "Silence!" so that the post-office has a long-established reputation as a formidable place. Mikhail Averyanich likes and respects Andrei Yefimich for his erudition and loftiness of spirit, but he is supercilious to everyone else, treating them as inferiors.

"Here I am!" he cries on entering the room. "How are you, my friend? Probably sick of me, hey?"

"Not at all, not at all," the doctor answers. "You know I'm always glad to see you."

The friends sit down on the sofa in the study, smoking in silence for a while.

"What about a little beer, Darya?" asks the doctor.

The first bottle is drunk in the same silence. The doctor looks pensive, while Mikhail Averyanich seems to be in high glee, like one who has a piece of very amusing information to impart. It is usually the doctor who opens the conversation.

"Isn't it a pity," he begins quietly and slowly, with a gentle shake of his head and without looking at his friend's face (he never looks at anyone's face), "isn't it a pity, I say, my dear Mikhail Averyanich, that there is not a soul in our town who cares about interesting and intelligent conversation or is capable of it? It is a great privation to us. Even the educated classes do not rise above the trivial; their mental development, I assure you, is in no way superior to that of the lower classes."

"Quite right. I agree."

"You are aware, of course," the doctor continues in his quiet level voice, "that everything in this world but the superior spiritual manifestations of the human mind is insignificant and uninteresting. It is the mind which draws the boundary-line between the human and the animal, giving us a glimpse of the divine nature of the former, and to a certain extent even taking the place of nonexistent immortality. Proceeding from this premise, we may say that the mind is the only source of enjoyment. We neither see nor hear of anything in the shape of a mind round us, and that means we are deprived of enjoyment. True, we have our books, but they cannot take the place of conversation and personal contact. If you will allow me to use a metaphor—and not a very happy one, I fear—I would say books were printed music, and conversation—singing."

"Quite right."

Silence ensues. Darya, an expression of dumb grief on her face, comes out of the kitchen and stands listening in the door-way, her cheek propped on her fist.

"Ah," sighs Mikhail Averyanich. "And you think people have minds nowadays!"

And he speaks of the old times when life was wholesome, gay, full of interest, of the educated classes of old Russia, who set such a high value on honour and friendship. People lent one another money without any receipts and it was considered a disgrace not to hold out a helping hand to a friend in need. And the campaigns, the adventures, the skirmishes, the friendships, the women! And the Caucasus—what a country! There was the wife of a battalion commander, an eccentric woman who dressed up as an officer and rode into the mountains every evening without a guide. They said she was carrying on an affair with some prince in a mountain village.

"Holy Mother!" sighs Darya.

"And how we drank! How we ate! And what desperate liberals we all were!"

Andrei Yefimich listens to him without taking in the meaning of the words; he is thinking of something else as he sips at his beer.

"I often dream about intelligent people, and converse with them," he suddenly says, interrupting Mikhail Averyanich. "My father gave me a splendid education, but, influenced by the ideas of the 60's, made me go in for medicine. I sometimes think that if I had not obeyed him I would by now be in the very centre of some intellectual movement. I would probably be a member of a university staff. Of course, the mind is not immortal and is transient like everything else, but I have already explained to you why I rate it so highly. Life is simply a miserable trap. As soon as a thinking individual reaches maturity and becomes capable of conscious thought, he cannot help feeling that he is caught in a trap from

which there is no way out. When you come to think of
it he has been summoned against his will and owing to
purely accidental causes, from the state of non-existence. . . . What for? If he tries to find out the meaning
and aim of his existence, he either gets no answer, or
is told all manner of absurdities; he knocks, and no one
opens to him; then death comes to him—also against his
will. And just as prisoners, united by a common misfortune, feel happier when they can be together, people with
a turn for analysis and generalizations are mutually attracted and, not noticing that they are in a trap, manage to while away the time in the exchange of lofty, un-
fettered thoughts. In this respect the mind is the source
of incomparable satisfaction."

"Quite true."

Avoiding his interlocutor's eye, Andrei Yefimich goes
on talking in a soft hesitating voice about intelligent folk
and the joys of conversing with them, Mikhail Averyanich listening to him attentively and occasionally contributing his "Quite true."

"But don't you believe in the immortality of the soul?"
the postmaster suddenly asks.

"I do not, my dear Mikhail Averyanich, I neither
believe in it nor have I any reason for such a belief."

"To tell the truth, I have my doubts about it, myself.
On the other hand, I have a feeling I will never die, you
know. Hi, old man, I say to myself sometimes, it's time
to be dying! But a little voice whispers: don't believe
it, you will never die."

Soon after nine Mikhail Averyanich leaves. As he
stands in the hall struggling into his heavy coat, he
says with a sigh:

"To think what a hole fate has thrown us into! And
the worst of it is, we shall have to die here, too. Oh,
dear!"

VII

After seeing his friend out, Andrei Yefimich sits at his desk and resumes his reading. Not a sound breaks the stillness of the night, time itself seems to have stopped and to be watching over the doctor and his book, as if the whole world consisted of nothing but this book and the lamp with its green shade. The doctors' rough, bucolic features gradually light up with a smile of affection and respect for the manifestations of the human mind. "Why, oh why is not man immortal?" he thinks. Why all these brain centres and convolutions, eyesight, speech, self-awareness, genius, if they are only destined to mingle with the soil, and finally cool together with the earth's crust and whirl round the sun for billions of years, without aim or reason? Surely it was not necessary, just for the sake of this cooling and whirling, to summon from oblivion man with his lofty, almost divine mind, and then, as if in bitter jest, to turn him into clay!

Metabolism! Who but a coward could find consolation in this substitute of immortality? The unconscious processes which go on in nature are at a lower level than even human stupidity, for there is a certain amount of consciousness and will in stupidity, whereas there is absolutely nothing underlying those processes. Only a coward, whose fear of death is greater than his self-respect, could solace himself with the thought that his body will go on living in a blade of grass, in a stone, in a toad. . . . To see immortality in metabolism is just as ridiculous as to foretell a brilliant future for a violin-case after the valuable instrument has become broken and useless."

Every time the clock strikes the hour, Andrei Yefimich leans back in his arm-chair and closes his eyes for a moment to concentrate on his thoughts for a while. Under the influence of the lofty ideas expounded in the book he has just been reading, he begins unconsciously

to analyze his life, past and present. The past disgusts
him and he prefers not to think of it. And the present
is just like the past. He knows that while his thoughts
whirl round the sun with the cooling crust of the earth,
in the large building a few paces from the doctor's
rooms, people are languishing in disease and filth; at
this very moment, perhaps, someone is lying awake,
fighting vermin, another has just been infected with erysipelas or is moaning from a tight bandage pressing on
his wound; perhaps some of the patients are playing
cards and drinking vodka with the nurses. Twelve thousand men and women were deceived last year; the whole
of hospital life is based on theft, quarrels, gossip, favour-
itism, and shameless quackery, just as it was twenty
years ago, and the hospital is still a highly immoral es-
tablishment, detrimental to the health of citizens. Andrei
Yefimich knows that behind the bars in Ward No. 6, Nikita beats the patients, and Moses goes out into the
streets every day, asking for alms.

At the same time, he knows, too, that the science
of medicine has shown miraculous development during
the last twenty-five years. While studying at the University it had seemed to him that medicine would soon be
sharing the fate of alchemy and metaphysics, but now,
in his nightly readings, this same medicine affects him
deeply, exciting in him a wonder amounting to ecstasy.
What unexpected brilliancy, what a revolution! Thanks
to antiseptics, operations are now performed which the
great Pirogov himself considered impossible even *in spe.*
Ordinary Zemstvo doctors are not afraid of performing
resections of the knee joint, only one person in a hundred dies after abdominal operations, and stone is regarded as too trivial even to mention in print. Syphilis can
be radically cured. And there is the theory of hered-
ity, hypnotism, the discoveries of Pasteur and Koch,
hygiene, statistics, and our Russian Zemstvo medical
organizations! Psychiatry with its modern classification

of disease, the new methods of diagnosis and treatment —all this towers mountain-high over the past. Mental cases are no longer doused with cold water or confined in strait jackets; they are treated as human beings and we read in the papers that theatrical performances and balls are actually got up for their entertainment. Andrei Yefimich knows that modern views and taste make an abomination like Ward No. 6 possible only in a town two hundred versts away from a railway station, where the mayor and town councillors are half-educated men, who regard the doctor as a high priest to be implicitly believed, even were he to pour molten lead into a patient's mouth; in any other place the public and the papers would long ago have razed the little Bastille to the ground.

"But what's the good?" Andrei Yefimich asks himself, opening his eyes wide. "What has come of it all? Antiseptics, Koch, and Pasteur have brought about no essential change. Mortality and disease remain where they were. Theatricals and balls are got up for mental cases, but they are not released from confinement. So it is all nonsense and vanity, and there is no essential difference between the best Viennese clinic and my hospital."

Nevertheless grief and a feeling akin to envy prevent him from remaining indifferent. But perhaps this feeling is to be attributed to exhaustion. He drops his heavy head on to the page, slipping his hands under his cheek for greater comfort, and goes on thinking:

"I am serving an evil cause, and I receive my salary from people whom I deceive; I am dishonest. But I am nothing in myself, only a particle in a necessary social evil; all district officials are bad and draw salaries for doing nothing.... Therefore it is the epoch and not myself which is to blame for my dishonesty.... If I were to be born two hundred years later, I would be different."

When the clock strikes three, he puts out his lamp and goes to his bedroom. He is not a bit sleepy.

A year or two ago the Zemstvo resolved, in a fit of generosity, to contribute a sum of three hundred rubles annually for the increasing of the hospital's medical staff till such time as a Zemstvo hospital should be opened, and district medical officer Yevgeny Fedorovich Khobotov was invited by the municipality to aid Andrei Yefimich in his duties. The new doctor was quite a young man, under thirty, tall and dark, with broad cheek-bones and small eyes, probably of non-Russian origin. He arrived in our town without a kopek in his pocket, with a small trunk and a plain young woman with a baby in her arms whom he called his cook. Yevgeny Fedorovich wears a peaked cap and high-boots, and goes about in the winter in a sheepskin jacket. He soon made friends with Sergei Sergeich, the medical assistant, and with the cashier, but the rest of the officials he calls, for some reason, aristocrats, and keeps away from them. He only has one book in his whole apartment—*The Latest Prescriptions of the Viennese Clinic for 1881*. He never goes to see a patient without taking this book with him. He plays billiards in the club in the evenings, but does not care for cards. He is extremely fond of using expressions such as "Here's a pretty kettle of fish!" "Come now, man was made to be merry!" and the like.

He goes to the hospital twice a week, makes the rounds of the wards and receives out-patients. The fact that, while there are no antiseptics, there is a plentiful supply of cupping glasses, stirs him to indignation, but he does not introduce any new methods for fear of offending Andrei Yefimich. He is convinced that his colleague Andrei Yefimich is a knave, suspects him of being very rich, and secretly envies him. He would gladly supplant him.

IX

One spring evening towards the end of March when
there was no more snow on the ground and the starlings
were singing in the hospital yard, the doctor went to
the gate to see off his friend the postmaster. Just then
Moses the Jew entered the yard, returning from one of
his usual excursions. He had no cap on and wore galoshes straight on his bare feet; in his hand he carried a
small bag holding the alms he had collected.

"Won't you give me a kopek?" he asked the doctor,
shivering with cold, but smiling.

Andrei Yefimich who never knew how to refuse, gave
him a ten-kopek piece.

"How appalling!" he thought as he looked at the
man's bare legs and thin raw ankles. "In such damp
weather. . . ."

Moved by a feeling of mingled pity and disgust, he
followed the Jew into the annexe, glancing from his bald
pate to his ankles. On the doctor's entrance, Nikita jumped
from off the rubbish heap and stood at attention.

"Good evening, Nikita!" Andrei Yefimich said in his
gentle voice. "What about giving that Jew a pair of
boots or something; he might catch cold, you see."

"Very good, Sir. I will report it to the superintendent."

"Yes, do! Ask him in my name. Tell him I asked."

The door from the passage into the ward was open.
Ivan Dmitrich was lying on his bed, propped on one el-
bow, listening anxiously to the unfamiliar voice. All at
once he recognized the doctor. Shaking with rage, he
leaped up, his face red and furious, his eyes starting
from the sockets, and ran out into the middle of the
room.

"The doctor has come!" he cried, and burst out laughing. "At last! I congratulate you, gentlemen: the doctor
has deigned to pay us a visit! The damned scoundrel!"
he almost squealed, stamping his foot in a frenzy never

before witnessed in the ward. "Kill the scoundrel! No, killing is too good for him! Throw him into the privy."

Andrei Yefimich put his head in at the door and asked quietly:

"What for?"

"What for?" shouted Ivan Dmitrich, walking towards him with a menacing look and pulling the flaps of his robe round him with a convulsive gesture. "What for? You're a thief!" he cried in loathing, puckering up his lips as if he were going to spit. "Quack! Hangman!"

"Don't get excited," said Andrei Yefimich, smiling apologetically. "I assure you I never stole anything in my life, and for the rest, you are probably exaggerating grossly. I see you are angry with me. Try and be calm and tell me without getting worked up, what makes you so angry?"

"Why do you keep me here?"

"Because you are ill."

"Yes, I am ill. But there are scores and hundreds of madmen enjoying their freedom only because you are too ignorant to distinguish them from normal men. Why then must I, and these wretches, be cooped up here for the sins of others, like so many scapegoats? You yourself, your assistant, the inspector and the whole hospital rabble, are infinitely lower, morally, than any one of us, why then must *we* be here, and not you? What sort of logic is this?"

"Moral values and logic have nothing to do with it. Everything depends on chance. Those who are put here, stay here, and those who are not, enjoy their liberty, that's all. There is neither morality nor logic in the fact that you are a mental patient and I a doctor, nothing but mere chance."

"I don't understand such nonsense," said Ivan Dmitrich in a hollow voice, seating himself on the side of his bed.

Moses, whom Nikita did not dare to search in the doctor's presence, spread out his crusts, papers and bones on his bed and, still shivering with cold, began talking to himself in Jewish in a rapid sing-song. He probably thought he had opened a shop.

"Let me out!" said Ivan Dmitrich in a breaking voice.

"I can't do that."

"But why can't you? Why not?"

"Because it is not in my power. Ask yourself what would be the good of my letting you out? Supposing I do, the towns-people or the police would stop you and bring you back."

"Yes, yes, you are right," said Ivan Dmitrich, rubbing his forehead. "It's terrible! What am I to do? What —tell me what!"

His voice and his youthful face, intelligent despite his grimacing, appealed to Andrei Yefimich. He longed to say something kind to the young man, to calm him. He sat down on the bed beside him, thought a while, and then said:

"You ask me what you are to do? The best thing for you to do would be to run away. Unfortunately it would be useless. You would be detained. When society resolves to protect itself from criminals, mental patients, and other embarrassing folk, it is invincible. There is only one line of behaviour open to you: reconcile yourself to the fact that your presence here is necessary."

"It is no good to anyone."

"Since there are such things as prisons and lunatic asylums, there must be people to fill them. If it's not you, it's me, if not me, someone else. Wait—in that distant future time when there are no longer either prisons or lunatic asylums, there will be no more barred windows or hospital gowns. The time is sure to come, sooner or later."

Ivan Dmitrich smiled scornfully.

"You don't mean it, of course," he said, narrowing his eyes. "What is the future to such gentlemen as yourself and your help-mate Nikita? But you may be sure that better times will come, Sir! My expressions may be trite, and you may laugh, but the dawn of a new life will break out in all its brilliancy, truth will triumph, and—we, too, will see the light! I shall not see it, I shall be dead by then, but other men's great-grandchildren will see it. I welcome them from the bottom of my heart, and rejoice, rejoice for their sake! Forward! God help you, friends!"

Ivan Dmitrich, his eyes shining, rose, stretching out his arms towards the window, and went on speaking in agitated tones:

"From behind these bars I send you my blessing! Long live Truth! I rejoice!"

"I see no reason for rejoicing," said Andrei Yefimich who, while considering Ivan Dmitrich's exaltation somewhat theatrical, liked him for it. "There will be no more prisons and lunatic asylums, and truth, as you are pleased to say, will triumph, but the essence of things will not change, and the laws of nature will remain the same. People will fall ill, grow old and die just as they do now. However brilliantly the dawn lights up your life, in the end you will be shut up in a coffin and thrown into a hole in the ground."

"And what about immortality?"

"Rubbish!"

"You don't believe in it, but I do. Dostoyevsky, or maybe it was Voltaire, said if there were no God, men would have invented him. And it is my deepest conviction that if there is no such thing as immortality, sooner or later the great human mind will invent it."

"Well said," cried Andrei Yefimich, smiling with pleasure. "It's a good thing you have faith. With a faith like yours one can be happy even when cooped within four walls. But you are an educated man, I see?"

"Yes, I have been to the University, though I did not graduate."

"I see you are a man who knows how to think. You can find solace in your thoughts in any circumstances. Thought, unshackled, profound striving for a full comprehension of life, together with utter contempt for the stupid bustle of the world—these are blessings higher than any mankind has ever known. And you may possess them in spite of all the barred windows in the world. Diogenes lived in a barrel and yet he was happier than kings."

"Your Diogenes was a fool," said Ivan Dmitrich sullenly. "Why do you talk to me of Diogenes and the comprehension of something or other?" he said, leaping to his feet in sudden fury. "I love life, I love it passionately! I suffer from persecution mania, I am tortured by constant, harassing fears, but there are moments when I am seized with a thirst for life, and then I am afraid I shall go mad. I want to live, oh, how I want to live!"

He crossed the room in his excitement and said, lowering his voice:

"Sometimes in my dreams I am visited by ghosts. People come to see me, I hear voices and music, and I think I am somewhere in the woods or on the sea-shore, and I long for bustle, for cares.... Tell me, what's going on there?" he suddenly broke off. "What is going on in the outside world?"

"Do you want me to tell you about our town, or the world in general?"

"Well, tell me about the town to begin with, and then about the world in general."

"Very well. There is nothing but boredom in town.... There is not a soul with whom one could talk, to whom one could listen. No fresh people. As a matter of fact, a young doctor, one Khobotov, has been sent us recently."

"Yes, I know. I was there when he came. An oaf, I suppose."

"Well, he is not a cultured man. It's quite funny, you know. . . . Judging from what one hears, there is no stagnation in our cities, there is intellectual activity, and that means there must be real people, but somehow the specimens they send us are not up to much. Unhappy town!"

"Unhappy, indeed!" sighed Ivan Dmitrich, and then laughed. "And the world? What do they write about in the magazines and papers?"

It was dark in the ward by now. The doctor rose to his feet, and stood telling Ivan Dmitrich what the papers said abroad and in Russia, what was the trend of modern thought. Ivan Dmitrich listened attentively, asking a question now and then, when all of a sudden, as if he had just remembered something terrible, clutched his head in his hands and lay down on his bed with his back to the doctor.

"Don't you feel well?" asked Andrei Yefimich.

"You won't get another word out of me," said Ivan Dmitrich rudely. "Leave me alone!"

"Why, what's the matter?"

"Leave me alone, I tell you! What the devil?"

With a sigh and a shrug, Andrei Yefimich left the ward. As he passed through the passage, he said:

"It would be nice if the place were cleaned up a bit, Nikita. . . . It smells awful."

"Very good, Sir!"

"A nice young man," mused Andrei Yefimich on his way home. "The first man I find I can talk to, after all these years. He can talk rationally, and is interested in the only things worth noticing."

Sitting reading that night, and later, in bed, he kept thinking about Ivan Dmitrich, and on waking up next morning he remembered he had made the acquaintance of an intelligent, interesting person, and decided to pay him another visit at the first opportunity.

X

Ivan Dmitrich was lying on his bed in the same pose as the day before, his hands pressed to his temples, his knees drawn up. His face was turned to the wall.

"How are you, my friend?" said Andrei Yefimich "You are not asleep?"

"In the first place, I am not your friend," mumbled Ivan Dmitrich into his pillow, "and in the second place, you need not trouble yourself; you will not get a word out of me."

"Funny..." muttered Andrei Yefimich, somewhat abashed. "We had such a nice talk yesterday, till you suddenly took offence and wouldn't go on.... I must have expressed myself badly, or said something that runs counter to your convictions...."

"Do you really expect to be believed?" said Ivan Dmitrich, sitting up and looking at the doctor at once mockingly and anxiously; his eyelids were red. "You had better go somewhere else to spy and cross-examine, you won't get anything out of me. I realized what you came here for, yesterday."

"What an idea!" chuckled the doctor. "D'you mean to say you think I am a spy?"

"Yes, I do.... Either a spy or a doctor set to watch over me, it's all the same."

"Well, you are—excuse me, but you are a funny chap!"

The doctor sat on a stool by the bed and shook his head reproachfully.

"Well, now, supposing you're right," he began, "supposing I really were trying, as you say, to get something out of you, in order to betray you to the police. You would be arrested and tried. But do you think it would be any worse for you in the court or in prison? And if you are deported, or even given hard labour, do you think that would be worse than this annexe? I don't believe it would. . . . What is there for you to be afraid of, then?"

The words evidently made an impression on Ivan Dmitrich. He seemed to relax.

It was a little after four, the time of day when Andrei Yefimich usually paced up and down his room, and Darya asked him if he were ready for his beer. It was a still, bright evening.

"I was taking my after-dinner walk and thought I'd drop in to see you," said the doctor. "A real spring day."

"What month is it? March?"

"Yes, the end of March."

"Is it very dirty out?"

"Not very. The garden paths have dried up."

"It would be nice to drive out of town in a carriage on a day like this," said Ivan Dmitrich, rubbing his red-rimmed eyes, as if he had just wakened from a slumber, "and to return home, to a warm, comfortable study and . . . to get a decent doctor to treat my headaches. . . . I have forgotten what it is to live like a human being. It's so squalid here! Unbearably squalid!"

He was enervated and languid from the excitement of the day before and seemed to bring out the words reluctantly. His fingers shook and you could see by his face that his head was aching violently.

"There is no difference between a warm comfortable study and this ward," said Andrei Yefimich. "Men must seek peace and satisfaction not in the world outside them, but in themselves."

"What do you mean?"

"The ordinary man looks for good or evil in outward things such as a carriage or a study, the thinking man looks for them within himself."

"Go and preach your philosophy in Greece, where it is always warm and the air is fragrant with orange-blossom—that sort of thing doesn't suit our climate. Who was I speaking about Diogenes to? You?"

"Yes, yesterday."

"Diogenes did not need a study or a warm room, simply because it was warm anyhow. He could loll in his barrel eating oranges and olives. If he had lived in Russia he would have begged to be taken into a house not only in December, but even in May. The cold would have sent him into contortions."

"Not at all. Cold, just like any other pain, can be ignored. Marcus Aurelius said: 'Pain is the lively conception of pain; with the aid of your will-power you can alter this conception, shake it off, stop complaining, and the pain will be gone.' And he is right. The sage, or even merely the thinking man is distinguished precisely by contempt for suffering; he is always content, and nothing surprises him."

"Then I must be an idiot, for I suffer, am discontented, and am continually amazed at human baseness."

"You're wrong there. If you tried to get at the root of things more often, you would realize how trivial the external things which agitate us really are. You must strive for a comprehension of life, that is the only blessing."

"Comprehension..." said Ivan Dmitrich, wincing. "The external, internal.... Excuse me, but I do not understand this sort of thing. All I know is," he said rising and looking angrily at the doctor, "that God created me of warm blood and nerves. Yes, Sir! And organic matter, if it has any vital capacity, must react to irritation. And I do react! I react to pain with tears and cries, to baseness with indignation, to vileness with disgust. And that, in my opinion, is life! The lower the organism, the less sensitive it is, and the feebler its reaction to irritation; and the higher it is, the more sensitive and energetic its reaction to reality. How is it you don't know that? A doctor not to know such elementary things! For a man to be able to despise suffering, always to be content, and wonder at nothing, he must have reached this stage," here Ivan Dmitrich pointed at the fat peasant, "or else have become so hardened by suffering as to have lost his sensitiveness to it, in other words, to have ceased to live. Excuse me," he went on irately, "I am no sage, no philosopher, I understand nothing about such things. I am in no state to argue."

"Oh, but you argue very well."

"The stoics whose teaching you travesty were no doubt remarkable men, but their philosophy has been at a standstill these two thousand years, and has not advanced an inch, and cannot advance, for it is an unpractical, unrealistic, philosophy. It was popular with the minority who spent their lives in studying and savouring different teachings, but the majority never understood it. A philosophy which preaches indifference to riches and comforts, contempt for suffering and death, is utterly incomprehensible to the majority, for the majority have never known either riches or comforts; for them to despise suffering would be tantamount to despising life itself, for man's whole existence consists of sensations of hunger, cold, mortification, loss, and a Hamlet-like fear of death. The whole of life is made up of these sensations: and while life may be burdensome and loathsome, no one ever despised it. And so, I repeat, the teaching of the stoics has no future, and from time immemorial to our own days the only things which show any progress are the power to struggle, sensibility to pain, and the ability to react to irritation."

Ivan Dmitrich suddenly lost the thread of his argument, and stopped short, rubbing his forehead in vexation.

"I wanted to say something very important, but it has escaped me," he said. "What was I talking about? Oh, yes! This is what I wanted to say: one of the stoics sold himself into slavery to redeem his neighbour. So you see the stoic reacted to an irritant, for in order to perform a magnanimous feat like destroying one's self for the sake of another, one must possess a soul capable of feeling indignation and compassion. Here, in this prison I have forgotten all I ever knew, or I would remember other examples. Take Christ, if you like! Christ reacted to reality by weeping, smiling, mourning, flying into a rage and grieving; he did not meet suffering with a smile, he did not despise death, but prayed in the Garden of Gethsemane that the cup might pass." Here Ivan Dmitrich laughed and sat down.

"Supposing you are right, and peace and content lie within man, not outside him," he said. "Supposing it is right to despise suffering and wonder at nothing. But what right have *you* to preach this doctrine? Are you a sage, a philosopher?"

"No, I am not a philosopher, but everyone ought to preach this doctrine, for it is rational."

"Ah, but I want to know why you should consider yourself an authority on comprehension, contempt for suffering and the like? Have you ever suffered? Have you the slightest idea what suffering is? Excuse me for asking it, but were you ever flogged in childhood?"

"No, my parents disapproved of corporal punishment."

"And *my* father used to flog me unmercifully. He was a violent man, an official, he had a long nose and a yellow neck and suffered from piles. But let us speak about you. All your life no one ever so much as touched you with his little finger, no one intimidated you, no one oppressed you; and you are as strong as a horse. You grew up under your father's wing, were educated on his money and then got a sinecure. For over twenty years you have been enjoying a warm, well-lighted apartment free of charge; you keep a servant and have a perfect right to work only when you feel like it, or even not to work at all. You are a lazy, passive man by nature and have therefore tried to organize your life so as to avoid all trouble and superfluous movement. You have dele-

gated all your work to your assistant and other scoundrels, yourself enjoying quiet and warmth, saving money, reading, feasting your mind on all manner of sublime nonsense, and," Ivan Dmitrich shot a glance at the
doctor's red nose, "drinking. In a word, you have seen
nothing of life, know nothing about it, and have only a
theoretical knowledge of reality. You despise suffering
and allow nothing to surprise you for a very simple reason: all your *vanitas vanitatum*, the external and the internal contempt of life, suffering and death, comprehension, true blessings, all this philosophy suits the
Russian idler better than any other. You see a peasant
beat his wife, for instance. Why interfere? Let him beat
her, they'll both die sooner or later; besides, it is himself that the bully degrades, and not his victim. Of course
it is stupid and indecorous to drink, but—those who
drink and those who do not drink alike die. A woman
comes to you with toothache.... Well, and what of it?
Pain is nothing but our conception of pain, besides we
can't expect to live without ever ailing, we shall all of
us die; therefore, go thy ways, wench, and let me think
and drink in peace. A young man comes to you for advice, he wants to know what he is to do, how to live;
another person would pause to think before answering
him, but you have your answer ready: strive for comprehension, or for the true blessing, as you call it. But
what is this mystical 'true blessing'? There is, of course,
no answer to this. We are kept here behind bars, beat-
en, allowed to rot, but all this is splendid and rational,
for there is no difference between this ward and a warm
comfortable study. A convenient philosophy, indeed!
There is nothing to do about it, your conscience is clear,
and you feel you are a true sage.... No, Sir, that is not
philosophy, that is not thought, that is not the broad
view, it is merely laziness, fatalism, mental torpor....
Yes, indeed!" cried Ivan Dmitrich with renewed vehem-
ence. "You despise suffering, but if your little finger

were to be squeezed in the door, you would probably cry at the top of your voice!"

"Perhaps I wouldn't," said Andrei Yefimich, smiling gently.

"Wouldn't you just! Now if you were suddenly smitten down with paralysis, or some fool or bounder, taking advantage of his rank and social position, insulted you publicly, and you knew he would escape unpunished, then you would know what it means to advise people to go in for comprehension and true blessings."

"This is very original," said Andrei Yefimich with a delighted laugh, rubbing his hands together. "I admire your turn for generalizations, and the way you just now described my character is simply brilliant! Talking to you affords one the greatest pleasure, I assure you. Well, I heard you out, now be so good as to listen to me. . . ."

XI

They went on talking for almost an hour, and the conversation must have made a great impression on Andrei Yefimich. He paid daily visits to the annexe now. He went there in the mornings, and after dinner, and often darkness would overtake him as he sat conversing with Ivan Dmitrich. At first Ivan Dmitrich was distant with him, suspecting him of evil intentions and openly avowing his dislike for him, but soon he got used to him and changed his harsh tone for one of indulgent irony.

Soon the rumour spread about the hospital that doctor Andrei Yefimich habitually visited Ward No. 6. No one—neither the assistant, nor Nikita, nor the nurses—could understand why he went there, why he stayed there by the hour, what he found to talk about there, and why he never wrote out a prescription. His behaviour seemed strange. He was often out now, when Mikhail Averyanich came, and Darya did not know what to make of it, for the doctor had become irregular about his beer and was sometimes actually late for dinner.

One day, towards the end of June, Doctor Khobotov went to see Andrei Yefimich about something; not finding him at his house, he went into the yard to look for him; there he was told the doctor was in the mental ward. Going into the annexe, and stopping in the passage, Khobotov overheard the following conversation:

"We shall never agree, and you will never convert me to your faith," Ivan Dmitrich was saying querulously. "You know nothing of reality, you have never suffered, you have only, like a leech, fed on the sufferings of others, whereas I have done nothing but suffer from the day I was born. Therefore I will be frank with you: I feel that I am your superior and consider myself more competent in all respects. It is not for you to teach me."

"I have not the slightest desire to convert you," answered Andrei Yefimich quietly and sadly, as if grieved at being misinterpreted. "And that is not the point, my friend. The fact that I have not suffered and you have has nothing to do with the question. Both suffering and joy are transient; we may ignore them, they do not matter. The point is that you and I can think; we see in one another individuals capable of thought and argument, and this creates sympathy between us, however different our views. If you could only know how sick I am of the universal madness, mediocrity, stupidity, and how happy I am every time I converse with you, dear friend! You are intelligent, and therefore I enjoy your company."

Khobotov opened the door an inch and peeped in: Ivan Dmitrich in his night-cap was sitting on the bed, and beside him was the doctor. The madman grimaced, starting continually and convulsively wrapping his robe round him while the doctor sat motionless, his head drooping, his face flushed, helpless, mournful. Khobotov shrugged his shoulders, smiled and exchanged glances with Nikita. The latter, too, shrugged his shoulders.

Next day Khobotov brought the medical assistant with him. They both stood in the passage, listening to the conversation.

"Our old man seems to have run amok!" said Khobotov as they went out of the annexe.

"God forgive us, miserable sinners," sighed the pious Sergei Sergeich, carefully avoiding the puddles in the yard, so as not to soil his brilliantly polished boots. "To tell you the truth, my dear Yevgeny Fedorovich, I have long been expecting this!"

XII

Soon after the visit of his colleague to the ward Andrei Yefimich became conscious of an atmosphere of mystery surrounding him. Hospital assistants, nurses and patients encountered him with enquiring looks, and fell to whispering when he had passed. The superintendent's little girl, Masha, whom he used to enjoy meeting in the garden of the hospital, now when he approached smilingly to stroke her hair, ran away from him. Mikhail Averyanich the postmaster no longer answered his harangues with the usual "quite right," but muttered, with unaccountable confusion: "Certainly, certainly," and looked at him thoughtfully and sadly; for some reason he began advising his friend to stop drinking beer and vodka, though always in a roundabout way as behoved a man of his breeding, throwing out hints and telling him now about his battalion commander, a fine fellow he was, now about their regimental priest, a good chap, too, both of whom had made themselves ill by drinking, and recovered as soon as they gave it up. Once or twice his colleague, Khobotov, paid him a visit; he, too, advised Andrei Yefimich to give up drinking and without any apparent reason suggested he might take potassium bromide.

In August Andrei Yefimich received a letter from the mayor, summoning him on extremely important business.

When he got to the town-hall, Andrei Yefimich found assembled there the military chief, the inspector of the district school, a member of the council, Khobotov, and a fair, corpulent gentleman who was introduced to him as a doctor. This doctor, who had a difficult Polish name, lived at the stud-farm thirty versts away and was only passing through the town.

"We have an application here which has some reference to you," said the member of the council, turning to Andrei Yefimich after the greetings were over and everyone was seated round the table. "Yevgeny Fedorovich here says there is not enough room for the dispensary in the main building, and that it ought to be transferred to one of the wings. It is not the actual change that worries us but the fact that the wing would have to be repaired in that case."

"Yes, repairs are needed badly," said Andrei Yefimich, pausing to think for a moment. "If, for instance, the corner wing were to be used for the dispensary, I suppose at least five hundred rubles would be required. Unproductive expenditure...."

Everyone was silent for a while.

"I had the honour of telling you ten years ago," went on Andrei Yefimich quietly, "that the hospital in its present state is a luxury beyond the means of our town. It was built in the forties, and things were different in those years. The City Council spends much too much on unnecessary buildings and superfluous nominations. If things were run differently I am sure we could have two model hospitals for the same money."

"Well, then, let us run things differently," said the member of the council eagerly.

"I had the honour of expressing my opinion before: let the Zemstvo take over the medical organization."

"Oh yes, give the Zemstvo our funds, by all means, so that it can steal the money," said the fair-haired doctor, laughing.

"No doubt, no doubt," agreed the member of the council, also laughing.

Andrei Yefimich turned a dull and jaundiced eye on the fair-haired doctor and said:

"We must be fair."

There was another pause. Tea was served. The military chief, for some reason greatly embarrassed, stretched his arm across the table to touch the hand of Andrei Yefimich.

"You seem to have quite forgotten us, Doctor," he said. "But you're a regular recluse, I know; you do not play cards and are indifferent to women. We are dull companions for you."

Everyone began saying how dull every man who was worth anything must find the town. No theatres, no music, and at the last ball held at the club there had been twenty women and only two partners for them. The young men do not dance, preferring to crowd round the refreshment-bar or play cards. Without looking at anyone, Andrei Yefimich began saying in his slow, quiet voice, how sad, how exceedingly sad it was that the citizens wasted their energy, their souls and their minds on cards and gossip and, unable and unwilling to spend their time in interesting conversation or in reading, refused to enjoy the delights of the mind. The mind alone was interesting and remarkable, everything else was mean and trivial. Khobotov listened to his colleague with great attention, and suddenly interrupted him with the question:

"What is the date, Andrei Yefimich?"

Having received an answer, he and the fair-haired doctor went on to ask Andrei Yefimich what day of the week it was, how many days there were in a year and whether it was true that there was a wonderful prophet in Ward No. 6. Their tone was that of examiners aware of their own incompetency.

In answer to the last question Andrei Yefimich flushed slightly and said:

"Yes, he is a sick man, but he is very interesting."

No more questions were asked after that.

As he was putting on his coat in the hall, the military chief came up to him, and patting him on the shoulder, sighed and said:

"Time we old folk began to think about resting."

As he left the town-hall, Andrei Yefimich realized that he had been summoned before a commission called to investigate his mental state. Remembering the questions which had been put to him, he flushed crimson, and for the first time in his life felt a kind of bitter pity for the science of medicine.

"Good Lord," he thought as he remembered the way the doctors had examined him, "they have so very recently attended their lectures on psychiatry, and answered their examinations—why, why then this utter ignorance? They have not an inkling of what psychiatry is!"

And for the first time in his life he felt insulted and angry.

On the evening of that very day Mikhail Averyanich came to see him. Without stopping to greet him, he walked up to him, took both his hands in his own, and said in a deeply-moved voice:

"Dearest friend, prove to me that you believe in the sincerity of my feeling for you, and consider me your friend. . . . Dearest friend!" and not letting Andrei Yefimich speak, he went on excitedly: "I love you for your learning and the nobility of your soul. Now listen to me, my friend. Professional ethics compel the doctors to keep the truth from you, but I am a soldier, and will be blunt: you are not well! Excuse me, dear friend, but that is the truth, and it has been noticed by those round you for quite a time. Yevgeny Fedorovich has just been telling me that in the interests of your health you must have rest and distraction. Quite true! Splendid! I am going on leave in a few days and mean to get some fresh air. Give me a proof of your friendship—come with me! Come, and we will revive our youth!"

"I feel perfectly well," said Andrei Yefimich after a pause. "And I cannot accompany you. Let me prove my friendship for you in some other way."

To go away, for no reason, leaving his books, and Darya, and his beer, to break up the routine which had been established these twenty years, at first seemed a mad, fantastic idea. But then he remembered what had been said in the town-hall and how depressed he had felt on his way home, and the thought of leaving the town for a while, the town where stupid people regarded him as a madman, suddenly appealed to him.

"Where do you intend to go?" he asked.

"To Moscow, Petersburg, Warsaw.... I spent five years in Warsaw, and they were the happiest years of my life. What a wonderful town! Do come with me, dear friend!"

XIII

A week later Andrei Yefimich was offered a rest, in other words asked to send in his resignation, which he did with the utmost unconcern, and in another week he was seated by the side of Mikhail Averyanich in the mail coach, driving to the nearest railway station. It was cool, still weather, the sky was blue, the air transparent. They covered the two hundred versts to the station in two days, putting up twice for the night.

If they were served tea in dirty glasses at the posting stations, or their horses were not harnessed quickly enough, Mikhail Averyanich would go red in the face, tremble from head to foot and shout: "Silence! No arguing!" And in the coach he talked interminably about his travels in the Caucasus and Poland. The adventures he had had! The people he had met! He spoke so loudly, and his eyes grew so round with astonishment, that anyone might have thought he was lying. To crown all, he breathed right into Andrei Yefimich's face, and laughed into his ear. This made the doctor uncomfortable and prevented him from concentrating on his thoughts.

They travelled third class for the sake of economy, choosing a carriage for non-smokers. Half of the passengers belonged to their own class. Mikhail Averyanich was soon on a friendly footing with them all and, stepping from bench to bench, assured them in a loud voice they should refuse to travel on those atrocious roads. Swindling all round! How different from riding, now: you make a hundred versts in a day and feel fresh and well after it. Our poor crops were of course due to the draining of the Pinsk marshes. Disorder prevailed everywhere. He got excited, talked loud and would not let anyone else put in a word. His incessant prattle, interspersed with loud laughter and expressive gesticulations, wearied Andrei Yefimich.

"Which of us ought to be considered mad?" he thought irritably. "I, who try not to be a burden to my fellow-passengers, or this egoist who thinks he is the most intelligent and interesting person in the railway carriage and won't let anyone enjoy a moment's peace?"

When they got to Moscow, Mikhail Averyanich donned a military jacket with no epaulettes, and trousers with red piping on the hems. He went about in a military cap and overcoat, and soldiers saluted him in the streets. Andrei Yefimich now saw in him a man who had managed to squander all the good qualities of the country gentleman, retaining only the bad ones. He was fond of being served even when there was no necessity for it. The box of matches would lie on the table before him, and he would see it was there, and yet he would shout to the servant to hand it to him; he thought nothing of going about in his underclothes in front of the maid; he said "thou" to all servants, even when they were old men, calling them fools and oafs when he was in a bad temper. Andrei Yefimich knew this was typical of country gentlemen, but it disgusted him.

Mikhail Averyanich began by taking his friend to pray at the "Iverskaya Shrine." He prayed fervently, bowing to the very ground, with tears in his eyes, and when he had finished praying, he heaved a profound sigh and said:

"One may not be a believer, but prayer does one good. Kiss the image, old chap."

Andrei Yefimich bent down awkwardly and obeyed, but Mikhail Averyanich pursed his lips, shook his head from side to side, and whispered a prayer, the tears welling into his eyes again. After this they went to the Kremlin, had a look at the Tsar-Cannon and the Tsar-Bell, which they actually touched with their finger-tips, admired the view over the river and paid visits to the Cathedral of the Saviour and to the Rumyantsev museum.

They dined at the Testov restaurant. Mikhail Averyanich studied the menu long, patting his whiskers, and said to the waiter, assuming the tone of a gourmet very much at home in restaurants:

"Let us see what you mean to give us today, old chap!"

XIV

The doctor went everywhere, looked at everything, ate and drank, but all he felt was irritation with Mikhail Averyanich. He was tired of his friend's continual presence, he was longing to escape from him, hide from him, but Mikhail Averyanich considered it his duty to stick to his side and provide him with every possible distraction. When there was nothing to look at, he amused him with conversation. Andrei Yefimich bore it all for two days, but on the third day he told his friend he did not feel well and wished to stay at home all day. His friend said in that case he would stay at home, too. He quite agreed that they needed a rest, or they would walk

themselves off their feet. Andrei Yefimich lay down on a
sofa with his back to the room listening with clenched
teeth to his friend, who was eagerly trying to assure
him that France would smash Germany sooner or later,
that Moscow was full of swindlers, and that you cannot
judge a horse from its points alone. The doctor was conscious of palpitations and a buzzing in his ears, but was
too polite to ask his friend to leave him, or to stop talking. Fortunately Mikhail Averyanich got tired of being at
home and went out for a stroll after dinner.

Finding himself alone, Andrei Yefimich gave himself
up to the sensation of peace. How good it was to be lying
motionless on a sofa, conscious of being alone in the
room! True happiness is inconceivable without solitude.
The fallen angel must have betrayed God from a longing
for that solitude which is denied to angels. Andrei Yefimich wanted to think about the things he had seen and
heard during the last days, but could not get Mikhail
Averyanich out of his head.

"And to think he asked for leave and came away with
me out of sheer friendship and generosity!" thought the
doctor irritably. "What can be worse than this sort of
friendly patronage! He is kind and generous and gay, but
—there you are—a bore. A dreadful bore. It is the same
with him as with those people who never say anything
that is not wise or good, and who nevertheless make you
feel how stupid they are."

On the days that followed Andrei Yefimich pleaded
indisposition and did not go out of the room. He lay with
his face to the wall, suffering when his friend tried to
divert him with his talk, resting in his absence. He was
angry both with himself for having taken this journey,
and with his friend, who became more and more talkative
and familiar every day, so that Andrei Yefimich was unable to tune his mind to serious and sublime thoughts.

"I am being persecuted by that reality of which Ivan
Dmitrich spoke," he thought, angry with himself for his

inability to rise above the trivial. "But that's all nonsense. . . . When I get home, everything will go on as
before."

It was the same in Petersburg; he stayed in the hotel
room for days on end, lying on the sofa, and only getting up to drink beer.

Mikhail Averyanich kept saying they ought to hurry
on to Warsaw.

"Why should I go to Warsaw, my dear friend?" said
Andrei Yefimich imploringly. "Go without me, and let me
go home! Please do!"

"Not for the world!" protested Mikhail Averyanich.
"It's such a wonderful town. I spent the five happiest
years of my life there!"

Andrei Yefimich, too weak to insist, grudgingly accompanied his friend to Warsaw. Here he kept his room
and lay on the sofa, furious with himself, with his friend,
and with the hotel servants, who stubbornly refused to
understand Russian, while Mikhail Averyanich, as usual
bursting with health and spirits, went about the town
from morning till night looking up old friends. Sometimes he stayed out all night. Once, after a night spent
in some unknown place, he returned early in the morning,
in a state of great excitement, red-faced and dishevelled.
He paced the room for a long time, muttering inco-
herently, then halted and said:

"Honour above all!"

After pacing up and down a little longer he clutched
at his head and said in tragic tones:

"Yes, honour above all other considerations! I curse
the hour in which I conceived the idea of visting this Ba-
bylon! Dearest friend," he said turning to the doctor,
"you may well despise me: I have lost money gambling!
Give me five hundred rubles!"

Andrei Yefimich counted out five hundred rubles and
handed them in silence to his friend. The latter, still red
with shame and rage, uttered an incoherent and quite

superfluous vow, put on his cap and went out. Returning two hours later, he dropped into an arm-chair, sighed noisily and said:

"My honour is saved! Let us go, my friend! I do not wish to remain another minute in this accursed town. Swindlers! Austrian spies!"

It was November, and the snow lay deep in the streets by the time the friends returned from their travels. Doctor Khobotov now filled the place which had formerly belonged to Andrei Yefimich; he was still living in his old rooms, waiting for Andrei Yefimich to come back and vacate the hospital apartments. The plain woman he called his cook was already living in one of the hospital wings.

The town was excited by fresh rumours about the hospital. They said the plain woman had quarrelled with the inspector and that the latter had crawled before her on his knees, begging her pardon.

On the very day of his arrival Andrei Yefimich was obliged to go and look for rooms.

"Dearest friend," said the postmaster timidly to him, "forgive me if I am indiscreet, but how much money have you?"

Andrei Yefimich counted up his money and said:

"Eighty-six rubles."

"That was not what I meant," said Mikhail Averyanich, perplexed by the doctor's answer and embarrassed. "I wanted to know how much money you had altogether?"

"Well, and I tell you: eighty-six rubles.... That's all."

Although Mikhail Averyanich considered the doctor an honest and high-minded man, he had been sure the latter had at least twenty thousand rubles put away somewhere. Now, on finding out that Andrei Yefimich was a pauper and did not have the means to live, he suddenly wept and flung his arms round his friend.

XV

Andrei Yefimich went to live in the house of a woman of the lower middle classes whose name was Belova. There were only three rooms in the little house, not counting the kitchen. Two of the rooms, which looked out on the street were occupied by the doctor, and Darya, the landlady and her three children lived in the third room and the kitchen. Sometimes the landlady's sweetheart came to spend the night, a drunken fellow who was often very violent, terrifying Darya and the children. When he sat on a chair in the kitchen demanding vodka, the place would seem terribly cramped and the doctor would take the crying children into his room out of compassion, making up beds for them on the floor, and this gave him great satisfaction.

He got up at eight as he had always done, drank his tea, and settled down to read his old books and magazines. He had no money to buy new ones. Either because the books were old, or, perhaps, owing to his changed surroundings, reading no longer took him out of himself, indeed it exhausted him. So as not to be idle he drew up a detailed catalogue of his books, sticking labels on their backs, and finding the mechanical occupation more absorbing than reading. The monotonous laborious work in some strange way seemed to lull his thoughts; he worked away, his mind a blank, and time passed rapidly. He even found peeling potatoes or sorting buckwheat in the kitchen with Darya quite entertaining. On Saturdays and Sundays he went to church. Leaning against the wall with closed eyes, he listened to the choir and thought of his father, his mother, the University, the various religions; he felt soothed and melancholy, and when he left the church was sorry the service was over so soon.

Twice he went to the hospital to see Ivan Dmitrich and have a talk with him. But both times he found him in a state of extraordinary excitement and rage; he begged

to be left alone, saying he was sick of empty prattle,
and that for all the suffering he had undergone he begged
of the accursed, base people only one recompense—solitary confinement. Was he to be denied that, too? Both
times, as Andrei Yefimich took his leave and bade him
good night, Ivan Dmitrich barked out:

"Go to the devil!"

Andrei Yefimich could not make up his mind whether
he should go to him a third time, or not, though he
wanted very much to do so.

In the old days Andrei Yefimich used to employ the
time after dinner in pacing the floor and thinking, now
he lay on the sofa with his face to the wall till the time
came for evening tea, giving himself up to trivial
thoughts which he could not shake off. He was mortified
at not having been allotted either a pension or a grant
after over twenty years of service. True, he did not consider his work had been honest, but all who had served
were entitled to a pension, whether honest or not. The
modern idea of justice consisted in the very fact that
rank, orders and pensions were awarded not for moral
qualities or abilities, but for service, whatever it had been
like. Why then should he alone be made an exception?
He had no money at all. He was ashamed to pass the
shop, and meet the shop-keeper's eye. He owed thirty-two
rubles for beer. They owed Belova the landlady, too. Darya secretly sold his old clothes and books, telling the
landlady that the doctor was expecting a large sum of
money very soon.

He was furious with himself for having spent a thousand rubles on his trip, all his savings! How handy that
thousand would have been now! And he was vexed at
not being left alone. Khobotov considered it his duty to
visit his ailing colleague every now and then. Everything about him disgusted Andrei Yefimich: his well-nourished countenance, his ill-bred, condescending tone, the
way he called him "colleague," his high-boots; but most

revolting of all was that Khobotov considered it his duty
to look after Andrei Yefimich, and thought he was really
giving him medical treatment. Every time he came he
brought with him a bottle of potassium bromide and grey
powders.

Mikhail Averyanich, too, considered it his duty to visit
his friend and try to distract him. He would enter Andrei Yefimich's room with an air of familiarity and forced
hilarity, assuring him he looked very well and was obviously on the mend, thank God, which only meant he
considered his friend's case hopeless. He had not paid
back the money he borrowed in Warsaw, and burdened
by a heavy sense of shame and strain tried to laugh still
louder and tell still funnier stories. His funny stories
and his conversation now seemed endless and were a torture both to Andrei Yefimich and himself.

During his visits Andrei Yefimich usually lay down
on the sofa with his back to him, listening to him and
clenching his teeth; he felt layers of scum forming on
the surface of his soul, and every time his friend visited
him the layers seemed to rise higher and higher, until
they almost suffocated him.

In order to stifle these base feelings he forced himself
to dwell on the thought that sooner or later he himself,
Khobotov, and Mikhail Averyanich, would perish without
leaving the slightest imprint behind them. If one could
imagine some spirit a million years hence flying through
space past the globe, it would see nothing but clay and
bare rocks. Culture, moral law, everything would have
perished and not so much as a blade of grass would grow.
What then were his mortification, his sense of shame
before the shop-keeper, the insignificant Khobotov, the
oppressive friendship of Mikhail Averyanich? Mere trifling rubbish.

But such reasoning was no longer any consolation to
him. The moment he evoked the image of the globe a
million years hence, Khobotov would appear in his high-

boots from behind a naked rock, or Mikhail Averyanich,
roaring with laughter; he could even hear the embarrassed whisper: "As for the Warsaw debt, dear friend, I
will pay you back in a few days. . . . I really will."

XVI

One day Mikhail Averyanich came to see Andrei
Yefimich in the afternoon, when the latter was lying on
the sofa. Khobotov happened to arrive together with the
potassium bromide. Andrei Yefimich drew himself into a
sitting position with an effort, supporting himself on the
sofa with his hand.

"My dear chap," began Mikhail Averyanich, "you look
much brighter than you did yesterday. Why, you look
splendid, absolutely splendid!"

"Time you were thinking of getting better, colleague,"
Khobotov joined in with a yawn. "You must be sick of
the whole thing yourself!"

"Why, we'll be as sound as a bell soon!" cried Mikhail
Averyanich gleefully. "We'll live another hundred years,
you see if we don't!"

"I don't know about a hundred, but he's certainly
good for another twenty years," said Khobotov reassur-
ingly. "Tut-tut, colleague, chin up. . . . Keep up your
spirits!"

"Ho-ho!" roared Mikhail Averyanich, "we'll yet show
you the stuff we're made of! You'll see! Next summer,
God willing, we'll rush off to the Caucasus and ride all
over its mountains—hoppitty-hoppitty-hop! And when
we come back from the Caucasus, who knows but we
might not have a wedding!" Mikhail Averyanich gave a
sly wink. "We'll marry you off, old chap, see if we
don't. . . ."

Andrei Yefimich suddenly felt the scum rise to his
throat; his heart thumped terrifically.

"How vulgar all this is!" he said, rising abruptly and

walking towards the window. "Can't you see how vulgar you are?"

He had meant to speak gently and mildly, but despite himself he doubled his fists and raised them above his head.

"Leave me alone!" he shouted at the top of his voice, red in the face and shaking all over. "Get out! Both of you! Out!"

Mikhail Averyanich and Khobotov both got up and stared at him, first in perplexity, then with awe.

"Get out, both of you!" Andrei Yefimich went on shouting. "Stupid men! Fools! I do not want your friendship, or your medicine either, you fool! Vulgar! Disgusting!"

Exchanging bewildered glances, Khobotov and Mikhail Averyanich backed to the door, and out into the passage. Andrei Yefimich snatched up the bottle of potassium bromide and hurled it after them; the bottle broke with a clatter on the threshold.

"Go to the devil!" he cried in a sobbing voice, running after them into the passage. "To the devil!"

After his visitors had left, Andrei Yefimich, shaking as if he had the ague, lay on the sofa, saying over and over again: "Stupid people! Fools!" When he calmed down, he at once thought how bad Mikhail Averyanich must be feeling now, how mortified, and how awful it all was. Such a thing had never happened to him before. Where were his intelligence and tact, his comprehension and philosophical indifference?

The doctor could not sleep all night for shame and vexation with himself, and in the morning, about ten o'clock, he went to the post-office, to apologize to the postmaster.

"We will not dwell on what has happened," said the deeply moved Mikhail Averyanich, sighing, and pressing his hand warmly. "Let bygones be bygones. Lyubavkin!" he cried so loudly as to make all the office clerks and clients start. "Bring a chair! Can't you wait, you?" he shouted at a poor woman who was handing in a registered letter through the bars. "Don't you see I'm busy? Let bygones be bygones," he went on affectionately, turning to Andrei Yefimich. "Do sit down, dear friend, I beg you."

For a whole minute he sat rubbing his knees in silence, then said:

"I didn't take offence for a moment. I realize what it is to be ill. The doctor and I were quite alarmed by your attack yesterday, we had a long talk about you. Dearest friend, why don't you take your illness seriously? You must not go on like this, really! Forgive me a friend's frankness," Mikhail Averyanich lowered his voice to a whisper, "but you live in the most undesirable surroundings: cramped, filth all round, no care, no means of taking treatment.... My dear friend, the doctor and I both implore you to take our advice; go to the hospital! The food is wholesome there, you'll be taken care of and your disease treated. Yevgeny Fedorovich, who between you and me is very *mauvais ton*, is a clever doctor, for all that, and one can rely on him. He promises to look after you."

Andrei Yefimich was moved by the tone of heartfelt concern and by the tears that suddenly gleamed on the postmaster's cheeks.

"My most esteemed friend, don't believe them!" he whispered, putting his hand on his heart. "Don't believe them! It's all lies! All that is wrong with me is that in the course of twenty years I have met only one intelligent man in our town, and he is mad. I'm not a bit ill, I have simply been caught in a vicious circle from which there is no way out. I don't care about anything, do as you like."

"Go to the hospital, my friend!"

"I don't care where I go—you can bury me alive if you like."

"Promise me you will obey Yevgeny Fedorovich in everything, old man!"

"All right, I promise. But I tell you again, my dear Sir, I am caught in a vicious circle. From now on everything, even the sincerest sympathy of my well-wishers tends to only one thing—my destruction. I am perishing, and I have the courage to realize it."

"But you'll get better, old chap!"

"What's the use of talking like that?" said Andrei Yefimich testily. "Almost everyone has to go through this sort of thing towards the end of his life. Whether you are told your kidneys are in a bad way, or that your heart is dilated, and you begin taking medical treatment, or whether they say you are mad or a criminal—in a word, as soon as people's attention is drawn to you, you may be sure you have entered a vicious circle from which you will never be able to escape. If you try to get out you will find yourself still deeper in. You had better give up, for no human effort will save you. At least that is my opinion."

In the meantime a crowd had formed on the other side of the counter. Not to keep them waiting any longer, Andrei Yefimich got up and began to say good-bye. Mikhail Averyanich made him repeat his promise, and saw him to the door.

That same evening Khobotov came unexpectedly, in his sheepskin jacket and high-boots and said, just as if nothing had happened:

"I've come to you on business, colleague. I want to ask you to join me in a consultation—feel like coming?"

Thinking Khobotov intended to divert him by the walk, or even to give him a chance to earn a little money, Andrei Yefimich put on his coat and cap, and went out with him. He was glad of the opportunity to expiate his fault of the day before, and felt grateful towards Khobotov, who said not a word about the incident, evidently

bent on sparing his feelings. He was quite surprised to
find so much tact in a man so utterly unrefined.

"Where is your patient?" asked Andrei Yefimich.

"At the hospital. I have been wanting to show him
to you for some time. . . . An extremely curious case."

They entered the hospital yard, and skirting the main
building walked towards the annexe where the mental
cases were housed. For some reason neither spoke all
this time. When they entered the wing, Nikita sprang up
and stood at attention as usual.

"One of them here has a complication in the lung,"
murmured Khobotov, as he entered the ward together
with Andrei Yefimich. "You wait for me in here, I'll be
back in a minute. I'll just go and fetch my stethoscope."

And out he went.

XVII

It was growing dark. Ivan Dmitrich lay on his bed,
his face half-buried in the pillow; the man with the palsy
sat motionless, quietly weeping and moving his lips. The
fat peasant and the former mail-sorter were asleep. It
was quiet in the room.

Andrei Yefimich sat on the side of Ivan Dmitrich's
bed, waiting. But half an hour passed, and instead of
Khobotov, Nikita entered the ward, holding a dressing-
gown, some underclothes and slippers in his arms.

"Change your clothes, Your Honour," he said quietly.
"This is your cot," he added, pointing to an unoccupied
bed which had evidently just been brought in. "You'll get
over it, God willing, don't worry."

Andrei Yefimich understood it all. Without a word, he
walked over to the bed pointed out by Nikita, and sat
on it; realizing that Nikita was waiting for him, he
stripped himself naked, feeling horribly embarrassed.
Then he began pulling the hospital clothes on; the drawers

were much too short, the shirt too long, and the dressing-gown smelt of smoked fish.

"You'll get over it, God willing," repeated Nikita.

Taking up Andrei Yefimich's clothes in his arms, he went out, closing the door behind him.

"It's all the same," thought Andrei Yefimich, bashfully drawing the skirts of the gown round him, "it's all the same ... frock-coat, uniform, or this gown...."

But his watch? The note-book which he kept in his side-pocket? His cigarettes? Where had Nikita taken his clothes to? He would probably never again for the rest of his life put on trousers, waistcoat and boots. All this seemed strange and even incomprehensible at first. Andrei Yefimich was still true to his conviction that there was not the slightest difference between the house of his landlady Belova and Ward No. 6, that everything in the world was nonsense, vanity of vanities, and yet his hands shook and his feet turned cold, and the thought that Ivan Dmitrich would wake up and see him in the hospital robe made his heart sink. He got up, took a few paces across the room, and sat down again.

Half an hour passed, then an hour, and he felt sick and weary of sitting there; was it possible to live a whole day, a week, and even years here, like all these people? Well, he had sat for a while, had then walked about, and sat down again; he could go up to the window and look out, and pace the room once more. And then what? Just sit there like a graven image all the time? No, no, that was quite impossible!

Andrei Yefimich lay down, but got up immediately, wiping the cold sweat from his brow with his sleeve and feeling as he did so that his face smelt of smoked fish.

"It's some misunderstanding," he said, throwing out his arms in bewilderment. "I must speak to them, it's a misunderstanding...."

Just then Ivan Dmitrich woke up. He sat up, propping his cheeks on his fists. He spat on the floor. Then he glanced languidly at the doctor, evidently not understanding anything at first; but the next moment the expression of his drowsy face became triumphant and cruel.

"So, they got you here, too, old chap!" he said, his voice hoarse with sleep, and one eye not quite open. "Glad to see you! Instead of sucking the blood of others, your blood will be sucked now. Splendid!"

"It's some misunderstanding," muttered Andrei Yefimich, alarmed by Ivan Dmitrich's words; he shrugged his shoulders and repeated once more: "It must be some misunderstanding...."

Ivan Dmitrich spat again, and lay down.

"Accursed life!" he grumbled. "And what makes it so galling and mortifying is that this life will end, not in recompense for suffering, not with an apotheosis, like it does at the opera, but in death; a couple of attendants will come and pick up the dead body by the arms and legs and take it to the cellar. Ugh! Never mind.... Our day will come in the other world.... My ghost will return and scare those swine. I'll make their hair turn grey."

Just then Moses came back, and, observing the doctor, stretched out his hand:

"Give me a kopek!"

XVIII

Andrei Yefimich walked up to the window and looked out at the field. It was getting quite dark, and on the right the moon was rising, cold and crimson. Not far from the hospital fence, some seven hundred feet, not more, stood a tall white building, surrounded by a stone wall. It was the prison.

"So this is reality!" thought Andrei Yefimich, and he was afraid.

Everything was terrible: the moon, the prison, the inverted nails on the top of the fence and the far-away flame coming from the kilns; behind his back someone sighed. Andrei Yefimich turned and saw a man with stars and orders sparkling all over his chest; the man was smiling and winking roguishly. This, too, was terrible.

Andrei Yefimich tried to tell himself that there was nothing unusual in the moon, or in the prison building, that people who were mentally sound wore orders, that in time everything would rot and turn to clay, but he was suddenly overcome by despair and, seizing the bars on the window with both his hands, tried to shake them. The grating was strong and did not give in the least.

Then, in his effort to shake off his terror, he walked over to Ivan Dmitrich's bed and sat down on the side of it.

"I have lost heart, dear friend," he muttered, shaking and wiping the cold sweat off his brow. "Lost heart."

"Try philosophizing," said Ivan Dmitrich derisively.

"My God, my God...! Oh, yes.... You were pleased to remark once that, while there is no school of philosophy in Russia, everyone philosophizes, even the common herd. But what harm does the philosophy of the common herd do anyone?" Andrei Yefimich's voice sounded as if he were going to cry, or trying to move his room-mate to pity. "Why then this malignant laugh, dear friend? And what is there left for the common herd to do but philosophize, since it can find no satisfaction? An intelligent, well-educated, proud, independent human being has no option but to become a doctor in a stupid dirty little town, and devote himself to cupping, leeches and mustard plasters for the rest of his life! The quackery, the narrowness, the vulgarity! Oh, my God!"

"You are talking nonsense! If you don't like being a doctor, why didn't you become a minister of state?"

"No, no, there's nothing one can do! We are weak, my friend.... I was indifferent, I reasoned cheerfully and sanely, but the moment I feel the rude touch of life, I lose heart ... *prostration.* ... We are weak, wretched. ... You, too, my friend! You are intelligent and high-minded, you imbibed noble impulses with your mother's milk, but you had hardly begun life when you wearied and fell ill. ... Weak, weak!"

Something insistent, in addition to his fear and sense of ignominy had begun to gnaw at Andrei Yefimich with the onset of darkness. At last he realized that this was his desire for beer and cigarettes.

"I'll leave you for a moment, my friend..." he said. "I'll tell them to give us a light.... I cannot stand it.... I simply can't...."

Andrei Yefimich went towards the door and opened it, but immediately Nikita leaped up and barred the way.

"Where are you going? None of that!" he said. "Time you were in bed!"

"I only want to go out for a few minutes, just for a stroll in the yard!" said Andrei Yefimich, completely taken aback.

"No, no, it's not allowed. You know it yourself."

And Nikita slammed the door, leaning his back against it.

"But how would my going out hurt anyone?" asked Andrei Yefimich, shrugging his shoulders. "I can't understand, Nikita, I simply must go out!" he said, his voice breaking. "I must!"

"Don't you go infringing the peace now," admonished Nikita.

"It's a disgrace!" shouted Ivan Dmitrich suddenly, leaping up. "What right has he to prevent people going out? The law states distinctly enough, I'm sure, that no one can be deprived of his liberty without a trial! It's sheer violence! Absolutely arbitrary!"

"Of course it's arbitrary!" said Andrei Yefimich, encouraged by the unlooked-for support. "I want to get out, I must! He has no right to prevent me! Let me out, I tell you!"

"Do you hear, you brute?" cried Ivan Dmitrich, thumping the door with his fist. "Open the door, or I'll break it down! You butcher!"

"Open the door!" cried Andrei Yefimich, shaking all over. "I insist!"

"Go on!" answered Nikita from the other side of the door. "Go on!"

"At least go and call Yevgeny Fedorovich! Tell him I ask him to step in for a minute!"

"He'll come without being called tomorrow."

"They'll never let us out!" said Ivan Dmitrich. "They'll leave us here till we rot! Oh, God, can it be true there is no hell in the next world, and that these scoundrels will be forgiven? Where is justice? Open the door, you knave, I'm suffocating!" he shouted hoarsely, throwing his weight against the door. "I'll beat out my brains! Murderers!"

Nikita opened the door abruptly and shoved Andrei Yefimich rudely aside, using his arms and one knee, then, brandishing his fist brought it down on Andrei Yefimich's face. An enormous salt wave seemed to engulf Andrei Yefimich from head to foot and drag him towards his bed; there really was a salty taste in his mouth; evidently his gums were bleeding. He waved his arms as if striving to emerge and caught at the back of someone's bed, feeling at the same time that Nikita struck him twice on the back.

Ivan Dmitrich gave a sharp cry. So he, too, was being beaten.

Then all was quiet. The moon shed its pale light through the bars, and on the floor lay a shadow which looked like a net. Everything was terrifying. Andrei Yefimich lay down, trying not to breathe, waiting, terrified, for another blow. He felt as if someone had taken a scythe, thrust it into his body and turned it several times in his chest and stomach. The pain made him bite into his pillow and clench his teeth, when all of a sudden, flashing through the chaos and filling his mind, came one thought, terrible, unbearable: the pain he was now experiencing must have been felt for years on end, day in day out, by all these people, now looking like black shadows in the moonlight. How was it that for over twenty years he had not known of it or had wished not to know of it? He had not known, had not had the slightest idea of the pain, therefore he was not to blame, but his conscience, as rude and implacable as Nikita, sent a cold shiver down his spine. He leapt up, wanting to cry at the top of his voice and rush out to kill Nikita, Khobotov, the superintendent and medical assistant, and then himself, but no sound came from his mouth, and his legs would not obey him; panting for air, he wrenched at his dressing-gown and shirt, tearing them, and fell back in his bed, unconscious.

XIX

He woke up next morning with throbbing head and a ringing in his ears; every bone in his body ached. The memory of his own weakness the night before caused him no shame. He had behaved like a coward, even allowed himself to be frightened by the moon and given vent, with complete sincerity, to thoughts and feelings he had never suspected in himself. That idea, for instance, of dissatisfaction making the common herd philosophize. But he did not care about anything, now.

He neither ate nor drank, but lay motionless and speechless on his bed.

"I don't care," he thought, when they questioned him. "I won't answer them. ... I don't care."

After dinner Mikhail Averyanich came to see him, bringing a packet of tea and a pound of jujubes. Darya came too, to stand for an hour by his bed-side with the expression of dumb grief on her face. And Dr. Khobotov visited him. He brought a bottle of potassium bromide with him and told Nikita to fumigate the ward with something or other.

Towards evening, Andrei Yefimich died from an apoplectic stroke. First he felt a feverish chill and nausea; something loathsome seemed to be spreading all over his body, right up to his finger-tips, rising from his stomach to his head and penetrating into his eyes and ears. Everything turned green before him. Andrei Yefimich understood that this was the end and remembered that Ivan Dmitrich, Mikhail Averyanich and millions of others believed in immortality. Supposing there were such a thing? But he felt no desire for immortality, and only devoted a passing thought to it. A herd of reindeer which he had been reading about the day before rushed past him, extraordinarily beautiful and graceful; then a country woman stretched out her hand to him, holding a registered letter. . . . Mikhail Averyanich said something. Then everything disappeared and Andrei Yefimich lost consciousness for ever.

Two attendants came, picked him up by his arms and legs, and took him into the chapel. There he lay on the table, with open eyes, and in the night the moon shone on him. The next morning Sergei Sergeich came, prayed with great piety before the crucifix and closed the eyes of his former chief.

Two days later Andrei Yefimich was buried. Only Mikhail Averyanich and Darya attended the funeral.

1892

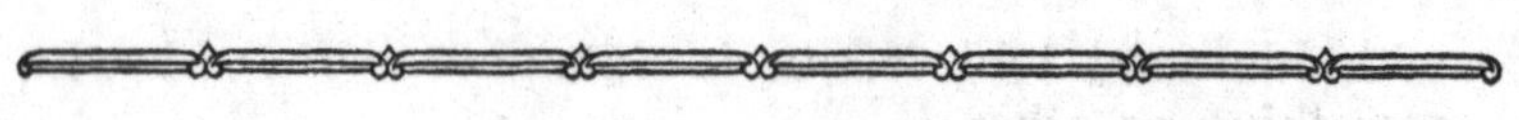

THE HOUSE WITH THE MANSARD

AN ARTIST'S STORY

I

All this happened six or seven years ago when I was living in the province of T., on the estate of a landed proprietor called Belokurov, a young man who rose very early, went about in a full-skirted peasant coat, drank beer of an evening, and was always complaining that he never met with sympathy anywhere. He lived in an annexe in the garden, and I took up my quarters in the old mansion, in a huge pillared ball-room, with no furniture but a wide sofa on which I slept, and a table at which I played patience. All the time, even in still weather, the ancient stoves hummed, and during thunderstorms the whole house shook as if it were on the point of falling to pieces; this was rather alarming, especially on stormy nights, when the ten great windows were lit up by lightning.

Doomed as I was to a life of idleness, I did nothing whatever. For hours at a time I looked out of the window at the sky, the birds, the garden walks, read whatever the post brought me, and slept. Sometimes I left the house and roamed about till late at night.

On my way home from one of these rambles, I happened upon an estate I had never seen before. The sun was setting and the shades of evening lay over the flowering rye. Two rows of ancient, towering fir-trees, planted close together so that they formed almost solid walls, enclosed a walk of sombre beauty. I climbed easily over some railings and made my way along this walk, my feet slipping on the carpet of pine-needles which lay an inch thick on the ground. It was still and dark, but for the brilliant gold of the sunlight, shimmering rainbow-like in the spiders' webs. The fragrance spread by the fir-trees was almost overpowering. I soon turned into a long avenue of lime-trees. Here, too, everything spoke of neglect and age. Last year's leaves rustled mournfully underfoot, and shadows lurked in the twilight between the trunks of the trees. On my right, in an ancient orchard, an oriole warbled feebly and listlessly—the bird, like everything else here, was probably old. And then the lime-trees came to an end in front of an old house with a verandah and a mansard, and suddenly I had a view of the courtyard, a big pond with a bathing-place on the bank, a huddle of green willows, and, in the midst of a village on the other side of the pond, a high, narrow belfry, the cross on its top lit up in the last rays of the departing sun.

For a moment I was under the spell of something familiar, something I had known long ago, as if I had seen this panorama before, at some time during my childhood.

A sturdy white stone gateway, adorned with lions, led from the courtyard into the open fields, and in this gateway stood two girls. The older of the two, slender, pale, very pretty, with a great knot of auburn hair on the top of her head and a small, obstinate mouth, looked very severe, and scarcely took any notice of me, the other, who looked extremely young, hardly more than seventeen or eighteen, was pale and slender, too, but her mouth was large and she looked shy, gazing at me from great wondering eyes and dropping out a word or two in English as I passed by; and it seemed to me that I had known these charming faces, too, at some distant time. I returned home, feeling as if I had had a delightful dream.

One afternoon, a few days later, Belokurov and I were walking about in front of the house, when the tall grass rustled beneath the wheels of a light carriage, turning into the yard. In it sat one of the girls I had seen, the older one. She had brought a subscription list for aid to the victims of a fire. Not looking at us, she told us gravely, and in much detail the number of houses burned in the village of Siyanovo, the number of men, women and children rendered homeless, and the temporary measures proposed by the committee, of which she was a member, for rendering aid to the victims. After giving us the list to sign, she put it away and prepared to take her leave immediately.

"You've quite forgotten us, Pyotr Petrovich," she said to Belokurov, putting out her hand to him. "Come and see us, and if Monsieur N. (she named me) would like to make the acquaintance of some of his admirers, my mother and I would be very glad to see him."

I bowed.

When she had gone Pyotr Petrovich began telling me about her. He said she came from a good family, and was called Lydia Volchaninova, and both the estate on which she lived with her mother and sister, and the village on the other side of the pond, were called Shelkovka. Her father had occupied a prominent post in Moscow, and had died with the rank of privy councillor. Though quite well-off, the Volchaninovs lived in the country all the year round, and Lydia taught in the Zemstvo school in her home village of Shelkovka, receiving a monthly salary of twenty-five rubles. She made this money suffice for her personal expenditure, and was proud to earn her own living.

"A very interesting family," said Belokurov. "We must pay them a visit. They would be very pleased if you went."

One day after dinner—it was some saint's day—we remembered the Volchaninovs, and set off to Shelkovka. We found the mother and both daughters at home. The mother, Yekaterina Pavlovna, must once have been good-looking, but had grown stouter than her age warranted, was short-winded, melancholy and absent-minded. She tried to entertain me with talk about art. Having learned from her daughter that I might visit Shelkovka, she had hastily recalled two or three landscapes of mine which she had seen at exhibitions in Moscow, and now asked me what I had intended to express by them. Lydia, or, as she was called at home, Leda, spoke more to Belokurov than to me. Her face grave and unsmiling, she asked him why he did not work in the Zemstvo, and why he had never been at a single one of its meetings.

"It's not right, Pyotr Petrovich," she said reproachfully. "Really it isn't—you ought to be ashamed of yourself."

"Quite true, Leda, quite true," agreed her mother. "It's not right."

"Our whole district is in the hands of Balagin," continued Leda, turning to me. "He is the chairman of the local board and has put his nephews and sons-in-law into all the district posts, and does whatever he likes. We must resist. We young people ought to make up a strong party, but you see what our young people are like. It's too bad, Pyotr Petrovich!"

Zhenya, the younger sister, said nothing while the Zemstvo was being discussed. She took no part in serious conversation, not being considered as a grown-up person by the family, among whom she went under the childish pet name of Missie, because that was what she had called

her governess, when she was a little girl. She kept looking at me with curiosity, telling me all about the origi-
nals of the family album I was looking through—"That's
my uncle . . . that's my godfather," she said, touching the
portraits with her finger, her shoulder brushing artlessly
against mine, giving me a clear view of her slight un-
developed breasts, her slender shoulders, her plait, and
her whole thin figure, tightly drawn in at the waist by
her belt.

We played croquet and tennis, walked about the garden, drank tea, and afterwards sat a long time over supper. After the huge empty pillared ball-room I felt quite
at ease in the comfortable little house in which there were
no oleograph pictures on the walls, and they said "you"
not the familiar "thou" to the servants. Leda and Missie
made the atmosphere seem pure and youthful, and everything breathed integrity. At supper Leda again talked
to Belokurov about the Zemstvo, Balagin, and school
libraries. She was lively, sincere, strong in her convictions. She was an interesting talker, though she spoke a
great deal, and very loud—perhaps because she was accustomed to addressing classes. My friend Pyotr Petrovich, on the other hand, still clung to the habit of his
student days—the habit of turning every conversation
into an argument. He held forth listlessly, tediously, and
at length, with an obvious desire to show off his intelligence and his progressive views. He gesticulated and
knocked a sauce-boat over with his cuff, and a large pool
formed on the table-cloth, but no one but myself seemed
to notice it.

When we set off for home it was dark and still.

"Good breeding does not consist in not upsetting
sauce on the table, but in not noticing if someone else
does," sighed Belokurov. "Yes, they're a delightful, cultured family. I've lost touch with nice people—I've deteriorated. There's so much to do, so much!"

He spoke of the work to be done if you wanted to be

a model landlord. And I thought what a lazy, unmanageable fellow he was. When he spoke of serious things he interspersed his speech with painfully emphatic "er-er's" and he did everything in the same way as he spoke— slowly, always getting behind, never finishing anything in time. I did not believe he was a bit practical, if only because when I gave him letters to post he kept them in his pocket for weeks.

"And the worst of it is," he muttered, as he walked by my side, "you work and work, and meet with no sympathy from anyone. No sympathy whatever."

II

I got into the habit of visiting the Volchaninovs. My usual place there was on the lowest of the steps leading to the verandah. I was devoured by remorse, deploring my life which was passing so rapidly and trivially, and continually telling myself that it would be a good thing if I could tear out my heart, which was such a heavy burden to me. And all the time there was talk going on on the verandah, the sound of skirts rustling, and pages being turned. I soon grew accustomed to the knowledge that Leda received patients, gave out books and went often to the village with a parasol over her uncovered head in the day-time, and in the evening talked in a loud voice about the Zemstvo and schools. Whenever this girl slender, good-looking, invariably severe, with her small, daintily curved mouth, began talking about practical things, she would preface her remarks by saying to me coldly:

"This won't interest you."

Me she disliked. She disliked me for being a landscape painter and not trying to show the needs of the people in my pictures, and also because she felt I was indifferent to all in which she believed so firmly. I remember riding along the shores of the Lake of Baikal, and meeting a Buryat girl in a shirt and blue denim trousers, riding astride. I asked her to sell me her pipe, but she only glanced contemptuously at my European features and hat, and, too bored to spend more than a minute talking to me, galloped past with a wild whoop. And Leda, too, felt there was something alien in me. She gave no outward signs of her dislike, but I could feel it, and, seated on the lowest step of the verandah, gave way to my irritation and said that to treat the peasants without being oneself a doctor, was to deceive them, and that when one had any amount of broad acres, it was easy to be charitable.

But her sister Missie had not a care in the world, and like myself, passed the time in complete idleness. The moment she got up of a morning she began reading, seated in a deep arm-chair on the verandah, her feet scarcely reaching the floor, or secluded herself with her book in the lime-tree walk, or passed through the gate into the fields. She read all day, scanning the pages avidly, and only an occasional weary and listless glance, and the extreme pallor of her face showed that this reading was a mental strain. When I arrived and she caught sight of me, she would blush faintly, eagerly relinquish her book, and, fixing her great eyes on my face, begin to tell me what had happened since she last saw me— that the chimney had been on fire in the servants' quarters, that one of the workmen had caught a big fish in the pond, and so on. On week-days she usually wore a coloured blouse and a dark-blue skirt. She and I used to stroll about, pick cherries for jam, or go rowing, and when she jumped up to reach a cherry, or bent over the oars, her thin, delicate arms showed through her wide sleeves. Or I would sketch, and she would stand by, watching admiringly.

One Sunday in the end of July, I set off for the Volchaninovs at about nine o'clock in the morning. I walked about the park, keeping as far from the house as possible, looking for mushrooms, which were very plen-

tiful that summer, and marking the places where I found
them with sticks, so as later to gather them with Zhenya. A warm wind was blowing. I could see Zhenya and
her mother, both in light-coloured Sunday dresses, coming home from church, Zhenya holding her hat on
against the wind. Then I heard sounds which meant
they were having tea on the verandah.

For a carefree individual like myself, always seeking an excuse to be idle, these summer Sunday mornings on our country-estates hold a special charm. When
the garden, green and sparkling with dew, lies radiant
and happy in the rays of the sun, when the oleanders
and the mignonette in the flower-beds near the house
spread their perfume, and the young folk, just returned
from church, are having tea in the garden, and everyone is so cheerful and so charmingly dressed; when I
remind myself that all these healthy, well-nourished,
good-looking people will do nothing at all the livelong
day, I long for life to be always like this. This particular
morning I was thinking these same thoughts and walking about the garden, ready to stroll about aimlessly,
with nothing to do, the whole day, the whole summer.

Zhenya appeared with a basket over her arm. Her
expression showed that she had known, or at any rate
felt, that she would find me in the garden. We gathered
mushrooms and talked, and when she put a question to
me she went in front, so as to see my face.

"There was a miracle in the village yesterday," she
said. "Lame Pelageya has been ill a whole year, no doctors or medicine were any use, and yesterday a wise
woman whispered over her, and she isn't ill any more."

"That's nothing," I said. "We ought not to look for
miracles only when people are ill or old. Isn't health a
miracle in itself? And life? Everything we don't understand is a miracle."

"And aren't you frightened by things you can't understand?"

"No. I approach phenomena I don't understand boldly, I don't give in to them. I am above them. A human
being should rate himself higher than lions, tigers and
stars, higher than the whole of nature, even higher than
things which we cannot understand and regard as miraculous, otherwise he is not a man, but a mouse, afraid
of everything."

Zhenya supposed that, being an artist, I knew a
great deal, and could divine accurately what I did not
know. She wanted me to waft her to some exquisite eternal sphere, to that higher world where, she believed, I was
quite at home, and she spoke to me of God, of life everlasting, of miracles. And I, unwilling to admit that myself
and my imagination would perish altogether after death,
would reply: "Yes, human beings are immortal," "Yes,
life everlasting awaits us." And she would listen, believing me without demanding proofs.

As we were going back to the house she suddenly
came to a halt and said:

"Isn't Leda splendid? I adore her and would sacrifice
my life for her at a moment's notice. But why—" Zhenya
put a finger on my coat-sleeve, "why do you always argue with her? Why are you so irritable?"

"Because she's wrong."

Zhenya shook her head disapprovingly, and tears
came into her eyes.

"How hard that is to understand," she said.

At that moment Leda, who had just returned from
somewhere or other, stood by the porch with a riding-crop
in her hand—slender, pretty, lit up by the rays of the
sun—giving orders to a workman. She received two or
three patients, in great haste, talking loudly, and then
went from room to room looking extremely business-like
and preoccupied, opening one wardrobe after another,
and going to the mansard. They looked for her to call her
to dinner for a long time, and by the time she came we
had finished our soup. Somehow I recall all these trivial

details affectionately, and I have the liveliest remem-
brance of this day, though nothing particular happened
on it. After dinner Zhenya read, reclining in a deep arm-
chair, and I sat on the lowest step of the verandah. Nobody spoke. The sky was enveloped in clouds, and there
was a light drizzle. It was warm, the wind had long fall-
en, and it seemed as if this day would go on for ever.
Yekaterina Pavlovna, who was still heavy with sleep,
came on to the verandah, holding a fan.

"Oh, Mamma," said Zhenya, kissing her hand. "It's
bad for you to sleep in the day-time!"

They adored each other. When one of them went into
the garden, the other was sure to appear on the verandah, and call out, her glance travelling among the trunks
of the trees: "Coo-ee, Zhenya!" or "Mamma, where are
you?" They always said their prayers together, and they
were equally devout, understanding each other perfectly,
even when they said nothing. And their opinions of other
people were the same. Yekaterina Pavlovna very soon
got fond of me, too, and when I did not come for two
or three days she would send to know if I was well. She,
too, inspected my sketches admiringly, and told me everything that happened as freely and frankly as Missie,
not infrequently confiding her domestic secrets in me.

She went in awe of her eldest daughter. Leda had no
caressing ways, and only talked about serious things. She
lived her own special life and was for her mother and
her sister the sacred, somewhat enigmatic figure that
the admiral, sequestered in his cabin, is for sailors.

"Our Leda is a fine person, isn't she?" the mother
often said.

And now, while the rain fell gently, we talked about
Leda.

"She's marvellous," said the mother, adding in con-
spiratorial undertones, glancing timidly around, "there
are very few like her, but, you know, I begin to be rather
alarmed. Schools, dispensaries, books—are all very well,

but why go to extremes? She's nearly twenty-four, it's time for her to be thinking seriously about her future. All those books and dispensaries make one blind to the passage of time.... It's time for her to get married."

Zhenya, pale from her reading, her hair rumpled, raised her head and said, as if to herself, but looking at her mother:

"We are all in the hands of God, Mummie."

And plunged into her book again.

Belokurov appeared in his peasant jacket and embroidered shirt. We played croquet and tennis, and when it got dark sat long round the supper-table, Leda again talking about schools and about Balagin, who had got the whole district into his hands. When I left the Volchaninovs that evening I carried away an impression of a long, long, idle day, and told myself mournfully that everything comes to an end in this world, however long it is. Zhenya saw us to the gate, and, perhaps because I had spent the whole day with her from morn till eve, I began to feel I should be lonely without her, to realize how dear this whole charming family was to me. And for the first time that summer the desire to paint a picture rose in me.

"Why should *your* life be so dull and colourless?" I asked Belokurov, as we walked home together. "*My* life is dull, boring, monotonous, because I'm an artist, a crank, I have been eaten up with envy, remorse, and disbelief in my own work from my youth up. I shall always be poor, I am a tramp, but you—you are a healthy, normal man, a landowner, a gentleman—why is your life so dreary, why do you get so little out of it? What is there to prevent you from falling in love with Leda or Zhenya, for instance?"

"You forget I love another woman," replied Belokurov.

I knew he meant Lyubov Ivanovna, the woman who

lived with him in the annexe. Every day I saw this lady, stout, chubby-faced, pompous, rather like a Michaelmas goose, walking about the garden, wearing Russian national costume and bead necklaces, always carrying an open parasol, and always being called by the servant to have a meal, or take tea. Three years before she had rented one of the annexes for the summer, and had remained there with Belokurov, apparently for the rest of her life. She was about ten years older than Belokurov, and kept him well in hand, so that before going anywhere he had to ask her permission. She often sobbed, in hoarse, masculine tones, and I had to send and tell her that if she did not stop I would give up my room; and then she would stop sobbing.

When we got home Belokurov sat on my sofa, thinking, his brows knitted, while I paced up and down the room, a prey to soft agitation, for all the world as if I were in love. I felt a desire to talk about the Volchaninovs.

"Leda is only capable of loving some member of the Zemstvo, somebody as keen on hospitals and schools as herself," I said. "But for a girl like that a man should be willing to walk about in iron boots, like the lover in the fairy-tale, not to speak of becoming a member of the Zemstvo. And Missie? What a darling that Missie is!"

With many an "er," Belokurov embarked upon protracted reflections on pessimism—the disease of our times. He spoke confidently, and by his tone it might have been thought that I was arguing with him. An endless, monotonous, sun-bleached steppe is not more dreary than a single individual who sits in one's room talking and talking, as if he never meant to stop.

"It's not a matter of pessimism or optimism," I said irately. "The point is that ninety per cent of people have no brains."

Belokurov took this remark as a personal affront, and went away offended.

"The Prince is staying at Malozemovo, and sends you greetings," said Leda to her mother. She had just come back from some visit and was taking off her gloves. "He was very interesting. He promised to raise the question of a medical post at Malozemovo at the next meeting of the council, but he says there's not much hope. Excuse me," she said, turning to me. "I keep forgetting this sort of thing can't be very interesting to you."

I felt a surge of irritation.

"Why not?" I asked, shrugging my shoulders. "You don't care to know my opinion, but I assure you this question interests me intensely."

"Does it?"

"Yes, it does. In my opinion a medical post is not required in Malozemovo."

My irritation communicated itself to her. Looking at me from narrowed eyes, she said:

"What is required then—landscape paintings?"

"Landscapes are not required, either. Nothing is required."

She had drawn off her gloves and was opening the newspaper which had just been brought from the post-office. A minute after she said quietly, obviously trying to keep her feelings under control:

"Last week Anna died in childbirth; if there had been a medical-aid post in the neighbourhood she would be alive now. I can't help thinking that even landscape-painters should deign to have some convictions in this respect."

"I have extremely definite convictions in this respect, I assure you," I replied, but she hid from me behind the newspaper, as if not wishing to hear me. "In my opinion medical-aid posts, schools, libraries, dispensaries, only serve the cause of enslavement, under existing circumstances. The people are fettered by heavy chains, and you do nothing to break them asunder, only add new links—there you have my convictions."

She raised her eyes to my face and smiled scornfully, but I went on, endeavouring to pin down my basic idea.

"What matters is not that Anna died in childbirth, but that Anna, Martha, and Pelageya must stoop over their work from morning to night, fall sick from onerous toil, spend their whole lives worrying over their hungry, sickly children, in fear of death and disease, dose themselves all their lives, fade early, age early, and die in filth and stench. As soon as their children grow up, they follow the example of their mothers, and hundreds of years pass like this, millions of people living in worse conditions than animals, merely to gain a crust of bread, to live in perpetual fear. And the true horror of their situation is that they never have time to think of their souls, of themselves as images of God. Hunger, cold, physical terror, perpetual toil, are like snow-drifts cutting off all paths to spiritual activities, to everything distinguishing human beings from animals and making life worth living. You go to their aid with hospitals and schools, but this does not deliver them from their chains, on the contrary, it enslaves them still. more, since, by introducing fresh superstitions into their lives, you increase their demands, not to mention the fact that they have to pay the Zemstvo for their leeches and their books, and, consequently, to work still harder."

"I shall not argue with you," said Leda, lowering the newspaper. "I have heard all this before. I will only say one thing—one can't just sit and do nothing. True, we are not saving humanity and perhaps we make many mistakes, but we do what we can, and—we are right. The loftiest and most sacred task of a cultured person is to serve his neighbours, and we endeavour to do so to the best of our abilities. You don't like what we do, but one can't please everyone, after all."

"True, Leda, true," said her mother.

She was always timid in the presence of Leda, glancing nervously at her when she spoke, afraid of saying something foolish or inappropriate. And she never contradicted her, always agreeing with her: "True, Leda, true."

"Peasant literacy, books full of wretched moralizings and popular maxims, and medical-aid posts can no more lessen their ignorance or their mortality rate than the light from your windows can light up this huge garden," I said. "You give them nothing, merely by your interference in the lives of these people creating fresh demands, fresh motives for working."

"But goodness me, something must be done!" said Leda irately, and the tone in which she spoke showed that she considered my arguments trifling and contemptible.

"People must be freed from heavy physical labour," I said. "Their burden must be lightened, they must be given a breathing-space, so that they do not have to spend their whole lives at the stove and the wash-tub, or working in the fields, but have time to think of their souls, too, and of God, and get a chance to display their spiritual abilities. Every individual has a spiritual vocation—the continual search for the truth and significance of life. Free them from coarse, physical toil, let them feel that they have liberty, then you will see the mockery that these books and dispensaries really are. When a person feels his true vocation, the only things that can satisfy him are religion, science, art—and not such trifles."

"Free them from toil!" mocked Leda. "As if that were possible!"

"Yes. Undertake some of their work yourself. If we all, town and country dwellers, all without exception, agreed to take our part in the labour on which the mass of humanity spend their time for the satisfaction of physical requirements, perhaps each one of us would not have to work more than two or three hours a day. Think how it would be if we all, rich and poor alike, worked only three hours a day, and had the rest of the time to ourselves! And think what it would mean if, in order to depend still less on our bodies and work still less, we were to invent machinery to substitute toil, and try to reduce the number of our requirements to a minimum! We would harden ourselves and our children, so that they need not fear hunger and cold, and we need not worry constantly over their health, as Anna, Martha, and Pelageya do. Just think, if we did not take medicine, and maintain dispensaries, tobacco factories and distilleries—what a lot of spare time we should have as a result! We could devote this time in united work on science and art. Just as the peasants sometimes repair the roads in a body, we could, all together, by general consent, search for the truth and meaning of life, and—of this I am sure—the truth would very soon be discovered, humanity would be freed from the perpetual, agonizing, oppressive fear of death—and even from death itself."

"But you contradict yourself," said Leda. "You preach science, and reject the idea of literacy."

"The literacy which enables a person to do no more than spell out tavern-signs, and every now and then read books he cannot understand, has existed in our country since the time of Rurik; Gogol's Petrushka has long been able to read, and yet the country-side is just as it was in Rurik's time. It is not literacy that we need, but leisure for the full display of our spiritual abilities. It is not schools, but universities that we need."

"You deny medicine."

"Yes. It would only be required for the study of disease as a natural phenomenon, and not for its cure. If treatment is required, let it be, not of disease, but of its causes. Remove the main cause—physical labour, and there will be no more diseases. I do not recognize that science which aspires to heal," I continued excitedly. "True science and art aim not at temporary, partial measures, but at what is eternal and general. They seek for the truth and meaning of life, they seek God, the soul, and when they are fastened down to the needs of the moment, to dispensaries and libraries, they can only complicate and burden life. We have plenty of doctors, chemists and lawyers, and there are plenty of literate persons now, but no biologists, mathematicians, philosophers, poets. Our brains, our spiritual energy, are wasted on the satisfaction of temporary, passing needs. . . . Scientists, writers and painters work with a will; thanks to them the comforts of life increase daily, our physical demands multiply, and yet we are far from the truth, and man still remains the most predatory, the uncleanest of animals, and everything tends towards the degeneracy of humanity as a whole and the irreparable loss of vitality. In such conditions the life of the artist is meaningless and the more talented he is the worse and the more incomprehensible his function, since superficially it would appear that he works for the entertainment of a predatory, unclean animal, by supporting the existing order of things. And I don't want to work, and I won't. . . . Nothing is wanted, let the world rattle to smithereens. . . ."

"Go away, Missie," said Leda to her sister, apparently considering my words unsuited to the hearing of so young a girl.

Zhenya glanced mournfully from her sister to her mother, and went away.

"People usually say nice things like that when they wish to justify their own indifference," said Leda. "It's much easier to deny the usefulness of hospitals and schools, than to cure and to teach. . . ."

"True, Leda, true," said her mother.

"You say you will throw up painting," continued
Leda. "Apparently you rate your work very high. Let's
stop arguing, we shall never agree, for I rate the most im-
perfect of those libraries and dispensaries, you have just
referred to so contemptuously, higher than all the landscape paintings in the world." And she turned abruptly to
her mother, and began speaking in quite a different voice.
"The Prince has got very thin and has changed greatly
since he was last here. They're sending him to Vichy."

She talked to her mother about the Prince, to avoid
talking to me. Her face was flushed, and to conceal her
agitation, she bent low over the table as if she were
short-sighted, and pretended to be reading the paper.
My presence was evidently disagreeable to her. I took
my leave and went home.

<h2 style="text-align:center">IV</h2>

It was very still in the courtyard. The village on the
other side of the pond was already asleep, not a light
was to be seen, but for the pale reflections of the stars
shimmering almost imperceptibly on the surface of the
pond. At the gates with the lions Zhenya stood motionless, waiting to see me out. "They're all asleep in the
village," I said, trying to make out her features in the
darkness, but only seeing a pair of dark, mournful eyes
fixed on my face. "The inn-keeper and the horse-thieves
are peacefully asleep, but we, respectable folk, irritate
one another and argue."

It was a melancholy August night, melancholy, because there was a hint of autumn in the air. The moon
was rising from behind a crimson cloud, but it scarcely
lit up the road, on either side of which extended the
autumn fields. Shooting stars darted continually about
the sky. Zhenya walked beside me along the road and
tried not to look up, so as not to see the shooting stars,
which for some reason or other frightened her.

235

"I think you are right," she said, shivering in the evening dampness. "If all of us, all together, were to devote ourselves to spiritual activities, we would soon discover everything."

"Of course. We are higher beings, and if we really appreciated the power of human genius and lived only for higher aims, we should at last become like gods. But that will never be—humanity is degenerating, and soon there will not be a trace of genius left."

When we were out of sight of the gates, Zhenya stood still and hastily pressed my hand.

"Good night," she said, shivering. She had nothing but a thin blouse over her shoulders, and cringed with cold. "Come tomorrow."

The thought of being alone, in this irritated state of dissatisfaction with myself and others, terrified me. I, too, began trying not to look at the shooting stars.

"Stay with me a little longer," I said. "Do!"

I was in love with Zhenya. Perhaps I had fallen in love with her for her way of meeting me and seeing me off, for the tender, admiring glances she cast at me. Her pale face, thin neck and arms, her delicacy, her idleness, her books, held a wistful appeal for me. And her mind? I suspected her of having an unusual brain, I admired her broad-mindedness, perhaps because she thought differently from the severe beauteous Leda, who did not like me. Zhenya liked me as an artist, I had conquered her heart by my talent, and I desired passionately to paint for her alone, dreaming of her as my little queen, who would, together with me, hold sway over these villages, fields, this mist, and evening glow, this country-side, so delightful, so exquisite, amidst which I had till now felt so hopelessly lonely and superfluous.

"Wait a little longer," I pleaded. "Only a few minutes."

I took off my coat and put it over her chilly shoulders. Afraid of looking funny and ugly in a man's coat, she laughed and threw it off, and I put my arms round her and began showering kisses on her face, shoulders and hands.

"Till tomorrow," she whispered, embracing me cautiously, as if afraid to disturb the stillness of the night. "We have no secrets from one another, I shall have to tell my mother and sister everything, immediately.... Oh, dear, I'm so frightened! Mamma's all right, Mamma is fond of you—but Leda!"

She ran back towards the gate.

"Good-bye!" she cried.

I stood listening to her retreating footsteps for a minute or two. I did not want to go home, and there was no reason for going there. I stood deep in thought for a short time, and then sauntered slowly back, to have another look at the house in which she lived, the dear innocent old house, with its mansard windows looking down at me as if they were eyes, as if they understood everything. I passed the verandah, sat on a bench near the tennis-court, in the darkness beneath an ancient willow, and looked at the house from there. In the windows of the mansard, where Missie's room was, a light shone brilliantly, and then turned a sober green—someone had put a shade on the lamp. Shadows moved.... My heart was filled with tenderness, calm and content— delighted to discover that I was capable of falling in love—and yet at the same time I was worried by the thought that at this moment, a few paces away, Leda lived in one of the rooms of this house, Leda who disliked, perhaps detested me. I sat there waiting for Zhenya to appear, straining my ears, and it seemed to me I could hear talking in the mansard.

About an hour passed. The green light went out and the shadows could no longer be seen. The moon now rode high over the house and lit up the sleeping garden and deserted walks. The dahlias and roses in the bed in front of the house stood out distinctly, but they all looked the same colour. It grew really cold. I went out of the garden, picked up my coat from the road, and wandered slowly homewards.

When I went to the Volchaninovs the next afternoon, the glass door into the garden was wide open. I sat down on the verandah, hoping Zhenya would suddenly appear on the tennis-court, or on one of the paths, listening for the sound of her voice from the house. Then I went into the drawing-room, and after that the dining-room. Not a soul was in sight. From the dining-room I made my way through the long passage into the hall, and back again. There were several doors opening into the passage, and from one of the rooms could be heard the voice of Leda:

"The crow had somewhere found a bit of—" she was saying loudly, in a sing-song voice—dictating probably. "... a bit of cheese. ... The crow— Who's there?" she cried suddenly, hearing my steps.

"It's me."

"Oh. Excuse me I can't come to you just now, I'm giving Dasha her lesson."

"Is Yekaterina Pavlovna in the garden?"

"No. She and my sister left this morning on a visit to my aunt in the Penza province. And in the winter they'll probably go abroad," she added, after a short pause. "A crow had ... somewhere ... found ... a bit of cheese. ... Written that down?"

I went into the hall and stood there, staring vacantly at the pond and the distant village, my ears still assailed by the words: "...a bit of cheese. ... The crow had somewhere found a bit of cheese...."

I went off the estate by the road I had approached it from the first time, but in reverse—from the courtyard to the garden, past the house, till I got to the lime-tree avenue. ... Here a small boy ran after me and gave me a note. "I told my sister everything and she insists that we part," I read. "I had not the heart to grieve her by disobedience. May God send you happiness—forgive me! If you only knew how bitterly Mamma and I are crying."

Then came the fir walk, the broken railings.... In the field where the rye had been in bloom and the quail had given its cries, there now wandered cows and hobbled horses. Here and there on hillocks the winter crops showed green. A prosaic everyday mood enveloped me and I was ashamed of all I had said at the Volchaninovs', and once more life became a tedious affair. When I got home I packed up my things, and left for Petersburg that evening.

I never saw the Volchaninovs again. Not so long ago I met Belokurov in the train on my way to the Crimea. He was still wearing his peasant coat and embroidered shirt, and when I asked him how he was, he replied: "Quite well, thanks to your prayers!" We had a talk. He had sold his estate and bought another, a smaller one, in the name of Lyubov Ivanovna. He could not tell me much about the Volchaninovs. Leda still lived at Shelkovka and taught in the village school. She had gradually contrived to gather round her a circle of people in sympathy with her ideas, and these composed a powerful party, and at the last Zemstvo meetings they had black-balled Balagin, who till then had kept the whole district in his hands. All he could tell me of Zhenya was that she did not live at home, and he did not know where she was.

I have begun to forget the house with the mansard, but every once in a while, painting or reading, I recall for no apparent reason the green light in the window, the sound of my own steps echoing in the nocturnal fields, that night I returned home, in love, chafing my cold hands. Still less frequently, in moments of loneliness and melancholy, I yield to vague memories, till I gradually begin to feel that I, too, am remembered, that I am being waited for, and that we shall meet....

Missie ... where are you?

1896

YONICH

I

When fresh arrivals to the town of S. complained of boredom and the monotony of life there, the old-established inhabitants pointed out in its favour that S. was a most interesting town, that it had a library, a theatre, and a club, that balls were given there, and, finally, that there were many clever, interesting and pleasant families whose acquaintance could be made. And they would point to the Turkin family as an example of all that was cultured and talented.

The Turkins lived in the main street, next door to the Governor's residence, in a house which was their own property. The head of the family, Ivan Petrovich, a stout, handsome, dark-haired man with side-whiskers, got up private theatricals for charitable purposes and took the part of old generals, and coughed to extremely humourous effect. He had a store of anecdotes, charades, and proverbs, was fond of a joke, indeed, was quite a wag, and it was impossible to tell from his expression whether he was serious or joking. His wife, Vera Yosifovna, was a gaunt, pleasant-faced lady who wore pince-nez and wrote stories and novels, which she was always ready to read aloud to visitors. They had a daughter called Yekaterina

Ivanovna, a young lady who played the piano. In a word, each member of the family had some gift or other. The Turkins were the soul of hospitality and showed off their talents light-heartedly, with frank simplicity. The big stone-built house was always cool in the summer, its back windows looking out on an old, shady garden, where nightingales sang in the spring. When there was company the house would ring with the sound of knives being sharpened in the kitchen, and the smell of fried onions would perfume the yard, giving promise of an abundant and tasty supper.

And Dr. Dmitri Yonich Startsev, the newly appointed Zemstvo medical officer, was told, as soon as he took up his residence in Dyalizh, some nine versts from S., that, as a cultured man, he simply must make the acquaintance of the Turkins. He was introduced to Ivan Petrovich in the street one winter day. They discussed the weather, the theatre, and the cholera epidemic, and an invitation followed. So on one of the spring church-holidays—the Ascension it was—Startsev, having seen all his patients for the day, set off for the town in search of relaxation and to make some necessary purchases while he was about it. He went on foot, at a leisurely pace (he had not yet set up his own carriage), singing to himself the whole way:

"Ere I had learned to drink of tears from the chalice of life."

He dined in town, walked about the park, and, the invitation of Ivan Petrovich coming into his head, decided to go to the Turkins and see what sort of people they were.

"Howdy! Howdy!" said Ivan Petrovich, who met him in the porch. "Delighted to see such a welcome visitor! Come in, I'll introduce you to my better half. I was telling him, Vera," he went on, after introducing the doctor to his wife, "I was telling him he has no earthly right to stick in his hospital, it's his duty to bestow his leisure on society. I'm right, darling, aren't I?"

"Sit here," said Vera Yosifovna, pointing to a chair
next to herself. "You can make up to me. My husband is
as jealous as Othello, but we will try to be discreet,
won't we?"

"Little witch!" murmured Ivan Petrovich tenderly, im-
printing a kiss on her brow. "You've chosen a very good
moment for your visit," he said, turning to his visitor
again. "My better half has just finished a great enormous
novel, and she's going to read it aloud to us this evening."

"Jean, ducky," said Vera Yosifovna to her husband.
"*Dites que l'on nous donne du thé.*"

Startsev was next introduced to Yekaterina Ivanovna,
an eighteen-year-old damsel, strikingly like her mother,
and equally thin and pleasant-faced. Her expression was
still childish, and she had a slender delicate frame. And
her virginal breasts, already beginning to develop, held
in their beauty and healthiness, a suggestion of spring,
the genuine spring. Afterwards they sat down to have
tea, with jam, honey, sweets, and some wonderful biscuits
which fairly melted in the mouth. With the approach of
dusk visitors began dropping in, and Ivan Petrovich, his
eyes smiling, said to every one of them: "Howdy! Howdy!"
When everybody had come they seated themselves in the
drawing-room with grave faces and Vera Yosifovna read
her novel. It began with the words: "'Twas bitter cold. . . ."
The windows were wide-open and the sound of knives
clanging in the kitchen came through them, together with
the smell of frying onions. . . ."

It was very peaceful sitting in the soft arm-chairs,
with the lights blinking lazily in the semi-dark of the
drawing-room. And it was hard to realize, on this summer evening, with the sound of voices and laughter coming from the street, and the fragrance of lilac wafted in
from the garden, that "'twas bitter cold" and that the setting sun could be lighting up with its cold rays the snowy
plain and the solitary wayfarer. Vera Yosifovna read how

the young and beautiful countess got up schools, hospitals and libraries in her native village, and how she fell in love with the roving artist, describing things that never happen in real life, and yet it was so pleasant and comforting to listen to her, while calm delightful thoughts passed through one's mind, that nobody wanted to get up. . . .

"Not badsome!" said Ivan Petrovich softly.

And one of the visitors, who had been listening, with his thoughts somewhere far, far away, said almost inaudibly:

"Yes, indeed. . . ."

An hour passed, and another. In the town park, nearby, an orchestra was playing, and a choir was singing. When Vera Yosifovna closed her note-book nobody spoke for five minutes, all listening to "Luchinushka," which the choir was singing, and the song spoke to them of what was lacking in the novel, and of real life.

"Do you publish your works in the periodicals?" Startsev asked Vera Yosifovna.

"No," she replied. "I don't publish them at all. I write them and put them away in a cupboard. Why should I publish them? We have enough to live on," she added by way of explanation.

And for some reason or other everyone sighed.

"And now you play us something, Kitten," Ivan Petrovich said to his daughter.

The lid of the grand piano was raised, the books were in readiness, on the music rack, and the instrument was opened. Yekaterina Ivanovna sat down and struck the keys with both hands. Then she struck them again with all her might, and again, and yet again. Her shoulders and breasts quivered, and she went on pertinaciously striking the keys in the same place, as if she did not mean to stop till she had driven them inside the piano. The drawing-room filled with thunder; everything thundered—the floor, the ceiling, the furniture. . . . Yekaterina Ivanovna played an intricate passage, the whole interest of which lay in its difficulty. It was long and monotonous, and Startsev, as he listened, pictured to himself rocks tumbling from the summit of a high mountain; they kept tumbling, tumbling, one after the other, and he wished they would stop, though he found Yekaterina Ivanovna, rosy with the exertion, strong, energetic, a lock of hair falling over her forehead, exceedingly attractive. After a winter in Dyalizh, amongst sick people and peasants, it was very pleasant, very novel, to be sitting in a drawing-room, looking at this youthful, elegant, and, no doubt pure creature, and listening to these loud, tiresome, but nevertheless cultured sounds. . . .

"Well, Kitten, you surpassed yourself today," said Ivan Petrovich with tears in his eyes, when his daughter, finishing her piece, got up. 'You'll never improve upon that, Denis, if you die in the attempt.' "

Everyone surrounded her, congratulating her, marvelling, vowing that they had not heard such music for ages, while she listened in silence, with a slight smile on her face, her whole figure expressing triumph.

"Splendid! Wonderful!"

And Startsev, too, yielding to the general enthusiasm, cried: "Splendid!"

"Where did you study?" he asked Yekaterina Ivanovna. "At the conservatoire?"

"No, I'm only preparing for the conservatoire, in the meantime I'm taking lessons here, from Madame Zavlovskaya."

"Did you graduate from the high school here?"

"Oh, no," Vera Yosifovna answered for her. "We had teachers for her at home, you will agree that there might be bad influences in the high school or at a boarding-school. While a girl is growing she ought to be under the influence of no one but her mother."

"But I intend to go to the conservatoire," said Yekaterina Ivanovna.

"Oh, no, our Kitten loves her mamma. Our Kitten would not grieve her papa and mamma."

"I will go, I will!" said Yekaterina Ivanovna, with humorous petulance, stamping her foot.

At supper-time it was the turn of Ivan Petrovich to show off his talents. Smiling with his eyes alone, he related anecdotes, joked, set comic problems which he solved himself, all the time speaking in his own peculiar language, which he had acquired by long practice in waggishness, and which had apparently now become a habit with him: *splendiferous, not badsome, I thank thee humblesomely.*

But this was not all. When the guests, sated and happy, flocked into the hall to look for their coats and walking-sticks, the footman Pavel, or as they called him, Pava, a fourteen-year-old boy with a cropped head and chubby cheeks, hovered around them.

"Perform, Pava, perform!" said Ivan Petrovich.

Pava threw himself into an attitude, raised one hand and uttered in tragic accents :

"Perish, unhappy female!"

And everyone laughed.

"Amusing!" thought Startsev, as he went out of the house.

He went to a restaurant for a drink of beer, and then walked back to Dyalizh. All the way home he hummed:

"The melting accents of your tender voice. . . ."

After his six-mile walk he went to bed without the slightest sensation of fatigue, telling himself that he could have walked another six miles with pleasure.

"Not badsome!" he remembered, laughing, as he fell asleep.

II

Startsev kept meaning to visit the Turkins again, but he had a great deal to do in the hospital and could never find an hour or two to spare. Over a year passed thus in work and solitude. And one day a letter in a blue envelope came to him from the town. . . .

Vera Yosifovna had long suffered from headaches, but of late, with Kitten threatening every day to go to the conservatoire, the attacks had become more and more frequent. All the doctors in the town visited the Turkins, and at last the turn of the Zemstvo doctor had come. Vera Yosifovna wrote him a touching letter, asking him to come and ease her sufferings. Startsev visited her, and after this began to be often, very often at the Turkins. . . . He really did manage to help Vera Yosifovna a little, and all visitors were told that he was an extraordinary, a marvellous doctor. But it was no longer on account of her headaches that he went to the Turkins. . . .

It was a holiday. Yekaterina Ivanovna had finished her long, tedious exercises on the piano. Then they all sat long at the dining-room table, drinking tea. Ivan Petrovich was in the middle of a funny story when there was a ring at the front door, and he had to go out to meet some visitor. Startsev took advantage of the moment of bustle to whisper, in great agitation, in the ear of Yekaterina Ivanovna:

"Do not torture me, for God's sake, I implore you. Let's go into the garden."

She shrugged her shoulders as if she were surprised and did not understand what he wanted, but she got up and went out.

"You practise three or four hours," he said, following her. "Then you sit with your mamma, and there's never a chance to speak to you. Give me just one quarter of an hour, I implore you!"

Autumn was approaching, and the old garden was still and melancholy, the walks strewn with dark leaves. The days were drawing in.

"I haven't seen you for a whole week," continued Startsev. "And if you only knew what suffering that is for me! Let's sit down. I want to speak to you."

They had their favourite place in the garden—a bench
beneath an ancient spreading maple. And now they sat
down on this bench.

"What is it you want?" Yekaterina Ivanovna asked
in a cold, business-like voice.

"I haven't seen you for a whole week, it's ages since
I heard your voice! I long passionately, I thirst for your
voice! Speak!"

He was captivated by her freshness, by the innocent
expression in her eyes, her naive cheeks. Even in the fit
of her dress he found something extraordinarily sweet,
something in its simple and innocent grace that was
touching. And at the same time, despite this innocence,
she seemed to him very clever, wise beyond her years.
He could talk to her about literature, art, or anything
he liked, could complain to her about life and people,
despite the fact that she sometimes started laughing
in a very disconcerting manner in the middle of a
serious conversation, or ran back to the house. Like almost
all the girls in S., she was a great reader (there was very
little reading done in S., and the local librarians declared
that but for the girls and the young Jews they might as
well close the library), and this caused Startsev infinite
delight. Every time he saw her he asked her eagerly what
she had been reading the last few days, and listened
entranced when she told him.

"What have you been reading this week, since we last
met?" he now asked her. "Do tell me."

"I've been reading Pisemsky."

"Which of his books?"

"*A Thousand Souls*," replied Kitten. "And what
a funny name Pisemsky has—Alexei Feofilaktich!"

"Where are you going?" cried Startsev in alarm, when
she suddenly got up and went towards the house. "I
simply must have a talk with you, there's something I
must tell you.... Stay with me—if only five minutes, I
implore you!"

She halted as if intending to speak, then thrust a note awkwardly into his hand and ran into the house, where she immediately sat down to the piano again.

"Be in the cemetery at Demetti's tomb, at eleven to-night," read Startsev.

"Now that really is silly," he thought, when he had recovered from his surprise. "Why the cemetery? What ever for?"

It was all perfectly clear: Kitten was trying to fool him. Nobody in his senses would make an appointment at night, a long way from town, when they could so easily meet in the street, or in the municipal park. And did it become him, a Zemstvo medical officer, an intelligent, highly-respected individual to be sighing after a girl, receiving notes, roaming about cemeteries, committing follies which a modern schoolboy would laugh at? What would this affair lead to? What would his colleagues say, if they discovered it? Such were the thoughts of Startsev, as he threaded his way among the tables in the club, and yet at half past eleven he suddenly started off for the cemetery.

He now had his own carriage and pair, and a coach-man named Panteleimon, who sported a velveteen waist-coat. The moon was shining. It was still and warm, but with an autumnal warmth. In the suburb of the town, near the slaughter-house, dogs were howling. Startsev left his carriage at the outskirts of the town, in a side-street, and went on foot to the cemetery. "Everyone has his peculiarities," he told himself. "Kitten is a queer girl, and who knows?—perhaps she really meant it. perhaps she'll be there." And he yielded to the intoxication of this vain, feeble hope.

The last part of the way was across a field. The cemetery was a dark strip in the distance, like a belt of woods, or a great park. A white stone wall came into sight, and then a gate.... In the moonlight the in-scription over the gate could be read: "Your hour, too, will strike." Startsev pushed open the wicket-gate, and found himself in a broad alley lined on either side by white crosses and monuments and tall poplars, all casting long black shadows across his path. Everything was black or white, the drowsy trees spreading their branches over the white stones. It seemed to be lighter here than in the field. The leaves of the maples looked like paws, and stood out in bold relief against the yellow sand of the alley and the white tombstones, and the inscriptions on the monuments were clearly visible. Startsev was struck by the thought that he was seeing for the first time in his life a thing which he would probably never again see— a world unlike any other world, a world in which the moonlight was as soft and sweet as if this place were its cradle, where there was no life, none at all, but where, in every darkling poplar, in every grave, could be felt the presence of mystery, fraught with the promise of eternal life—still and exquisite. From the tombstones, the fading flowers, and the autumnal smell of decaying leaves, sorrow and peace seemed to be wafted.

All round was silence. The stars gazed down from the sky as if in profound humility and Startsev's footsteps struck a harsh discordant note. It was only while the church clock was striking the hour, and he was imagining himself dead, buried for all time, that he felt as if somebody were looking at him, and fancied for a moment that this was not peace and stillness, but the profound melancholy of non-existence, suppressed despair....

Demetti's monument was in the form of a chapel, with an angel on the roof. Some time in the past an Italian operatic troupe had visited the town of S., and one of the singers had died, and been buried here, and this monument erected to her memory. Nobody in the town remembered her any more, but the lamp hanging over the entrance to her tomb reflected the moonlight and seemed to be burning.

There was no one in sight. And who would be coming
here at midnight? But Startsev waited, and, as if the
moonlight had kindled his passion, waited ardently,
picturing to himself kisses, embraces.... He sat beside
the tomb about half an hour, and then began walking up
and down one of the side paths, his hat in his hand,
waiting, wondering how many of the women and girls
in these graves had been beautiful and fascinating, had
loved, burned with passion at nights, as they yielded to
their lovers' caresses. What a sorry jest Mother Nature
plays upon human beings, and how humiliating to have
to acknowledge this! Startsev, pondering all these things,
felt a desire to cry out that he must have love, that he
must have love at all costs! He no longer contemplated
white slabs of marble, but bodies, he saw their forms
hiding bashfully in the shadows of trees, he could feel
their warmth, and at last the amorous languor became
unbearable.

And suddenly, as if a curtain had been lowered, the
moon went behind a cloud and darkness fell on all around.
Startsev could hardly find the gateway, for it was by now
as dark as an autumn night, and he wandered about for
an hour and a half looking for the side-street in which
he had left his carriage.

"I'm so tired I can hardly stand," he told Panteleimon.

And sinking luxuriously into the seat he said to
himself:

"I shouldn't let myself get so fat."

III

The next day he went to the Turkins' in the evening
fully intending to propose. But the moment was unsuit-
able, since the hairdresser was in Yekaterina Ivanovna's
bedroom, doing her hair. She was going to a dance at
the club.

Once more a long time had to be spent in the dining-
room over tea. Ivan Petrovich, seeing that his guest was

pensive and dull, drew some papers from his waistcoat pocket and read aloud a letter from a German steward, written in excruciatingly funny, broken Russian.

"And they'd probably give her a pretty good dowry," thought Startsev, listening abstractedly.

After his sleepless night he was in a state of bewilderment, as if he had been given something sweet and soporific to drink. There was a sensation at once dreamy, joyful and warm in his heart, but a cold and heavy particle in his brain was arguing:

"Stop before it is too late. Is she a match for you? She is spoilt and wilful, sleeps till two in the afternoon, and you are a sexton's son, a Zemstvo doctor...."

"Well, what about it?" he thought.

"Besides, if you marry her," continued the particle, "her relations will make you give up your work in the Zemstvo, and come to live in the town."

"Well," he thought, "and why not live in the town? They'll give her a dowry and we'll set up house...."

At last Yekaterina Ivanovna came looking so fresh and pretty in her low-cut ball dress, and Startsev gazed his fill at her, falling into such an ecstasy that he could not utter a word and could only look at her and laugh.

She began saying good-bye all round and he—there was nothing for him to stay for—got up, saying it was time for him to go home. His patients were waiting for him.

"Too bad!" said Ivan Petrovich. "Off you go, then! And you might as well give Kitten a lift!"

Out of doors it was dark and drizzling, and they could only discover where the carriage was from the sound of Panteleimon's hoarse coughing. The hood of the carriage was raised.

Ivan Petrovich joked incessantly as he helped his daughter into the carriage and bade them a facetious farewell. "Off with you! Goodeebye!"

They drove off.

"I went to the cemetery yesterday," said Startsev. "How ungenerous and cruel of you it was...."

"You were at the cemetery?"

"Yes, and I waited almost two hours. I suffered...."

"Serve you right—can't you understand a joke?"

Yekaterina Ivanovna, delighted to have fooled her admirer so successfully and to be loved so ardently, laughed loudly, and the next moment cried out in alarm, for the horses turned sharply in at the club gates, and the carriage lurched. Startsev put his arm round her waist. In her fright she leaned against him, and he could not refrain from pressing passionate kisses on her lips and chin, and holding her still more tightly.

"That'll do," she said coldly.

And a moment later she was no longer in the carriage, and the policeman standing by the brightly lighted entrance to the club, shouted brutally to Panteleimon:

"What are you waiting for, dolt? Move on!"

Startsev went home, but soon came out again. In another man's frock-coat, and a stiff white tie which puckered up and slipped to one side, he was sitting at midnight in the club drawing-room, and saying ecstatically to Yekaterina Ivanovna:

"Oh, how little do those know who have never loved! It seems to me that no one has ever yet described love faithfully, indeed it is practically impossible to describe this tender, joyous, torturing feeling, and whoever has experienced it, if only once, will never try to put it into words. Why go in for preliminaries, for descriptions? Why all this superfluous eloquence? My love is boundless.... I beg you, I implore you, " Startsev ended up, getting it out at last, "to be my wife!"

"Dmitri Yonich," said Yekaterina Ivanovna, looking extremely grave, after a slight pause. "Dmitri Yonich, I am very grateful to you for the honour, I respect you, but..." she rose and went on speaking in a standing position, "but, forgive me, I cannot be your wife. Let us speak plainly. You know very well, Dmitri Yonich, that I love art most of all in life, I love music madly, I adore it, I have consecrated my whole life to it. I want to be a musician, I want fame, success, liberty, and you want me to go on living in this town, to continue this dull, futile life, which has become intolerable to me. Just somebody's wife? No, thank you! A person should aspire to some lofty, brilliant aim, and family life would bind me for ever. Dmitri Yonich" (she smiled faintly, for when she pronounced the name "Dmitri Yonich," she could not help remembering "Alexei Feofilaktich"), "Dmitri Yonich, you are a kind, generous, clever man, you are better than all the rest—" here tears welled up in her eyes, "I feel for you with all my heart, but ... but, I'm sure you understand...."

She turned away to prevent herself from crying, and went out of the drawing-room.

Startsev's heart no longer fluttered nervously. Going out of the club into the street the first thing he did was to tear off his stiff tie and take a deep breath. He was somewhat abashed, his vanity had received an affront— he had not anticipated a refusal—and he could not believe that all his dreams, torments and hopes had come to such a banal end, like the final scene of some little comedy acted by amateurs. He was so sorry for his feelings, for this love of his, that he felt like sobbing, or bringing his umbrella down with all his strength on the broad shoulders of Panteleimon.

For three days everything went wrong with him, he neither ate nor slept, but when the news reached him that Yekaterina Ivanovna had gone to Moscow to enter the conservatoire he quieted down and lived as before.

Afterwards, when he happened to remember how he had roamed about the cemetery, or how he had driven all over the town looking for a frock-coat, he stretched lazily and said:

"What a to-do!"

IV

Four years passed. Startsev had a big practice in the town. Every morning he hastily examined his patients in Dyalizh, and then drove to his town patients, and now he drove not in a carriage-and-pair, but behind three horses with jingling bells, and returned home late at night. He had grown fat and ponderous and avoided walking, which gave him palpitations. Panteleimon had grown fat, too, and the broader his girth became, the more mournfully he sighed and complained of his bitter lot: "Always on the move."

Startsev visited many houses and met many people, but he never grew intimate with any of them. The conversation, views, the very look of the townsfolk, irritated him. He had gradually learned that so long as he played cards and supped with a man in the town of S., the latter would be peaceable, good-humoured and even comparatively intelligent, but the moment the conversation turned to anything but food, say to politics or science, he would either be utterly bewildered, or begin to air a philosophy so stupid and cruel that one could only leave him alone and go away. When Startsev tried to talk even with a liberal-minded man about the fact that humanity, thank God, is progressing and that in time we shall be able to dispense with passports and capital punishment, his interlocutor would shoot him an oblique, mistrustful glance, and ask: "So people will be able to cut one another's throat in the street as much as they like, then?" And when Startsev said during supper or tea that everyone ought to work, that life without work was impossible, all present took it as a reproach, and began arguing insistenly. And with it all, these ordinary people did nothing, nothing whatever, and interested themselves in nothing, and it was impossible to find anything to talk to them about. And Startsev evaded conversation, only eating and playing vint with them, and when he happened to be in a house where some

254

domestic event was being celebrated, and they invited him to take part in it, he would sit down and eat in silence, staring at his plate. For everything said on these occasions was uninteresting, unjust, stupid, and he would be irritated and excite himself; but he held his tongue, and because he always stared at his plate in severe silence, he was known in the town as a "jumped-up Pole," although there was not a drop of Polish blood in his veins.

He avoided such entertainments as the theatre and concerts, but played vint every evening, for about three hours with complete enjoyment. There was yet another amusement into which he was gradually and imperceptibly drawn: this was to take out of his pockets of an evening all the bank-notes accumulated during his rounds; and these notes with which his pockets were crammed—some yellow, some green, some smelling of scent, some of vinegar, incense, or fish—sometimes amounted to as much as seventy rubles. When he had several hundred of them he paid the money into his account at the Mutual Credit Society.

In the four years since the departure of Yekaterina Ivanovna he had only been twice at the Turkins, on the invitation of Vera Yosifovna, who was still being treated for headaches. Yekaterina Ivanovna came back to stay with her parents every summer, but he never saw her—somehow it did not come about.

And now four years had passed. One still, warm morning a letter was brought to the hospital. Vera Yosifovna wrote to Dmitri Yonich that she missed him very much, and that he simply must come and see her and ease her sufferings, and that today happened to be her birthday. At the bottom of the letter was a postscript: "I join in Mamma's request. K."

Startsev thought it over and in the evening went to the Turkins. Ivan Petrovich greeted him with his usual "Hullo-ullo-ullo!" smiling with his eyes alone, and added: "Bon-joursky!"

Vera Yosifovna, who had aged considerably, and
was now white-haired, pressed Startsev's hand, sighed
affectedly, and said:

"You don't want to make up to me, Doctor, you never
come to see us, I'm too old for you. But the young one
is here now, perhaps she will be more fortunate."

And Kitten? She was thinner and paler, but still
lovelier and more graceful. She was Yekaterina Ivanovna now, not a Kitten. Her freshness and expression
of child-like innocence had vanished. There was something new, something timid and guilty in her glance, as
if she no longer felt at home here, in the Turkin house.

"We haven't met for ages," she said, putting her
hand into his, and it was obvious that her heart was
beating violently. Looking fixedly and with curiosity into
his face, she continued: "You've got quite stout! You're
darker and more manly looking, but on the whole you
haven't changed much."

He still found her attractive, extremely attractive, but
there was something lacking in her now, or something
superfluous, he could not say exactly what, but whatever it was it prevented him from feeling as he had
before. He did not like her pallor, her new expression,
her faint smile, her voice, and very soon he was disliking her dress, the chair in which she sat, disliking something in the past, when he had almost married her.
He remembered his love, the hopes and dreams which
had agitated him four years ago, and he felt awkward.

There was tea and a cream tart. Vera Yosifovna read
her novel aloud, read of what never happens in real life,
and Startsev listened, and sat looking at her beautiful
grey head and waiting for her to finish.

"It is not the person unable to write stories who is
mediocre," he said to himself, "but the person who writes
them and is unable to conceal the fact."

But Ivan Petrovich said: "Not badsome!"

Then Yekaterina Ivanovna played long and noisily

and when she stopped everybody took a long time thanking and applauding her.

"It's a good thing I didn't marry her, after all," thought Startsev.

She looked at him, obviously expecting him to ask her to go into the garden, but he said nothing.

"Let's talk," she said, going over to him. "How are you getting on? What kind of a life do you have? I've been thinking about you all these days," she continued nervously. "I wanted to write to you, to go to see you in Dyalizh, I had determined to, but then I changed my mind—goodness knows what you feel about me now! I waited so impatiently for you to come today. Do come out into the garden."

They went out into the garden and sat down on the bench under the ancient maple-tree, as they had done four years ago. It was dark.

"Well now, how are you getting on?" said Yekaterina Ivanovna.

"I'm all right, thanks," replied Startsev.

He could not think of anything else to say. They sat in silence.

"I'm all worked up," said Yekaterina Ivanovna, putting her hand over her face. "Take no notice! I'm so glad to be home, so glad to see everyone, and I can't get used to it. What memories! I thought you and I would talk our heads off all night!"

He could see her face and her brilliantly shining eyes, and here, in the dark, she seemed younger than in the room, even her former child-like expression seemed to have come back. He could see she was looking at him with a naive curiosity, as if she wanted to get closer to him, to understand this man who had once loved her so ardently, so tenderly, and so vainly. Her eyes thanked him for that love. And he, too, recalled all that had happened down to the most trifling detail, how he had roamed about the cemetery, and how, in the small hours, exhausted, he had gone back to his home; and suddenly he felt sad, regretting the past. A flame flickered in his soul.

"Do you remember that night I took you to the club?" he said. "It was raining, dark. . . ."

The flame in his soul grew bigger, and now he felt a desire to talk, to bewail his life. . . .

"Ah me!" he sighed. "You ask me about my life. How do we live here? We don't live. We grow old and fat, we let ourselves go. One day follows another, life passes, drab and dingy, without any striking impressions or thoughts. . . . The day goes in making money, the evenings at the club, in the company of card-players, drinkers, blusterers, all of whom I detest. What sort of a life is that?"

"But you have your work, a noble aim in life. You used to be so fond of talking about your hospital. I was an odd sort of creature then, fancying myself a great pianist. All young ladies play the piano nowadays, and I did, too, like everyone else, but there was nothing special about me. I'm as much a pianist as Mamma is a novelist. I did not understand you then, of course, but afterwards, in Moscow, I often thought of you. I never thought of anything else. What a joy to be a Zemstvo doctor, to help sufferers, to serve the people! What a joy!" repeated Yekaterina Ivanovna enthusiastically. "When I thought about you in Moscow you seemed to me an ideal, lofty character. . . ."

Startsev remembered the notes he produced with such satisfaction from his pockets every evening, and the flame in his soul died down.

He got up to go back to the house. She took his arm.

"You're the best person I have ever known," she continued. "We will see one another and talk, won't we? Promise me that. I am not a real pianist, I am under no illusions about myself, and I will never play or talk about music in front of you."

When they re-entered the house and Startsev saw, in the lighted room, her face, the mournful, penetrating, grateful glance she bestowed on him, he felt a little uneasy, but assured himself once more:

"It's a good thing I didn't marry her."

He took his leave.

"You have no earthly right to leave before supper," said Ivan Petrovich, seeing him off. "It's extremely pee-kay-yulier on your part. Come on now, perform!" he cried, turning to Pava in the hall.

Pava, no longer a little boy, but a young man with a moustache, struck an attitude, raised his hand, and said in tragic accents:

"Perish, unhappy female!"

All this only irritated Startsev now. As he got into his carriage and looked out at the dark house and garden, once so dear to him, everything came back to him with a rush—Vera Yosifovna's novels, Kitten's noisy execution on the grand piano, Ivan Petrovich's witticisms, and Pava's tragic pose, and he asked himself, since the most talented people in the whole town were so mediocre, what was to be expected of the town itself?

Three days later Pava brought him a letter from Yekaterina Ivanovna.

"You never come to see us. Why?" she wrote. "I'm afraid you have changed towards us. I'm afraid, and the very thought terrifies me. Soothe me, come and tell me that everything is all right.

"I must see you. Your Y. T."

He read the letter, thought a moment, and said to Pava:

"Say I can't come today, my good man. I'm very busy. I'll come in a day or two."

But three days passed, and then a week, and still he did not go. Once, while driving by the Turkin house in his carriage, he told himself that he ought to look in,

if only for a few minutes, but reflected a little... and
drove by.

He never went to the Turkins again.

V

A few more years passed. Startsev had become still
stouter, quite obese, short of breath, and had to throw
back his head when he walked. It was a sight to see him
drive by, red-faced and chubby, his three horses jingling their bells, Panteleimon on the box seat, red-faced
and chubby, too, with rolls of fat on the back of his
neck, his arms extended straight in front of him as if
they were of wood, shouting to drivers coming towards
him: "Keep to the r-r-right!" Not a human being, but
some heathen god seemed to be passing by. His practice
in the town was now so extensive that he never had a
breathing space; he had a country-estate, and two
houses in the town, and had his eye on another, still
more profitable. Whenever he heard, in the Mutual Credit Society, of a house soon to be sold at auction, he
would enter it with scant ceremony, pass through all
the rooms, quite regardless of the half-dressed women and
children in them who looked at him in astonishment and
terror, tap with his stick on each door, asking:

"Is this the study? Is this a bedroom? And what
room is this?"

And all the while he would breathe heavily and mop
his perspiring brow.

He had many cares, but he did not throw up his post
as a Zemstvo doctor; the prey of avarice, he desired to get
what he could everywhere. He was now always referred
to as "Yonich," both in Dyalizh and the town. "Where's
Yonich off to?" or "Hadn't we better call in Yonich?"

His voice, no doubt owing to the layers of fat around
his throat, had become shrill and squeaky. His disposition, too, had changed, he had become irritable and

disagreeable. While examining his patients he would often lose his temper, bang impatiently on the floor with his stick, and exclaim, in his unpleasant voice:

"Kindly restrict yourself to answers to my questions. Don't talk unnecessarily."

He lives alone. His life is tedious, nothing interests him.

His love for Kitten was the only, probably the last joy, he ever knew during the whole of his sojourn in Dyalizh. He plays vint at the club of an evening, and then sits at a big table all by himself and has supper. He is always waited on by Ivan, the oldest and most respected of all the club servants. They bring him Lafitte number 17, and everyone, the managing staff, the chef, the footmen, know his likes and dislikes, and do their best to humour him, otherwise, which God forbid, he will suddenly fly into a rage and start knocking on the floor with his stick.

During supper he occasionally turns and joins in some conversation.

"What are you talking about? Eh? Who?"

And if the conversation at the next table should happen to turn on the Turkins, he asks:

"Are you talking about the Turkins? The ones whose daughter plays the piano?"

And that is about all there is to be said about him.

And the Turkins? Ivan Petrovich has not aged or altered in any way, he still jokes and relates funny stories. Vera Yosifovna reads her novels to her visitors with as much gusto and frankness as ever. And Kitten practises four hours a day. She has aged perceptibly, is often ill, and goes to the Crimea every autumn with her mother. When he sees them off, Ivan Petrovich wipes his eyes as the train draws out of the station, crying after it: "Goodeebyee!"

And he waves his handkerchief.

1898

THE MAN WHO LIVED IN A SHELL

The sportsmen, overtaken by darkness on the outskirts
of the village of Mironositskoye, decided to spend the
night in a shed belonging to Prokofy, the village elder.
There were two of them, Ivan Ivanich, the veterinary
surgeon, and Burkin, the high-school teacher. Ivan Ivanich bore a strange, hyphenated name: Chimsha-Himalaisky; the name did not seem to suit him, and everyone
called him simply by his name and patronymic—Ivan
Ivanich; he lived at a stud-farm not far from the town,
and was now hunting for the sake of an outing in the
fresh air. The high-school teacher Burkin spent every
summer on the estate of Count P. and was regarded by
the inhabitants of those parts as quite one of themselves.

Neither of them slept. Ivan Ivanich, a tall, lean old
man with a long moustache, sat outside the door, in the
moonlight, smoking his pipe. Burkin lay inside, on the
hay, concealed by the darkness.

They whiled away the time by telling each other stories. They spoke of Mavra, the wife of the village elder,
a perfectly healthy and by no means unintelligent woman, who had never been out of her native village in
her life. She had never seen a town or a railway, and

had spent the last ten years sitting by her stove, only venturing out at night.

"Is it so very strange, though?" said Burkin. "There are plenty of people in this world who are recluses by nature and strive, like the hermit-crab or the snail to retreat within their shells. Perhaps this is just a manifestation of atavism, a return to the times when our forbears had not yet become social animals, and inhabited solitary caves. Or perhaps such people are one of the varieties of the human species, who knows? I am no naturalist, and it is not for me to attempt to solve such problems; all I want to say is that people like Mavra are by no means rare phenomena. Why, only a month or two ago there died in our town a colleague of mine, Belikov, a teacher of Greek. You must have heard of him. He was famous for never stirring out of his house, even in the best weather, without an umbrella, galoshes and a wadded coat. His umbrella he kept in a case, he had a case of grey suède for his watch, and when he took out his pen-knife to sharpen a pencil, he had to draw it out of a case, too; even his face seemed to have a case of its own, since it was always hidden in his turned-up coat-collar. He wore dark glasses, and a thick jersey, and stopped up his ears with cotton wool, and when he engaged a droshky, made the izvozchik put up the hood. In fact, he betrayed a perpetual, irrepressible urge to create a covering for himself, as it were a case, to isolate him and protect him against external influences. Reality irritated and alarmed him and kept him in constant terror, and, perhaps to justify his timidity, the disgust which the present aroused in him, he always praised the past, and things which had never had any existence. Even the dead languages he taught were merely galoshes and umbrellas between himself and real life.

" 'How beautiful, how sonorous is the Greek language!' he would say with a beatific expression; and by way of proof he would half-close his eyes, raise a finger and murmur: 'An-thro-pos!'

"Belikov tried to keep his thoughts in a case, too. Only those circulars and newspaper articles in which something was prohibited were comprehensible to him. When instructions were circulated forbidding school-boys to be in the streets after 9 p. m., or an article was published in which indulgence in carnal love was condemned, everything was clear and definite for him—these things were prohibited once and for all. In his eyes permission and indulgence always seemed to contain some doubtful element, something left unsaid, vague. If a dramatic circle or a reading-room or a café were allowed to be opened, he would shake his head and say gently:

"'It's a very fine thing no doubt, but ... let's hope no evil will come of it.'

"The slightest infringement or deviation from the rules plunged him in dejection, even when it could not possibly concern him. If one of his colleagues were late for prayers, or rumours of a trick played by some school-boys reached his ears, if a *dame de classe* were seen late at night in the company of an officer, he would be profoundly agitated, repeating constantly that he was afraid it would lead to no good. At the meetings of the teachers' council he fairly tormented us with his circum-spection and suspicions, his apprehensions and sugges-tions (typical of a mind encased): the young people in both the girls' and boys' schools behave disgracefully, make a terrible noise in the class-rooms—supposing the authorities get to hear of it, he hoped no evil would come of it, and wouldn't it help matters if we expelled Petrov from the second form, and Yegorov from the fourth? And what do you think? With his sighs and moans, his dark glasses on his little, white face—a ferrety sort of face, you know—he managed to depress us all to such an extent that we yielded, gave Petrov and Yegorov low marks for behaviour, had them put in the lock-up, and, finally, expelled. He had an old habit of visiting us in our homes. Going to the rooms of a fellow-teacher, he would sit down and say nothing, with a watchful air. After an hour or so of this, he would get up and go. He called this 'keeping on friendly terms with one's colleagues,' and it was obvious that he found it an uncongenial task and only came to see us because he considered it his duty as a fellow-teacher. We were all afraid of him. Even the headmaster was. Just think! Our teachers are on the whole a decent, intelligent set, brought up on Turgenev and Shchedrin, and yet this mite of a man, with his eternal umbrella and overshoes, managed to keep the whole school under his thumb for fifteen years! And not only the school, but the entire town! Our ladies gave up their Saturday private theatricals for fear of his finding out about them; the clergy were afraid of eating meat or playing cards in his presence. Under the influence of men like Belikov the people in our town have begun to be afraid of everything. They are afraid to speak loudly, write letters, make friends, read books, help the poor, teach the illiterate...."

Ivan Ivanich cleared his throat as if in preparation for some weighty remark, but first he relit his pipe and glanced up at the moon, and only then said, in unhurried tones:

"Quite right. A decent, intelligent set, reading Turgenev, Shchedrin and Buckle and all those, and yet they submitted, they bore with him.... That's just it."

"Belikov and I lived in the same house," went on Burkin, "on the same floor; his door was just opposite mine, we saw quite a lot of one another, and I had a pretty good idea of what his home-life was like. It was the same story: dressing-gown, night-cap, shutters, bolts and bars, a long list of restrictions and prohibitions, and the same adage—let's hope no evil will come of it! Lenten fare did not agree with him, but he could not eat meat or people might say that Belikov did not observe

Lent. So he ate pike fried in butter—it was not fasting but neither could it be called meat. He never kept female servants for fear of people getting 'notions,' but employed a male cook, Afanasy, an old man of about sixty, drunken and crazy, who knew how to cook from having served as a batsman some time in his life. This Afanasy was usually to be seen standing outside the door with folded arms, always muttering the same thing over and over again with a deep sigh:

" 'Ah, there's a sight of *them* about, nowadays!'

"Belikov's tiny bedroom was like a box, and there was a canopy over the bed. Before going to sleep he always drew the bedclothes over his head; the room was hot and stuffy, the wind rattled against the closed doors and moaned in the chimney; sighs were heard in the kitchen, ominous sighs. . . .

"And he would lie trembling under his blanket. He was afraid that some evil would come, that Afanasy would murder him, that thieves would break in, and his very dreams were haunted by these fears; and in the mornings, when we walked side by side to the school, he was always pale and languid and it was obvious that the crowded school he was approaching was the object of his terror and aversion, and that it was distasteful for him, a recluse by nature, to have to walk by my side.

" 'They make such a noise in the class-rooms,' he would say, as if trying to find an explanation for his heaviness of heart. 'It's quite disgraceful.'

"And what do you think? This teacher of Greek, this hermit-crab once nearly got married."

Ivan Ivanich turned his head sharply towards the shed.

"You don't mean it!" he said.

"Yes, he nearly got married, strange as it may sound. We were sent a new teacher for history and geography, one Kovalenko, Mikhail Savvich, a Ukrainian. He brought his sister Varya with him. He was young, tall, dark-complexioned, with enormous hands and the sort of face that goes with a deep voice; as a matter of fact he had a deep, booming voice, as if it came from a barrel.... His sister, who was not so young, thirty or thereabouts, was also tall; willowy, black-browed, red-cheeked, she was a peach of a girl, lively and noisy, always singing Ukrainian songs, always laughing. On the slightest provocation she would burst out into a ringing ha-ha-ha! The first time we became really acquainted with brother and sister, if I am not mistaken, was at our headmaster's name-day party. Suddenly, among the severe, conventional, dull teachers who make even going to parties a duty, a new Venus rose from the foam, one who walked about with arms akimbo, laughed, sang, danced.... She sang with great feeling 'The Winds Are Blowing,' following it with another song, then another, and we were all charmed, even Belikov. He sat beside her, and said, with a honeyed smile:

" 'The Ukrainian tongue, in its sweetness and delightful sonority is reminiscent of the ancient Greek.'

"The lady was flattered, and began telling him with sincere feeling about her farmstead in the Gadyachi uyezd, where her Mummie lived and where there were such pears, such melons and such pumpkins! Pumpkins are called marrows in the Ukraine, and they make a delicious *borshch* with blue egg-plant and red capsicum, ever so good, you know!

"We sat round her, listening, and the same thought struck us all.

" 'Why shouldn't these two get married?' said the headmaster's wife to me in a low voice.

"For some reason everyone suddenly realized that our Belikov was a bachelor and we wondered how it was that we had never remarked, had completely overlooked, so important a detail in his life. What was his attitude to woman, how did he solve this vital problem for himself? We had never thought about it before; perhaps none of us could admit the idea that a man who wore overshoes all the year round and slept under a canopy was capable of loving.

" 'He's well over forty, and she's thirty. . .' the headmaster's wife went on. 'I think she would take him.'

"The things one does out of sheer boredom in the provinces, the absurd, useless things! And all because what ought to be done, never is done. Why, why did we feel we had to marry off this Belikov, whom nobody could imagine in the role of a married man? The headmaster's wife, the inspector's wife, and all the ladies who had anything to do with the school, brightened up, and actually became handsomer, as if they had at last found an object in life. The headmaster's wife took a box in the theatre, and whom do we behold in this box but Varya, fanning herself with an enormous fan, radiant, happy, and at her side Belikov, small and huddled up, as if he had been extracted from his room with pincers. I myself gave a party, to which the ladies insisted on my inviting Belikov and Varya. In a word, we started the ball rolling. The idea of marriage, it appeared, was by no means disagreeable to Varya. Her life with her brother was far from happy, they did nothing but wrangle all day long. I'll give you a typical scene in their lives: Kovalenko stalks along the street, tall and massive, wearing an embroidered shirt, his forelock tumbling over his brow from beneath the peak of his cap; a parcel of books in one hand, a gnarled walking-stick on the other. He is followed by his sister, also carrying books.

" 'But, Misha, you haven't read it!' she shouts. 'You haven't, I tell you, I am absolutely certain you never read it!'

" 'And I tell you I have!' Kovalenko shouts back, knocking with his stick on the pavement.

" 'For goodness' sake, Misha! What makes you so cross? It's only a matter of principle, after all!'

" 'And I tell you I *have* read it!' shouts Kovalenko, still louder.

"And at home, whenever anyone came to see them, they would start bickering. She was probably sick of such a life, and longing for a home of her own, and then—her age: there was no time for picking and choosing, a girl would marry anyone, even a teacher of Greek. It's the same with all our girls, by the way—they'd marry anyone, simply for the sake of getting married. However that may be, Varya was beginning to show a marked liking for this Belikov of ours.

"And Belikov? He visited Kovalenko in the same way that he visited the rest of us. He would go to see him, and sit saying nothing. And there he would sit in silence, while Varya sang 'The Winds are Blowing,' gazing at him from her dark eyes, or suddenly breaking out into her 'ha-ha-ha!'

"In affairs of the heart, especially when matrimony is involved, suggestion is all-powerful. Everyone—his colleagues, the ladies—began assuring Belikov that he ought to marry, that there was nothing left for him in life but marriage; we all congratulated him, uttering with solemn countenances various commonplaces to the effect that marriage was a serious step, and the like; besides, Varenka was by no means plain, she might even be considered handsome, and then she was the daughter of a councillor of state, she had a farmstead of her own and, still more important, was the first woman who had ever treated him with affection. So he lost his head and persuaded himself it was his duty to marry."

"That was the moment to take his umbrella and overshoes away from him!" put in Ivan Ivanich.

"Ah, but that proved to be impossible! He placed Varenka's photograph on his desk, kept coming to me to talk about Varenka, family life, and the seriousness of marriage, went often to the Kovalenkos', but did not change his way of living in the least. On the contrary,

the decision to marry seemed to have a painful effect on
him, he grew thinner, paler and seemed to retreat still
further into his shell.

"'I find Varvara Savvishna an agreeable girl,' he
said to me with his faint, crooked smile, 'and every man
ought to get married, I know, but ... it's all so sudden,
you know.... One must think....'

"'What's there to think about?' I answered. 'Get married, that's all.'

"'No, no, marriage is a serious step, one ought to
weigh one's future duties and responsibilities first...
so's to make sure no evil will come of it.... It worries
me so, I can't sleep at night. And to tell you the truth,
I am somewhat alarmed—they have such a strange way
of thinking, she and her brother, their outlook, you know,
is so strange, and then she is so sprightly. Supposing I
marry and get mixed up in something....'

"And he put off proposing to her, putting it off from
day to day, much to the disappointment of the headmaster's wife and the other ladies; he kept weighing his future duties and responsibilities, walking out with Varenka almost every day, probably thinking the situation
demanded it of him, and coming to me to discuss family life in all its aspects. Very likely he would have
proposed in the end, contracting another of those stupid, unnecessary marriages, which are made here by the
thousand, out of sheer boredom and for want of something better to do, if *ein kolossalische Skandal* had not
suddenly broken out. I must tell you that Varenka's brother, Kovalenko, had contracted a hatred for Belikov
from the very first day of their acquaintance, and could
never stand him.

"'I can't understand you,' he would say, shrugging
his shoulders, 'how can you tolerate that sneak of a man,
that mug? How can you live here, gentlemen? The atmosphere is stifling, poisonous. Do you call yourselves teachers, pedagogues? You're nothing but a pack of place-

hunters. Your school is not a temple of science, but
a charitable institution, there's a sickly smell about it,
like in a policeman's booth. No, my friends, I shan't be
long with you, I'll be going back to my farmstead, to
catch crayfish and teach the Ukrainian lads. Yes, I'll go
away, and you may stay with your Judas, and be
damned to him!'

"Another time he would roar with laughter first in a
deep bass, and then in a shrill soprano till the tears came
to his eyes.

" 'Why does he sit there? What does he want—sitting and staring?'

"He gave Belikov a nickname of his own: vampire-
spider.

"Naturally we avoided mentioning to him that his
sister was about to marry this 'spider.' When the headmaster's wife hinted to him that it would be nice to see
his sister settled down with such a solid and respected
person as Belikov, he knitted his brows and said:

" 'It's none of my business. She may marry a snake
for all I care. I'm not one to meddle in other people's
affairs.'

"Now, hear what happened later. Some wag drew a
caricature: Belikov in his overshoes, the ends of his trousers turned up, his umbrella open over his head and Varya walking arm-in-arm with him; beneath the drawing
there was an inscription: 'The Anthropos in Love.' The
expression of his face, you know, was very true to life.
The artist must have sat up several nights over his work,
for the teachers of both the schools, the girls' and the
boys' and of the seminary, and all the town officials
received a copy. Belikov received one, too. The caricature had the most depressing effect on him.

"One day we went out of the house together, it happened to be the first of May and a Sunday and the whole
school, pupils and masters, were to meet in front of the
school and walk to a wood outside the town—well, we

went out, he looking very green about the girls and as black as thunder.

"'What cruel, malicious people there are in the world,' he said, and his lips quivered.

"I could not help feeling sorry for him. We walked on, when who should we see but Kovalenko riding a bicycle, followed by Varenka, also on a bicycle, panting, red-faced, but very jolly and happy.

"'We'll be there before all of you!' she cried. 'Isn't it a glorious day? Wonderful!'

"They were soon out of sight. My Belikov, no longer green but deathly pale, was struck dumb. He stopped and stared at me.

"'What can the meaning of this be?' he asked. 'Or do my eyes deceive me? Is it proper for schoolteachers and women to ride bicycles?'

"'There's nothing improper about it,' I said. 'Why shouldn't they ride bicycles?'

"'But it is insufferable!' he cried. 'How can you talk like that?'

"The shock he had received was too great, refusing to go any further, he turned homewards.

"All the next day he kept nervously rubbing his hands together and starting, and you could see by his face that he was not well. He left school before lessons were over—a thing he had never done before. And he did not eat any dinner. Towards evening he dressed warmly, though it was a real summer day, and shuffled off to the Kovalenkos. Varenka was not in, but her brother was.

"'Take a seat, please,' said Kovalenko coldly, knitting his brows; he had just got up from his afternoon nap, his face was still heavy with sleep, and he felt awful.

"After sitting in silence for about ten minutes, Belikov began:

"'I have come to relieve my mind. I am very, very unhappy. A certain unknown lampoonist has made a

drawing in which he ridicules me and a certain other
person near to us both. I consider it my duty to assure
you that it is not my fault. I have done nothing to give
grounds for such ridicule, on the contrary, I have behaved like a thorough gentleman all the time.'

"Kovalenko sat silent and lowering. After a short
pause Belikov went on in his low plaintive voice:

" 'And there's something else I have to say to you.
I am a veteran and you are only beginning your career,
and it is my duty as an older colleague of yours to warn
you. You ride a bicycle and this is a highly reprehensible
amusement for one who aspires to educate the young.'

" 'Why?' asked Kovalenko in his deep bass voice.

" 'Does it require explanation, Mikhail Savvich, I
should have thought it was self-evident. If the master is
to go about riding a bicycle, there is nothing left for the
pupils but to walk on their heads. And since no circular
permitting this has been issued, it is wrong. I was as-
tounded yesterday! I nearly fainted when I saw your sister. A young lady on a bicycle—preposterous!'

" 'What exactly do you want from me?'

" 'I only want to warn you, Mikhail Savvich. You are
young, you have your life before you, you must be very,
very careful, and you are so reckless, so very reckless!
You go about in embroidered shirts, are constantly seen
carrying all sorts of books about the streets, and now
this bicycle. The fact that you and your sister have been
seen riding bicycles will be made known to the headmaster, it will reach the patron's ears.... And that's no
good.'

" 'It is no man's business whether my sister and I
ride bicycles or not!' said Kovalenko, flushing up. 'And
if people stick their noses into my domestic and family
affairs they can go to hell.'

"Belikov turned pale and rose to his feet.

" 'Since you assume such a tone with me, I cannot go
on,' he said. 'And I would beg you to be careful what

you say about our superiors in my presence. The authorities must be treated with deference.'

" 'And did I say anything wrong about the authorities?' asked Kovalenko, looking at him with hatred. 'Leave me alone, Sir. I am an honest man, and have nothing to say to a person like you. I abhor snakes.'

"Belikov fidgeted nervously and began hastily putting on his coat, an expression of horror on his face. Never in his life had anyone spoken so rudely to him.

" 'You may say what you like,' he said as he passed on to the landing. 'But I must warn you: somebody may have overheard us, and to prevent our conversation from being misrepresented, and the possible consequence of this, I shall have to report the purport of our conversation to the headmaster ... its main points. It is my duty.'

" 'What? Report? Go on, then!'

"Kovalenko grasped him by the collar and gave him a push, and Belikov rolled down the stairs, his galoshes knocking against the steps. The staircase was long and steep, but he arrived at the bottom unhurt, rose to his feet and felt the bridge of his nose to see if his glasses were unbroken. But while he was rolling down the steps, Varenka, accompanied by two other ladies, entered the porch; they all three stood at the bottom of the stairs, looking at him—and for Belikov that was the worst of all his sufferings. He would a great deal sooner have broken his neck, and both legs, than appear in a ridiculous light. Now the whole town would know of it, the headmaster would be told, and probably the patron, too. And who knows what that would lead to! Someone might draw another caricature and it would end in his having to resign....

"When he got up, Varya recognized him, and looking at his ridiculous face, his rumpled coat, his overshoes, without the faintest idea what had happened, but supposing that he must have slipped, she could not help bursting out with her loud 'ha-ha-ha!'

"This buoyant resonant 'ha-ha' was the end: the end of Belikov's courting and of his earthly existence. He never again saw Varenka. The first thing he did when he got home was to remove her photograph from the top of his desk, then he lay down on his bed, never to leave it.

"Three days later Afanasy came to ask me whether he should send for the doctor, for his master was behaving very strangely. I went to see Belikov. He was lying under his canopy, covered by a blanket, mute; he answered my questions with a monosyllabic 'yes' or 'no,' and not a word more. There he lay, while Afanasy, morose and frowning, stumped round the bed, heaving deep sighs and reeking of spirits like a tavern.

"A month went by and Belikov died. Everybody, that is to say, the two schools and the seminary, went to his funeral. Now, as he lay in his coffin, the expression on his face was gentle, pleasing, even cheerful, as if he were glad at last to be put into a case which he would never have to leave. Yes, he had achieved his ideal! As if in his honour the day was cloudy and wet, and we all wore galoshes and carried umbrellas. Varya was at the funeral, too, and shed a tear when the coffin was lowered into the grave. I have noticed with Ukrainian women that they must either laugh or weep, they do not admit of any intermediate moods.

"I must confess that it is a great pleasure to bury individuals like Belikov. But we returned from the cemetery with long, 'lenten' faces; none of us wished to show our relief, a relief like that we felt long ago, in childhood, when the grown-ups went away and we could run about the garden for an hour or two enjoying perfect freedom. Ah, freedom! A hint of it, the faintest hope of attaining it, gives wings to our souls, doesn't it?

"We returned from the cemetery in good spirits. But hardly a week passed before everyday life, bleak, fatiguing, meaningless life, neither forbidden in one circu-

lar nor sanctioned in another, resumed its usual course;
and things were no better than they had been before.
After all, when you come to think of it, though we have
buried Belikov, there are still plenty of men who live in
a shell, and there are plenty, as yet unborn."

"Yes, indeed," said Ivan Ivanich as he lit his pipe.

"And plenty as yet unborn!" repeated Burkin.

The high-school teacher came out of the shed. He was
short, corpulent, quite bald, with a long black beard
reaching nearly to his belt; two dogs came out with him.

"What a moon!" he said, looking up.

It was past midnight. The whole of the village was
visible on the right, the long street extending for five
versts or so. Everything was plunged in profound, calm
sleep; not a sound, not a stir, it seemed incredible that
nature could be so calm. When we gaze upon a wide
village street on a moonlit night, with its dwellings and
hayricks and sleeping willows, a great peace descends
on our souls; in its serenity, sheltered by the shadows
of the night from all toil, cares and grief, the village
seems gentle, melancholy and beautiful, the very stars
seem to look down upon it kindly, and there seems to be
no more evil in the world, and all is well. To the left,
where the village ended, stretched the fields; one could
look far into them, to the very horizon, and all was silent
and motionless there, too, and the vast plain was flooded
with moonlight.

"Yes, indeed," repeated Ivan Ivanich. "And is not our
living in towns, in our stuffy, cramped rooms, writing
our useless papers, playing vint, isn't that living in an
oyster-shell, too? And the fact that we spend all our life
among drones, litigious boors, silly, idle women, talk
nonsense and listen to nonsense, is not that our oyster-
shell, too? I could tell you a highly instructive yarn, if
you'd care to listen...."

"I think it's time we went to sleep," said Burkin.
"Keep it for tomorrow."

They went to the shed and lay down. They snuggled into the hay and began to doze when a light footstep was heard outside. Somebody was walking about not far from the shed; a few steps, then a stop, and then again the light steps. The dogs growled.

"It's Mavra having a walk," said Burkin.

The steps were heard no more.

"To have to look on and listen to people lying," said Ivan Ivanich as he turned on his side, "and then to be called a fool for tolerating all those lies; to swallow insults, humiliations, not to dare to speak up and declare yourself on the side of honest, free men, to lie yourself, to smile, and all for the sake of a crust of bread and a snug corner to live in, for the sake of some miserable rank—no, no, life is intolerable!"

"This is quite another theme, Ivan Ivanich," said the schoolmaster. "Let's go to sleep."

In ten minutes Burkin was asleep. But Ivan Ivanich kept sighing and tossing on the hay; then he got up, went out again, squatted down by the door, and lit his pipe.

1898

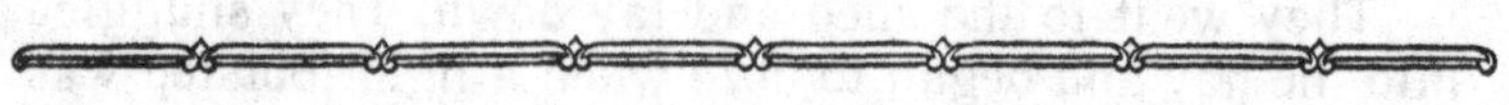

GOOSEBERRIES

The sky had been covered with rain-clouds ever since the early morning; it was a still day, cool and dull, one of those misty days when the clouds have long been lowering overhead and you keep thinking it is just going to rain, and the rain holds off. Ivan Ivanich, the veterinary surgeon, and Burkin, the high-school teacher, had walked till they were tired, and the way over the fields seemed endless to them. Far ahead they could just make out the windmill of the village of Mironositskoye, and what looked like a range of low hills at the right extending well beyond the village, and they both knew that this range was really the bank of the river, and that further on were meadows, green willow-trees, country-estates; if they were on the top of these hills, they knew they would see the same boundless fields and telegraph-posts, and the train, like a crawling caterpillar in the distance, while in fine weather even the town would be visible. On this still day, when the whole of nature seemed kindly and pensive, Ivan Ivanich and Burkin felt a surge of love for this plain, and thought how vast and beautiful their country was.

"The last time we stayed in Elder Prokofy's hut," said Burkin, "you said you had a story to tell me."

"Yes. I wanted to tell you the story of my brother."

Ivan Ivanich took a deep breath and lighted his pipe as a preliminary to his narrative, but just then the rain came. Five minutes later it was coming down in torrents and nobody could say when it would stop. Ivan Ivanich and Burkin stood still, lost in thought. The dogs, already soaked, stood with drooping tails, gazing at them wistfully.

"We must try and find shelter," said Burkin. "Let's go to Alekhin's. It's quite near."

"Come on, then."

They turned aside and walked straight across the newly reaped field, veering to the right till they came to a road. Very soon poplars, an orchard, and the red roofs of barns came into sight. The surface of a river gleamed, and they had a view of an extensive reach of water, a windmill and a whitewashed bathing-shed. This was Sofyino, where Alekhin lived.

The mill was working, and the noise made by its sails drowned the sound of the rain; the whole dam trembled. Horses, soaking wet, were standing near some carts, their heads drooping, and people were moving about with sacks over their heads and shoulders. It was wet, muddy, bleak, and the water looked cold and sinister. Ivan Ivanich and Burkin were already experiencing the misery of dampness, dirt, physical discomfort, their boots were caked with mud, and when, having passed the mill-dam, they took the upward path to the landowner's barns, they fell silent, as if vexed with one another.

The sound of winnowing came from one of the barns; the door was open, and clouds of dust issued from it. Standing in the door-way was Alekhin himself, a stout man of some forty years, with longish hair, looking more like a professor or an artist than a landed proprietor. He was wearing a white shirt, greatly in need of washing, belted with a piece of string, and long drawers with

no trousers over them. His boots, too, were caked with
mud and straw. His eyes and nose were ringed with dust.
He recognized Ivan Ivanich and Burkin, and seemed
glad to see them.

"Go up to the house, gentlemen," he said, smiling.
"I'll be with you in a minute."

It was a large two-storey house. Alekhin occupied the
ground floor, two rooms with vaulted ceilings and tiny
windows, where the stewards had lived formerly. They
were poorly furnished, and smelled of rye-bread, cheap
vodka, and harness. He hardly ever went into the upstairs rooms, excepting when he had guests. Ivan Ivanich and Burkin were met by a maid-servant, a young
woman of such beauty that they stood still involuntarily
and exchanged glances.

"You have no idea how glad I am to see you here, dear
friends," said Alekhin, overtaking them in the hall. "It's
quite a surprise! Pelageya," he said, turning to the maid,
"find the gentlemen a change of clothes. And I might
as well change, myself. But I must have a wash first, for
I don't believe I've had a bath since the spring. Wouldn't
you like to go and have a bathe while they get things
ready here?"

The beauteous Pelageya, looking very soft and delicate,
cate, brought them towels and soap, and Alekhin and
his guests set off for the bathing-house.

"Yes, it's a long time since I had a wash," he said,
taking off his clothes. "As you see I have a nice bathing-place, my father had it built, but somehow I never
seem to get time to wash."

He sat on the step, soaping his long locks and his
neck, and all round him the water was brown.

"Yes, you certainly . . ." remarked Ivan Ivanich, with
a significant glance at his host's head.

"It's a long time since I had a wash. . ." repeated
Alekhin, somewhat abashed, and he soaped himself
again, and now the water was dark-blue, like ink

Ivan Ivanich emerged from the shed, splashed noisily into the water, and began swimming beneath the rain, spreading his arms wide, making waves all round him, and the white water-lilies rocked on the waves he made. He swam into the very middle of the river and then dived, a moment later came up at another place and swam further, diving constantly, and trying to touch the bottom. "Ah, my God," he kept exclaiming in his enjoyment. "Ah, my God...." He swam up to the mill, had a little talk with some peasants there and turned back, but when he got to the middle of the river, he floated, holding his face up to the rain. Burkin and Alekhin were dressed and ready to go, but he went on swimming and diving.

"God! God!" he kept exclaiming. "Dear God!"

"Come out!" Burkin shouted to him.

They went back to the house. And only after the lamp was lit in the great drawing-room on the upper floor, and Burkin and Ivan Ivanich, in silk dressing-gowns and warm slippers, were seated in arm-chairs, while Alekhin, washed and combed, paced the room in his new frock-coat, enjoying the warmth, the cleanliness, his dry clothes and comfortable slippers, while the fair Pelageya, smiling benevolently, stepped noiselessly over the carpet with her tray of tea and preserves, did Ivan Ivanich embark upon his yarn, the ancient dames, young ladies, and military gentlemen looking down at them severely from their gilded frames, as if they, too, were listening.

"There were two of us brothers," he began. "Ivan Ivanich (me), and my brother Nikolai Ivanich, two years younger than myself. I went in for learning and became a veterinary surgeon, but Nikolai started working in a government office when he was only nineteen. Our father, Chimsha-Himalaisky, was educated in a school for the sons of private soldiers, but was later promoted to officer's rank, and was made a hereditary nobleman and given a small estate. After his death the estate had to

be sold for debts, but at least our childhood was passed
in the freedom of the country-side, where we roamed
the fields and the woods like peasant children, taking
the horses to graze, peeling bark from the trunks of lime-
trees, fishing, and all that sort of thing. And anyone who
has once in his life fished for perch, or watched the
thrushes fly south in the autumn, rising high over the village on clear, cool days, is spoilt for town life, and will
long for the country-side for the rest of his days. My
brother pined in his government office. The years passed
and he sat in the same place every day, writing out the
same documents and thinking all the time of the same
thing—how to get back to the country. And these long-
ings of his gradually turned into a definite desire, into
a dream of purchasing a little estate somewhere on the
bank of a river or the shore of a lake.

"He was a meek, good-natured chap, I was fond of
him, but could feel no sympathy with the desire to lock
oneself up for life in an estate of one's own. They say
man only needs six feet of earth. But it is a corpse, and
not man, which needs these six feet. And now people are
actually saying that it is a good sign for our intellectuals to yearn for the land and try to obtain country-
dwellings. And yet these estates are nothing but those
same six feet of earth. To escape from the town, from the
struggle, from the noise of life, to escape and hide one's
head on a country-estate, is not life, but egoism, idleness, it is a sort of renunciation, but renunciation without faith. It is not six feet of earth, not a country-estate,
that man needs, but the whole globe, the whole of nature, room to display his qualities and the individual
characteristics of his soul.

"My brother Nikolai sat at his office-desk, dreaming of eating soup made from his own cabbages, which
would spread a delicious smell all over his own yard,
of eating out of doors, on the green grass, of sleeping
in the sun, sitting for hours on a bench outside his gate,

and gazing at the fields and woods. Books on agriculture, and all those hints printed on calendars were his delight, his favourite spiritual nourishment. He was fond of reading newspapers, too, but all he read in them was advertisements of the sale of so many acres of arable and meadowland, with residence attached, a river, an orchard, a mill, and ponds fed by springs. His head was full of visions of garden paths, flowers, fruit, nesting-boxes, carp-ponds, and all that sort of thing. These visions differed according to the advertisements he came across, but for some reason gooseberry bushes invariably figured in them. He could not picture to himself a single estate or picturesque nook that did not have gooseberry bushes in it.

"‘Country life has its conveniences,’ he would say. ‘You sit on the verandah, drinking tea, with your own ducks floating on the pond, and everything smells so nice, and ... and the gooseberries ripen on the bushes.’

"He drew up plans for his estate, and every plan showed the same features: a) the main residence, b) the servant’s wing, c) the kitchen-garden, d) gooseberry bushes. He lived thriftily, never ate or drank his fill, dressed anyhow, like a beggar, and saved up all his money in the bank. He became terribly stingy. I could hardly bear to look at him, and whenever I gave him a little money, or sent him a present on some holiday, he put that away, too. Once a man gets an idea into his head, there’s no doing anything with him.

"The years passed, he was sent to another gubernia, he was over forty, and was still reading advertisements in the papers, and saving up. At last I heard he had married. All for the same purpose, to buy himself an estate with gooseberry bushes on it, he married an ugly elderly widow, for whom he had not the slightest affection, just because she had some money. After his marriage he went on living as thriftily as ever, half-starving his wife, and putting her money in his own bank account. Her first husband had been a postmaster, and she was used to pies and cordials, but with her second husband she did not even get enough black bread to eat. She began to languish under such a regime, and three years later yielded up her soul to God. Of course my brother did not for a moment consider himself guilty of her death. Money, like vodka, makes a man eccentric. There was a merchant in our town who asked for a plate of honey on his deathbed and ate up all his bank-notes and lottery tickets with the honey, so that no one else should get it. And one day when I was examining a consignment of cattle at a railway station, a drover fell under the engine and his leg was severed from his body. We carried him all bloody into the waiting-room, a terrible sight, and he did nothing but beg us to look for his leg, worrying all the time—there were twenty rubles in the boot, and he was afraid they would be lost."

"You're losing the thread," put in Burkin.

Ivan Ivanich paused for a moment, and went on: "After his wife's death my brother began to look about for an estate. You can search for five years, of course, and in the end make a mistake and buy something quite different from what you dreamed of. My brother Nikolai bought three hundred acres, complete with gentleman's house, servants' quarters, and a park, as well as a mortgage to be paid through an agent, but there were neither an orchard, gooseberry bushes, nor a pond with ducks on it. There was a river, but it was as dark as coffee, owing to the fact that there was a brick-works on one side of the estate, and bone-kilns on the other. Nothing daunted, however, my brother Nikolai Ivanovich ordered two dozen gooseberry bushes and settled down as a landed proprietor.

"Last year I paid him a visit. I thought I would go and see how he was getting on there. In his letters my brother gave his address as Chumbaroklova Pustosh or Himalaiskoye. I arrived at Himalaiskoye in the afternoon. It was very hot. Everywhere were ditches, fences, hedges, rows of fir-trees, and it was hard to drive into the yard and find a place to leave one's carriage. As I went a fat ginger-coloured dog, remarkably like a pig, came out to meet me. It looked as if it would have barked if it were not so lazy. The cook, who was also fat and like a pig, came out of the kitchen, barefoot, and said her master was having his after-dinner rest. I made my way to my brother's room, and found him sitting up in bed, his knees covered by a blanket. He had aged, and grown stout and flabby. His cheeks, nose and lips protruded—I almost expected him to grunt into the blanket.

"We embraced and wept—tears of joy, mingled with melancholy—because we had once been young and were now both grey-haired and approaching the grave. He put on his clothes and went out to show me over his estate.

" 'Well, how are you getting on here?' I asked.

" 'All right, thanks be, I'm enjoying myself.' "

"He was no longer the poor, timid clerk, but a true proprietor, a gentleman. He had settled down, and was entering with zest into country life. He ate a lot, washed in the bath-house, and put on flesh. He had already got into litigation with the village commune, the brick-works and the bone-kilns, and took offence if the peasants failed to call him 'Your Honour.' He went in for religion in a solid, gentlemanly way, and there was nothing casual about his pretentious good works. And what were these good works? He treated all the diseases of the peasants with bicarbonate of soda and castor-oil, and had a special thanksgiving service held on his name-day, after which he provided half a pail of vodka, supposing that this was the right thing to do. Oh, those terrible half pails! Today the fat landlord hauls the peasants before the Zemstvo representative for letting their sheep graze on his land, tomorrow, on the day of rejoicing, he treats them to half a pail of vodka, and they drink

and sing and shout hurrah, prostrating themselves before him when they are drunk. Any improvement in his
conditions, anything like satiety or idleness, develops the
most insolent complacency in a Russian. Nikolai Ivanich, who had been afraid of having an opinion of his
own when he was in the government service, was now
continually coming out with axioms, in the most ministerial manner: 'Education is essential, but the people
are not ready for it yet,' 'corporal punishment is an evil,
but in certain cases it is beneficial and indispensable.'

"'I know the people and I know how to treat them,'
he said. 'The people love me. I only have to lift my little
finger, and the people will do whatever I want.'

"And all this, mark you, with a wise, indulgent
smile. Over and over again he repeated: 'We the gentry,'
or 'speaking as a gentleman, and seemed to have quite
forgotten that our grandfather was a peasant, and our
father a common soldier. Our very surname—Chimsha-
Himalaisky—in reality so absurd, now seemed to him a
resounding, distinguished, and euphonious name.

"But it is of myself, and not of him, that I wish to
speak. I should like to describe to you the change which
came over me in those few hours I spent on my brother's
estate. As we were drinking tea in the evening, the cook
brought us a full plate of gooseberries. These were not
gooseberries bought for money, they came from his own
garden, and were the first fruits of the bushes he had
planted. Nikolai Ivanich broke into a laugh and gazed
at the gooseberries, in tearful silence for at least five
minutes. Speechless with emotion, he popped a single
gooseberry into his mouth, darted at me the triumphant
glance of a child who has at last gained possession of
a longed-for toy, and said:

"'Delicious!'

"And he ate them greedily, repeating over and over
again:

"'Simply delicious! You try them.'

"They were hard and sour, but, as Pushkin says: 'The lie which elates us is dearer than a thousand sober truths.' I saw before me a really happy man, one whose dearest wish had come true, who had achieved his aim in life, got what he wanted, and was content with his lot and with himself. There had always been a tinge of melancholy in my conception of human happiness, and now, confronted by a happy man, I was overcome by a feeling of sadness bordering on desperation. This feeling grew strongest of all in the night. A bed was made up for me in the room next to my brother's bedroom, and I could hear him moving about restlessly, every now and then getting up to take a gooseberry from a plate. How many happy, satisfied people there are, after all, I said to myself! What an overwhelming force! Just consider this life—the insolence and idleness of the strong, the ignorance and bestiality of the weak, all around intolerable poverty, cramped dwellings, degeneracy, drunkenness, hypocrisy, lying.... And yet peace and order apparently prevail in all those homes and in the streets. Of the fifty thousand inhabitants of a town, not one will be found to cry out, to proclaim his indignation aloud. We see those who go to the market to buy food, who eat in the day-time and sleep at night, who prattle away, marry, grow old, carry their dead to the cemeteries. But we neither hear nor see those who suffer, and the terrible things in life are played out behind the scenes. All is calm and quiet, only statistics, which are dumb, protest: so many have gone mad, so many barrels of drink have been consumed, so many children died of malnutrition.... And apparently this is as it should be. Apparently those who are happy can only enjoy themselves because the unhappy bear their burdens in silence, and but for this silence happiness would be impossible. It is a kind of universal hypnosis. There ought to be a man with a hammer behind the door of every happy man, to remind him by his constant knocks

that there are unhappy people, and that happy as he
himself may be, life will sooner or later show him its
claws, catastrophe will overtake him—sickness, poverty,
loss—and nobody will see it, just as he now neither sees
nor hears the misfortunes of others. But there is no man
with a hammer, the happy man goes on living and the
petty vicissitudes of life touch him lightly, like the wind
in an aspen-tree, and all is well.

"That night I understood that I, too, was happy and
content," continued Ivan Ivanich, getting up. "I, too,
while out hunting, or at the dinner table, have held forth
on the right way to live, to worship, to manage the people. I, too, have declared that without knowledge there
can be no light, that education is essential, but that bare
literacy is sufficient for the common people. Freedom is
a blessing, I have said, one can't get on without it, any
more than without air, but we must wait. Yes, that is
what I said, and now I ask: In the name of what must
we wait?" Here Ivan Ivanich looked angrily at Burkin.
"In the name of what must we wait, I ask you. What is
there to be considered? Don't be in such a hurry, they
tell me, every idea materializes gradually, in its own
time. But who are they who say this? What is the proof
that it is just? You refer to the natural order of things,
to the logic of facts, but according to what order, what
logic do I, a living, thinking individual, stand on the
edge of a ditch and wait for it to be gradually filled up,
or choked with silt, when I might leap across it or build
a bridge over it? And again, in the name of what must
we wait? Wait, when we have not the strength to live,
though live we must and to live we desire!

"I left my brother early the next morning, and ever
since I have found town life intolerable. The peace and
order weigh on my spirits, and I am afraid to look into
windows, because there is now no sadder spectacle for
me than a happy family seated around the tea-table.
I am old and unfit for the struggle, I am even incapable

of feeling hatred. I can only suffer inwardly, and give
way to irritation and annoyance, at night my head burns
from the rush of thoughts, and I am unable to sleep.…
Oh, if only I were young!"

Ivan Ivanich began pacing backwards and forwards,
repeating:

"If only I were young still!"

Suddenly he went up to Alekhin and began pressing
first one of his hands, and then the other.

"Pavel Konstantinich," he said in imploring accents.
"Don't *you* fall into apathy, don't *you* let your conscience
be lulled to sleep!· While you are still young, strong,
active, do not be weary of well-doing. There is no such
thing as happiness, nor ought there to be, but if there
is any sense or purpose in life, this sense and purpose
are to be found not in our own happiness, but in something greater and more rational. Do good!"

Ivan Ivanich said all this with a piteous, imploring
smile, as if he were asking for something for himself.

Then they all three sat in their arm-chairs a long
way apart from one another, and said nothing. Ivan
Ivanich's story satisfied neither Burkin nor Alekhin. It
was not interesting to listen to the story of a poor clerk
who ate gooseberries, when from the walls generals and
fine ladies, who seemed to come to life in the dark, were
looking down from their gilded frames. It would have
been much more interesting to hear about elegant people, lovely women. And the fact that they were sitting
in a drawing-room in which everything—the swathed
chandeliers, the arm-chairs, the carpet on the floor,
proved that the people now looking out of the frames had
once moved about here, sat in the chairs, drunk tea,
where the fair Pelageya was now going noiselessly to
and fro, was better than any story.

Alekhin was desperately sleepy. He had got up early,
at three o'clock in the morning, to go about his work on
the estate, and could now hardly keep his eyes open. But

he would not go to bed, for fear one of his guests would relate something interesting after he was gone. He could not be sure whether what Ivan Ivanich had just told them was wise or just, but his visitors talked of other things besides grain, hay, or tar, of things which had no direct bearing on his daily life, and he liked this, and wanted them to go on....

"Well, time to go to bed," said Burkin, getting up. "Allow me to wish you a good night."

Alekhin said good night and went downstairs to his own room, the visitors remaining on the upper floor. They were allotted a big room for the night, in which were two ancient bedsteads of carved wood, and, an ivory crucifix in one corner. There was a pleasant smell of freshly laundered sheets from the wide, cool beds which the fair Pelageya made up for them.

Ivan Ivanich undressed in silence and lay down.

"Lord have mercy on us, sinners," he said, and covered his head with the sheet.

There was a strong smell of stale tobacco from his pipe, which he put on the table, and Burkin lay awake a long time, wondering where the stifling smell came from.

The rain tapped on the window-panes all night.

1898

THE LADY WITH THE DOG

I

People were telling one another that a newcomer had been seen on the promenade—a lady with a dog. Dmitri Dmitrich Gurov had been a fortnight in Yalta, and was accustomed to its ways, and he, too, had begun to take an interest in fresh arrivals. From his seat in Vernet's outdoor café, he caught sight of a young woman in a toque, passing along the promenade; she was fair and not very tall; after her trotted a white pomeranian.

Later he encountered her in the municipal park, and in the square, several times a day. She was always alone, wearing the same toque, and the pomeranian always trotted at her side. Nobody knew who she was, and people referred to her simply as "the lady with the dog."

"If she's here without her husband, and without any friends," thought Gurov, "it wouldn't be a bad idea to make her acquaintance."

He was not yet forty, but had a twelve-year-old daughter and two schoolboy sons. He had been talked into marrying in his second year at college, and his wife now looked nearly twice as old as he was. She was a tall, black-browed woman, erect, dignified, imposing, and, as she said of herself, a "thinker." She was a great reader, omitted the "hard sign"* at the end of words in her letters, and called her husband "Dimitri" instead of Dmitri; and though he secretly considered her shallow, narrow-minded, and dowdy, he stood in awe of her, and disliked being at home. It was long since he had first begun deceiving her and he was now constantly unfaithful to her, and this was no doubt why he spoke slightingly of women, to whom he referred as *the lower race.*

He considered that the ample lessons he had received from bitter experience entitled him to call them whatever he liked, but without this "lower race" he could not have existed a single day. He was bored and ill-at-ease in the company of men, with whom he was always cold and reserved, but felt quite at home among women, and knew exactly what to say to them, and how to behave; he could even be silent in their company without feeling the slightest awkwardness. There was an elusive charm in his appearance and disposition which attracted women and caught their sympathies. He knew this and was himself attracted to them by some invisible force.

Repeated and bitter experience had taught him that every fresh intimacy, while at first introducing such pleasant variety into everyday life, and offering itself as a charming, light adventure, inevitably developed, among decent people, (especially in Moscow, where they are so irresolute and slow to move) into a problem of excessive complication leading to an intolerably irksome situation. But every time he encountered an attractive woman he forgot all about this experience, the desire for life surged up in him, and everything suddenly seemed simple and amusing.

* Certain progressive intellectuals omitted the hard sign after consonants in writing, thus anticipating the reform in the Russian alphabet introduced later on.—*Tr.*

One evening, then, while he was dining at the restaurant in the park, the lady in the toque came strolling up and took a seat at a neighbouring table. Her expression, gait, dress, coiffure, all told him that she was from the upper classes, that she was married, that she was in Yalta for the first time, alone and bored.... The accounts of the laxity of morals among visitors to Yalta are greatly exaggerated, and he paid no heed to them, knowing that for the most part they were invented by people who would gladly have transgressed themselves, had they known how to set about it. But when the lady sat down at a neighbouring table a few yards away from him, these stories of easy conquests, of excursions to the mountains, came back to him, and the seductive idea of a brisk transitory liaison, an affair with a woman whose very name he did not know, suddenly took possession of his mind.

He snapped his fingers at the pomeranian, and when it trotted up to him, shook his forefinger at it. The pomeranian growled. Gurov shook his finger again.

The lady glanced at him and instantly lowered her eyes.

"He doesn't bite," she said, and blushed.

"May I give him a bone?" he asked, and on her nod of consent added in friendly tones: "Have you been long in Yalta?"

"About five days."

"And I am dragging out my second week here."

Neither spoke for a few minutes.

"The days pass quickly, and yet one is so bored here," she said, not looking at him.

"It's the thing to say it's boring here. People never complain of boredom in God-forsaken holes like Belyev or Zhizdra, but when they get here it's: 'Oh, the dullness! Oh, the dust!' You'd think they'd come from Grenada to say the least of it."

She laughed. Then they both went on eating in silence, like complete strangers. But after dinner they left the restaurant together, and embarked upon the light, jesting talk of people free and contented, for whom it is all the same where they go, or what they talk about. They strolled along, remarking on the strange light over the sea. The water was a warm, tender purple, the moonlight lay on its surface in a golden strip. They said how close it was, after the hot day. Gurov told her he was from Moscow, that he was really a philologist, but worked in a bank; that he had at one time trained himself to sing in a private opera company, but had given up the idea; that he owned two houses in Moscow. . . . And from her he learned that she had grown up in Petersburg, but had got married in the town of S., where she had been living two years, that she would stay another month in Yalta, and that perhaps her husband, who also needed a rest, would join her. She was quite unable to explain whether her husband was a member of the gubernia council, or on the board of the Zemstvo, and was greatly amused at herself for this. Further, Gurov learned that her name was Anna Sergeyevna.

Back in his own room he thought about her, and felt sure he would meet her the next day. It was inevitable. As he went to bed he reminded himself that only a very short time ago she had been a schoolgirl, like his own daughter, learning her lessons, he remembered how much there was of shyness and constraint in her laughter, in her way of conversing with a stranger—it was probably the first time in her life that she found herself alone, and in a situation in which men could follow her and watch her, and speak to her, all the time with a secret aim she could not fail to divine. He recalled her slender, delicate neck, her fine grey eyes.

"And yet there's something pathetic about her," he thought to himself as he fell asleep.

A week had passed since the beginning of their acquaintance. It was a holiday. Indoors it was stuffy, but the dust rose in clouds out of doors, and people's hats blew off. It was a thirsty day and Gurov kept going to the outdoor café for fruit-drinks and ices to offer Anna Sergeyevna. The heat was overpowering.

In the evening, when the wind had dropped, they walked to the pier to see the steamer come in. There were a great many people strolling about the landing-place; some, bunches of flowers in their hands, were meeting friends. Two peculiarities of the smart Yalta crowd stood out distinctly—the elderly ladies all tried to dress very young, and there seemed to be an inordinate number of generals about.

Owing to the roughness of the sea the steamer arrived late, after the sun had gone down, and it had to manoeuvre for some time before it could get alongside the pier. Anna Sergeyevna scanned the steamer and passengers through her lorgnette, as if looking for someone she knew, and when she turned to Gurov her eyes were glistening. She talked a great deal, firing off abrupt questions and forgetting immediately what it was she had wanted to know. Then she lost her lorgnette in the crush.

The smart crowd began dispersing, features could no longer be made out, the wind had quite dropped, and Gurov and Anna Sergeyevna stood there as if waiting for someone else to come off the steamer. Anna Sergeyevna had fallen silent, every now and then smelling her flowers, but not looking at Gurov.

"It's turned out a fine evening," he said. "What shall we do? We might go for a drive."

She made no reply.

He looked steadily at her and suddenly took her in his arms and kissed her lips, and the fragrance and dampness of the flowers closed round him, but the next moment he looked behind him in alarm—had anyone seen them?

"Let's go to your room," he murmured.

And they walked off together, very quickly.

Her room was stuffy and smelt of some scent she had bought in the Japanese shop. Gurov looked at her, thinking to himself: "How full of strange encounters life is!" He could remember carefree, good-natured women who were exhilarated by love-making and grateful to him for the happiness he gave them, however short-lived; and there had been others—his wife among them—whose caresses were insincere, affected, hysterical, mixed up with a great deal of quite unnecessary talk, and whose expression seemed to say that all this was not just love-making or passion, but something much more significant; then there had been two or three beautiful, cold women, over whose features flitted a predatory expression, betraying a determination to wring from life more than it could give, women no longer in their first youth, capricious, irrational, despotic, brainless, and when Gurov had cooled to these, their beauty aroused in him nothing but repulsion, and the lace trimming on their underclothes reminded him of fish-scales.

But here the timidity and awkwardness of youth and inexperience were still apparent; and there was a feeling of embarrassment in the atmosphere, as if someone had just knocked at the door. Anna Sergeyevna, "the lady with the dog," seemed to regard the affair as something very special, very serious, as if she had become a fallen woman, an attitude he found odd and disconcerting. Her features lengthened and drooped, and her long hair hung mournfully on either side of her face. She assumed a pose of dismal meditation, like a repentant sinner in some classical painting.

"It isn't right," she said. "You will never respect me any more."

On the table was a water-melon. Gurov cut himself a slice from it and began slowly eating it. At least half an hour passed in silence.

Anna Sergeyevna was very touching, revealing the purity of a decent, naive woman who had seen very little of life. The solitary candle burning on the table scarcely lit up her face, but it was obvious that her heart was heavy.

"Why should I stop respecting you?" asked Gurov. "You don't know what you're saying."

"May God forgive me!" she exclaimed, and her eyes filled with tears. "It's terrible."

"No need to seek to justify yourself."

"How can I justify myself? I'm a wicked, fallen woman, I despise myself and have not the least thought of self-justification. It isn't my husband I have deceived, it's myself. And not only now, I have been deceiving myself for ever so long. My husband is no doubt an honest, worthy man, but he's a flunkey. I don't know what it is he does at his office, but I know he's a flunkey. I was only twenty when I married him, and I was devoured by curiosity, I wanted something higher. I told myself that there must be a different kind of life I wanted to live, to live.... I was burning with curiosity ... you'll never understand that, but I swear to God I could no longer control myself, nothing could hold me back, I told my husband I was ill, and I came here.... And I started going about like one possessed, like a madwoman ... and now I have become an ordinary, worthless woman, and everyone has the right to despise me."

Gurov listened to her, bored to death. The naive accents, the remorse, all was so unexpected, so out of place. But for the tears in her eyes, she might have been jesting or play-acting.

"I don't understand," he said gently. "What is it you want?"

She hid her face against his breast and pressed closer to him.

"Do believe me, I implore you to believe me," she
said. "I love all that is honest and pure in life, vice is
revolting to me, I don't know what I'm doing. The common people say they are snared by the devil. And now
I can say that I have been snared by the devil, too."

"Come, come," he murmured.

He gazed into her fixed, terrified eyes, kissed her, and
soothed her with gentle affectionate words, and gradually she calmed down and regained her cheerfulness.
Soon they were laughing together again.

When, a little later, they went out, there was not a
soul on the promenade, the town and its cypresses
looked dead, but the sea was still roaring as it dashed
against the beach. A solitary fishing-boat tossed on the
waves, its lamp blinking sleepily.

They found a droshky and drove to Oreanda.

"I discovered your name in the hall, just now," said
Gurov, "written up on the board. Von Diederitz. Is your
husband a German?"

"No. His grandfather was, I think, but he belongs
to the Orthodox church himself."

When they got out of the droshky at Oreanda they
sat down on a bench not far from the church, and looked
down at the sea, without talking. Yalta could be dimly
discerned through the morning mist, and white clouds
rested motionless on the summits of the mountains. Not
a leaf stirred, the grasshoppers chirruped, and the monotonous hollow roar of the sea came up to them, speaking of peace, of the eternal sleep lying in wait for us all.
The sea had roared like this long before there was any
Yalta or Oreanda, it was roaring now, and it would
go on roaring, just as indifferently and hollowly, when
we had passed away. And it may be that in this con-
tinuity, this utter indifference to life and death, lies the
secret of our ultimate salvation, of the stream of life

on our planet, and of its never-ceasing movement towards perfection.

Side by side with a young woman, who looked so exquisite in the early light, soothed and enchanted by the sight of all this magical beauty—sea, mountains, clouds and the vast expanse of the sky—Gurov told himself that, when you came to think of it, everything in the world is beautiful really, everything but our own thoughts and actions, when we lose sight of the higher aims of life, and of our dignity as human beings.

Someone approached them—a watchman, probably—looked at them and went away. And there was something mysterious and beautiful even in this. The steamer from Feodosia could be seen coming towards the pier, lit up by the dawn, its lamps out.

"There's dew on the grass," said Anna Sergeyevna, breaking the silence.

"Yes. Time to go home."

They went back to the town.

After this they met every day at noon on the promenade, lunching and dining together, going for walks, and admiring the sea. She complained of sleeplessness, of palpitations, asked the same questions over and over again, alternately surrendering to jealousy and the fear that he did not really respect her. And often, when there was nobody in sight in the square or the park, he would draw her to him and kiss her passionately. The utter idleness, these kisses in broad daylight, accompanied by furtive glances and the fear of discovery, the heat, the smell of the sea, and the idle, smart, well-fed people continually crossing their field of vision, seemed to have given him a new lease of life. He told Anna Sergeyevna she was beautiful and seductive, made love to her with impetuous passion, and never left her side, while she was always pensive, always trying to force from him the admission that he did not respect her, that he did not love her a bit, and considered her just an ordinary woman. Almost every night they drove out of town, to Oreanda, the water-fall, or some other beauty-spot. And these excursions were invariably a success, each contributing fresh impressions of majestic beauty.

All this time they kept expecting her husband to arrive. But a letter came in which he told his wife that he was having trouble with his eyes, and implored her to come home as soon as possible. Anna Sergeyevna made hasty preparations for leaving.

"It's a good thing I'm going," she said to Gurov. "It's the intervention of fate."

She left Yalta in a carriage, and he went with her as far as the railway station. The drive took nearly a whole day. When she got into the express train, after the second bell had been rung, she said:

"Let me have one more look at you.... One last look. That's right."

She did not weep, but was mournful, and seemed ill, the muscles of her cheeks twitching.

"I shall think of you ... I shall think of you all the time," she said. "God bless you! Think kindly of me. We are parting for ever, it must be so, because we ought never to have met. Good-bye—God bless you."

The train steamed rapidly out of the station, its lights soon disappearing, and a minute later even the sound it made was silenced, as if everything were conspiring to bring this sweet oblivion, this madness, to an end as quickly as possible. And Gurov, standing alone on the platform and gazing into the dark distance, listened to the shrilling of the grasshoppers and the humming of the telegraph wires, with a feeling that he had only just waked up. And he told himself that this had been just one more of the many adventures in his life, and that it, too, was over, leaving nothing but a memory.... He was moved and sad, and felt a slight remorse. After all, this young woman whom he would never again see had not been really happy with him. He had been friendly and affectionate with her, but in his whole behaviour, in the tones of his voice, in his very caresses, there had been a shade of irony, the insulting indulgence of the fortunate male, who was, moreover, almost twice her age. She had insisted in calling him good, remarkable, high-minded. Evidently he had appeared to her different from his real self, in a word he had involuntarily deceived her....

There was an autumnal feeling in the air, and the evening was chilly.

"It's time for me to be going north, too," thought Gurov, as he walked away from the platform. "High time!"

III

When he got back to Moscow it was beginning to look like winter, the stoves were heated every day, and it was still dark when the children got up to go to school and drank their tea, so that the nurse had to light the lamp for a short time. Frost had set in. When the first snow falls, and one goes for one's first sleigh-ride, it is pleasant to see the white ground, the white roofs; one breathes freely and lightly, and remembers the days of one's youth. The ancient lime-trees and birches, white with rime, have a good-natured look, they are closer to the heart than cypresses and palms, and beneath their branches one is no longer haunted by the memory of mountains and the sea.

Gurov had always lived in Moscow, and he returned to Moscow on a fine frosty day, and when he put on his fur-lined overcoat and thick gloves, and sauntered down Petrovka Street, and when, on Saturday evening, he heard the church bells ringing, his recent journey and the places he had visited lost their charm for him. He became gradually immersed in Moscow life, reading with avidity three newspapers a day, while declaring he

never read Moscow newspapers on principle. Once more
he was caught up in a whirl of restaurants, clubs, banquets, and celebrations, once more glowed with the flat-
tering consciousness that well-known lawyers and actors
came to his house, that he played cards in the Medical
Club opposite a professor.

He had believed that in a month's time Anna Sergeyevna would be nothing but a vague memory, and
that hereafter, with her wistful smile, she would only
occasionally appear to him in dreams, like others before
her. But the month was now well over and winter was
in full swing, and all was as clear in his memory as
if he had only parted with Anna Sergeyevna the day
before. And his recollections grew ever more insistent.
When the voices of his children at their lessons reached
him in his study through the evening stillness, when he
heard a song, or the sounds of a musical-box in a restaurant, when the wind howled in the chimney, it all came
back to him: early morning on the pier, the misty mountains, the steamer from Feodosia, the kisses. He would
pace up and down his room for a long time, smiling at
his memories, and then memory turned into dreaming,
and what had happened mingled in his imagination with
what was going to happen. Anna Sergeyevna did not
come to him in his dreams, she accompanied him everywhere, like his shadow, following him everywhere he
went. When he closed his eyes, she seemed to stand before him in the flesh, still lovelier, younger, tenderer
than she had really been, and looking back, he saw himself, too, as better than he had been in Yalta. In the
evenings she looked out at him from the bookshelves,
the fire-place, the corner, he could hear her breathing,
the sweet rustle of her skirts. In the streets he followed women with his eyes, to see if there were any
like her. . . .

He began to feel an overwhelming desire to share his
memories with someone. But he could not speak of his

love at home, and outside his home who was there for him to confide in? Not the tenants living in his house, and certainly not his colleagues at the bank. And what was there to tell? Was it love that he had felt? Had there been anything exquisite, poetic, anything instructive or even amusing about his relations with Anna Sergeyevna? He had to content himself with uttering vague generalizations about love and women, and nobody guessed what he meant, though his wife's dark eyebrows twitched as she said:

"The role of a coxcomb doesn't suit you a bit, Dimitri."

One evening, leaving the Medical Club with one of his card-partners, a government official, he could not refrain from remarking:

"If you only knew what a charming woman I met in Yalta!"

The official got into his sleigh, and just before driving off turned and called out:

"Dmitri Dmitrich!"

"Yes?"

"You were quite right, you know—the sturgeon was just a *leetle* off."

These words, in themselves so commonplace, for some reason infuriated Gurov, seemed to him humiliating, gross. What savage manners, what people! What wasted evenings, what tedious, empty days! Frantic card-playing, gluttony, drunkenness, perpetual talk always about the same thing. The greater part of one's time and energy went on business that was no use to anyone, and on discussing the same thing over and over again, and there was nothing to show for it all but a stunted, earth-bound existence and a round of trivialities, and there was nowhere to escape to, you might as well be in a mad-house or a convict settlement.

Gurov lay awake all night, raging, and went about the whole of the next day with a headache. He slept badly on the succeeding nights, too, sitting up in bed, thinking, or pacing the floor of his room. He was sick of his children, sick of the bank, felt not the slightest desire to go anywhere or talk about anything.

When the Christmas holidays came, he packed his things, telling his wife he had to go to Petersburg in the interests of a certain young man, and set off for the town of S. To what end? He hardly knew himself. He only knew that he must see Anna Sergeyevna, must speak to her, arrange a meeting, if possible.

He arrived at S. in the morning and engaged the best room in the hotel, which had a carpet of grey military frieze, and a dusty ink-pot on the table, surmounted by a headless rider, holding his hat in his raised hand. The hall porter told him what he wanted to know: von Diederitz had a house of his own in Staro-Goncharnaya Street. It wasn't far from the hotel, he lived on a grand scale, luxuriously, kept carriage-horses, the whole town knew him. The hall porter pronounced the name "Drideritz."

Gurov strolled over to Staro-Goncharnaya Street and discovered the house. In front of it was a long grey fence with inverted nails hammered into the tops of the palings.

"A fence like that is enough to make anyone want to run away," thought Gurov, looking at the windows of the house and the fence.

He reasoned that since it was a holiday, her husband would probably be at home. In any case it would be tactless to embarrass her by calling at the house. And a note might fall into the hands of the husband, and bring about catastrophe. The best thing would be to wait about on the chance of seeing her. And he walked up and down the street, hovering in the vicinity of the fence, watching for his chance. A beggar entered the gate, only to be attacked by dogs, then, an hour later, the faint, vague sounds of a piano reached his ears. That would be Anna Sergeyevna playing. Suddenly the front door opened and an old woman came out, followed by a familiar white pomeranian. Gurov tried to call to it, but his heart beat violently, and in his agitation he could not remember its name.

He walked on, hating the grey fence more and more, and now ready to tell himself irately that Anna Sergeyevna had forgotten him, had already, perhaps, found distraction in another—what could be more natural in a young woman who had to look at this accursed fence from morning to night? He went back to his hotel and sat on the sofa in his room for some time, not knowing what to do, then he ordered dinner, and after dinner, had a long sleep.

"What a foolish, restless business," he thought, waking up and looking towards the dark window-panes. It was evening by now. "Well, I've had my sleep out. And what am I to do in the night?"

He sat up in bed, covered by the cheap grey quilt, which reminded him of a hospital blanket, and in his vexation he fell to taunting himself.

"You and your lady with a dog ... there's adventure for you! See what you get for your pains."

On his arrival at the station that morning he had noticed a poster announcing in enormous letters the first performance at the local theatre of *The Geisha*. Remembering this, he got up and made for the theatre.

"It's highly probable that she goes to first-nights," he told himself.

The theatre was full. It was a typical provincial theatre, with a mist collecting over the chandeliers, and the crowd in the gallery fidgeting noisily. In the first row of the stalls the local dandies stood waiting for the curtain to go up, their hands clasped behind them. There, in the front seat of the Governor's box, sat the Governor's daughter, wearing a boa, the Governor himself hiding modestly behind the drapes, so that only his hands were

visible. The curtain stirred, the orchestra took a long
time tuning up their instruments. Gurov's eyes roamed
eagerly over the audience as they filed in and occupied
their seats.

Anna Sergeyevna came in, too. She seated herself in
the third row of the stalls, and when Gurov's glance fell
on her, his heart seemed to stop, and he knew in a flash
that the whole world contained no one nearer or dearer
to him, no one more important to his happiness. This
little woman, lost in the provincial crowd, in no way
remarkable, holding a silly lorgnette in her hand,
now filled his whole life, was his grief, his joy,
all that he desired. Lulled by the sounds coming from
the wretched orchestra, with its feeble, amateurish
violinists, he thought how beautiful she was ... thought
and dreamed....

Anna Sergeyevna was accompanied by a tall, round-
shouldered young man with small whiskers, who nodded
at every step before taking the seat beside her and
seemed to be continually bowing to someone. This must
be her husband, whom, in a fit of bitterness, at Yalta, she
had called a "flunkey." And there really was something
of the lackey's servility in his lanky figure, his side-
whiskers, and the little bald spot on the top of his head.
And he smiled sweetly, and the badge of some scientific
society gleaming in his buttonhole was like the number
on a footman's livery.

The husband went out to smoke in the first interval,
and she was left alone in her seat. Gurov, who had taken
a seat in the stalls, went up to her and said in a trembling voice, with a forced smile: "How d'you do?"

She glanced up at him and turned pale, then looked
at him again in alarm, unable to believe her eyes,
squeezing her fan and lorgnette in one hand, evidently
struggling to overcome a feeling of faintness. Neither
of them said a word. She sat there, and he stood beside
her, disconcerted by her embarrassment, and not daring

to sit down. The violins and flutes sang out as they
were tuned, and there was a tense sensation in the atmosphere, as if they were being watched from all the boxes.
At last she got up and moved rapidly towards one of
the exits. He followed her and they wandered aimlessly
along corridors, up and down stairs; figures flashed by
in the uniforms of legal officials, high-school teachers
and civil servants, all wearing badges; ladies, coats
hanging from pegs flashed by; there was a sharp
draught, bringing with it an odour of cigarette-stubs.
And Gurov, whose heart was beating violently, thought:

"What on earth are all these people, this orchestra
for?...."

The next minute he suddenly remembered how, after
seeing Anna Sergeyevna off that evening at the station,
he had told himself that all was over, and they would
never meet again. And how far away the end seemed
to be now!

She stopped on a dark narrow staircase over which
was a notice bearing the inscription "To the upper
circle."

"How you frightened me!" she said, breathing heavily, still pale and half-stunned. "Oh, how you frightened
me! I'm almost dead! Why did you come? Oh, why?"

"But, Anna," he said, in low, hasty tones. "But,
Anna.... Try to understand ... do try...."

She cast him a glance of fear, entreaty, love, and
then gazed at him steadily, as if to fix his features firmly in her memory.

"I've been so unhappy," she continued, taking no
notice of his words. "I could think of nothing but you
the whole time, I lived on the thoughts of you. I tried
to forget—why, oh, why did you come?"

On the landing above them were two schoolboys,
smoking and looking down, but Gurov did not care, and,
drawing Anna Sergeyevna towards him, began kissing
her face, her lips, her hands.

"What are you doing, oh, what are you doing?" she said in horror, drawing back. "We have both gone mad. Go away this very night, this moment. . . . By all that is sacred, I implore you. . . . Somebody is coming."

Someone was ascending the stairs.

"You must go away," went on Anna Sergeyevna in a whisper. "D'you hear me, Dmitri Dmitrich? I'll come to you in Moscow. I have never been happy, I am unhappy now, and I shall never be happy—never! Do not make me suffer still more! I will come to you in Moscow, I swear it! And now we must part! My dear one, my kind one, my darling, we must part."

She pressed his hand and hurried down the stairs, looking back at him continually, and her eyes showed that she was in truth unhappy. Gurov stood where he was for a short time, listening, and when all was quiet went to look for his coat, and left the theatre.

IV

And Anna Sergeyevna began going to Moscow to see him. Every two or three months she left the town of S., telling her husband that she was going to consult a specialist on female diseases, and her husband believed her and did not believe her. In Moscow she always stayed at the "Slavyanski Bazaar," sending a man in a red cap to Gurov the moment she arrived. Gurov went to her, and no one in Moscow knew anything about it.

One winter morning he went to see her as usual (the messenger had been to him the evening before, but had not found him at home). His daughter was with him for her school was on the way, and he thought he might as well see her to it.

"It is three degrees above zero," said Gurov to his daughter, "and yet it is snowing. You see it is only above zero close to the ground, the temperature in the upper layers of the atmosphere is quite different."

"Why doesn't it ever thunder in winter, Papa?"

He explained this, too. As he was speaking, he kept reminding himself that he was going to a rendezvous and that not a living soul knew about it, or, probably, ever would. He led a double life—one in public, in the sight of all whom it concerned, full of conventional truth and conventional deception, exactly like the lives of his friends and acquaintances, and another which flowed in secret. And, owing to some strange, possibly quite accidental chain of circumstances, everything that was important, interesting, essential, everything about which he was sincere and never deceived himself, everything that composed the kernel of his life, went on in secret, while everything that was false in him, everything that composed the husk in which he hid himself and the truth which was in him—his work at the bank, discussions at the club, his "lower race," his attendance at anniversary celebrations with his wife—was on the surface. He began to judge others by himself, no longer believing what he saw, and always assuming that the real, the only interesting life of every individual goes on as under cover of night, secretly. Every individual existence revolves around mystery, and perhaps that is the chief reason that all cultivated individuals insisted so strongly on the respect due to personal secrets.

After leaving his daughter at the door of her school Gurov set off for the "Slavyanski Bazaar." Taking off his overcoat in the lobby, he went upstairs and knocked softly on the door. Anna Sergeyevna, wearing the grey dress he liked most, exhausted by her journey and by suspense, had been expecting him since the evening before. She was pale and looked at him without smiling, but was in his arms almost before he was fairly in the room. Their kiss was lingering, prolonged, as if they had not met for years.

"Well, how are you?" he asked. "Anything new?"

"Wait I'll tell you in a minute.... I can't...."

She could not speak, because she was crying. Turning away, she held her handkerchief to her eyes.

"I'll wait till she's had her cry out," he thought, and sank into a chair.

He rang for tea, and a little later, while he was drinking it, she was still standing there, her face to the window. She wept from emotion, from her bitter consciousness of the sadness of their life; they could only see one another in secret, hiding from people, as if they were thieves. Was not their life a broken one?

"Don't cry," he said.

It was quite obvious to him that this love of theirs would not soon come to an end, and that no one could say when this end would be. Anna Sergeyevna loved him ever more fondly, worshipped him, and there would have been no point in telling her that one day it must end. Indeed, she would not have believed him.

He moved over and took her by the shoulders, intending to fondle her with light words, but suddenly he caught sight of himself in the looking-glass.

His hair was already beginning to turn grey. It struck him as strange that he should have aged so much in the last few years. The shoulders on which his hands lay were warm and quivering. He felt a pity for this life, still so warm and exquisite, but probably soon to fade and droop like his own. Why did she love him so? Women had always believed him different from what he really was, had loved in him not himself but the man their imagination pictured him, a man they had sought for eagerly all their lives. And afterwards when they discovered their mistake, they went on loving him just the same. And not one of them had ever been happy with him. Time had passed, he had met one woman after another, become intimate with each, parted with each, but had never loved. There had been all sorts of things between them, but never love.

And only now, when he was grey-haired, had he fallen in love properly, thoroughly, for the first time in his life.

He and Anna Sergeyevna loved one another as people who are very close and intimate, as husband and wife, as dear friends love one another. It seemed to them that fate had intended them for one another, and they could not understand why she should have a husband, and he a wife. They were like two migrating birds, the male and the female, who had been caught and put into separate cages. They forgave one another all that they were ashamed of in the past, in their present, and felt that this love of theirs had changed them both.

Formerly, in moments of melancholy, he had consoled himself by the first argument that came into his head, but now arguments were nothing to him, he felt profound pity, desired to be sincere, tender.

"Stop crying, my dearest," he said. "You've had your cry, now stop. . . . Now let us have a talk, let us try and think what we are to do."

Then they discussed their situation for a long time, trying to think how they could get rid of the necessity for hiding, deception, living in different towns, being so long without meeting. How were they to shake off these intolerable fetters?

"How? How?" he repeated, clutching his head. "How?"

And it seemed to them that they were within an inch of arriving at a decision, and that then a new, beautiful life would begin. And they both realized that the end was still far, far away, and that the hardest, the most complicated part was only just beginning.

1899

IN THE GULLY

I

The village of Ukleyevo lay in a gully, and all that could be seen of it from the highroad and the railway station were the belfry and the chimneys of the cotton-printing works. When travellers asked what village that was, they were told: "It's the place where the sexton ate up all the caviare at the funeral."

At some funeral in the family of the mill-owner Kostyukov, an old sexton noticed, amidst other delicacies, a jar of caviare, and fell upon it with avidity. People nudged him, tugged at his sleeve, but he took no notice, only ate and ate in a kind of trance. There were four pounds in the jar and he ate it all. It happened ages ago, and the sexton had long been dead and buried, but every one remembered how he ate up all the caviare. Whether it was that life here was so eventless, or that the only thing which ever made an impression on the villagers was this insignificant incident, which occurred ten years before, nothing else was ever related of the village of Ukleyevo.

Fevers raged here, and even in the summer sticky mud lingered, especially at the foot of the fences, over which bowed ancient willows, spreading wide shadows. There was always a smell of factory refuse, and of the acetic acid used in finishing the prints. The factories— three cotton-mills and a tanning works—were not situated in the village itself, but on its outskirts and even beyond. They were small enterprises, employing not more than four hundred workers altogether. The water in the river stank continually from the tannery discharges; the meadowlands were polluted by refuse, the peasants' cattle suffered from anthrax, and the tannery was condemned. It was considered as closed, but worked in secret, with the connivance of the head of the rural police and district medical officer, each of whom the owner paid ten rubles a month. There were only two decent brick-built houses with iron roofs in the whole village; one of them belonged to the volost board of administration, in the other, a two-storey building, lived Tsibukin, Grigory Petrovich, who came from a lower middle-class family of the town of Yepifanovo.

Grigory kept a grocery shop, but that was merely a blind, his real occupation was the sale of vodka, cattle, hides, grain, hogs, in a word anything that came his way; thus, for instance, when magpie's wings for ladies' hats were in vogue abroad, he got thirty kopeks a pair for them; he bought up timber, lent money on interest, and was altogether a resourceful old man.

He had two sons. The elder, Anisim, was in the detective division of the police forces, and was away most of the time. The younger, Stepan, went in for trade and helped his father; but his help was not much depended on, for he was deaf and sickly. His wife Aksinya was a handsome, agile woman who wore a bonnet and carried an umbrella on Sundays and saints' days, rose early and went to bed late, rushing about all day long, her skirt tucked up and a bunch of keys jingling at her belt, from the store-house to the cellar, and from the cellar to the shop, and old Tsibukin watched her with joy, his eyes lighting up whenever he saw her, at the same time deploring that she had not married his elder son instead of the younger, the deaf one, who could hardly be expected to appreciate feminine loveliness.

The old man was of a domestic turn, prizing his family above everything in the world, especially his elder son, the detective, and his daughter-in-law. As soon as she became the wife of the deaf man, Aksinya showed herself an exceedingly business-like woman; she knew whom to allow credit for goods purchased, and whom to refuse it, kept the keys herself, not even trusting her husband with them, clicked away at the abacus, looked the horses in the mouth like a proper farmer, and was always either laughing or shouting; and whatever she did, or said, the old man could only admire, murmuring:

"There's a daughter-in-law for you! There's a beauty!"

He had been a widower for some time, but a year after his son's marriage had not been able to stand it any longer, and had married, too. A girl who lived thirty versts from Ukleyevo was chosen for him; her name was Varvara Nikolayevna, and she came of good family. She was not very young, but still good-looking, and attractive. The moment she was settled in her little room on the top floor, the whole house seemed to light up, as if new panes had been put in the windows. Lamps were lighted in front of the icons, table-cloths, white as snow, were spread on every table, red flowers appeared on window-sills and in the front garden, and at dinner every one had a plate to himself instead of eating out of a common bowl. Varvara Nikolayevna had a sweet, affectionate smile, and everything in the house seemed to smile back at her. For the first time beggars, pilgrims, and pious mendicants were seen in the yard, beneath the windows were heard the piteous wails of Ukleyevo women, the apologetic coughs of sickly, hollow-cheeked men,

sacked from the factory for drinking. Varvara relieved
their sufferings with money, bread, and old clothes, and
later, when she began to feel more sure of herself,
even smuggled various articles from the shop for them.
The deaf son saw her take two packets of tea from the
shop, and this upset him greatly.

"Mother has taken two ounces of tea," he told his
father afterwards. "Where shall I enter it?"

The old man did not answer him, but stood silent for
a few moments, his brows twitching; then he went upstairs to speak to his wife.

"Varvara dear," he said affectionately, "if you ever
want anything from the shop, take it. Take anything
you like, don't think twice about it."

And the next day, the deaf son shouted to her as he
was running across the yard:

"If you need anything, Mother, take it!"

There was something novel in her alms-giving, something as cheerful and bright as the lamps before the
icons and the red flowers. At Shrovetide, or on the three-
day holiday of the local patron-saint, when the peasants
were sold tainted beef from a barrel which stank so
that one could hardly stand beside it, and drunken men
handed scythes, caps and their wives' shawls over the
counter, when the mill-hands, bemused by bad vodka,
wallowed in the mud, and sin seemed to rise over everything in a thick mist, it was nice to think that somewhere in the house was a quiet, cleanly woman who had
nothing to do with tainted beef or vodka; on such dreary,
foggy days her alms acted as a safety valve in machinery.

The days in the Tsibukin household passed in perpetual cares. Before the sun rose, Aksinya could be
heard puffing and blowing in the entry as she washed
her face, the samovar would be boiling in the kitchen,
droning away as if warning of evil to come. The old
man, Grigory Petrovich, natty and small in his long

black coat, print trousers and shining high-boots, stumped about the rooms like the father-in-law in the popular song. Then the shop would be unlocked. As soon as was light a racing sulky was brought up to the porch, and the old man jumped briskly into it, pulling his big peaked cap over his ears, to look at him, no one would have said he was fifty-six. His wife and daughter-in-law went out to see him off, and at such moments, in his good, well-brushed coat, with the enormous black stallion, which had cost him three hundred rubles, har-nessed to the sulky, the old man did not like to have the peasants coming up to him with their complaints and requests; he had a fastidious dislike for peasants, and when he saw one waiting for him by the gate, he would shout angrily:

"What are you standing there for? Get out!"

Or if it happened to be a beggar, he would shout:

"The Lord will provide!"

Then he would drive off on his own business. His wife, a black apron over her dark dress, would put the rooms in order, or help in the kitchen. Aksinya stood behind the counter in the shop, and the clinking of bot-tles and coins, Aksinya's laughing and scolding, the angry retorts of the customers when she cheated them, could be heard from the yard; and it was obvious that a secret trade in vodka was already going on in the shop. The deaf son either sat in the shop, or walked about the street without his cap, glancing absently from the huts to the sky. Tea was drunk about six times dur-ing the day, and at least four meals were served. And in the evening, after the day's takings had been counted and entered in the books, everyone went to bed and slept soundly.

The three cotton mills in Ukleyevo were linked by telephone with the houses of the owners—Khrimins Senior, Khrimins Junior, and Kostyukov. The line had been extended to the volost board as well, but very soon ceased to work, owing to bugs and cockroaches in the apparatus. The volost elder could scarcely read and write and began every word with a capital letter, but when the telephone went out of order, he said:

"Yes, yes, it will be hard to do without a telephone."

The Khrimins Senior were constantly at law with the Khrimins Junior, while the Khrimins Junior often quarrelled among themselves and also went to law; during their quarrels the mills would stop working for a month or two, until they made it up again; this afforded much entertainment to the people of Ukleyevo, for every quarrel caused a great deal of talk and gossip. On holidays Kostyukov and the Khrimins Junior went for drives, tearing about Ukleyevo and running over calves. On those days Aksinya, dressed in her best, would walk up and down in front of the shop, her starched petticoats rustling; the Juniors would whisk her into their carriage, pretending to carry her off against her will. Then old Tsibukin would drive out to show off his new steed, taking Varvara with him.

In the night, after the drive, when other people had gone to bed, the strains of an expensive concertina could be heard in the yard of the Juniors, and if there was a moon, the music stirred and rejoiced people's hearts, and Ukleyevo no longer seemed such a hole.

II

The eldest son, Anisim, visited his home very seldom, only on special holidays, but he often sent gifts, and letters, penned in a stranger's exquisite hand, always covering a whole sheet of note-paper, and written in the form of a petition. These letters were full of expressions which Anisim would never have used in talking: "Honoured Parents, I hereby transmit a packet of herb tea for the satisfaction of your physical requirements." Every letter was signed *Anisim Tsibukin*, in a scrawl

which looked as if written with a spoilt nib, and under
the signature, in the same excellent handwriting, was
the word "Agent."

The letters were read aloud several times over, and
the old man, deeply affected and flushed with emotion,
would say:

"There, he wouldn't stay at home, but went in for
learning! Well, never mind! Each to his own, I say!"

One day, just before Shrovetide, a hard sleety rain
began to fall; the old man and Varvara went to the
window to look out, when whom should they see but
Anisim driving up in a sleigh from the station! Nobody
had expected him. He came into the room in a state of
anxiety and concealed dread which never seemed to
abate for a moment; but he bore himself with a kind
of airy familiarity. He was in no hurry to leave, and
it looked as if he had lost his job. Varvara seemed to be
glad of his visit; she cast him sly glances, sighing and
wagging her head:

"How's this, for goodness sake!" she exclaimed.
"Okh-ch'k-ch'k, the lad is twenty-seven if he is a day,
and still a bachelor!"

From the next room it sounded as if she were saying
nothing but okh-ch'k-ch'k, okh-ch'k-ch'k over and over
again in her low monotonous voice. She held whispered
conferences with the old man and Aksinya, and they,
too, assumed a sly, mysterious expression, as if they
were conspirators.

It was decided that Anisim should marry.

"Your youngest brother has been married a long
time," said Varvara, "and you go about alone, like a
cock at the market. That won't do, you know. God willing, you'll marry, then you can go back to your work if
you like, and your wife will stay at home and help us.
There's no order in your life, my boy, you've forgotten
what it is to have order in your life. Oh, you town lads!"

When any of the Tsibukins decided to get married,

the most beautiful brides were sought out for them, for
they were rich people. This time, too, a beautiful girl
was found for Anisim. He himself was insignificant and
unattractive; short of stature, with a weak rickety
frame; he had fat puffy cheeks, which he seemed to be
always blowing out, a pair of unblinking, sharp eyes,
and a reddish, sparse beard, and when he fell into a reverie, he would stuff it into his mouth and chew at the
ends; and by way of a finishing touch he was a constant
drinker, as both his face and gait betrayed. Nevertheless,
when told that a wife was chosen for him, and that she
was very beautiful, he said:

"Well, I'm not such a fright myself, am I? Nobody
will deny that we Tsibukins are a good-looking lot."

Hard by the town lay the village of Torguyevo. One
half of it had lately become part of the town, while the
other half remained a village. In the town half there
lived, in her own house, a widow-woman; she had a sister who was very poor and went out to work by the day,
and this sister had a daughter Lipa, who worked by
the day, too. Lipa's beauty was already being talked
about in the town, and it was nothing but her appalling
poverty that put people off; the general opinion was
that some elderly man, perhaps a widower, would marry
her despite her poverty, or simply take her to live with
him, and then her mother would be fed, too. Varvara
made enquiries about Lipa among the match-makers,
and then set out for Torguyevo.

The showing of the bride was duly held in the house
of Lipa's aunt, with food and drink served, and Lipa
in a new pink gown, specially made for the occasion;
and she wore a crimson ribbon like a tongue of flame
in her hair. She was thin, fragile, pale, with tender,
delicate features, and her skin was tanned from working in the fields; a timid melancholy smile hovered
round her lips, and she had the child's glance, trustful
and inquisitive.

She was very young, just a little girl with unformed breasts, but old enough to be wedded. She was beautiful—there was no gainsaying that. The only thing that could be said against her was that she had big, masculine hands, which now hung idle at her sides like great red claws.

"We can overlook the dowry," said the old man to the aunt, "we took a wife for our son Stepan from a poor family, too, and now we can't praise her enough. She does everything well, both in the house and in the shop."

Lipa stood by the door, her whole attitude expressing: "You may do what you like with me, I trust you," while her mother, the charwoman, hid in the kitchen, overcome by timidity. Once, in her youth, a merchant whose floors she was washing, stamped his foot at her, so that she was almost numb with terror, and ever since had been unable to shake off her fear. Her hands and knees, her very cheeks would shake with fear. She sat in the kitchen, trying to hear what the visitors were saying, and kept crossing herself, pressing her fingers to her forehead and glancing at the icon. Anisim, slightly drunk, opened the door into the kitchen now and then, calling out negligently:

"Why don't you come out to us, dear mother of ours? We miss you!"

And Praskovya, pressing her hands to her lean, shrivelled breast, answered every time:

"Oh, sir, you are very kind...."

After the bride-show a day was fixed for the wedding. Anisim walked about the rooms of his home, whistling. Then he would suddenly remember something, fall into a deep reverie and stare at the floor with a fixed, penetrating gaze, as if trying to see through it and deep into the earth below. He expressed neither satisfaction that he was to be wed—and that very soon, at Easter—nor a desire to see his betrothed, but only went about whistling softly. And it was obvious that he was only marrying to please his father and stepmother, and because it was the custom of the village that a son should marry, so that there should be someone to help in the house. When the time came for him to leave, he seemed to be in no hurry, and his behaviour as a whole was not what it had been during his former visits—he spoke with more airy familiarity than ever, and was always saying the wrong things.

III

In the village of Shikalovo lived two dressmakers, sisters, both belonging to the Khlysty sect. They were given the order to make the wedding-clothes and often came to the Tsibukin home to try on the dresses, sitting long over their tea afterwards. Varvara had a brown dress with black lace and bugles, and Aksinya a light green one with a yellow front and a long train. When the dressmakers had finished their work, Tsibukin paid them, not in money but with goods from the shop, and they departed with sad countenances, carrying away in their bundles tallow candles and tins of sardines for which they had no use at all, and when they got to the fields outside the village, they sat down on a mound and wept.

Anisim arrived three days before the wedding, all dressed in new clothes. He wore shiny rubber galoshes and a red cord with beads at the ends instead of a tie, and had flung his new coat over his shoulders without putting his arms into the sleeves.

After praying gravely in front of the icons, he greeted his father and gave him ten silver rubles and ten half-rubles; he gave the same to Varvara, but Aksinya he gave twenty quarter-ruble coins. The main charm of these presents lay in the fact that every coin was new and shone brightly in the sun. In his efforts to appear grave and dignified, Anisim strained the muscles of his face, puffing out his cheeks; he smelt strongly of spirits, he had evidently visited the refreshment-room at every station. And again, there was the airy familiarity, the something superfluous about the man. Anisim and his father had tea and a bite of food, while Varvara played with the brand-new rubles in her hands, and asked after friends from her village who had gone to live in the town.

"All are well, thanks be to God," answered Anisim. "True, there was an incident in the domestic life of Ivan Yegorov; his old woman, Sofia Nikiforovna died. Consumption. They ordered the funeral feast at the confectioner's—two and a half rubles per head. There was wine, too. There were a few muzhiks from our parts, you know, and they were fed for two and a half rubles each, too. But they ate nothing. As if a muzhik could appreciate sauces!"

"Two and a half rubles!" exclaimed the old man, shaking his head.

"Of course! It's not the village, you know. You step into a restaurant for a snack, order a dish or two, others drop in, you take a drop with them, and suddenly it's the dawn, and there you are—kindly pay up three or four rubles each! And if Samorodov's there, he likes to wind up with coffee and brandy, and brandy costs sixty kopeks a glass."

"How he lies!" exclaimed the old man admiringly.

"Oh, I always go about with Samorodov now. He's the one who writes my letters for me. He's a wonderful writer! And if I were to tell you, Mother," Anisim went on cheerfully, addressing Varvara, "what sort of man this Samorodov is, you wouldn't believe me. We all call him Mukhtar, he's just like an Armenian, dark all over. I can see right through him, I know all his affairs as well as I know the palm of my hand, Mother, and he feels it, and sticks to me, we are inseparable, him and me. He's a bit afraid of me, and yet he can't live without me. Wherever I go, he goes. I have a wonderful eye, Mother. For instance, a peasant is selling a shirt at the rag-market. 'Stop!' I cry, 'it's stolen goods!' And I'm quite right—it turns out to be stolen goods."

"How d'you know?" asked Varvara.

"I don't know, I have an eye, I suppose, I know nothing about the shirt, but it kind of draws me. Ha! It's stolen, and that's all! They always say at the office when they see me go out: 'There goes Anisim to shoot snipe!' That's what they call looking for stolen goods. Oh, yes, anyone can steal, it's keeping the things that's hard! The world is large, but there's no place for stolen goods in it."

"They stole a ram and two lambs last week from the Guntarevs in our village," said Varvara with a sigh. "And there's no one to look for the thief."

"Why, I might look into this. I don't say I won't."

The day of the wedding came, a chilly April day, but bright and cheerful. From early in the morning troikas and two-horse vehicles tore about Ukleyevo, bells jingling and bright-coloured ribbons streaming from the shaft-bows and the horses' manes. The rooks, disturbed by the noise, cawed among the willow-trees, and the starlings sang incessantly, as if they were delighted that the Tsibukins were having a wedding.

In the house the tables were already laden with enormous fishes, hams, stuffed game, tins of sprats, and pickles of every kind, and innumerable bottles of wine and vodka; a smell of smoked sausage and musty tinned lobster hung over it all. And the old man stumped round the tables sharpening the blade of one knife against another. Everyone was calling for Varvara, asking for this and that, and she, breathing heavily, and looking thoroughly flustered, kept running in and out of the kitchen, where the chef from Kostyukovs, and the head-cook from the Khrimins Junior had been working since day-break. Aksinya, her hair curled, wearing nothing over her stays, her new boots squeaking, rushed about the yard like a whirlwind, so swiftly that all people saw was an occasional flash of her bare knees and exposed bosom. Oaths and imprecations could be heard amidst the din; passers-by stopped at the wide-open gate; and underlying everything was the sense that something out-of-the-way was in preparation.

"They've gone to fetch the bride!"

The jingling of bells was heard, gradually receding beyond the village. Soon after two the crowd pressed forward, and the jingling of the bells was again heard— they were bringing the bride. The church was full, the candles in the overhead sconces were lighted, and the choir, by special request of old Tsibukin, sang with the music in their hands. The glare of the lamps and the coloured dresses almost blinded Lipa, who felt as if the loud voices of the singers were tapping on her skull like little hammers; the stays which she was wearing for the first time in her life squeezed her, and her new boots were tight, and she looked as if she had just come out of a swoon and did not yet understand where she was. Anisim, in his black coat, with the red cord he wore in place of a tie, seemed to be deep in thought, gazing fixedly at one place, and when the choir started singing in loud voices, he crossed himself hastily. He was deeply moved and he would have liked to cry. He had known this church ever since he was a little boy; his mother used to take him in her arms to receive the holy sacrament here, and later he used to sing in the choir-stalls with the boys; how well he knew every nook, every icon! And now he was being married here, being married because it was the right thing to do, but he was not thinking of that just now, the fact that this was his wedding had somehow quite escaped his mind. He could hardly see the icons for tears, he felt a weight at his heart; he prayed, imploring God to allow the disaster hanging over his head and ready at any moment to burst out, to pass away, as rain-clouds during a drought sometimes pass over a village, without letting a drop of rain spill. He had committed so many sins in the past, so many sins, everything was so hopeless, so irrevocably spoilt, that it seemed incongruous to ask for forgiveness. And yet he did ask to be forgiven, too, and even sobbed aloud once, but no one took any notice, for they thought he was drunk.

A child's frightened voice cried out:

"Mummie dear, do take me away, please do!"

"Quiet, there!" shouted the priest.

The crowd ran after the wedding party as it left the church; near the shop, by the gate, in the yard, and pressing against the walls beneath the windows there was a crowd, too. The women came to congratulate the young couple. The moment the newly-wed couple crossed the threshold, the singers, who stood ready in the entry with their music, began singing loudly; the musicians, sent for from the town for the occasion, struck up. The Don champagne was being handed round in tall glasses, and the carpenter and building-contractor Yelisarov, a tall lean old man with brows so thick that his eyes were hardly visible, addressed the couple:

"Anisim—and you, child—love one another, walk in the sight of God, and the Divine Mother will never abandon you." He buried his face in old Tsibukin's shoulder and gave a sob. "Let us weep, Grigory Petrovich, let us weep for joy!" he piped out in his high voice, and suddenly laughed and went on in a loud bass: "Ho-ho-ho! This bride of yours is beauteous, too! Everything is as it should be, all smooth, no rattling, the mechanism in order, all the screws in their places."

He was from the Yegoryevsk district, but had worked in the mill at Ukleyevo and in the neighbourhood from his youth, and felt he belonged to the place. It seemed to those who knew him that he had always been as old and lean and lanky as he was now, no one remembered calling him by any other name but "Spike." Perhaps it was owing to his forty years of work in the factories on nothing but repairs that he judged both human beings and inanimate objects according to a single standard—their durability: were they in need of repair? This time, too, before sitting down to the table, he tried several chairs to see whether they were strong enough; he even touched the salmon before eating it.

After tossing off the champagne they all sat down to table. The guests talked as they drew their chairs in. The choir sang in the passage, the band played, and at the same time the women gathered in the yard began singing the ritual-song in unison, and there was a wild, appalling mixture of sounds, enough to make one's head go round.

Spike fidgeted in his chair, shoving his elbows into his neighbours, interrupting everyone, laughing and weeping by turns.

"Children, dear children," he muttered hurriedly. "Aksinya dear, Varvara, let us live in peace with one another, peace and quiet, my beloved little axes...."

He was not accustomed to drinking and the first glass of gin made him drunk. This bitter, nauseating drink, brewed of goodness knows what, stupefied everyone who drank it, like a blow on the head. Speech became thick and incoherent.

Round the table were assembled the local clergy, the foremen from the factories with their wives, merchants and tavern-keepers from neighbouring villages. The volost elder and volost clerk, who had been working together these fourteen years and had never signed a single paper or let a single person leave their office, without deceiving or injuring someone, were both here, sitting side by side, fat and sleek, and they seemed to be so saturated with lies that the very skin on their faces looked like the skin of swindlers. The clerk's wife, a

meagre, cross-eyed woman, had brought all her children with her and sat there like some bird of prey,
glancing from plate to plate, pouncing on whatever
came her way, and cramming into her own and her
children's pockets.

Lipa sat as if petrified, her face wearing the same
expression as it had in the church. Anisim had not exchanged a single word with her since they had made one
another's acquaintance, so that he did not even know
what her voice was like; and now he sat next to her,
silently drinking gin, and when he got drunk, addressed
Lipa's aunt across the table.

"I have a friend, his name is Samorodov. He's not
like anyone else. An honorary citizen, and knows how
to talk. But I see right through him, Auntie, and he
knows it. Let us drink the health of Samorodov, Auntie!"

Varvara walked round the table, pressing the guests
to eat; she was bewildered and exhausted, but pleased
that there was such a lot of food and everything was so
grand—nobody could say anything, now. The sun went
down, but the feasting went on; the guests hardly knew
what they were putting into their mouths, nobody could
hear what was said, and only every now and then, when
the music stopped for a moment, a woman's voice could
be distinctly heard from the yard.

"Blood-suckers, tyrants, a plague on you!"

In the evening there was dancing to the strains of
the band. The Khrimins Junior came, bringing their own
wine, and one of them went through the quadrille with
a bottle in each hand and a glass between his teeth, to
the intense amusement of the company. Some varied
the step of the quadrille by squatting down and shooting out their legs in the Russian manner; the green-clad
Aksinya flashed by, raising a wind with her train. One
of the dancers stepped on the flounce at the bottom of
her dress, ripping it off, and Spike shouted:

"You've broken the plinth! Children, children!"

Aksinya had innocent grey eyes and an unblinking gaze, and an innocent smile played constantly over her features. In those unblinking eyes, in the tiny head poised on the long neck, and in the litheness of her figure, there was something snake-like; the yellow front of her green dress, her constant smile, made her look like an adder, rearing its length out of the young rye in spring to peep at the passer-by. The Khrimins treated her with easy familiarity, and it was only too clear that there were long established intimate relations between her and the eldest of the brothers. But her deaf husband saw nothing, and did not even look at her; he sat with his knees crossed, eating nuts, and cracking the shells with a noise like a pistol shot.

Then old Tsibukin stepped out into the middle of the floor waving his handkerchief to show that he wished to dance, too; and a murmur passed from room to room, and was caught up in the yard:

"Himself is going to dance! Himself!"

It was Varvara who danced, while the old man merely waved his handkerchief to the music and tapped his heels, but the eager crowd outside pressing against the windows and peeping through the panes was delighted, for the moment forgiving him all—his riches and his injustices.

"Go it, Grigory Petrovich!" they shouted from the yard. "Stick to it! There's life in the old dog yet! Ha-ha!"

It was after one when the rejoicings came to an end. Anisim staggered up to the musicians and singers, presenting each with a new half-ruble piece by way of a farewell gift. And the old man, not quite reeling, but lurching unsteadily, saw off the guests, telling each:

"The wedding cost two thousand rubles."

While the party was dispersing it was discovered that someone had left his old coat in the place of the good new one of the Shikalov tavern-keeper, and Anisim, suddenly on the alert, shouted:

"Stop! I'll find it this instant! I know who took it! Stop, I say!"

He rushed out into the street, trying to overtake one of the guests; he was caught and led home, where they pushed him, drunk, crimson with rage, soaked in sweat, into the room, where the aunt had already undressed Lipa; then the door was locked on them.

IV

Five days passed. Anisim went upstairs to bid Varvara good-bye before leaving. The lamps in front of the icons were all lit, and there was a smell of incense; Varvara was sitting by the window, knitting a red woollen stocking.

"Well, you haven't stayed very long with us," she said. "Tired of us, I suppose? We have a good life, here, we live in plenty, and we gave you a decent wedding, everything was as it should be; the old man says it cost two thousand. In a word, we live like true merchants, but it's dreary here. We treat the people badly. It makes my heart ache, my friend, to see how we treat them, how we treat them, by God! Whether we barter a horse, buy something, or hire help, it's always deceit, nothing but deceit. Deception on every hand. The vegetable oil in our shop is bitter, rancid—tar would be sweeter! Now, tell me, don't you think we could afford to sell good oil?"

"To each his own, Mother."

"But when we come to die? Oh, couldn't you speak to your father, couldn't you now?"

"Why don't you speak to him yourself?"

"Ah! When I tell him my mind, he answers me, just like you, with those very words: 'to each his own.' But in the next world nobody will ask what belonged to you and what to others. The judgement of the Lord is just."

"Of course nobody will ask about that," said Anisim
and sighed. "There is no God, Mother. So there'll be
no one to ask."

Varvara looked at him in amazement, laughing, and
throwing out her arms. Her frank astonishment, and
the way she looked at him as if she thought he must be
mad, made him uneasy.

"Well, perhaps there is a God, but no one believes
any more," he said. "When I was being married, I felt
funny. It was like when one takes an egg from under
the hen, and suddenly hears the chicken cheep inside,
and I heard my conscience cheep, and while the wedding was going on, I thought: 'There *is* a God!' But
when I left the church, it all passed. And how should I
know whether there is a God, or not? When we were
children we were not taught such things, and while the
baby is still at its mother's breast, it hears nothing but
the words: 'to each his own.' Father doesn't believe in
God, either. Do you remember you told me once about
some sheep being stolen from the Guntorevs? Well, I
found out all about it: a Shikalovo peasant stole them;
yes, it was he who stole them, but the hides found their
way to Father's shop. . . . There's religion for you!"

Anisim winked and shook his head.

"The village elder doesn't believe in God, either,"
he went on, "nor do the clerk and the sexton. And if
they do go to church and fast, it is only so that people
won't talk and in case the Day of Judgement comes
after all. Some people say the end of the world is at
hand, for men have become weak, no longer honour
their parents and all that. But that's nonsense. This is
what *I* think, Mother: all our troubles come from people having no conscience any more. I see through people,
Mother, I know them. When I see a stolen shirt, I know
it is stolen. A man sits in a tavern, and you may think
he's just drinking his tea, but I see, not only that he's
drinking tea, but that he has no conscience. You can go

about all day long, and never meet a man who has a conscience. And all because nobody knows whether there is a God, or not.... Well, Mother, good-bye. Keep your health and spirits, and think kindly of me."

Anisim bowed to the ground before Varvara.

"We thank you for everything, Mother," he said. "You are very good for our family. You are a decent woman, and I am greatly pleased with you."

Deeply moved, Anisim left the room, but turned back once more, and said:

"Samorodov has got me mixed up in a certain affair: it will either make me rich, or ruin me. In case anything happens, Mother, I hope you will console my parent."

"Don't say that! God is merciful. But, Anisim, I wish you would be a little kinder to your wife, you look at one another like wild beasts; never a smile, never!"

"She's such a strange girl," said Anisim with a sigh. "She understands nothing, and never says a word. She's very young, she must grow up."

A tall well-fed white stallion harnessed to a gig was waiting for him at the porch.

Old Tsibukin sprang jauntily into the gig, and took the reins. Anisim kissed Varvara, Aksinya and his brother. Lipa was standing on the porch, too; she stood motionless, looking away, as if she had merely sauntered on to the porch and had not come to see her husband off. Anisim walked up to her and touched her cheek with his lips, ever so lightly.

"Good-bye," he said.

She did not look at him, but a strange smile crept over her face; her features twitched and everyone felt sorry for her, without quite knowing why. Anisim, too, sprang into the carriage and sat down, arms akimbo, like one confident of his good looks.

While the gig climbed the side of the gully, Anisim kept looking back, at the village. It was a warm, sunny day. The cattle had been taken out to graze for the first time that year, and the women and girls accompanying them were dressed up as for a holiday. A red bull bellowed loud, rejoicing in its freedom, pawing the ground with its hoofs. Everywhere, down below, and up above, the larks were singing. Anisim looked back at the church, so graceful and white—it had just been whitewashed—and remembered how he had prayed in it five days ago; then he looked at the school with its green roof, at the stream in which he used to bathe and fish, and his heart leaped with joy, and he wished a wall would suddenly rise from the ground and prevent him from going any further, leaving him with nothing but the past.

When they got to the station they went up to the refreshment-room and had a glass of sherry each. The old man put his hand into his pocket to get out his purse, but Anisim said:

"My treat!"

The old man was moved, patted him on the shoulder and winked at the barman, as if to say: "See what a son I have!"

"I wish you would stay at home, Anisim, and help me with my business," he said. "You would be invaluable to me! I would plaster you with gold, Son."

"No, no, Father, I can't."

The sherry was sour and smelt of sealing-wax, but they had another glass each.

When he returned from the station the old man hardly recognized his youngest daughter-in-law. The moment her husband left the house, Lipa was transformed into a cheerful young woman. Barefooted, in a worn skirt, her sleeves pulled high up her arms, she was washing the steps of the porch and singing in a high, silvery voice; and when she carried out the heavy tub of dirty water, and looked up at the sun with her childlike smile, she was like a lark herself.

An old workman who happened to pass the porch just then, shook his head and cleared his throat.

"What daughters-in-law God has sent you, Grigory Petrovich!" he said. "Real treasures!"

V

On the eighth of July, which was a Friday, Lipa and Yelisarov, nicknamed Spike, were walking back from the village of Kazanskoye, where they had been to celebrate the day of the Kazan Madonna, the patron saint of the church there. Far behind them came Lipa's mother, Praskovya, for she was a sick woman, and short of breath. It was getting on towards evening.

"O-o-oh!" exclaimed Spike in astonishment as he listened to Lipa. "O-o-oh! Well?"

"I am very fond of jam, Ilya Makarich," Lipa was saying. "So I sit in the corner, drinking tea and eating jam. Or else I have my tea with Varvara Nikolayevna, and she tells me something sad and beautiful. They have ever so much jam—four jars! 'Eat up, Lipa, don't stint yourself!' they keep saying."

"Ha! Four jars!"

"Yes. They are rich. They eat white bread with their tea, and as much meat as you like. They are rich, but I am afraid all the time, Ilya Makarich. Oh, I'm so afraid!"

"What are you afraid of, child?" asked Spike, looking back to see if Praskovya was very far away.

"At first, after the wedding, I was afraid of Anisim Grigorich. He was all right, he never did me any harm, but whenever he came near me, it made my skin creep, right to my bones. And I lay awake every night, trembling and praying. And now it's Aksinya I'm afraid of, Ilya Makarich. She's all right, really, she smiles all the time, but sometimes, she looks out of the window, and her eyes are fierce, with a green light in them, like

sheep's eyes in a dark shed. The Khrimins Junior keep
on at her: 'Your old man has a plot of land in Butyekino, about forty dessiatins or so,' they say, 'the soil is
mostly sand, and there is a stream there. Why shouldn't
you build a brick-works of your own, Aksinya,' they
say, 'and we would be your partners.' Brick costs
twenty rubles a thousand now. They'd make a pile.
Yesterday at dinner Aksinya said to the old man: 'I
want to build a brick-works in Butyekino, and start
business on my own.' She said it smiling-like. But Grigory Petrovich's face went all dark; you could see he
didn't like it. 'So long as I'm alive,' he said, 'there will
be no separate trading. We must all slide together.' She
gave him such a look, and gnashed her teeth.... And
when the fritters were served, she wouldn't have any."

"Ha!" exclaimed Spike. "She wouldn't?"

"And I'd like to know when she sleeps," Lipa went
on. "She lies down for half an hour, and then up she
gets and starts walking about the place, walking, walking, looking into every nook and corner, to see if the
peasants haven't burnt or stolen anything. She frightens
me, Ilya Makarich! And the Khrimins Junior didn't go
to bed after the wedding, they went straight to the law-
courts in the town; and people say it's all Aksinya's
fault. Two of the brothers promised to build a works
for her, and the third is displeased, and so the mill
didn't work for almost a month, and my uncle Prokhor
was out of work and went from house to house begging
crusts. 'Why don't you go and work in the fields,' I says
to him, 'or saw wood, instead of disgracing yourself
like that!' and he says, 'I've forgotten what it is to work
like an honest peasant. I can't work in the fields any
more, Lipa.' "

They halted at the young aspen grove to rest and let
Praskovya catch up with them. Yelisarov had been
working as contractor for a long time, but he had no
horse, and walked all over the district on foot, carrying

a little sack containing bread and onions, and striding
along rapidly on his long legs, his arms swinging. It
was quite hard to keep up with him.

On the edge of the copse was a milestone. Yelisarov
touched it to see if it was as strong as it looked. Praskovya joined them, breathing heavily. Her wizened, per-
manently alarmed face was now radiantly happy: she
had been to church like other people, afterwards walking about the fair drinking *pear-kvass*. This sort of thing
did not happen often in her life, and it seemed to her
that today was the only happy day she had ever had.
After resting, all three walked on side by side. The sun
was setting, its rays penetrating the copse, lighting up
the trunks of the trees. From somewhere ahead came
the hum of voices. The girls from Ukleyevo were a long
way in front, lingering in the copse, probably looking
for mushrooms.

"Hi, lasses!" shouted Yelisarov. "Hi, my beauties!"
His cry was greeted with laughter.

"Spike's coming! Spike! Old fogey!"

And the echo laughed, too. And now they had left
the copse behind. The tops of the factory chimneys could
be seen and the cross on the belfry flashed in the sun:
it was the village, "the place where the sexton ate up
all the caviare at the funeral." They would soon be home
now; they only had to descend into the great gully. Lipa
and Praskovya, who had been walking barefoot, sat
down to put on their boots; the contractor sat in the
grass beside them. Seen from above, Ukleyevo, with
its willows, its white church and its little river looked
picturesque and peaceful, but the mill roofs, painted a
sombre colour in the interests of economy, spoilt the effect. On the opposite slope of the gully could be seen
rye—in sheaves, in stocks, as if flung down in the storm,
or, where it had only just been mowed, in near rows; the
oats were ripe, too, and gleamed in the rays of the setting
sun with a pearly lustre. Harvesting was in full swing.

Today was a holiday, tomorrow they would gather in the
rye and the hay, and the next day would be Sunday, a
holiday again; every day the thunder rumbled somewhere far away, the air was sultry and as if it were
soon going to rain, and as they gazed at the field, each
thought—if only the grain is harvested in time—and
there was joy and a happy tumult in each breast.

"Hay-makers are getting good money this year," said
Praskovya. "A ruble forty kopeks a day!"

And all the while people kept streaming back from
the fair at Kazanskoye; women, mill-workers in new
caps, beggars, children.... A farm-cart went by, raising a cloud of dust, a horse which its owners had been
unable to sell trotting behind, looking as if it were glad
it had not been sold; now an obstreperous cow was led
by the horns; another cart passed, loaded with drunken
peasants, their legs dangling over the sides. An old
woman led by the hand a little boy in a big cap and
enormous high-boots; the boy, though exhausted by the
heat and the heavy boots, which did not allow his knees
to bend, blew incessantly with all his might into a toy
trumpet; they had already descended the slope and
turned into the street, but the trumpet could still be
heard.

"Something's come over our mill-owners," said Yelisarov. "Mercy on us! Kostyukov is angry with me.
'You've used too many shingles on the cornices,' he says.
'Too many?' asks I. 'I used as many as were needed,
Vassily Danilich,' I says. 'I don't eat shingles with my
porridge, you know.' 'How dare you,' says he, 'speak
to me like that? You fool,' he says, 'you this and that!
You forget yourself! It was I who made a contractor
of you!' 'Ha,' says I, 'and what of it? I got tea to drink
every day before I was a contractor, didn't I?' 'You're
a pack of swindlers, all of you...' says he. I held my
peace. *We* are swindlers in this world, I thought to myself, but you will be swindlers in the other. Ho-ho! Next

day he wasn't so rough. 'Don't be angry with me, Makarich,' says he, 'for what I said to you. If I did say something I shouldn't have, after all, I am a merchant of the first guild, and your superior, and you should bear with me.' 'It's true you are a merchant of the first guild, and I am only a carpenter,' says I. 'But St. Joseph was a carpenter, too. It's a worthy occupation, one that is pleasing to the Lord, and if you choose to consider yourself my superior, you're welcome, Vassily Danilich.' And then, after that talk of ours, I got to thinking: which of us is the superior? The merchant of the first guild, or the carpenter? The carpenter, children, the carpenter!"

Spike thought for a while, and then added:

"Yes, my children. He who labours and endures, he is the superior."

The sun had now set, and a dense mist, white as milk, was rising above the stream, the churchyard and the clearings round the mills. Now, with darkness coming on apace, and the lights shimmering below, while the mist seemed to be concealing a bottomless abyss, Lipa and her mother, born into utter poverty, and reconciled to live in poverty all their days, giving up to others everything but their meek, timid souls, may have felt, for one short moment that they, too, in this vast mysterious universe, in the infinite chain of living creatures, meant something, were superior beings; they enjoyed sitting on the top of the slope, and smiled blissfully, forgetting for a moment that they would have to go down into the gully sooner or later.

At last they were home again. The hay-makers were sitting on the ground near the gate, and in front of the shop. The Ukleyevo peasants did not usually hire themselves out to Tsibukin, who had to get his hay-makers from other villages, and it seemed in the half-light as if all round sat men with long black beards. The shop was open, and the deaf man could be seen through the

door playing draughts with a boy. The hay-makers were
singing softly, almost inaudibly, every now and then
breaking off to demand in loud voices their wages for
the day before, but they were not paid for fear they
might go away before morning. Beneath the boughs of
a birch-tree growing in front of the porch, old Tsibukin
sat in his shirt sleeves, drinking tea with Aksinya; a
lighted lamp stood on the table.

"Ga-a-a-ffer!" one of the hay-makers on the other side
of the gate sang out in a taunting voice. "Give us half—
only half! Ga-a-a-ffer!"

And then there was laughter and more soft, almost
inaudible singing.... Spike sat down at the table to
have some tea.

"So we went to the fair," he began relating. "We had
a good time, children, a very good time, thanks be to
God. But something very unpleasant happened. Sasha
the smith bought some tobacco, and handed a half-ruble
piece to the merchant. And the coin turned out to be a
false one." Spike looked round him as he spoke; he meant
to speak in a whisper, but everyone could hear what he
said in his hoarse, half-smothered voice. "And it turned
out to be a false one. 'Where did you get it?' they asked
him. 'Anisim Tsibukin,' he says, 'gave it me, at the
wedding....' So they called the policeman, and he took
him away.... Look out, Petrovich, mind you don't have
trouble, people talk, you know...."

"Ga-a-a-ffer!" came in the same taunting voice from
the gate. "Ga-a-a-ffer!"

Then there was silence.

"Ah, children, children..." murmured Spike rapidly
and he got up; he was overcome with drowsiness.
"Thanks for the tea and sugar, my children. Time to go
to bed. I'm a-mouldering, I am, and all my beams are
rotting. Ho-ho!"

Before going away, he said:

"It means the time has come to die!" And he gave a

sob. Old Tsibukin did not finish his tea but sat on, thinking; he seemed to be still listening to the sound of Spike's steps, though he was already far away by now in the street.

"Sasha the smith must have been lying," said Aksinya, guessing at his thoughts.

He went into the house, returning in a few minutes with a small bundle in his hands. He unwrapped it and brand-new rubles gleamed on the table. Taking one up, he put it between his teeth, then flung it on the tray; then he picked up another, and flung it down, too....

"The coins *are* false..." he said, looking at Aksinya, in a kind of wonder. "They're the ones... The ones Anisim brought, his present. Here, child, take it," he whispered, shoving the bundle into her hands, "take it and throw it into the well.... Who wants them? And see there is no talk. There may be trouble.... Take the samovar away, put out the lamp...."

Lipa and Praskovya sat in the shed, watching the lights go out, one by one; only in the top storey, in Varvara's window, shone the red and blue lamps in front of the icons, and they seemed to bring peace, content and innocence. Praskovya could never get used to the idea that her daughter had married a rich man, and when she came to see her, she crouched timidly in the entry, smiling ingratiatingly, and they would send her out some tea and sugar. Lipa could not get used to it, either, and after her husband had gone away, did not sleep on her own bed, but laid herself down anywhere, in the kitchen, or the shed, and every day she scrubbed the floors and did the washing, and imagined she was still a hired worker. This time, too, after she and her mother returned from their pilgrimage, they had their tea with the cook and then went into the shed and lay down on the floor, between the wall and the sleigh. It was dark there, and smelt of harness. The lights went out round the house, then the deaf man could be heard

locking up the shop, and the hay-makers settling down
to sleep in the yard. Far away, at the Khrimins Junior,
someone was playing on the expensive concertina.

And when they were waked up by someone's footsteps, it was light, for the moon had risen; Aksinya was
standing in the entrance of the shed, holding her bed-
clothes in her arms.

"It'll be cooler in here," she said, stepping in and
lying down almost on the threshold, her whole figure lit
in the moonlight.

She did not sleep and kept sighing heavily, tossing
about in the heat, throwing off almost all her clothes;
and in the magical light of the moon, what a beautiful,
what a proud animal she looked! A short time elapsed,
and footsteps were again heard; the old man, all in
white, appeared in the door-way.

"Aksinya!" he called out. "Are you there?"

"Well, what is it?" she answered crossly.

"I told you to throw the money into the well—did
you?"

"I'm not such a fool as to fling good stuff like that
into the water! I gave it to the hay-makers...."

"Oh, my God!" said the old man, consternation in
his voice. "You stubborn wench.... Oh, God!"

He brought his hands together in a gesture of despair and walked away, muttering to himself. A little
later Aksinya sat up, heaved a deep sigh of irritation,
gathered up her bed-clothes and went out of the shed.

"Why did you marry me into this house, Mother!"
said Lipa.

"Everyone must marry, child. It is ruled by others,
not ourselves."

They were ready to give themselves up to feelings
of inconsolable grief. But there was someone, they felt,
high up in the sky, looking down upon them from the
blue, where the stars were, seeing all that went on in
Ukleyevo, watching over it. And great as the evil was,

the night was still and lovely, and there was justice in
God's universe, and there would be justice, as still and
beautiful as the night, and everything on the earth was
only waiting to be merged with justice, as the moonlight merges with the night.

And both, their peace restored, pressed close against
one another and fell asleep.

VI

News had long arrived that Anisim was in prison
for counterfeiting and circulating false coins. Months
passed by, more than half a year, the long winter was
over, and spring had begun, and everyone in the house
and in the village had got used to the idea of Anisim
being in prison. And whoever happened to pass the
house or the shop in the night remembered that Anisim
was in prison; and whenever they tolled the bell for the
dead, people somehow remembered again that he was
in prison, awaiting his trial.

A shadow lay over the entire household. The walls
of the house seemed to have become darker, the roof
was rusty, the heavy, green, iron-bound shop-door was
warped; and old Tsibukin himself seemed to have grown
darker. He had long stopped having his hair cut or his
beard trimmed, and there was a shaggy growth all over
his cheeks, and he no longer leaped into his gig with a
jaunty air, or shouted to the beggars: "The Lord will
provide!" His strength was declining, and this showed
itself in everything about him. People no longer feared
him so much, and the policeman drew up a statement
in his shop, although he got the same solid bribe as before; the old man had been summoned three times to
the town, to be tried for trading in spirits without a
license, and the trial had been put off three times owing
to non-appearance of witnesses, and the old man was
worn out.

He often went to see his son in prison, hired a lawyer for his defence, sent applications somewhere, bought a church-banner. He presented the warden of the prison in which Anisim was confined with a silver glass-holder bearing an enamelled inscription: "The soul knoweth its measure," and a long silver spoon.

"There is no one for us to turn to, no one," Varvara went about saying. "We ought to ask one of the gentry to write to the chief authorities.... If only they would let him out before the trial.... Why should the lad languish there?"

She, too, was grieved, but she had become stouter and sleeker, and she lit the icon-lamps as usual, and saw that everything in the house was in order, and treated visitors to jam and apple jelly. Aksinya and her deaf husband worked as usual in the shop. A new enterprise was afoot—the building of a brick-works at Butyekino—and Aksinya went there almost every day in the gig; she drove herself, and when she met anyone she knew, she reared her head like a snake in the young rye, and smiled her naive, mysterious smile. And Lipa played all the time with her baby, born just before Lent. It was a tiny baby, thin and sickly, and it seemed strange that it could cry and look about and that people regarded it as a human being, and called it Nikifor. It would lie in its cradle, and Lipa would walk away to the door, and say, with a bow:

"Good day to you, Nikifor Anisimich!"

And she would rush back to it, and kiss it, then walk back to the door again, bow and say:

"Good day to you, Nikifor Anisimich!"

And the baby would kick out with its little red legs, laughing and crying at the same time, just like Yelisarov the carpenter.

At last a day was appointed for the trial. The old man set out for the town five days before the time. Then it was said that peasants from the village had been sent for as witnesses; Tsibukin's old workman went, too, having also received a summons.

The trial was to be held on Thursday, but Sunday passed, and the old man had not returned, and there was no news. Towards evening on Tuesday, Varvara sat at the open window listening for the old man to come back. Lipa was playing with the baby in the next room. She dandled it, gleefully crooning:

"You'll grow up big, big! You'll grow to be a man and we'll go and hire ourselves out to work together! Together, together!"

"Oh!" said Varvara, shocked. "What's this about going out for hire, you silly? He'll grow up to be a merchant!"

Lipa began singing softly, but very soon forgot herself, and started all over again:

"You'll grow big, big! And we'll go out to work together!"

"There you are—at it again!"

Lipa stopped in the the door-way with Nikifor in her arms, and asked:

"Why do I love him so, Mother? Why is he so dear to me?" and her voice broke, and her eyes glistened with tears. "Who is he? What is he? Light as a feather, such a teeny-weeny thing, and I love him as if he were a real human being. Look, he can't say anything, not a thing, and I understand everything he wants, just by looking at his eyes."

Varvara listened again: the sound of the evening train coming into the station reached her ears. The old man might be in it. She neither heard nor understood what Lipa was saying, and did not notice the minutes go by, but sat trembling, not so much from fear, as from violent curiosity. She heard a cart clatter noisily past, loaded with peasants. It was the witnesses returning from the station. The old workman jumped out of the cart as it drove past the shop, and walked into the yard.

She could hear people greeting him in the yard, questioning him. . . .

"Debarred from all rights and property," he answered loudly. "Siberia, hard labour, six years."

Aksinya could be seen coming out of the shop by the back entrance; she had been selling kerosene, and had the bottle in one hand, and the funnel in another, while between her teeth she held some silver coins.

"And where's Dad?" she lisped.

"At the station," answered the workman. "He'll come home when it gets darker, he says."

When it was known in the house that Anisim was sentenced to hard labour, the cook began wailing in the kitchen at the top of her voice, as if for the dead, for she considered that decency required this of her.

"Why do you leave us, Anisim Grigorich, my bright eagle?"

The dogs were roused and began barking. Varvara ran up to the window, and stood there rocking herself from side to side in her grief; she shouted to the cook, straining her voice:

"Sto-op it, Stepanida, sto-o-op it! Don't torture us, for Christ's sake!"

No one remembered to heat the samovar, they all seemed to have lost their heads. Lipa was the only one who had no idea what had happened, and she went on fondling over the baby.

When the old man returned from the station, nobody asked him anything. He said a word of greeting, and then walked through the rooms in silence; he refused supper.

"There's no one for us to turn to," said Varvara when they were alone. "I told you you should have asked some of the gentry, you wouldn't listen to me then. . . . You should have sent in a petition. . . ."

"I did what I could!" said the old man, with a wave of his hand. "After the sentence was read, I went up to the gentleman who defended Anisim. 'You can't do anything now,' he said, 'it's too late.' And Anisim said those very words: 'Too late.' But still, as I was leaving the court, I spoke to a lawyer; I gave him some money on account.... I'll wait a week, and then go up again. We are in God's hands."

Once more the old man went through the rooms in silence, and when he got back to Varvara, said:

"I must be ill. My head is misty-like. I don't seem to be able to think clearly."

Then he closed the door so that Lipa should not hear him, and said:

"I'm worried about my money. Remember Anisim brought me those new ruble and half-ruble pieces just before the wedding, the week after Easter? I put away one bundle, but the rest I mixed with my own money.... When my uncle Dmitry Filatich (God rest his soul!) was alive, he used to go buying goods, sometimes to the Crimea, sometimes to Moscow. And he had a wife, and that wife while he was away, buying goods, like I said, used to go about with other men. And they had six children. And when my uncle had taken a drop too much, he used to laugh and say: 'I can't make out which of them are mine and which aren't.' He was an easy-going man, you see. And I can't make out, which of my money is good, and which is false. It all seems false to me, now."

"Don't say that, for God's sake!"

"Yes, I go to buy myself a ticket at the station, take out three rubles to pay for it, and keep wondering if they aren't false ones. It makes me afraid. I must be ill."

"We are all in God's hands, say what you will," said Varvara with a shake of her head. "We must think about it, Petrovich.... Anything might happen, you're not a young man any more. If you were to die, your grandson might be badly treated. I keep worrying about Nikifor. The father's as good as gone, the mother's young and foolish.... You might at least leave him that plot of land, Butyekino, really you might, Petrovich! Think it over!" continued Varvara persuasively. "He's a pretty little thing, it would be a shame! Go tomorrow and write out a paper. What's the use of waiting?"

"Yes, I forgot about the boy..." said Tsibukin. "I haven't seen him today. He's a nice boy, is he? Well, well, let him grow up, God bless him!"

He opened the door and beckoned to Lipa with his forefinger. She came up with the baby in her arms.

"If there's anything you want, Lipa dear, you just ask for it," he said. "And eat whatever you like, we don't grudge you anything, all we want is that you should be well...." He made the sign of the cross over the baby. "And look after my grandson. I have lost my son, but I still have a grandson."

Tears poured down his cheeks, he gave a sob and walked away. Soon after he went to bed and, after seven sleepless nights, fell into a sound sleep.

VII

The old man was away in the town for several days. Somebody told Aksinya that he had gone to see a notary about his will, and had willed Butyekino, where she was baking her bricks, to his grandson Nikifor. She was told this in the morning, while the old man and Varvara were sitting in front of the porch, beneath the birch-tree, drinking tea. She locked both the street door and the yard door of the shop, gathered up all the keys in her possession, and flung them on the ground at the old man's feet.

"I will not work for you any more!" she cried in a loud voice and all of a sudden burst into tears. "It appears I'm not your daughter-in-law, but a mere servant! As it is everyone laughs: 'See what a fine servant the Tsibukins have found!' I never hired myself out to you! I'm not a beggar, not some jumped-up creature—I have a mother and a father."

Without wiping away her tears, she fixed her swimming eyes, blazing and squinting with resentment, on the old man's face shouting at the top of her voice, her face and neck crimson with the strain:

"I will serve you no more! I'm worn out! When it comes to working, sitting in the shop day after day, going for vodka in the night, it's me, but when it comes to giving away land, it's her, the convict's wife with her little devil! She's the mistress here, the lady, and I am her servant! Go on, leave everything to her, the gaol-bird and may it choke her, but I shall go home! Find yourselves another fool, accursed tyrants!"

Never in his life had the old man abused or punished his children and he could not even imagine that anyone belonging to his household could speak rudely to him, or treat him disrespectfully, and now he was terrified and ran into the house, where he hid behind a cupboard. But Varvara was so dumbfounded, she could not even get up and could only sit waving her arms as if warding off a bee.

"What's this, what's this?" she kept muttering in a horrified voice. "Must she shout so loud? People will hear her! If only she would be a little quieter.... Just a little!"

"You've given away Butyekino to the convict's wife," Aksinya went on shouting, "go on—give her everything, then, I don't want anything from you! To hell with you all! You're a gang of thieves! I've seen enough, and I'm sick of it! You've robbed passers-by, travellers, you scoundrels, you've robbed the old and the young! Who sold vodka without a license? And the false money? Your chests are crammed with false coins—and now you don't need me any more!"

A crowd had by now gathered before the wide-open gate and stood peering into the yard.

"Let people see!" cried Aksinya. "I'll shame you before them! I'll make you burn with shame! You shall

grovel at my feet! Hi, Stepan!" she called to the deaf
man. "Come home with me this minute! Come home to
my father and mother! I will not live with convicts! Pack
up everything!"

There was some washing hanging on a line across
the yard; she tore from it her petticoats and bodices, all
wet as they were, and thrust them into the deaf man's
arms. Then, in a frenzy, she dashed up and down, tearing everything off the line, throwing on the ground
everything which was not hers, and stamping on it.

"Oh-oh, stop her!" moaned Varvara. "What's the matter with her? Give her Butyekino, for Christ's sake!"

"What a wench!" they were saying at the gate.
"There's a wench for you! Did you ever see such a passion?"

Aksinya rushed into the kitchen, where the clothes
were being laundered. Lipa was alone, washing, the
cook having gone to the river to rinse the linen. Steam
was rising from the wash-tub and from a vat in front of
the stove, and the kitchen was dim and stuffy. There
was a heap of unwashed linen on the floor, and on a
bench beside the heap, so that if he fell he would not
hurt himself, lay Nikifor, kicking out with his red, skin-
ny legs. Just as Aksinya entered the kitchen, Lipa tugged
one of her chemises from the heap and dumped it
into the tub, reaching out for a great scoop full of boiling
water which was standing on the table. . . .

"Give it here!" said Aksinya, looking at her with hatred and snatching her chemise out of the tub. "It's not
for the likes of you to touch my linen. You're a convict's
wife, and ought to know your place, and what you are!"

Lipa gazed at her, too stunned to understand anything, but suddenly, catching the glance Aksinya cast
at the baby, she understood, and went stiff with horror.

"This is what you get for stealing my land!"

With these words, Aksinya grasped the scoop full of
boiling water and poured it over Nikifor.

A scream was heard, such a scream as had never before been heard in Ukleyevo, and it was hard to believe that so puny and frail a creature as Lipa could have screamed like that. Then a great stillness came over the yard. Aksinya went into the house in silence, smiling her curious innocent smile. ... The deaf man, who had been pacing up and down the yard with the washing in his arms, now began hanging it up on the line again, silently, unhurriedly. And until the cook returned from the river, no one dared to go into the kitchen and see what was going on there.

VIII

Nikifor was taken to the Zemstvo hospital, where he died towards evening. Without waiting for anyone to send for her, Lipa wrapped up the dead body of her child in a blanket and carried it home.

The hospital, a new one with large windows, stood on the top of the hill; it was all aglow with the rays of the setting sun and looked as if it was on fire. The village spread out beneath it. Lipa went down by the road, and seated herself by a small pond just outside the village. A woman had brought a horse to the water, but the horse would not drink.

"Why don't you drink?" the woman said softly, as if astonished. "What's the matter?"

A little boy in a red shirt was squatting right at the water's edge, washing his father's boots. And there was not another soul to be seen, either in the village, or on the hillside.

"It won't drink..." said Lipa, watching the horse.

And then the woman and the boy with the boots went away, and there was nobody in sight. The sun had gone to bed in a broad sheet of gold and crimson, and long clouds, red and purple, stretched across the sky, watching over its sleep. Somewhere in the distance, goodness knows where, the bittern boomed, and it sounded like the hollow, melancholy bellowing of a cow locked in a shed. The cry of the mysterious bird was heard every spring, and no one knew what sort of a bird it was, or where it lived. On the top of the hill, beside the hospital, in the bushes round the pond, on the other side of the village and all over the fields, nightingales were pouring out their song. The cuckoo was trying to tell somebody's age, losing count every time, and beginning all over again. In the pond frogs were calling to one another, in harsh, angry voices, and you could even make out the words: "Ee ti takava, ee ti takava!*" What a noise everywhere! One would think that all these creatures were shouting and singing on purpose, so that no one should sleep on this spring night, so that everyone, even the bad-tempered frogs, should cherish and enjoy every moment of it: after all, we only live once!

A silver crescent moon shone in the sky, which was studded with stars. Lipa had no idea how long she remained sitting by the pond, but when she got up and began walking, she could see that everyone in the village was in bed, and the lights were out. It was probably about twelve versts to Ukleyevo, and she was very weak, and could not give her mind to the task of finding the way. The moon shone, now in front of her, now on her left, now on her right, and the cuckoo, hoarse by now, went on shouting, as if laughing, and taunting her: "You've lost your way, you've lost your way!" Lipa walked fast and lost her head kerchief. . . . She gazed into the sky, wondering where her little boy's soul was—was he following her, or floating somewhere high up, near the stars, forgetful of his mother? How lonely it is in the fields of a night, amidst all this singing, when you cannot sing yourself, amidst incessant cries of joy, when you cannot rejoice yourself, when the moon looks

* You're just as bad!—*Tr.*

down from the sky, as lonely as yourself, not caring whether it is spring or winter, whether people are alive, or dead.... When there is grief in your heart it is hard to be alone. If only she could be with her mother, or with Spike or the cook, or with just anyone!

"Booh!" cried the bittern. "Boo-oo-h!"

And all of a sudden she distinctly heard a man's voice:

"Come on, Vavila, harness the horse!"

A few paces ahead, by the very road-side, a bonfire was burning, the flames had died down, and only the embers glowed. There was a sound of horses munching. In the dusk could be made out two carts, one with a barrel on it, the other, much lower, loaded with sacks, and the figures of two men; one of the men was taking a horse up to the cart, the other stood motionless in front of the fire, his hands clasped behind his back. Somewhere near the carts a dog growled. The man leading the horse stopped and said:

"Someone must be coming down the road."

"Quiet, Sharik!" shouted the other one to the dog.

And from his voice you could tell he was an old man. Lipa stopped and said:

"The Lord be with you!"

The old man approached her, and at first said nothing.

Then he said:

"Good evening!"

"Your dog won't bite me, will he, Gaffer?"

"No, no, you can pass. He won't touch you."

"I've been in the hospital," said Lipa, after a pause. "My little son died there. And I'm carrying him home."

Evidently what she said upset the old man, for he walked away from her and said hurriedly:

"Never mind, my dear. It was the will of God. Come on, lad!" he cried, addressing his companion. "Hurry up, can't you?"

"Your shaft-bow isn't here," answered the lad. "I can't find it."

"What's the good of you, Vavila!"

The old man picked up a coal and blew on it, so that his eyes and his nose were lit up, and then, after they had found the shaft-bow, he moved towards Lipa, still with the coal in his hand, and glanced at her; and his glance expressed compassion and tenderness.

"You're a mother," he said. "Every mother loves her child."

And he sighed and shook his head. Vavila threw something on the fire, and then stamped it out, and immediately all was intense darkness; the vision had disappeared, and once more there was nothing but the field, the star-studded sky, and the noisy birds, keeping each other awake. And the landrail was crying in the very place, so it seemed, where the fire had been.

But after a minute or two the carts, the old man and the lanky Vavila were visible again. The wheels creaked as the carts were dragged back into the road.

"Are you saints?" Lipa asked the old man.

"No. We live in Firsanovo."

"You looked at me, and my heart grew softer. And the lad with you is so quiet. So I thought to myself, they must be saints."

"Have you far to go?"

"To Ukleyevo."

"Get in, we'll take you as far as Kuzmenki. From there you can go straight on, we turn to the left."

Vavila got into the cart with the barrel, and the old man and Lipa into the other. They drove slowly, Vavila's cart leading the way.

"My boy suffered all day," said Lipa. "He looked so gently at me from his dear eyes, as if he wanted to say something, and couldn't. God in Heaven! Holy Mother of God! I kept falling to the ground from grief. I stood by his bed, and down I went. Tell me, Gaffer, why should a little baby have to suffer so much before dying? When grown-up people suffer, men or women, their sins are forgiven, but why should a little baby that has no sins suffer? Why?"

"Who can tell!" answered the old man.

They drove on in silence for half an hour.

"You can't know all, the why and the wherefore," said the old man. "A bird has two wings, and not four, because two are enough for it to fly with; and in the same way it is not given to man to know all there is to know, but only a half or a quarter. Man knows just what he needs to help him through life."

"I think I would feel better if I walked, Gaffer. The jolting shakes my heart."

"Never mind. Stay where you are."

The old man yawned, making the sign of the cross over his mouth.

"Never mind," he repeated. "Your grief is only half-grief. Life is long, there is yet good and evil to come. Oh, Great Mother Russia!" he exclaimed, looking from side to side of the road. "I have been all over Russia, and I have seen all there is to see in it, so you can believe me, my dear. There is good to come and there is evil. I went on foot all the way to Siberia, I've been on the river Amur, and on the Altai Mountains, I settled in Siberia and tilled the land there, and then I felt home-sick for Mother Russia and came back to my own village. We went back to Russia on foot; I remember once we crossed a river by the ferry, and I was so thin, so ragged, barefoot, freezing cold, sucking at a crust, and there was a gentleman on the ferry, God rest his soul if he's dead, and he looked at me with pity, and the tears rolled down his cheeks. 'Ah,' he said, 'black your bread, and black your life.' And when I came back I had neither house nor home, as they say; I had a wife, but I left her in Siberia, in the grave. And so I hired myself out by the day. And what do you think? After that there was

evil in my life and there was good. And I don't want to
die, my dear, I would like to live another twenty years,
so you see there must have been more good than
evil. Ah, but how great Mother Russia is!" he repeated
again, glancing from right to left, and looking backwards.

"Gaffer!" said Lipa, "when a person dies, how many
days does his soul walk about the earth?"

"Who can say? Wait, we'll ask Vavila, he has been
to school. They teach them everything there, nowadays.
Vavila!"

"Eh?"

"Vavila, when someone dies, how many days does
his soul roam the earth?"

Vavila first brought his horse to a standstill before
replying:

"Nine days. But when my Uncle Kirilla died, his soul
lived in our hut for thirteen days."

"How d'you know?"

"For thirteen days there was a rumbling in the stove."

"Very well. Go on," said the old man, and it was
clear he did not believe a word of it.

Near Kuzmenki the carts turned on to the highway,
and Lipa went on on foot. It was getting light. As she
was descending the slope into the gully, the church and
huts of Ukleyevo were hidden by the mist. It was cold,
and it seemed to her that the same cuckoo was still giving its call.

The cattle had not yet been driven out to pasture
when Lipa got home; everyone was still asleep. She sat
on the porch, waiting. The old man was the first to come
out; the moment he glanced at her, he understood all,
and for some time could not utter a word, and only stood
there mumbling.

"Ah, Lipa," he said at last. "You couldn't look after
my grandson...."

Varvara was roused from her sleep. She threw up

her hands and wept, and began to lay out the dead child
for its coffin.

"And such a sweet little boy as he was..." she kept
saying. "You only had one son, and you couldn't take
care of him, you little silly."

There were funeral services in the morning and
evening. The child was buried the next day, and after
the funeral the guests and the clergy fell on the food so
greedily that one might have thought they had had nothing to eat for days. Lipa served at table, and the priest,
raising his fork with a pickled mushroom on it, said
to her:

"Do not grieve over the infant. For of such is the
kingdom of heaven."

It was only after everyone had gone that Lipa really
understood there was no Nikifor any more, and never
would be—and, understanding, wept. She did not know
what room to go and weep in, for she felt there was no
place for her in the house since her boy had died, that
there was nothing for her to do here, that she was unwanted; and everyone else seemed to feel the same
about her.

"Well, what are you bawling about there?" shouted
Aksinya, appearing suddenly in the door-way; in honour
of the funeral she was all dressed in new clothes, and
her face was powdered. "Stop it!"

Lipa tried to stop, but only cried louder still.

"Do you hear me?" shouted Aksinya, stamping her
foot in her rage. "Who d'you think I'm talking to? Get
out of here, and never dare to show yourself here again,
felon! Get out!"

"Come, come," said the old man, rousing himself.
"Calm yourself, Aksinya dear.... 'Tis natural she should
weep.... Her child is dead...."

"Natural, natural!" repeated Aksinya, mockingly.
"She can stay the night, but by tomorrow let her pack

off! Natural!" repeated Aksinya once more, and laughing turned to go into the shop.

Early in the morning of the next day Lipa went back to Torguyevo, to her mother.

IX

Now the roof and iron door of the shop have been freshly painted and shine like new, gay geraniums blossom in the windows as formerly, and what happened three years ago in the Tsibukin household is almost forgotten.

Grigory Petrovich, the old man, is still considered the master but in reality everything has passed into Aksinya's hands; she it is who buys and sells, and nothing is done without her consent. The brick-works is doing well; owing to the demand for bricks for the railway their price has reached twenty-four rubles a thousand; women and girls take the bricks to the station and load the trucks, receiving twenty-five kopeks a day for this.

Aksinya has gone shares with the Khrimins, and the mill is now called "Khrimins Junior and Co." A tavern has been opened next to the station, and the expensive concertina is now heard in the tavern, and not in the factory; the postmaster, who has also set up in trade on his own, frequents the tavern, and so does the station-master. The Khrimins Junior have given the deaf man a gold watch which he is always taking out of his pocket and holding to his ear.

They say in the village that Aksinya has become very powerful; and this must be true, for when she drives to the works of a morning, with her innocent smile, good-looking, radiant with happiness, and orders people about all day long, you cannot help feeling her power. Everyone is afraid of her, at home, in the village and at the works. When she makes her appearance at the post-office, the postmaster leaps up, saying:

"Be seated, Ksenya Abramovna, do!"

A middle-aged landowner, a great dandy, in a coat of fine cloth and patent-leather top-boots, selling her a horse one day, was so entranced by her conversation that he let her have it at her own price. He held her hand long in his, and said, gazing into her mirthful, arch, innocent eyes:

"I would do anything in the world for a woman like you, Ksenya Abramovna! Only tell me when we could meet without anybody to disturb us."

"Why, whenever you like!"

Ever since, the middle-aged dandy drives up to the shop almost every day for a drink of beer. The beer is atrocious, bitter as wormwood. The landowner shakes his head but drinks it down.

Old Tsibukin does not interfere in business matters any more He never has any money in his pockets, for he cannot distinguish between false coins and genuine ones, but he says nothing about it, not wishing anyone to know of this failing of his He has become very absent-minded, and unless food is set before him, never thinks of asking for it: they have got used to sitting down to dinner without him, and Varvara often says:

"He's gone to bed without his supper again " And she says it calmly, for she has got used to it, too Winter and summer alike he goes about in his fur-coat, staying at home only on very hot summer days He usually walks about the village street, in his winter-coat with the collar turned up, taking the road leading to the station, or sits from morning to night on a bench outside the church gate. Sits there motionless Passers-by salute him, but he never answers their greetings, for he retains his dislike for peasants. When addressed, his answers are quite polite and rational, but always very brief.

They say in the village that his daughter-in-law has turned him out of his own house and starves him, and that he lives on alms; some rejoice in this rumour, others are sorry for the old man.

Varvara has grown still stouter, her complexion still more brilliant, she still goes in for charity, and Aksinya does not prevent her. So much jam is made every summer now that there is no time to eat it up before next year's berries ripen; so it candies, almost driving Varvara to tears, for she does not know what to do with it.

People have begun to forget about Anisim. Once a letter came from him, in verse, on a large sheet of paper, in the form of a petition, written in the same exquisite hand. Evidently his friend Samorodov is serving a sentence at his side. Beneath the verses was written in an ugly, almost illegible scrawl: "I'm ill all the time here very unhappy help me for the sake of Christ."

One sunny autumn afternoon old Tsibukin was sitting by the church gate, with the collar of his winter-coat turned up so that only the tip of his nose and the peak of his cap could be seen. At the other end of the long bench sat the contractor Yelisarov, and next to him the school-watchman Yakov, a toothless old man of about seventy. Spike and the watchman were talking.

"Children ought to support the old people... honour thy father and thy mother," said Yakov severely. "But she, his daughter-in-law, has turned her father-in-law out of his own house. The old man has nothing to eat or drink, and there's nowhere for him to go. He's had no food for three days."

"Three days!" exclaimed Spike.

"Yes. And there he sits, without a word. He's too weak to speak. Why hush it up? He ought to have the law on her. She'd get it, in the courts."

"Get what in the courts?" asked Spike, who did not catch the watchman's words.

"What's that you said?"

"She's not a bad wench, she works hard. Women

can't get along without that ... without a little sin, I mean."

"Turning him out of his own house," continued Yakov angrily. "Get a house of your own, I say, then turn people out of it. Who does she think she is? The pest!"

Tsibukin listened to them without stirring.

"What does it matter whether it's your own house, or someone else's, so long as it's warm and the women don't quarrel..." said Spike and laughed. "When I was young, I cherished my Nastasya. She was a quiet wench. And she used to go on at me: 'Buy a house, Makarich, buy a house! Buy a horse!' Even when she was dying, she kept saying: 'Buy yourself a droshky, Makarich, so as not to go about on foot.' But the only thing I ever bought her was gingerbread, nothing more."

"Her husband is deaf and a natural," Yakov went on, not heeding Spike. "A real natural, he has no more brains than a goose. What does he understand? You can hit a goose on the head, and still he won't understand."

Spike got up to go back to his home at the mill. Yakov got up, too, and they walked away together, still talking. When they were fifty paces or so away, old Tsibukin got up, and shuffled after them with uncertain steps, as if he were walking on ice.

The village was beginning to be plunged in twilight, and the sun shone only on the top of the road, which wound its way up the slope like a snake. Old women were returning from the woods, with children running beside them; they carried baskets filled with mushrooms. Women and young girls were coming back from the station where they had been loading bricks on trucks, and red brick-dust lay on their noses, and on their cheeks beneath the eyes. They were singing. In front of them went Lipa, singing in a piping voice, warbling away as she gazed up into the sky, as if she were delighted that the day, thank God, was over, and it was time to rest. Her mother, Praskovya, the day-labourer, walked with the crowd, carrying a bundle and as usual breathing heavily.

"Good evening, Makarich!" said Lipa, as she met Spike. "Good evening, dearie!"

"Good evening, Lipa dear!" answered Spike joyfully. "Wenches and lasses, be kind to the wealthy carpenter! Ho-ho! Oh, my children, my children!" Spike gave a sob. "Oh, my precious axes!"

Spike and Yakov went on, and everyone could hear them talking. Then the crowd encountered old Tsibukin, and there was a sudden lull. Lipa and her mother were at the back now, and as the old man approached them, Lipa bowed low before him and said:

"Good evening, Grigory Petrovich!"

Her mother bowed, too. The old man stopped, gazing at them in silence; his lips trembled and his eyes filled with tears. Lipa took a piece of buckwheat pie out of her mother's bundle, and offered it to the old man. He accepted it and began eating.

The sun had gone down; it no longer lit up even the top of the road. It was getting dark and cold. Lipa and Praskovya went on their way, crossing themselves continually.

1900

THE BRIDE

I

It was already nine o'clock in the evening, and the full moon was shining over the garden. In the Shumin house the evening service ordered by the grandmother Marfa Mikhailovna was only just over, and Nadya, who had slipped out into the garden for a minute, could see a cold supper being laid in the dining-room, her grandmother in her billowing silk dress hovering about the table, Father Andrei, the Cathedral priest, talking to Nadya's mother, Nina Ivanovna, who looked very young seen through the window, by artificial light. Beside her stood Andrei Andreich, Father Andrei's son, listening attentively.

It was cool and still in the garden, and dark shadows lay peacefully on the ground. From a long way off, probably outside town, came the distant croaking of frogs. There was a feeling of May, the delightful month of May, in the air. One could draw deep breaths, and imagine that somewhere, far beyond the town, beneath the sky, above the tree tops, in the fields and woods, the spring was beginning its own life, that mysterious, exquisite life, rich and sacred, from which sinful mortals are shut out. It almost made one want to cry.

Nadya was now twenty-three; ever since she was

sixteen years old she had been dreaming ardently of marriage, and now at last she was betrothed to Andrei Andreich, the young man standing in the dining-room. She liked him, and the wedding was fixed for the seventh of July, but she felt no joy; she slept badly, her gaiety had deserted her. From the open windows of the basement kitchen came sounds of bustling and the clanging of knives, and the door, which closed with a hanging weight, banged constantly. There was a smell of roasting turkey and spiced cherries. And it seemed as if things would go on like this, without changing, for ever and ever.

Someone came out of the house and stood in the porch. It was Alexander Timofeich, or as everyone called him, Sasha, who had arrived from Moscow about ten days before, on a visit. Long ago, Maria Petrovna, an impoverished widow gentlewoman, small, slight and delicate, used to visit Nadya's grandmother, to whom she was distantly related, asking for charity. She had a son called Sasha. For some reason or other people said he was a fine artist, and when his mother died, Granny, for her own soul's salvation, sent him to the Komissarov school in Moscow. A year or two later he got himself transferred to an art school, where he remained something like fifteen years, till at last he scrambled through his final examinations in the architectural department; he never worked as an architect, but found occupation in a Moscow lithographical works. He came to stay almost every summer, usually very ill, to rest and recuperate.

He was wearing a long coat buttoned up to his neck and shabby canvas trousers with frayed hems. And his shirt was unironed, and his whole appearance was dingy. He was emaciated, with huge eyes and long, bony fingers, bearded, dark-skinned, and with it all, handsome. At the Shumins he felt as if he were among his own people, and was quite at home in their house. And the room he occupied on his visits had long been known as Sasha's room.

He caught sight of Nadya from the porch, and went out to her.

"It's nice here," he said.

"It's ever so nice. You ought to stay till the autumn."

"Yes, I know, I shall have to, I suppose. I shall probably stay with you till September."

He laughed for no apparent reason, and sat down beside her.

"I've been standing here watching Mama," said Nadya. "She looks so young from here. Of course I know my Mama has her weaknesses," she continued after a pause, "but just the same she's a marvellous woman."

"Yes, she's very nice," agreed Sasha. "In her way your Mama is of course very good and kind, but ... how shall I put it? I went into the kitchen this morning early and saw four servants sleeping right on the floor, no beds, only rags to lie on, a stench, bugs, cockroaches. ... Just the same as it used to be twenty years ago, not the slightest change. Granny's not to be blamed, of course, she's old—but your mother, with her French and her amateur theatricals. ... You'd think *she*'d understand."

When Sasha spoke he had a habit of holding up two long, bony fingers in the direction of his hearer.

"Everything here strikes me as so strange," he continued. "I'm not used to it, I suppose. Good heavens, nobody ever does anything! Your mother does nothing but stroll about like a grand-duchess, Granny does nothing at all, and nor do you. And Andrei Andreich, your fiancé, he does nothing, either."

Nadya had heard all this last year, and, she seemed to remember, the year before, and she knew it was the only way Sasha's mind could work; there was a time when it had amused her, but now for some reason it irritated her.

"That's old stuff, I'm sick of hearing it," she said, getting up. "Can't you think of anything new?"

He laughed and got up, too, and they both went back to the house. Good-looking, tall and slender, she seemed almost offensively well-dressed and healthy, as she walked by his side. She was conscious of it herself, and felt sorry for him, and almost apologetic.

"And you talk a lot of nonsense," she said. "Look what you just said about my Andrei—you don't know him a bit, really!"

"*My* Andrei.... Never mind your Andrei! It's your youth I grudge."

When they went into the dining-room everyone was just sitting down to supper. Nadya's grandmother, or, as everyone in the house called her, "Granny," a corpulent, plain old woman, with heavy eyebrows and a moustache, was talking loudly, and her voice and manner of speaking showed that it was she who was the real head of the house She owned a row of booths on the market-place, and the old house with its pillars and garden was hers, but every morning she prayed with tears that the Lord would preserve her from ruin. Her daughter-in-law, and Nadya's mother, Nina Ivanovna, blonde, tightly corsetted, who wore pince-nez and had diamond rings on all her fingers, Father Andrei, a lean, toothless old man who always looked as if he were just going to say something very funny, and Andrei Andreich, his son and Nadya's fiancé, a stout, handsome young man with curly hair, rather like an actor or an artist, were all three talking about hypnotism.

"You'll fatten up in a week here," Granny told Sasha. "But you must eat more. Just look at yourself!" she sighed. "You look awful. A real prodigal son, that's what you are."

"He wasted his substance with riotous living," interpolated Father Andrei, bringing out the words slowly, his eyes twinkling, "and he was sent into the fields to feed swine."

"I love my old Dad," said Andrei Andreich, patting

his father on the shoulder. "Dear old man. Good old man!"

Nobody said anything. Sasha suddenly burst out laughing, and pressed his napkin to his lips.

"So you believe in hypnotism?" Father Andrei asked Nina Ivanovna.

"I can't exactly say I believe in it," replied Nina Ivanovna, assuming a grave, almost severe expression. "But I have to acknowledge that there is much that is mysterious and incomprehensible in nature."

"I quite agree with you, though I am bound to add that faith narrows the sphere of the mysterious considerably for us."

An enormous juicy turkey was placed on the table. Father Andrei and Nina Ivanovna continued their conversation. The diamonds on Nina Ivanovna's fingers sparkled, and in her eyes sparkled tears, she was deeply moved.

"Of course I cannot venture to argue with you," she said. "But you will agree that there are many unsolved riddles in life."

"Not one, I assure you."

After supper Andrei Andreich played the violin, Nina Ivanovna accompanying him on the piano. He had graduated from the philological department of the university ten years before, but had no employment and no fixed occupation, merely playing at occasional charity concerts. In the town he was spoken of as a musician.

Andrei Andreich played and all listened in silence. The samovar steamed quietly on the table, and Sasha was the only one drinking tea. Just as twelve o'clock struck a fiddle-string snapped. Everyone laughed, and there was a bustle of leave-taking.

After saying good night to her fiancé, Nadya went upstairs to the rooms she shared with her mother (the ground floor was occupied by Granny). The lights were being extinguished downstairs, in the dining-room, but Sasha still sat on, drinking tea. He always sat long over his tea, in the Moscow way, drinking six or seven glasses one after another. Long after Nadya had undressed and got into bed she could hear the servants clearing the table, and Granny scolding. At last the house was quiet, but for an occasional sonorous cough from downstairs, in Sasha's room.

II

It must have been about two o'clock when Nadya waked up, for dawn was beginning to break. The night watchman's rattle could be heard in the distance. Nadya could not sleep, her bed seemed too soft to lie down in comfortably. As she had done on all the previous nights this May Nadya sat up in bed and gave herself up to her thoughts. The thoughts were just the same as those of the night before, monotonous, futile, insistent—thoughts of how Andrei Andreich had courted her and proposed, how she had accepted him and gradually learned to appreciate this good and clever man. But somehow or other now that there was only a month left till the wedding, she began to experience fear, uneasiness, as if something vaguely sad lay in wait for her.

"Tick-tock, tick-tock," rapped out the night watchman lazily. "Tick-tock. . . ."

Through the big old-fashioned window could be seen the garden, and beyond it lilac bushes, heavy with bloom, drowsy and languid in the cold air. And a dense white mist encroached silently upon the lilacs, as if intent on enveloping them. Sleepy rooks cawed from distant trees.

"Oh, God, what makes me so sad?"

Do all girls feel like this before their weddings? Who knows? Or could it be the influence of Sasha? But Sasha had been saying the same things over and over again, as if by rote, year after year, and what he said always sounded so naive and quaint. And why couldn't she get the thought of Sasha out of her head? Why?

The watchman had long stopped going his rounds. Birds began twittering beneath the window and in the tree tops, the mist in the garden cleared away, and now everything was gilded by the spring sunlight, everything seemed to be smiling. In a short time the whole garden, warmed by the caresses of the sun, had sprung to life, and drops of dew gleamed like diamonds on the leaves of the trees. And the old, neglected garden was young and gay for that one morning.

Granny was already awake. Sasha gave his harsh, deep cough. Downstairs the servants could be heard bringing in the samovar, moving chairs about.

The hours passed slowly. Nadya had been up and walking in the garden for a long time and the morning still dragged on.

And here came Nina Ivanovna, tearful, a glass of mineral water in her hand. She went in for spiritualism and homeopathy, read a great deal, and was fond of talking about her religious doubts, and Nadya supposed there must be some profound, mysterious significance in all this. She kissed her mother, and walked on at her side.

"What have you been crying about, Mama?" she asked.

"I read a book last night about an old man and his daughter. The old man worked at some office, and what d'you think, his chief fell in love with the old man's daughter! I haven't finished it, but I came to a place in it where I couldn't help crying," said Nina Ivanovna, and took a sip from her glass. "I remembered it this morning, and cried again."

"And I've been so depressed all these days," said Nadya after a pause. "Why can't I sleep?"

"I don't know, dearie. When I can't sleep I shut my eyes tight—like this—and imagine how Anna Karenina looked and spoke, or I try to imagine something historical, something from olden times. . . ."

Nadya felt that her mother did not understand her, that she was incapable of understanding her. She had never had this feeling before, it frightened her; she wanted to hide, and went back to her room.

At two o'clock everyone sat down to dinner. It was Wednesday, a fast-day, and Granny was served meatless *borshch* and bream with buckwheat porridge.

To tease Granny Sasha ate *borshch* as well as meat soup. He joked all through the meal, but his jokes were too elaborate and always intended to point a moral, and it was not funny at all when, before coming out with a witticism, he lifted his long, bony, dead-looking fingers; and when the thought that he was very ill and probably had not long to live crossed your mind, you felt so sorry for him, you could have cried.

After dinner Granny went to her room to rest. Nina Ivanovna played the piano for a short time, and then she went out of the room, too.

"Oh, Nadya dear," Sasha said, returning to his usual after-dinner topic, "if only you would listen to me! If only you would!"

She sat curled up in an old-fashioned arm-chair, closing her eyes, while he paced quietly up and down the room.

"If only you would go away and study," he said. "Enlightened, saintly people are the only interesting ones, the only ones who are needed. And the more such people there are, the sooner the kingdom of heaven will be on earth. Then not one stone will be left on another, in this town of yours everything will be turned topsy-turvy, everything will change, as if by magic. And there will be huge splendid buildings, beautiful parks, marvellous fountains, fine people. . . . But that's not the chief thing. The chief thing is that then there will be no crowd any more, as we now understand the word, that evil in its present aspect will disappear, for each individual will have faith, and know what he lives for, and nobody

will seek support from the crowd. Darling, little pet, go
away! Show them all that you have had enough of this
stagnant, dull, corrupt life! At least show yourself that
you have."

"I can't, Sasha, I'm going to get married."

"Never mind that! What does it matter?"

They went out into the garden and strolled about.

"Anyhow, my dear, you've simply got to think, you've
got to understand, how abhorrent, how immoral your
idle life is," continued Sasha. "Can't you see that to enable you and your Mama and your Granny to live in
idleness, others have to work for you, you are devouring the life of others, is that pure, now, isn't it filthy?"

Nadya wanted to say: "Yes, you are right," wanted
to tell him she understood, but tears came into her eyes
and she fell silent and seemed to shrink into herself; she
went to her room.

In the evening Andrei Andreich came and played the
violin a long time as usual. He was taciturn by nature,
and perhaps he loved his violin because while playing
he did not have to speak. Soon after ten, when he had his
coat on to go home, he took Nadya in his arms and showered passionate kisses on her face, shoulders, and hands.

"My dearest, my darling, my beautiful," he murmured. "Oh, how happy I am! I think I shall go mad
with joy!"

And this, too, she seemed to have heard long, long
ago, to have read it in some novel, some old, tattered
volume which no one ever read any more.

In the dining-room was Sasha, sitting at the table,
drinking tea from a saucer balanced on the tips of his
five long fingers. Granny was playing patience. Nina
Ivanovna was reading. The flame sputtered in the icon-
lamp, and everything seemed still and secure. Nadya
said good night and went up to her room, falling asleep
the moment she got into bed. But, just as the night before, she waked up at the first streak of dawn. She could

not sleep, something heavy and restless lay on her heart. She sat up and put her head on her knees, thinking about her fiancé, her wedding. . . . For some reason she remembered that her mother had not loved her husband, and now had nothing of her own, and was completely dependent on Granny, her mother-in-law. And try as she would, Nadya could not understand how it was that she had regarded her mother as something special, remarkable, had not seen that she was just an ordinary, unhappy woman.

Downstairs, Sasha, too, was awake—she could hear him coughing. A strange, naive creature, thought Nadya, and there is something absurd in his dreams, in all those splendid parks, and marvellous fountains. But there was so much that was beautiful in his naivety, in his very absurdity, that the moment she began to wonder if she ought to go away and study, her whole heart, her very being, was bathed in refreshing coolness, and she was plunged in ecstasy.

"Better not think. . ." she whispered. "Better not think about it."

"Tick-tock," the distant night-watchman rapped out on the board. "Tick-tock . . . tick-tock. . . ."

III

Towards the middle of June Sasha was suddenly overcome by boredom and began to talk about going back to Moscow.

"I can't live in this town," he said morosely. "No running water, no drainage! I can hardly bear to eat my dinner—the kitchen is indescribably filthy. . . ."

"Wait a little longer, Prodigal Son," Granny whispered. "The wedding will be on the seventh."

"I simply can't!"

"You said you would stay with us till September."

"And now I don't want to. I've got to work."

The summer had turned out cold and rainy, the trees were always dripping, the garden looked sombre and unfriendly, and the desire to get away and work was quite natural. Unfamiliar feminine voices could be heard in all the rooms, upstairs and downstairs, a sewing-machine whirred in Granny's room. It was all part of the bustle over the trousseau. Of winter-coats alone Nadya was to have six, and the cheapest of them, boasted Granny, had cost three hundred rubles. All this fuss irritated Sasha. He sat and sulked in his room. But they managed to persuade him to stay, and he promised not to leave before the first of July.

The time passed quickly. On St. Peter's day Andrei Andreich took Nadya after dinner to Moscow Street to have yet another look at the house which had long been rented and furnished for the young couple. It was a two-storey house, but so far only the upper floor had been furnished. In the ball-room, with its gleaming floor, painted to look like parquet, were bent-wood chairs, a grand piano, a music-stand for the violin. There was a smell of paint. On the wall was a large oil-painting in a gilt frame—a picture of a naked lady beside a purple vase with a broken handle.

"Beautiful picture," said Andrei Andreich with an awed sigh. "It's by Shishmachevsky."

Next came the drawing-room, in which were a round table, a sofa, and some arm-chairs upholstered in bright blue material. Over the sofa hung an enlarged photograph of Father Andrei with all his medals on, wearing a tall ceremonial hat. They passed into the dining-room with its side-board, and from there into the bedroom. Here, in the half-light, stood two beds side by side, and it looked as if those who had furnished the bedroom had taken it for granted that life would always be happy here, that it could not be otherwise. Andrei Andreich conducted Nadya through the rooms, never removing his arm from her waist. And she felt weak, guilty, hating all these rooms and beds and chairs, while the naked lady made her sick. She now saw quite clearly that she no longer loved Andrei Andreich, perhaps never had loved him. But she did not know how to say this, whom to say it to, and why to say it at all, and though she thought about it day and night she came no nearer to knowing. . . . He had his arm round her waist, spoke to her so kindly, so humbly, was so happy, walking about his home. And all she saw was vulgarity, stupid, naive, intolerable vulgarity, and his arm round her waist seemed to her cold and rigid, like an iron hoop. At any moment she was ready to run away, to burst into sobs, to jump out of the window. Andrei Andreich led her to the bathroom, touched a tap screwed into the wall, and the water gushed out.

"What do you think of that?" he said, and laughed. "I had them put up a cistern holding a hundred pails of water, so we shall have running water in our bathroom."

They walked about the yard for a while and then went out into the street, where they got into a droshky. The dust rose in thick clouds, and it looked as if it were just going to rain.

"Are you cold?" asked Andrei Andreich, narrowing his eyes against the dust.

She did not answer.

"Remember Sasha reproaching me for not doing anything, yesterday?" he said, after a short pause. "Well, he was right. Infinitely right. I do nothing, and there is nothing I know how to do. Why is it, my dear one? How is it that the very thought of one day wearing a cockade in my cap and going to an office makes me feel sick? How is it that I can't stand the sight of a lawyer, or a Latin teacher, or a town councillor? Oh, Mother Russia, Mother Russia! How many idlers and useless beings you still bear on your bosom! How many beings like myself, oh, long-suffering one!"

And he theorized about his own idleness, seeing it as a sign of the times.

"When we are married," he continued, "we'll go to live in the country, my dear one, we'll work. We'll buy a little plot of land with a garden and a stream, and we'll toil, observe life.... Oh, how lovely it will be!"

He took his hat off and his hair waved in the breeze, and she listened to him, thinking all the time: "Oh, God, I want to go home! Oh, God!" They overtook Father Andrei just before they got back to Nadya's home.

"Look, there's my father!" said Andrei Andreich joyfully, and he waved his hat. "I love my old Dad, really I do," he said, paying off the cabby. "Dear old man! Good old man!"

Nadya went into the house feeling out-of-humour and unwell, unable to forget that all the evening there would be visitors, that she would have to entertain them, to smile, to listen to the violin, to hear all sorts of nonsense and talk about nothing but the wedding. Granny, stiff and pompous in her silk dress, was sitting beside the samovar, looking very haughty, as she always did when there were visitors. Father Andrei came into the room with his subtle smile.

"I have the pleasure and virtuous consolation of seeing you in good health," he said to Granny, and it was hard to say whether he was in earnest or in jest.

IV

The wind knocked on the window-panes and on the roof. Whistling sounds could be heard, and the brownie in the chimney crooned his morose, plaintive song. It was one o'clock in the morning. Everyone in the house was in bed, but no one was asleep, and Nadya kept thinking she could hear the violin being played downstairs. There was a sharp report from outside, a shutter must have torn loose from its hinges. A minute later Nina Ivanovna came into the room in her chemise, holding a candle.

"What was that noise, Nadya?" she asked.

Nadya's mother, her hair in a single plait, smiling timidly, seemed on this stormy night older, plainer, and shorter than usual. Nadya remembered how, so very recently, she had considered her mother a remarkable woman and had felt pride in listening to the words she used. And now she could not for the life of her remember what those words had been—the only ones that came back to her were feeble and affected.

Bass voices seemed to be singing in the chimney, even the words "Oh, my God!" could be made out. Nadya sat up in bed, and tugged violently at her hair, sobbing.

"Mama, Mama!" she cried. "Oh darling, if you only knew what I was going through! I beg you, I implore you—let me go away!"

"Where to?" asked Nina Ivanovna, in bewilderment, and she sat down on the side of the bed. "Where d'you want to go?"

Nadya cried and cried, unable to bring out another word.

"Let me go away from this town," she said at last. "The wedding must not, will not, be, believe me. I don't love that man. . . . I can't bear to speak about him."

"No, my darling, no," said Nina Ivanovna quickly, frightened out of her wits. "Calm yourself. You're out of sorts. It'll pass. It often happens. You've probably had a quarrel with Andrei, but lovers' tiffs end in kisses."

"Go, Mama, go!" sobbed Nadya.

"Yes," said Nina Ivanovna, after a pause. "Only the other day you were a little girl, and now you're almost a bride. Nature is in a constant state of metabolism. Before you know where you are you'll be a mother yourself, and then an old woman, with a troublesome daughter like mine."

"My darling, you're kind and clever, and you're unhappy," said Nadya. "You're ever so unhappy—why do you say such commonplace things? Why, for God's sake?"

Nina Ivanovna tried to speak, but could not utter a word, only sobbed and went back to her room. Once more the bass voices moaned in the chimney, and Nadya was suddenly terrified. She jumped out of bed and ran into her mother's room. Nina Ivanovna, her eyelids swollen from crying, was lying in bed covered by a blue blanket, a book in her hands.

"Mama, listen to me," said Nadya. "Think, try to understand me, I implore you! Only think how shallow and humiliating our life is! My eyes have been opened, I see it all now. And what is your Andrei Andreich? Why, he's not a bit clever, Mama. Oh, God, oh, God! Only think, Mama, why, he's stupid!"

Nina Ivanovna sat up with a jerk.

"You and your grandmother keep torturing me," she said, with a gasping sob. "I want to live! To live!" she repeated, smiting her chest again and again. "Can't you let me have my freedom? I'm still young, I want to live, you've made an old woman of me!"

She cried bitterly and lay down, rolling herself up in the blanket, and looking just a silly, pathetic little thing. Nadya went back to her room and dressed, then she sat at the window to wait for morning to come. All night she sat there thinking, and someone seemed to be knocking at the shutter outside and whistling.

The next morning Granny complained that the wind had beaten down all the apples and split the trunk of an old plum-tree. It was a grey, dim, joyless morning, one of those days when you feel inclined to light the lamp from the very morning. Everyone complained of the cold, and the rain-drops tapped on the window-panes. After breakfast Nadya went to Sasha's room and, without a word, fell on her knees before a chair in the corner, covering her face with her hands.

"What's the matter?" asked Sasha.

"I can't go on like this, I can't!" she exclaimed. "I don't know how I could live here before, I simply can't understand it! I despise my fiancé, I despise myself, I despise this whole idle, empty life...."

"Come, come..." Sasha interrupted her, not yet realizing what she was talking about. "Never mind ... it's all right...."

"This life is hateful to me," continued Nadya. "I won't be able to bear another day here! I shall go away tomorrow. Take me with you, for God's sake!"

Sasha gazed at her for a moment in amazement. At last the truth dawned upon him, and he rejoiced like a child, waving his arms and shuffling in his loose slippers, as if he were dancing with joy.

"Splendid!" he said, rubbing his hands. "God, how fine that is!"

She gazed at him unblinkingly, from wide-open eyes, full of love, as if fascinated, waiting for him to come out immediately with something significant, something of infinite importance. He had not told her anything yet, but she felt that something new and vast, something she had never known before, was already opening before her, and she looked at him full of expectation, ready for anything, for death itself.

"I'm leaving tomorrow," he said after a pause. "You can come to the station to see me off. I'll take your things in my trunk and buy a ticket for you. And when the third bell rings, you can get into the train, and off we go. Go with me as far as Moscow, and go to Petersburg by yourself. Have you a passport?"

"Yes."

"You will never regret it—never repent it, I'm sure!" said Sasha enthusiastically. "You will go away and study, and afterwards things will take their own course. As soon as you turn your life upside down, everything will change. The great thing is to turn your life upside down, nothing else matters. So we're off tomorrow?"

"Oh, yes! For God's sake!"

Nadya, who imagined that she was profoundly stirred and that her heart had never before been so heavy, was quite sure that now, on the eve of departure, she would suffer, be racked with anguished thoughts. But she had hardly gone upstairs to her room and lain down on the bed when she fell fast asleep, and slept soundly, with a tear-stained face and a smile on her lips, till the very evening.

V

The droshky had been sent for. Nadya, in her hat and coat, went upstairs to have one last look at her mother, at all that had been hers so long. She stood in her room beside the bed, which was still warm, and then went softly into her mother's room. Nina Ivanovna was asleep, and it was very quiet in her room. After kissing her mother and smoothing her hair, Nadya stood for a minute or two.... Then she went downstairs with unhurried steps.

The rain was coming down in torrents. A droshky, dripping wet, stood in front of the porch, its hood raised.

"There's no room for you, Nadya," said Granny, when the servant began putting the luggage into the droshky. "I wonder you want to see him off in such weather! You'd better stay at home. Just look at the rain!"

Nadya tried to say something, but could not. Sasha helped her into the droshky, covering her knees with the rug. And now he was seated beside her.

"Good-bye! God bless you!" shouted Granny from the porch. "Mind you write when you get to Moscow, Sasha!"

"All right. Good-bye, Granny!"

"May the Queen of Heaven protect you!"

"What weather!" said Sasha.

It was only now that Nadya began to cry. It was only now that she realized she was really going away, a thing she had not quite believed, even when saying good-bye to Granny, or standing beside her mother. Good-bye, town! Everything came over her with a rush—Andrei, his father, the new house, the naked lady with the vase. But all this no longer frightened her or weighed upon her, it had become naive and trivial, it was re-treating farther and farther into the past. And when they got into the railway carriage and the train started, the whole of this past, so big and important, shrank to a little lump, and a vast future, scarcely perceptible till now, opened before her. The rain-drops tapped on the windows, there was nothing to be seen but the green fields, the telegraph-poles flashing by, the birds on the wires, and joy suddenly almost choked her. She remembered that she was going to be at liberty, to study, doing what used to be called in the old days: "Running away to the Cossacks." She laughed and cried and prayed.

"Come, come," said Sasha, smiling broadly. "Come, come!"

VI

Autumn passed, and after it winter. Nadya was now very homesick, and thought every day of her mother and Granny; she thought of Sasha, too. Letters from home were resigned and kindly, everything seemed to have been forgiven and forgotten. After passing her May examinations, she set off, well and happy, for home, breaking her journey at Moscow to see Sasha. He was just the same as he had been the year before—bearded, shaggy, still wearing the same long old-fashioned coat and canvas trousers, his eyes as large and beautiful as ever. But he looked ill and worried, he had got older and thinner, and coughed incessantly. And to Nadya he seemed dingy and provincial.

"Why, it's Nadya!" he cried, laughing joyfully. "My darling, my pet!"

378

They sat together in the litographical workshop, amidst the fumes of tobacco smoke and a stifling smell of ink and paint; then they went to his room, which reeked of smoke, too, and was littered and filthy. On the table, beside the cold samovar, was a broken plate with a bit of dark paper on it, and both floor and table were strewn with dead flies. Everything here showed that Sasha took no thought for his private life, lived in a continual mess, with utter contempt for comfort. If anyone had spoken to him about his personal happiness and private life, had asked him if there was anyone who loved him, he would have been at a loss to know what was meant, and would only have laughed.

"Everything passed off all right," said Nadya hurriedly. "Mama came to Petersburg in the autumn, to see me, she says Granny isn't angry, but keeps going into my room and making the sign of the cross on the walls."

Sasha looked cheerful, but coughed and spoke in a cracked voice, and Nadya kept looking at him, wondering if he was really seriously ill, or if it was her imagination.

"Sasha, dear Sasha," she said, "but you're ill!"

"I'm all right. A bit unwell—nothing serious...."

"For goodness' sake," said Nadya, in agitated tones, "why don't you go to a doctor? Why don't you take care of your health? My dear one, Sasha, dear," she murmured, and tears sprang into her eyes, and for some reason Andrei Andreich, and the naked lady with the vase, and the whole of her past, which now seemed as far off as her childhoood, rose before her mind. And she cried because Sasha no longer seemed to her so original, clever and interesting as he had last year. "Sasha dear, you are very, very ill. I don't know what I wouldn't give for you not to be so pale and thin! I owe you so much. You can have no idea what a lot you have done for me, Sasha darling! You are now the closest, the dearest person in my life, you know."

They sat on, talking and talking. And now, after a
winter in Petersburg, it seemed to her that something
outmoded, old-fashioned, finished, something, perhaps,
already half in the grave, could be felt in everything he
said, in his smile, in the whole of him.

"I'm going for a trip down the Volga the day after
tomorrow," said Sasha, "and then I'll go somewhere
and take *koumiss*. I want to try *koumiss*. A friend of
mine, and his wife, are going with me. The wife is a
marvellous person. I keep trying to persuade her to go
and study. I want her to turn her life topsy-turvy."

When they had talked themselves out, they went to
the station. Sasha treated her to tea and bought her
some apples, and when the train started, and he stood
smiling and waving his handkerchief, she could see by
just looking at his legs, how ill he was, and that he
was not likely to live long.

Nadya arrived at her native town at noon. As she
drove home from the station the streets seemed to her
disproportionately wide, the houses very small and
squat. There was hardly anyone about, and the only
person she met was the German piano-tuner in his rusty
overcoat. And the houses seemed to be covered with a
film of dust. Granny, now really old, and as stout and
plain as ever, put her arms round Nadya and cried for
a long time, with her face pressed against Nadya's
shoulder, as if she could not tear herself away. Nina Ivanovna, who had aged greatly, too, had become quite
plain and seemed to have shrunk, but she was as tight-
laced as ever and the diamonds still shone from her
fingers.

"My darling," she said, shaking all over. "My own
darling!"

Then they sat down and wept silently. It was easy
to see that both Granny and Mama realized that the past
was irrevocably lost. Gone were their social position,
their former distinction, their right to invite guests to

their house. They felt as people feel when, in the midst
of an easy, carefree life, the police break in one night
and search the house, and it is discovered that the master
of the house has committed an embezzlement or a forgery—and then farewell for ever to the easy, carefree life!

Nadya went upstairs and saw the same bed, the same
window with its demure white curtains, the same view
of the garden from the window, flooded with sunshine,
gay, noisy with life. She touched her table, sat down,
fell into a reverie. She had a good dinner, drinking tea
after it, with delicious thick cream, but something was
missing, there was an emptiness in the rooms, and the
ceiling struck her as very low. When she went to bed in the
evening, covering herself with the bed-clothes, there was
something ridiculous in lying in this warm, too soft bed.

Nina Ivanovna came in for a moment, and seated herself as the guilty do, timidly, with furtive glances.

"Well, Nadya, how is everything?" she asked. "Are
you happy? Really happy?"

"Yes, Mama."

Nina Ivanovna got up and made the sign of the cross
over Nadya and the window.

"As you see I have turned religious," she said. "I am
studying philosophy, you know, and I keep thinking,
thinking. . . . And many things are as clear as daylight
to me now. It seems to me that the most important thing
is to see life through a prism."

"Mama, how is Granny really?"

"She seems all right. When you went away with
Sasha and Granny read your telegram, she fell down on
the spot. After that she lay three days in bed without
stirring. And then she began praying and crying. But
she's all right now."

She got up and began pacing up and down the room.

"Tick-tock," rapped the watchman, "tick-tock."

"The great thing is for life to be seen through a prism,"
she said. "In other words life must be divided up in our

consciousness into its simplest elements, as if into the seven primary colours, and each element must be studied separately."

What more Nina Ivanovna said, and when she went away, Nadya did not know, for she soon fell asleep.

May passed, and June came. Nadya had got used to being at home again. Granny sat beside the samovar, pouring out tea and giving deep sighs. Nina Ivanovna talked about her philosophy in the evenings. She still lived like a dependent, and had to turn to Granny whenever she wanted a few kopeks. The house was full of flies and the ceilings seemed to be getting lower and lower. Granny and Nina Ivanovna never went out, for fear of meeting Father Andrei and Andrei Andreich. Nadya walked about the garden and the streets, looking at the houses and the drab fences, and it seemed to her that the town had been getting old for a long time, that it had outlived its day and was now waiting, either for its end, or for the beginning of something fresh and youthful. Oh, for this new, pure life to begin, when one could go straight forward, looking one's fate boldly in the eyes, confident that one was in the right, could be gay and free! This life was bound to come sooner or later. The time would come when there would be nothing left of Granny's house, in which the only way for four servants to live was in one room, in the basement, surrounded by filth—yes, the time would come when there would not be a trace left of such a house, when everyone would have forgotten it, when there would be no one left to remember it. Nadya's only distraction was the little boys in the next house who banged on the fence when she strolled about the garden and laughed at her shouting "There goes the bride!"

A letter came from Saratov, from Sasha. He wrote in his reckless, staggering handwriting that the trip down the Volga had been a complete success, but that he had been taken rather ill at Saratov, and had lost his voice, and been in hospital for the last fortnight. She understood what this meant, and a foreboding amounting almost to a conviction came over her. It vexed her that this foreboding and the thought of Sasha himself no longer moved her as formerly. She felt a longing to live, to be in Petersburg, and her friendship with Sasha seemed to belong to a past, which, while dear, was now very distant. She could not sleep all night, and in the morning sat at the window, as if listening for something. And there really did come the sound of voices from below—Granny was saying something in rapid, querulous tones. Then someone cried.... When Nadya went downstairs Granny was standing in the corner of the room praying, and her face was tear-stained. On the table lay a telegram.

Nadya paced up and down the room for a long time, listening to Granny's crying, before picking up the telegram and reading it. It said that yesterday morning, in Saratov, Alexander Timofeich, Sasha for short, had died of consumption.

Granny and Nina Ivanovna went to the church to order a service for the dead, and Nadya walked about the rooms for a long time, thinking. She realized clearly that her life had been turned topsy-turvy, as Sasha had wanted it to be, that she was lonely, alien, unwanted here, and that there was nothing she wanted here, the past had been torn away and vanished, as if burned by fire, and the ashes scattered to the winds. She went into Sasha's room and stood there.

"Good-bye, dear Sasha," she said. Life stretched before her, new, vast, spacious, and this life, though still vague and mysterious, beckoned to her, drawing her onward.

She went upstairs to pack, and the next morning said good-bye to her family, and left the town, gay and full of spirits—never to come back, she was sure.

1903

www.ingramcontent.com/pod-product-compliance
Lightning Source LLC
Chambersburg PA
CBHW012011050726
47590CB00009B/3144